SHE COULD NOT LET HER DEFENSES DOWN

"All this time you were alive," she said. "While I suffered thinking that you had died, you lived. I'm glad of that. For you, but not for me, I think."

"Oh, Minerva." His sigh seared her. "I love you."

She turned her head from his words.

"I love you, Minerva. I've never stopped loving you. If I could have come to you sooner, I would have. Trust me, please. Trust me that I'm the same man who left you, and that I want nothing more than to claim you now as I wanted to then."

"Oh, Gray, I want to."

"Then look at me."

"Give me time. Ti̲̲̲̲̲̲̲̲e to be sure."

He dre̲̲̲̲̲̲̲̲til his booted leg pres̲̲̲̲̲̲̲̲I will not let you go a̲̲̲̲̲̲̲̲d me?"

Stella Cameron

Wait For Me

WARNER BOOKS

A Time Warner Company

WARNER BOOKS EDITION

Cover design by Diane Luger

Warner Books, Inc.
1271 Avenue of the Americas
New York, NY 10020

Visit our Web site at
http://warnerbooks.com

W A Time Warner Company

Printed in the United States of America

First Printing: December, 1997

10 9 8 7 6 5 4 3 2 1

Chapter One

"Humility reduces a female to butter every time, old man. A fellow must be humble. Go to the girl, hat in hand, heart on sleeve, soul in the eye, adoration in every word—"

"Gray."

Gray Falconer blinked several times and frowned at his friend, Max Rossmara. "What?"

"The girl in question is Minerva Arbuckle?"

"You know it is. *She* is. That's why we're here. This is her home. Her parents' home." Gray felt exasperated.

"Quite. And Minerva is the very female you have rhap-sodized about all the way home from the West Indies? She who is most unlike any other woman? A sweet creature, but with a will of her own, and a strong head, and a fierce temper when aroused? The same Minerva Arbuckle who is ahead of her time, determined, and who will never allow another to persuade her of her own mind?"

Max had only grown more apt to annoy Gray in the years since their meeting at Eton.

Just in time to save Gray from searching out another

response, Mrs. Hatch, the Arbuckles' plump, phlegmatic housekeeper, appeared in the foyer of Willieknock Lodge where she'd left them—without a civil word—before going in search of her mistress.

"Well, Mrs. Hatch," Gray said, bestowing one of the smiles famous for shaking any female's reserve. "You left us so quickly I hadn't the time to tell you how very fine you're looking."

"I've the gout," Mrs. Hatch responded, sniffling, and hobbled to prove her point. "Hersel' says ye're to wait in the garden room. Daft, I call it. *Garden room.* Hoity-toity. Cold in there, too. No better then ye deserve, though. Disturbin' folks at such an hour." She turned away and shuffled past the foot of the no-nonsense mahogany staircase looming over an oppressive entry hall hung with so many paintings of nudes that the dark burgundy-colored wallpaper could barely be seen.

"I told you we shouldn't be making calls so late in the day," Max said. He paused to study a painting of a recumbent, raven-haired damsel of impressive proportions and said, "I say, Gray, look at these—"

"Yes," Gray said quickly. "Mr. Arbuckle is Mr. Porteous Arbuckle."

"Really?" Clearly Max failed to make any connection between Min's father and the paintings.

"The celebrated painter," Gray clarified. A man could be forgiven a small, judicious exaggeration. After all, Mr. Arbuckle was responsible for the paintings.

"Does he paint anything other than nudes?" Max cleared his throat. "I mean, I don't recall if he paints anything other than nudes."

"Doesna'," Mrs. Hatch said, leading the way from the hall, through a corridor lined with more tributes to billowing white flesh, toward a door fashioned of stained-glass panels. "Ye wouldna' get me takin' my clothes off the way those hussies do. All in the name o' art." She made a scoffing noise. "I wouldna' no matter how much the master begged."

Gray met Max's eyes, managed not to smile, and entered the garden room he remembered so well from the many hours he'd spent at Willieknock Lodge before leaving for the Falconer sugar plantations in the West Indies so long ago.

"That's that, then," Mrs. Hatch said when she'd deposited them amid raised, brick-lined beds devoid of anything but unlikely holly bushes, and the bare stalks of plants too fragile to stand the bone-chilling cold inside the glass walls and dome of the room. "Hersel' will be here when she's primped enough. Daft." Mrs. Hatch left with a mighty swishing of her black skirts.

Light in the garden room was low. Snow fell softly from a black sky onto the glass overhead, and nestled in here-and-gone puffs against the windows.

"Damn cold," Max muttered, shifting his wide shoulders inside a heavy coat of a cloth similar to Gray's black caped cloak. "I say we should have gone directly to Drumblade. You have much to share with your uncle, and you could have come here at an appropriate hour in the morning."

"Minerva would never have forgiven me had I wasted another moment in coming to her." The anticipation of seeing her caused warmth enough to shut out the night chill that permeated the room.

"You'd do well to tell her it all, then, Gray. The whole truth."

"Hush," Gray said, glancing over his shoulder. "I told you we must keep everything between us until I discover more." Even Max didn't know *everything*. Gray had considered it wise to keep his own counsel on some details of his abduction at sea, on his way home to England, and his subsequent detainment on a primitive island held by a murderous pirate band.

"They intended to kill you," Max said, undeterred by

Gray's exhortation to be cautious. "There could be no other explanation."

"Possibly." Gray had his own theories about the cut-throats' plans for his fate, but knew he must not reveal them yet. "I thank God that I was picked up from that pathetic raft."

"And I thank God for the amazing coincidence that put me aboard that ship. I wasn't to have sailed in her at all."

They'd marveled many times at the chance that had placed Max aboard the very vessel that came upon Gray's exhausted body.

"Max, bear with me. I know it's your way to have everything out in the open, but I know what I'm about here." He knew that his captors had been paid for their efforts, and that they'd been expected to kill him. He'd heard them in the dark of hot nights, drunk and planning to turn "Lord Ice-eyes," as they called him, into a bigger fortune than any they'd ever dreamed of before. They referred to his enemy as "Mr. No-name," and laughed while they congratulated themselves on outwitting that gentleman and causing him to keep them supplied with "fat boons," in exchange for their repeatedly broken promises to kill Gray.

"Of course it'll be the way you want it," Max said. "But I'd have thought you'd be chafing to see Drumblade. It's your home, man, and you almost bid it goodbye."

"I almost bid Min goodbye. My house and lands are dear to me, but not as dear as Minerva Arbuckle."

Heavy, hurrying footsteps approached and Janet Arbuckle, Minerva's mother, entered. A large lady with blue eyes and a great many blond ringlets bouncing about her ears, she rushed at Gray with outstretched arms. "My dear Mr. Falconer, our joy knows no bounds. We are beside ourselves with ecstasy."

Gray kept his teeth together and his lips smiling and took Mrs. Arbuckle's plump hands in his. "Ecstasy," he murmured. "I hope you are well."

"Oh, I've been far from well." She averted her face and bowed her head. "How could I be well while my dearest Minerva pined for you? How could I be other than destroyed when she has barely eaten a decent meal since she began to watch for you with less and less hope that you would ever return?"

"How indeed?" Max asked, his green eyes solemn. "Any woman awaiting Gray Falconer's return for long would be bound to fade away entirely."

Janet Arbuckle shot Gray's friend a suspicious glance. "And you are, sir?"

"Max Rossmara," Gray said hurriedly. "An old friend. He's also by way of being a neighbor."

Mrs. Arbuckle had already lost interest in Max. "Ahem." She produced a lace handkerchief and flapped it before her full, but pretty, face. "I do wonder if it mightn't be kinder to have you come back in the morning. Just to give me time to prepare Minerva."

Gray frowned and swung his cape back from his shoulders. "I doubt Minerva would be amused to discover I'd visited and gone away without seeing her." He propped a foot on the edge of a brick wall and rested a forearm on his thigh. The pose should assure Mrs. Arbuckle that he had no intention of going anywhere very soon.

Mrs. Arbuckle made a twittery noise, not unlike the canary Gray had once given Min. "Well, I'm sure you aren't to be dissuaded. Gentlemen can be so forceful." She smiled coyly. "But then, isn't that what we ladies find so irresistible?"

Max coughed and turned to stare through the glass at the snow-dotted darkness.

"Surely Min's been told I'm here," Gray said.

"Oh"—the lady raised plump shoulders shown off by an inappropriately frilly, off-the-shoulder dress in peach-colored silk—"she'll be along very soon, I'm sure."

More footsteps sounded in the corridor, and Gray stood up. His palms were suddenly damp.

A familiar high—soaring to even higher—laugh reached them, and Gray closed his eyes for a moment, anticipating the arrival of Porteous Arbuckle. Even the thought of the man made nerves in Gray's jaw twitch, and fixed his spine until it ached. That his wonderful Minerva was the product of such a couple would always bemuse him.

"What's this, then?" Porteous demanded, all but capering into view. "Hatch said I'd best come and deal with things. I said I pay *her* to deal with things, but she just walked away. *Walked away.*" He laughed again, slapping his knees through a paint-splotched blue smock.

"Mr. Arbuckle," Mrs. Arbuckle said severely. "We have visitors. Very welcome visitors, I may add." She went to her husband's side.

"I can't see anyone of importance," the man said, peering at Gray. "Who is this, then, m'dear?"

"Mr. Arbuckle," that gentleman's lady said, and delivered a kick to his skinny shin without making any attempt at disguising the blow. When he shrieked and hopped about, she caught him by the voluminous sleeve of his smock and jerked him back beside her. The top of his head, in a huge, floppy blue beret, reached her chin. "Gray Falconer has returned from his travels. Praise be, when we all thought something dreadful had happened to him. We are grateful that was not the case, aren't we, Mr. Arbuckle?"

Gray watched the man closely. Never deceived by the idiotic act, Gray regarded the other as almost certainly dangerous, but he could not risk giving his suspicions away. Given warning, Arbuckle might find a way to conceal the connections Gray was certain he had, and the treacherous steps he'd taken to rid himself of the man he'd never wanted as a son-in-law. Porteous Arbuckle didn't want any son-in-law at all. He was too dependent on his daughter's keen intelligence and her levelheaded ability to run his household and keep them from financial chaos. And he was just mad enough to kill for such a reason.

How would Minerva regard Gray if he unmasked her father as a would-be murderer? After all, she hadn't been present when the man had said, "I'll see you dead rather than married to my daughter." Afterward Arbuckle had laughed his manic laugh and denied ever having made such a threat, but Gray had heard, and Gray had suffered the painful evidence that the threat had been very real.

Later, Gray thought, he must deal with the question of how to handle the issue with Minerva later. That's why every move must be cautiously made.

"*Mr. Arbuckle,*" Mrs. Arbuckle said, treading on her husband's toe this time. When he howled, she shook her head until her ringlets flapped. "Do stop giving vent to your artistic temperament, my dear. Gray Falconer has returned."

Arbuckle stood quite still and looked at Gray. "Who?" There could be no mistaking shock on the man's face.

"*Gray Falconer.* He's your daughter's fiancé."

For a moment Arbuckle stared at a man he'd thought dead. "My daughter doesn't have a fiancé. She's a spinster. Who's that?" He pointed rudely at Max.

"Mr. Max Rossmara," Mrs. Arbuckle said. "He's a friend of Gray's."

"And who is he when he's not a friend of . . . whatever his name is?"

Max turned back from the windows, his color suspiciously high. His dark red hair glinted in the subdued light. "I'm estate commissioner to the Marquess of Stonehaven at Castle Kirkcaldy."

"Never heard of either of them."

"I'm sure not," Max said, deeply polite. "Dunkeld way. Somewhat beyond. Gray and I met at Eton, and we haven't seen much of each other since."

"Fortunate for you, I should say," Arbuckle announced, and earned himself a pinch to the cheek. He clapped a hand over his face and said, "*Dunkeld* way? Dunkeld way. No wonder I haven't heard of you, or it, or him, or whatever. You're a foreigner."

A foreigner? Dunkeld couldn't be more than thirty miles distant. Ballyfog lay between that village and Edinburgh.

Gray gave his attention to Mrs. Arbuckle once more. "What do you suppose is keeping Minerva?"

"The silliness," she said, with another exuberant shake of the head. "She'll give all that up now you're back."

"Good night to you," Porteous said. "Nice of you to pay your respects. Do have a safe trip to . . . wherever. Let yourself out, will you?" Without more parting words, he drew his slight stature up and strutted from the room without looking back.

Mrs. Arbuckle wound her handkerchief between her fingers and leaned forward from the waist. "Excuse Mr. Arbuckle. He hasn't been well. I'd better go to him."

Afraid he would be forced to leave without seeing Minerva, Gray said, "Please do take care of your husband. If you'd just direct me, I'll find Minerva. Is she busy with her piano?"

"Um, nooo."

"Her own painting, then. I always said she'd inherited some of her father's brilliance in that direction." Actually Minerva was an excellent watercolorist.

"Nooo," Mrs. Arbuckle said. "Gray, I really do think tomorrow might be preferable."

He allowed his desperation to show. "I need to see her. Surely you can understand my fervor to do so."

Another coy smile was his reward. "Of course. I'm not so old that I forget how these things are. I shall send you to her, but you must promise me you'll make allowances for the time she's spent awaiting your return. She's—*changed.* Somewhat changed. Quite changed."

"Really?"

"Yes, she"—Mrs. Arbuckle blinked rapidly—"she's the

dear girl you left but with a few minor, ummm, idiosyncrasies. Yes, that's what they are. Developed to help mask her desperate concern for you."

"I see."

"I'm sure you will. The third floor. She's taken it over and spends all of her time up there with her cousins."

Iona and Fergus Drummond, twins orphaned by Janet Arbuckle's brother and his wife, had lived with the Arbuckles since their early teens. "Thank you," Gray said. "Don't let me take up any more of your time. You've already been more than kind."

"No more kind than I should be. Oh, this is *wonderful*. Oh, how wonderful."

"Thank you," Gray said again.

Mrs. Arbuckle turned away, then turned back, a frown puckering her brow. "Now, you won't forget what I said? You must be patient with Minerva. Whatever she says, don't believe a word of it. She doesn't mean it."

Gray tried, but failed, to avoid Max's eyes. Max raised his arched brows.

"You know how difficult she can be," Mrs. Arbuckle continued. "And she has only become more so. In fact, she's positively infuriating sometimes. Frequently. Almost all the time."

"Don't worry." Gray was worried—just a little worried. "Leave her in my hands."

"Yes, yes, I'll do that. That's what I'll do. Leave her in your hands. Oh, yes, in your hands . . ." The lady's voice continued to a meaningless babble that faded as she got farther from the garden room.

"Right," Gray said. "The third floor. Big closed rooms are all I remember. Didn't think anyone went up there."

"Apparently the infuriating Minerva Arbuckle goes there now," Max said in deceptively even tones. "Are you still convinced she's going to turn to butter the moment she sets eyes on you?"

"Utterly convinced."

"Why?"

He considered. "It's best to be blunt at times like this."

Max crossed his arms. "Times like this?"

"When dealing with matters of the heart, and the head, and the soul, and the—"

"Quite. You be blunt, then, Gray."

"Min worships me." There was the slightest disquiet lurking amid his conviction, but it was nothing worth consideration. "She has worshiped me from the moment we met. And when I had to leave for the West Indies, she promised she'd be waiting for me when I returned."

Max made a humming noise, a habit of his of which Gray was not at all fond, before asking, "She promised she'd be waiting for you when you returned?"

"Yes." Irritation made itself felt.

"When you returned a year after you left?"

Rossmara could be a *damnably* irritating fellow. *"Yes."*

"But you're three years late."

Chapter Two

Women would be set free, or Minerva Arbuckle wasn't Minerva Arbuckle, who she most certainly was. One day all women would be as free as she made herself when she was working. Today she wore one of her favorite chiffon outfits. Light and loose, with no undergarments to restrict movement, the sleeves were full and the top separate from a divided skirt of slender cut that didn't quite reach her ankles. A turban with a good many feathers secured at one side was a purely whimsical touch.

"Now, Min?" Fergus Drummond asked, bending to the crank that turned a revolving dais he'd concocted mostly from the rescued parts of some discarded milling equipment.

Minerva stepped back and said, "Yes, now," and Fergus turned the crank slowly.

The dais itself—formerly the top of a round table—creaked ominously. Minerva reassured herself that no collapse of the contraption was imminent, and concentrated on her latest invention. On the latest version of her latest invention.

"Aesthetically pleasing," she pronounced. "Say you agree, Fergus. Oh, do stop slavering over your silly machine and pay attention."

Carrot-haired, blue-eyed, and freckled, Fergus stood up. His face red, he puffed and moved away to survey Minerva's masterpiece. "Aye. But if I can't turn my crank, I can't turn your dais thing, and you can't see the full sartorial splendor of your frightful frills and flounces, can you?"

"*These* frightful frills and flounces are a stroke for womanhood. They are the most innovative innovation to appear on the fashion scene in hundreds of years. My frills and flounces will keep the ankles of Scots womanhood *dry*. No more scuffing, bedraggled and mortified before the supercilious eyes of so-called *man*hood. How does it feel, Iona?"

"Um." Balanced atop the dais, and resplendent in a brown velvet gown, Iona pointed a tentative toe. "I suppose it feels fine."

"Of course it feels fine," Minerva told her.

Holding her arms out from a vast bustle (the gown was appropriated from Mama's castoffs), Iona surveyed herself. "I never thought brown a color that suited me."

"*Iona.*" Minerva waved her arms and circled. "Everyone knows brown is very good on redheads." Iona's hair was a similar carrot hue to her brother's. "Not that the suitability of brown velvet to your coloring is an issue here. Flip your skirts behind you. Not with your hand, silly. Use a foot, the way I taught you."

Dutifully Iona held her tongue between her teeth, concentrated until her frown grew deep and her eyes all but crossed, and batted at the hem of the dress with a slippered foot.

Minerva clapped her hands and laughed. "Perfect. Except that you appear to be preparing for some athletic feat, Iona. A painful athletic feat. So the initial test is a success. No one will have the faintest idea that there is anything different about this gown. All they will see will be the marvelous confidence of the female striding, undaunted, through gutters and puddles, across rain-wet pavement, and over sodden grass, a smile of triumph upon her face, needing the hand of no man to assist her."

Fergus mumbled. Fergus frequently mumbled.

"I don't see why a lady will feel any different, Min," Iona said. "Unless she's embarrassed because her skirts are inches too short."

"Pah!" Minerva laughed and twirled, enjoying the way her own self-styled costume moved so lightly and without impeding her. "The garment will be put into service by late spring. By then hems will have risen anyway. Mark that you heard the news from me first. Anyway, that's immaterial. Look to your waist."

Iona looked. "What?"

"Can I turn the thing again?" Fergus asked.

"Soon," Minerva assured him. "At your waist, Iona. See? That sly, brown satin ribbon with gold trim."

"This bow, you mean," Iona said, pulling on one side, then yelping.

With a scratching thump, a lace-trimmed petticoat descended to meet the dais. The garment settled in a stiff circle.

"That's it." Minerva clapped her hands again. "Exactly as I planned. The ribbon surrounds the waist. Tabs are suspended from the ribbon. The tabs hold up the petticoat. Untie the ribbon, and the petticoat lowers. But only to the extent I've planned. You see how I've fashioned large knots at the ends of the ribbons to stop them from sliding inside the eyelets."

Iona continued to frown but made no comment.

"And there you have it!" Minerva's glee knew no bounds. "Minerva Arbuckle's Mud Thwarter Hem. The whole world shall hear of it."

"Min," Iona said.

"Now for the final test. Unnecessary, but I insist on absolute thoroughness."

"Min," Iona repeated.

Iona tended to whine somewhat and was best ignored when in such moods. "The tray, Fergus. Hold my hands while he puts the tray beneath your feet, Iona."

"*Min.*"

"Be quick, Fergus. Iona grows restless. You know how she is when she's restless."

"Oooh," Iona moaned. "Oooh, Min."

A large metal pan with a deep lip was maneuvered beneath the dress and beneath Iona's feet. "You haven't asked what the petticoat's made of," Minerva said, so elated she could scarce concentrate at all. "It's canvas. Ships' canvas. Now, isn't that obvious. Of course, a material used for the sails of ships will keep a lady's hems dry. Oh, the deviousness of men. The foolishness of men. They knew this, but didn't want us to know it because they control us through the flapdoodle clothes they insist we wear. Don't let our arms move too much, because a man can only be shamed by the notion that any lady under his protection needs to move her arms at all. Outrageous nonsense!" She raised her own chiffon-clad arms and reveled in the way her sleeves slipped down to reveal her naked arms. "In truth they are afraid to give us freedom, because then they might not be able to control us so easily."

"Minerva," Iona said, whispering now. "Please, Minerva."

"Oh, all right. We'll be through soon enough, *then* you may go and relieve yourself."

"*Minerva*, this is taking so long."

"Oh, *really*. Fergus, the buckets. Quickly."

At twenty-two, Fergus was wiry and strong, and despite coloring and facial features so similar to those of his twin, he couldn't be more different in build. Iona was as fragile as he was sturdy. He picked up a large bucket in each hand and carried them to the dais. Then he emptied first one, then the other, of a great quantity of muddy water, filling the pan almost to the rim.

Minerva stood still.

Fergus stood still.

Iona hugged her middle and whimpered.

"Well?" Minerva asked. "Speak up, Iona."

Iona raised a foot. Then she raised the other foot. "It's cold. And wet."

"You should have worn boots," Fergus observed. "You should have made her wear boots, Min."

Minerva went closer and leaned to peruse the bottom of the gown. Dark water soaked the lace she'd used to camouflage the edge of the sail canvas. "The lace was a mistake," she said. "No lace."

Gradually the petticoat fell into tighter, soggier folds, and a wavy gray line rose around its width.

"Minerva," Iona said tentatively. "Did you think canvas didn't get wet?"

"Of course it doesn't. They use it at sea."

"It's getting wet. And heavy, and Min"—Iona's face creased with distaste—"it feels horrible."

"It can't feel as horrible as wet skirts."

"It *is* a wet skirt. A heavy, wet skirt. And it scratches. I'm cold." Her teeth chattered loudly. "I want to get out."

The choking noise Minerva heard made her furious. Fergus laughing. Fergus was a champion laugher, especially when he was confronted with the failed fruits of Minerva's labors.

"I shall make adjustments," Minerva announced. "Promptly. I already have a better idea. The canvas was too simple a solution. My next effort is more complex, but it will succeed."

"Not now." Iona's voice rose to a wail. "Help me out, Fergus."

Swallowing chuckles, Fergus dutifully handed his sister from her plinth to the old library steps that had been in the room when Minerva claimed it. Large, with a high gallery all around, her grandfather Arbuckle had converted the space from a schoolroom to his private library. The books still remained. Neither Mama nor Papa was fond of books, so they hadn't minded that Minerva wanted the library for her own retreat.

"Min, you must change," Iona said. With each shift, her skirts sounded like sodden sheets flapping before a stiff wind. "It isn't suitable for you to wear that foreign-looking thing. It hardly covers you. Tell her, Fergus."

"You've never found fault before," Minerva said shortly. "It allows me freedom of movement. I am a working woman. A woman who must move about freely as she works."

"*Trousers,*" Iona continued, worry etched into her pretty face. "Not seemly at all."

"Why are you suddenly critical?" Minerva asked. "And it's a divided skirt, not trousers. And you can mark my word that before long divided skirts will be commonplace among thinking women who refuse to be put down by men. It isn't *seemly* for a gentleman to catch a glimpse of an ankle. Pah! It's seemly enough for a gentleman to catch a glimpse of a lady's ankle if he can, and as long as no other gentleman catches a glimpse of an ankle he considers his property. Mark that I've told you this: divided skirts will become commonplace. And mark that it was I who told you that this entire Rule by Restriction that has been forced upon us by the male of the species is sexual in its implications."

"*Minerva.*"

"If you keep saying *Minerva* like that I shall change my name. Now. Are you telling me the canvas underskirt is completely out of the question?"

"Completely. Min"—Iona beckoned Minerva close—"oh, Min, this is terrible, isn't it? A disaster. But you're putting such a good face on it. Only, please don't say any more of those dreadful things about . . . *sexual.*"

Minerva smiled and hugged her gentle cousin. "You are such a silly goose, Iona. And you are not a baby anymore.

You are twenty-two, only three years younger than I. It's time we could discuss sexual matters without your face turning as red as that artist's model of Daddy's when we found them—well, you know."

Fergus had grown unnaturally still. He said, "Min," in a voice quite unlike his own.

"Oh, what is it, Fergus? What is the matter with *both* of you this evening? I declare you need more sleep. Go to bed at once and stay there until you feel well again. You are in poor spirits, and it pains me. I have pushed you both too hard. Forgive me, please."

"No," Fergus said. "It's not that, Min. Aren't you cold? You can all but see through that thing."

She looked down at herself. "No, of course I'm not cold. It must be something you've eaten." Minerva felt considerable concern. "I insist you leave me now and go to your beds. I'll tell Hatch to bring you bread and milk. And a brandy broth with lemon and honey. Go at once."

"Min—"

"Now," Minerva insisted, shooing them toward the door. "I'll clean up here."

Iona covered her strangely reddening face with both hands.

Fergus crossed his arms, braced his feet apart, and contrived to look like a strong tree that would require a very sharp ax to fell. "We can't leave you," he said. "You know we can't leave you unchaperoned."

"Catch this, Fergus, there's a good chap." A man spoke from the gallery behind Minerva. "Wrap it around her if you please."

Minerva spun about and looked up into the darkened recesses of the book-lined gallery. Two tall, shadowy figures stood there. A large black thing billowed in the air and fell, to be gathered up by Fergus, who was now as pink-cheeked as his sister.

"Let him put my cloak on you, please, Minerva," the voice said. "We shall all be more comfortable."

Blood left her head, left her dizzy.

It could not be him.

Fergus came to her side, the cloak spread in readiness to engulf her. Minerva batted it and Fergus away. "No," she told him, and the room blurred before her. "Don't touch me, please."

"No shoes," Fergus whispered. "And a turban with feathers in it. What'll he think?"

"What will who think?" She closed her eyes. This could not be. This was impossible.

"You know who," Fergus said. "No doubt you're in a blither, but please put on the cloak."

"Never," she said between clenched teeth. "This is a cruel trick. I had thought you above such viciousness."

"Put on—"

"I will *not* put on the cloak," she told Fergus. "Now, please. Leave me. All of you leave me. Your cruel jest wounds me. How could you twist my broken heart again?"

A silence followed, finally shattered by the thud of booted feet on the spiral staircase from the gallery. There was an entrance to the room up there.

Minerva opened her eyes and stared, and took several steps backward.

If the tall, exceedingly solid, and muscular man who stood before her was not Gray Falconer, then she was confronting his ghost—his tall, exceedingly solid, and muscular ghost. And that ghost possessed Gray's dark curly hair and the ice-gray eyes that could become warmer than any might ever expect gray ice to become. And the ghost was also gifted with Gray's wide, generous mouth, and the dimpled grooves in his cheeks, and the intriguing indentation at the center of his chin, and his square jaw. True, this . . . *creature* . . . looked older, but Gray would be older by four years than when he'd left Ballyfog for the West Indies. He was five years older than Minerva and would be almost thirty now.

"Minerva," the ghost said. "Oh, dearest Minerva."

Gray's softly deep and rumbly voice. She looked at his outstretched hands. Gray's large, long-fingered hands.

"Minerva, love of my life, I have come for you, just as I promised I would. You are as lovely as you have been in my dreams, and my dreams were all I had for so long."

She looked about. Yes, this was her library workroom, the place where she performed what Mama was pleased to call "silliness." And Iona was there. And Fergus. And the rickety dais topped with a pan of muddy water, the same muddy water that dripped slowly from Iona's skirts onto an old but valuable silk rug.

"You are overcome with joy," Gray said. He smiled, and his smile turned her heart. He continued, "I believe you have become a little unbalanced with the pressure of waiting for me, but I shall help you put all this silliness behind you."

Silliness. Mama's term.

"I am a happy man tonight, dearest. Only say you are happy, too, and my joy will be complete. And do consent to wearing my cloak, pet. You must be cold, dressed as you are. *Undressed* as you are. Did you think you would be attending a masquerade this evening perhaps? As a harem girl? Oh, it is long past time for me to care for you as you must be cared for. I had thought you a woman with a very strong mind. But then, that was before you were forced to live without the sight of me. Minerva, I should never have wished such a thing upon you. I have missed you so."

"Gray." The second man, also tall and with dark red hair and the most extraordinary green eyes, looked at his companion with concern. "I say, Gray, old man. I think we should put this off until the morning."

"What?" Gray—and it did seem to be Gray in the flesh rather than a ghost—glanced at the other man. "What in

God's name are you talking about? We're here now, aren't we?"

"Yes. And you are clearly not yourself. I assure you that you will thank me for putting the close to this encounter for the moment."

"I hardly think—"

"You're babbling, man," Gray was told summarily. "Making a cake of yourself."

"Damn your infernal nerve," Gray said.

"And cursing in front of ladies."

Minerva managed to take a full breath. "You didn't come when you said you would."

"I'm so sorry." Gray's voice, Gray's serious eyes.

"You stopped writing." Her legs grew weaker by the instant. "Not a word in so long. They said you were dead." Her voice sounded weak.

"Well." Gray spread his hands. "I'm not surprised, I suppose, given the circumstances. But—"

"The ship you were on came back to England safely. The captain said you had boarded, but then they thought you got off again."

"So they thought."

"You weren't dead at all."

"No. I . . . but there were circumstances that made it hard for me to write to you."

"I mourned. I wore black."

"Oh, my dearest Minerva."

"You aren't dead."

"No."

"You never were." She longed to flee but couldn't make her feet move. "For three years when you were, you weren't. Dead, that is."

"No, I wasn't."

Just like that. *No, I wasn't.* And sweet words, and smiles, and the evident expectation that she would think nothing of such extraordinary behavior. That she would, in fact, simply fly into his arms without question.

"Well," she told him. "In that case, since you aren't dead, you can just leave."

Chapter Three

The carriage topped a rise, the rise that gave Gray his first view of Drumblade. Softened by a quilt of snow, the uncompromising gray stone of the impressive Jacobean house took on a silver sheen in the moonlight.

He leaned closer to the window to capture his fill of the harshly beautiful home where he had been born on the same day his mother died. His father had also died at Drumblade, barely a year before Gray left for the plantations.

On the very day of his departure, on a journey he'd had no choice but to make, Minerva Arbuckle had promised she'd wait for him. At her father's insistence, they'd put off their betrothal. He'd pointed out that Gray was only to be gone a year and that he and Minerva had a lifetime before them, that more attention could be paid to planning that lifetime once Gray was returned. And this very day Arbuckle had pretended he didn't even recognize the man he'd known for years. Bitterness made an acid taste in Gray's mouth tonight. Behind Porteous Arbuckle's vague manner, his artistic temperament and its affectations, behind it all lay a conniving manipulator. With each passing day, each passing event, Gray became more convinced that he who wished him dead was a cavorting popinjay in paint-stained blue.

Seated opposite Gray in the coach, Max also watched their downhill progress toward Drumblade. "A fine house," he said. "You must have thought of this moment many times on that island."

"I thought of it," Gray said shortly. "I thought of other things a good deal more." He'd thought of Minerva and would continue to do so.

"Your Minerva," Max said, jostled by the wheels bouncing into frozen ruts. "She is very—unusual."

"She isn't herself." He took up his hat from the seat beside him and balanced it on his knee. "I blame myself— or perhaps I should blame that—" He closed his mouth. He must have a care. Max was entirely reliable, but there were things a man must do alone. To reveal Arbuckle as a monster in his daughter's eyes was out of the question. She might never recover from the horror. No, the monster's claws had already been blunted by failure. Now they must be removed in such a way that his crimes were hidden while they served to deter any further effort to interfere in his daughter's future—or in Gray's.

He felt Max watching him and made much of brushing off his hat with the sleeve of his jacket.

"She's fascinating, Gray," Max murmured. "That's what I should have said."

"Yes." Gray scarcely trusted himself to think too closely about his feelings for the one woman he'd ever loved. "We met when she was little more than a child. I thought her an impossible nuisance then. She came to Drumblade with her parents—to a garden party given by my father under pressure from my uncle. Uncle Cadzow insisted that it was time to stop hiding away—which my father did to a degree after my mother died." He did not add, *after I was born.* "This is a small enough community. All those of any position were invited, and many of no position at all, because that is the kind of man my father was."

"As are you," Max remarked. "And as my own father is. I love deeply the generosity of men and women who could, but who do not, affect any airs."

"Indeed." Gray had met Max's adoptive parents—Struan, Viscount Hunsingore, and his lovely Viscountess, Lady Justine. His own family were, and had been, wildly successful merchants elevated to the stature of landed gentry by their own endeavors. They had also always been people of huge generosity.

"So," Max said. "You met the incomparable Minerva at a garden party when she was a child."

"I couldn't stand her." Gray laughed. "She was like a gnat. No, like a moth—no, a rather attractive but sturdy butterfly who flitted about me, stared at me, questioned me incessantly. She simply would not be ignored." He smiled at the memory.

"And then?"

Gray raised a brow and kept his eyes on Drumblade. The coach bore down the last stretch of road leading to great gates where iron unicorns rampant stood sentry duty on either side.

"Then?" Max persisted.

"Then? Ah, then, yes. Whenever I ventured into Ballyfog—and anyone who lives in these parts must venture into Ballyfog frequently since nothing is far distant—whenever I went there little Miss Arbuckle managed to pop up before me. She was about twelve, and I, seventeen. You can imagine how enthralled I was with the attentions of a twelve-year-old."

"Aha," Max said. "But you remember those occasions."

"I remember them because the devious little madam was busily implanting herself under my skin. She burrowed into my nerves, bored into my bones, and took over my brain. Of course, I knew no such thing at first. In fact, I think I was twenty, and she fifteen, before revelation exploded. And it did explode, I assure you."

"Do tell."

Gray tapped his bottom lip with his cane. "The forward hussy kissed me."

"What?" Shifting to the edge of his seat, even in the almost dark interior of the coach, Max's eyes glinted with interest. "The devil you say."

"Yes, and I do say. That little miss who scarcely reaches my chin, even if she is *sturdy,* leaped out at me in the lane between Maudlin Manor and the McSporrans' cottage. She pretended to be injured, then, when I rushed to her aid, climbed upon a stile, threw her arms around my neck, and kissed me. What do you say to that?"

"Too bad she wasn't somewhat older, and beautiful."

"She was beautiful." Gray found he could no longer smile. "She was always beautiful, just as she is now."

Max didn't reply.

"Minerva has the kind of beauty you discover gradually. First there is the way she carries herself. Upright, graceful, smooth in the manner of her walk. Her eyes are marvelous. Very dark blue and large. Every thought she has passes through her eyes. And her features are soft, very soft. Her mouth . . . so soft and full."

"And so capable of delivering the vinegar," Max commented.

Gray smiled again. "That, too. She has the sharpest of wits, and tongues. But I have hurt her."

"You had no choice."

"I managed my return badly. I should have listened to you and approached more cautiously. She will come around, of course. Nothing has changed there. She has loved me since she was a little girl."

"One hopes that love is somewhat changed."

"Don't be facetious."

"I am never facetious. Your Minerva has"—Max

coughed—"she is exceedingly well-made. No doubt the pleasure of observing the blossoming of so lovely a body assisted you in deciding you loved her, too."

"Damn you!" An instant and Gray had Max by the cravat. "I don't like your suggestions. And I don't want to know that you've been looking at Minerva in that manner again. Do I make myself clear?"

"I say." Max gripped Gray's hand and worked it free. "No disrespect intended. Only compliment."

"I did not ever look upon Minerva Arbuckle with a lascivious eye."

"Of course not, old man."

"I have never had other than her best interests at heart."

"Indubitably."

"Her purity is my treasure. I will protect it always, just as I always have."

"Really?" Max asked, much too innocently.

The import of his own words embarrassed Gray. "I simply mean that I cherish her and would never willingly do anything to hurt her."

"I think you set yourself an impossible task," Max said. "She's angry and she is, as you've already admitted, headstrong. She may not be easily persuaded that there was nothing you could do to change what has happened."

"She will listen and understand."

"If you refuse to give her explanations?"

Therein rested the dilemma. "I will find a way."

"Will you listen to some advice?"

"From a bachelor? From a man who knows nothing of love?"

Max rested against the squabs, and Gray saw his handsome face in profile and cast in serious lines.

"Max? Have I offended you?"

"Let's just say that I know a great many things about a great many things. And nothing about a great many things.

Love is in the former category. In my case, there is no hope. And the topic is closed."

All men carried their secrets. Gray bowed his head. "I'd appreciate any advice you can give me."

"Very well," Max said. "Pursue her relentlessly. Refuse to be turned aside. If she slips from your grasp, chase her and capture her again. Woo her with those words and looks you spoke of, and with actions. If you love the girl, you must make her yours or you will suffer as long as you live."

In the wake of Max's speech, silence crowded the compartment. Gray couldn't look away from his friend's lean, shadow-etched features, his eyes that gazed but saw nothing. "Thank you," Gray said. "I'll heed your words." He'd intended to do exactly as Max proposed anyway, but the sadness he felt in the other man made him even more determined.

"I worry about you," Max said, stirring, and turning from the windows. "Your abduction was no isolated act. It wasn't a lark. You know that, don't you?"

"I've told you I do."

"Someone wanted you disposed of. They wanted you killed. That means you present a threat to someone, or to something that affects someone deeply."

"We've already had this discussion."

"And we'll probably have it many more times. How can we avoid it? I fear that your enemies won't be satisfied to give up on their scheme. Why should they? If they had some reason to want you dead before, why would that have changed?"

Nothing Max said was a new thought to Gray. He must change the subject. "Now I need to prepare myself for Uncle Cadzow. He was always a quiet man. Distant, but kind. He is very pious."

"So you said."

"He preferred to lead his own life. Very private. He's

dedicated himself to good works—often overseas. And in London, too, I understand. He speaks a great deal of the 'unsaved among us.' It didn't please him to be forced to come here and play guardian to me after my father died."

"Hardly guardian. You were twenty-four."

"It fell to him to administer the estates until my twenty-fifth birthday."

Max rested a hand on Gray's knee. "You didn't mention that. Cadzow's been at the reins, then? At the purse strings?"

"Yes." Gray shook his head. "I know what you're thinking. We'll have to look elsewhere for our villain. At least, I think we will. God is his master, not possessions. Cadzow's share in the business is minor, but provides him with more than any man could need. He's not a physical fellow, either. Never had enough energy to ride a horse unless he absolutely had to. Setting about a full-scale intrigue would be far too taxing—and completely contrary to his nature. He'll probably hand over the responsibility of everything to me as quickly as possible. Then he'll tell me where to send his very considerable allowance, and the revenue from his share of profits, and take himself off on some new mission."

The coach scrunched through packed snow to the porte cochere.

"It's close to nine," Max said. "Will he have retired?"

"Might be as well if he had," Gray said. "I could slip old Ratley—our butler—a guinea to deliver the news with Cadzow's morning chocolate."

"You think Cadzow's going to . . . what?"

"Damned if I know," Gray said, donning his hat in anticipation of the coachman opening the door. "But I'd as well he had apoplexy in bed as out of it. Save time."

Max chuckled, and followed Gray from the carriage.

"We'll announce ourselves," Gray told the coachman. "I'll send help for the luggage. Then you can go around to the stables. Someone will take care of you—find you a bed for the night."

The coachman muttered his thanks and set about unloading Max's trunks and the three valises that were all Gray had taken time to assemble in London before setting out for Scotland.

He walked up stone steps flanked by empty urns that overflowed with flowers in summertime. After a moment's pause, he rapped a panel on the great oak front door. The sensations that assailed him were confused. Home at last. But after so much that was almost impossible to think of without revulsion, and without the rushing back of the helplessness that had sometimes engulfed him even though he'd never given up working toward his escape to freedom.

The door opened slowly and a small, white-haired manservant with jutting brows that were still red raised his pointed face to look at the newcomers.

"Good evening, Ratley," Gray said. "It's good to see you, again."

Slowly, the man's mouth sagged open. His eyebrows moved up and down and he made chewing motions, swallowing between each one.

"Come now, Ratley," Gray said with a heartiness he didn't feel, "is that any way to welcome a wanderer?"

"Och, a wanderer is it, ye are? Hah. A ne'er-do-well gallivanter, more like. Takin' off when ye're needed in your home. Sendin' back a pack o' lies t'make the likes o' us mourn the loss o' ye. Shame on ye, Master Gray. Shame on ye." He clapped a hand over his heart. "Shame on ye for the shock ye've dealt a poor old man. Taken me years closer t'me grave, ye have."

Gray allowed Ratley to revel in his indignation before saying, very gently, "I've been misused, Ratley, old friend. I'll explain more of that later," and then suggesting, "Perhaps you'd tell me if my Uncle Cadzow has retired?"

Raising a gnarled fist to his brow, Ratley emitted a shuddering sigh. "Mr. Cadzow. I forgot Mr. Cadzow. Och, but it's a weary night we've ahead o' us. Wait till himsel' puts his eyes on ye. The shock'll likely kill him."

Similar unpleasant possibilities had certainly occurred to Gray.

Ratley opened the door wide and stood back to allow Gray and Max to enter. Gray got no farther than a few footsteps into the hall before he stood still and surveyed surroundings he'd once taken for granted. Suits of armor stood, gleaming, in rows on either side. Underfoot, great slabs of stone shimmered in the flickering light of a roaring fire at the distant end of the hall. An oaken chandelier, carved by grateful tenants of Drumblade lands in Gray's grandfather's time, hung from the open ceiling on the second floor above the hall. A staircase with marble banisters rose to that second floor, to a handsomely proportioned balcony from which corridors led to various wings.

When Max tapped his shoulder, Gray started, disoriented for the moment, and said, "I want Minerva here."

"Of course you do." Max smiled and settled a hand on the back of Gray's neck. "You've been through too much in too short a time. You need to sleep."

"My *God!*"

The roar of the voice he knew was Cadzow's snapped Gray sharply to attention.

"*Gad.*" Cadzow Falconer, still blond, but more bald than when Gray had last seen him, took tottering steps from the door to the green drawing room. He paused, tottered some more, and collapsed onto the bottom step of the stairs. He looked up, sought and found Gray's face, and covered his own eyes.

Helpless, Gray turned to Max, who shook his head and raised his palms.

"I'll get brandy," Ratley said, and pushed the front door shut.

"Our luggage," Max said.

"Think no more of it," Ratley instructed, and hurried into the room Cadzow had left.

Within seconds Gray decided, with something akin to horror, that Cadzow was crying.

"Praise be to God," the man said, his voice muffled. "I don't know how this can be, but I thank God. I dared to hope, but could not share my hope. Everyone thought you dead. In the end I had to accept that you were, and put out news to that effect. I never cared for you when you were a boy, did you know that?" Gray's uncle raised his plump, tear-streaked face. His blue eyes shone moistly. "I must tell you the truth. I was so consumed with the plight of those who did not know God that I never had any time for children. That's why I was never inclined to marry. I had no inclination to share my life with a woman—miserable creature that I am." He broke into fresh sobs that doubled him over.

"It's all right," Gray said, unable to think what else to say. "I'm not dead. I almost was, though."

"Oh, praise be," Cadzow said. "I've been adrift, my boy. A pathetic man of fifty trying to change his ways and be something he isn't. But I have changed a good deal. I promise you I have. If you'll allow me to be your friend. If we can be a family, I shall remain a changed man."

Gray approached and patted his uncle's arm awkwardly. "I'm touched, Uncle. I hadn't expected you to care this much." He hadn't been certain Cadzow would care at all one way or the other.

"I never wanted to run a business, Gray. You know as much. Good fortune willed that I should be the younger brother. That pointed me in the way I was to go—the Lord's way. My dear departed Ewan, your stalwart father, was the man to head the family fortunes, and he did so as brilliantly as anyone could. Without him I felt lost."

"I know," Gray told him. "As did I."

"But you were just such a one as Ewan. You were to take

over. If you knew how many times I cursed the decision to have you go to learn more about the plantations. They'd have done as well without you. But I thought you needed to see things firsthand out there. I'd been myself—for different reasons, it's true—but I found it such a very *different* place from any you had encountered. Ah, well."

If Gray had needed additional assurance of filial feeling on the man's part, he now had that assurance.

Cadzow stood up abruptly. "Oh, forgive me. Forgive me, dear nephew. You have a companion."

Gray introduced Max, who brought some semblance of Cadzow's natural caution to the fore in the form of quizzical appraisal. With the announcement that Max was related to the Rossmaras and was breaking his journey on his way to Kirkcaldy Castle, Cadzow's suspicious countenance cleared and he waved the two newcomers into the drawing room.

Once more Gray was drawn into the subtle snare of so many memories. A beautiful room favored by his father. Deep green velvet, well worn but beautiful, fabulously valuable furnishings painstakingly gathered by three generations of Falconers, silken carpets—green and gold—and silken hangings on the walls, except where leatherbound books rose, shelf upon shelf, to soaring plaster ceilings encrusted with clusters of carved fruits.

Flames curled over the ancient chimney breast. Atop the massive white marble fireplace, an ormolu clock that had once belonged to Gray's mother still ticked among Dresden shepherdesses and exquisite painted miniatures of Falconers no longer living.

A flashing swirl of red startled Gray. He'd been too preoccupied to notice a woman reclining on a chaise set into a draped alcove. That, so he'd been told, had once been his mother's favorite place to read.

"*Cadzow?*" The female, a stranger, whispered hoarsely as if reluctant to intrude. "Who is it? At this hour, who is it?" She stood up and fluffed out the skirts of her ornate satin gown.

"Eldora," Cadzow said, approaching her with an outstretched hand. "My pet, I want you to share my joy this evening. The best surprise. The most unexpected surprise. One I had stopped daring to hope might occur."

The surprise, Gray knew at once, was his own. His uncle might have changed, as he'd put it, but a great deal, but his having installed a female at Drumblade hadn't been among the possibilities that sprang to mind.

Taller than Cadzow by several inches, the woman was beautiful. Chestnut hair drawn severely back from a center part and coiled into sleek braids about each ear heightened her exotic good looks. Her eyes were a shade of brown that was more gold, and they were almond-shaped. She wore a good deal of paint, but in the manner of women skilled with that medium so that she took on a mysterious aspect, perhaps as if she were an actress of the dramatic variety.

Holding Cadzow's hand, she came silently forward. Gray could not help but note how the slow raising and lowering of her lashes reminded him of a particularly gorgeous cat lying in the sun.

And the body . . . Ah, yes, the body. Gray lifted his eyes from lush hips, and tiny waist, and magnificent breasts corsetted tantalizingly high, their pale tops visible through a modest covering of lace, to her eyes, and felt a jolt.

Empty.

He drew back his lips from his teeth. So his godly uncle, who had never shown much interest in females, had finally been lured by the flesh after all.

Gray bowed over the hand Cadzow conveyed into one of his and murmured, "Madam. Enchanted."

"It's miss! At least it's still miss, now. Tell him, Cadzy."

And a second shock was delivered. A silly, trilling voice—allowed full volume—raked Gray's nerves. He winced.

"Miss Eldora Makewell," Cadzow said, with every sign of adoration in his manner. "My very dear friend."

"And *companion*," Miss Makewell shrieked.

"And companion," Cadzow agreed, avoiding Gray's eyes. "This is my nephew, Gray Falconer, Eldora. He who I thought was lost, is found. I am beside myself with gratitude. Gray is the man who should be here, doing what I'm doing because I must. He will do it because he was born to do so. Praise be. Praise be."

Perhaps his uncle had changed in even more ways than were immediately evident. The man Gray left behind showed no deference—or even particular awareness—toward women. He had certainly never given any sign of wanting to share personal matters with one.

"I'm pleased to meet you, too, Miss Makewell," Max said, and Gray didn't have to see his friend's face to know he would be making an assessment based on anything but the quality of Miss Makewell's mind.

"You too, I'm sure," she said, and laughed again, bringing an ache to Gray's back teeth. "Tell them, Cadzy. You'd better, before they get themselves into trouble, and you know what I mean." She winked at Max and Gray. "We wouldn't want them to get the wrong idea, would we?"

"Eldora is a dear friend," Cadzow said, reddening. "We met in London when—"

"I'm an actress," Eldora said, and executed a deep curtsy, her free hand outstretched as if acknowledging accolades from an adoring audience. "Or I was until I decided the only stage I wanted to perform on was dear Cadzy's. And, ooh, Cadzy does have a stage worth performing on, if you know what I mean."

Gray couldn't as much as look at Cadzow.

Ratley had withdrawn to a corner, apparently to await the dispatch of ritual reacquaintance of relatives. Now he came forward and set a silver tray of brimming brandy goblets on a low table before the fire.

"I'm Cadzy's fiancée," Eldora announced, drawing herself up and hugging Uncle Cadzow to her side. "He's going to make me the happiest, proudest woman in all the land, aren't you, Cadzy?"

The poor man slid a sideways glance at Gray, lifted one corner of his mouth, and said, "We're so happy you're going to be present for the festivities." Then he quickly added, "Not that they'll be occurring in the near future, of course."

Eldora pressed Cadzow to her, pressed his face to her breast, stroked his head, and crooned. "He needs someone to love him, and I do. I always shall. And I can't tell you how happy I am that you're here to share our happiness. Ooh, Cadzy, isn't this lovely?"

Even if "Cadzy" had been moved to agree, he couldn't have done so. Gray noted where his uncle's mouth rested, and promptly looked away. "Thank you," he told anyone who cared. He was exhausted, and still bewildered about Minerva. He must find a way to see her again, and soon. "I'm sure everyone's too tired to think. No doubt you're in my rooms these days, Uncle. Ratley, would you—"

"I'm dashed well *not* in your rooms, m'boy," Cadzow announced, finally disengaging himself from Eldora. "Never. In my heart I never gave up on you, even when others seemed happy to do so."

"What others?" Gray asked without thinking.

Cadzow shook his head sharply. "Dashed tongue. Forget what I said. Ratley, see to your master's rooms. And to rooms for Mr. Rossmara." He waited until Ratley slipped quickly and quietly from the drawing room before saying, "I've got to know where you've been, Gray. I know you're tired. I can see it in your face. But I'm only human. Where, damn it?"

This was bound to come up, and would again, and again, and it was never likely to sound less outrageous. "On an island."

Cadzow frowned. "Yes. I know that."

"I'm not talking about the West Indies," Gray told him. "Although I think this island was thereabouts. A small island off the shipping lanes. Dense vegetation. Held by a band of pirates. The band of pirates who took me from my homebound ship in darkness without a soul noticing I was gone, evidently."

No one spoke for so long that Gray commenced to pacing, and glancing at his companions each time he reversed directions.

"That's impossible," Cadzow said at last. "You were actually *on* the ship to come home, you say."

"I was."

"But the ship arrived without you."

Exasperated, Gray stopped his pacing. "Of course it did."

"They said you'd never boarded. Or that if you had, you must have changed your mind."

Gray thought about that. "The devil they did. Perhaps . . . True, it happened on the first night out. We'd had no gathering since casting off, so they could have thought I'd got off again."

"But they said you'd *never* boarded, I tell you."

He'd never considered that the crew of the ship on which he'd intended to return home might have been involved. "I doubt we'll track them down easily."

"You were abducted, *kidnapped,* and taken to a private island?"

"Yes," he told his uncle. "And kept segregated. Not that I suppose I'd have cared to be otherwise. And by keeping me apart, and, therefore, largely alone, they gave me time to plan and prepare for my escape. Unfortunately, it takes a long time to turn the roof of a shack into a seaworthy raft without drawing undue attention."

Uncle Cadzow stared until his blue eyes bulged. He sat down abruptly on the nearest chair and reached trembling fingers for a goblet of brandy. This he downed, and then shook his head as if to make it more clear. "Horrible," he said finally. "You mean you were abducted and imprisoned—for *three* years?"

He had no wish to examine it all, not yet, not now. Now he wanted only to find another means of being with Minerva, alone. He had to get her away from Willieknock and her odious—possibly murderous—parent.

Shaken by the clear vision of what must be done, Gray took up a brandy himself and drank it as rapidly as had his uncle.

"I say, Gray," Max murmured. "Steady on, old man."

Gray smiled at him and clapped his shoulder. "A little extra courage for the moment," he said with an attempt at lightness that needed to sound more convincing than it felt. "Memories, you know. Still hard to deal with."

"Where is this island?" Cadzow demanded, his eyes blazing now. "We shall go there at once. With an army. We shall confront the blaggards. They'll regret meddling with any man by the name of Falconer."

"Uncle," Gray said, mildly enough. A slight fogginess followed the brandy. "I don't know where the island is. And perhaps it's for the best."

"For the best?" Max said. "Dash it all, Gray. Now I know you aren't yourself yet. We need to track 'em down and find out who is at the bottom of this dastardly thing. Don't you agree, sir? Someone paid these people to snaffle Gray. He heard them talking about it when they were drunk."

"The *devil* they did," Cadzow said, rising to his feet again, the color high in his cheeks. "Someone paid them to take Gray? But . . . no, it's too much. No, I cannot countenance such a thing, it's too monstrous."

"It's over," Gray said, weary now. "I'm only grateful I was able to outwit them."

"It is not over," Cadzow said sonorously. "Such evil

must be punished. These men. These *pirates*. They must have names. You were with them three years. There has to be something you can tell us to help us locate and punish them."

Gray shook his head. "You don't understand. They never spoke to me directly. They kept me in a pen. A pen with a shack in it. Food and water were handed to me over a fence of sticks and wire and palm fronds. Oh, I saw them from a distance, all right—when I could hear how drunk they were and was certain they wouldn't notice I was watching them through the trap I made for the purpose. But they gathered some distance away and had their quarters on the far side of a beach from mine. They felt safe enough. I had no means of escape—or so they thought."

"Fantastic," Cadzow whispered.

Eldora Makewell came to push her hand around his waist and look worriedly down at him. "It's dreadful," she said. "Can you credit such bad people, Cadzy?"

"Give me a name," Uncle Cadzow said. "Give me *something*, Gray. I shall not rest until they've been brought to justice."

Gray laughed shortly. " 'Cap'n.' Will that help? Or *Two*, or *Nine*, perhaps. They called each other numbers. Sometimes they'd raise their voices as if for my benefit and shout to each other. They were proud of their clever anonymity, I think. And they wanted me to know they were being paid for their filthy business—'by someone 'e trusts,' they'd shout, and then laugh."

"Why didn't they kill you?" Uncle Cadzow asked the question as if speaking a thought aloud, then looked horrified. "My God, what am I saying?"

"What any sane man would wonder about," Max told him. "Why didn't they just get him off the ship and drown him at once for that matter. So much more simple."

"Thank God you managed to escape."

Gray regarded Cadzow seriously. "I must thank God.

That I managed at all is a miracle. Slowly I contrived to lash together the poor sticks and fronds they used for the roof of my shack. Then I pulled pieces from the fence around the pen—I had to go slowly so they wouldn't notice what I was doing. So slowly I thought I might die of frustration. I needed stronger stuff, but had to make do with sheer mass, and thickness—and it worked. It floated—for a day and two nights, until I was found."

"Gray—"

"No." Gray cut Max off, but smiled to soften his own abruptness. "No more tonight, good friend. I have things to think about—in private. And I need to rest before I embark on putting my life back together. I'm sure you'll understand if I retire, Uncle—and Eldora." He could not fathom his uncle's choice in a wife after so many years, but since he had chosen, Gray would give the woman the appropriate respect.

Cadzow moved toward the bell pull, but paused, his back to the company.

"What is it, Cadzy?" Eldora asked. "Oh, you do look poorly, lovey."

"Gray." Cadzow turned around. "When you leave a place for four years, things change."

"Of course," Gray agreed, but he read discomfort in the other man's manner. "Even if it's only that everyone is four years older." He laughed and heard the hollowness of it.

Cadzow wiped a hand across his brow, disarranging the curls combed carefully forward around his face. "Hmm. Have you thought about Minerva Arbuckle at all since you left Ballyfog?"

The question took Gray by surprise. "Minerva?"

Cadzow smiled, and his lips trembled. "Oh, you were a boy before you left, really, weren't you. Nonsense, all that cub love stuff. You'll have grown up and learned a thing or two since then. No doubt you had your flings while you were in the Indies—found out there's more to a woman than anything a bit of a girl like the Arbuckle female could ever offer."

Anger would serve no purpose here. "I think it would be wiser not to continue this conversation," Gray said. "Minerva, and my feelings for her, are my affair."

The wavering smile deserted Cadzow. "Blast, I was afraid of that. Too much to hope that a constant fella like you would get over it."

Gray no longer felt fatigued. He did feel disquiet so deep it shook him. "Let's be straight with each other," he told his uncle. "You're trying to tell me something, without telling me. About Minerva. Out with it, please."

"Damn, this is awkward." Flipping aside the tails of his burgundy-colored coat, Cadzow sat down again. He hung his head forward. "Well, you'll have to know sooner or later. Better from me than from some stranger in the village. You remember Brumby McSporran?"

The McSporrans owned Ballyfog Cottage, had owned it as long as Gray could remember, although they rarely lived there. They were an unusual family who made their way in life by acting as caretakers for the large property called Maudlin Manor. Ballyfog Cottage was actually on Maudlin Manor land. The owner of Maudlin was an elderly single lady who had inherited the estate and never so much as visited it. So it was that the McSporrans held court as if they were owners rather than caretakers. A local joke had been that it would seem far more profitable to care for the empty houses of the rich than to care for the rich themselves.

Gray started and looked at the rest of the company. They looked expectantly back at him. "Of course I know the McSporrans. Angus and Drucilla."

"And Brumby," Cadzow said, frowning.

"And Brumby," Gray agreed. "Wanted to go on the stage, if I remember rightly. Nice enough fellow in his way. Indolent devil, but I rather liked him." Brumby was Gray's age or thereabouts.

"You've been gone four years," Cadzow said.

Surely this wasn't going in the direction it appeared to be going. "I think that's well established." Gray kept his tone even, but anger began to beat in his heart and in his gut. "Make your point."

"Tomorrow will be soon enough for more discussion." A bright, completely unconvincing smile only served to make Cadzow appear more anxious. "Enough of this for now."

"I think not." Gray put himself in front of his uncle. "We'll finish the subject, if you don't mind."

"Gray," Max said. "Things are raw right now."

Gray ignored him. "Uncle?"

"Well, as I said, you've been gone four years. For three years there's been no word from you. Natural for a girl to seek comfort somewhere."

"Minerva?" Gray backed up. "And Brumby McSporran?"

"Well," Cadzow blustered. "After all, the parents are close. The Arbuckles and the McSporrans. Always have been. Welcome to each other, I always said. Queer crew, if you ask me. You're better off out of that one."

Close. The Arbuckles and the McSporrans. Always have been.

And it would certainly be easier for old man Arbuckle to keep his beloved daughter where he wanted her, under his thumb, if she were married to the son of the couple who all but lived at Willieknock when they weren't living in some stranger's empty house, wouldn't it? Brumby McSporran, for all his declared thespian aspirations, had never left his parents' sides for a day, let alone to set up his own home. With little enough coercion, the younger McSporran could doubtless be persuaded to go as far as establishing married residence with the Arbuckles, or, at least, leaving his wife there most of the time. The entire scenario sickened Gray.

"They aren't already married?" He couldn't countenance such a thing.

Uncle Cadzow said, "No."

"Gray," Max said, his voice strained. "Gray, old chap, you don't look well."

Although the effort cost him dearly, Gray smiled. "Just exhausted, as everyone's already decided. You all stay and get more acquainted. I'm going to renew my friendship with familiar things."

Max came toward him and said, "I'll come with you."

"Not a bit of it," Gray told him, reaching the door. "Keep him here and do the duty for me, Uncle Cadzow. Tell Max the family secrets. I'll see you all in the morning."

He let himself out of the drawing room and closed his eyes, drawing energy from the calm place he'd learned to form at the center of his being. The entire horror must have been a plot on the part of at least Porteous Arbuckle, if not also Janet and, possibly, the older McSporrans. Gray didn't believe Brumby had that sort of daring—or insanity—in him.

There was only one thing for it. Rekindling Minerva's love for him wouldn't be difficult. He'd seen her eyes, seen that her anger with him was tempered by that love even then. The bigger challenge would be to separate her from her poisonous family without alienating her from himself in the process.

Chapter Four

Great clouds of vapor shot skyward with each snorting breath the mare took. Minerva rode astride tonight and pressed her knees against Agatha's bulging sides, urging the reluctant creature onward.

Leaving the lights of Ballyfog behind in its tight valley, Minerva huddled inside her cloak and listened to the crunch of Agatha's hoofs in the snow. A glitter of freezing particles flittered through the air. Clouds had moved in, and the moon's light came and went like a cape of silver used to sweep the land with coy strokes. The darkness between didn't frighten Minerva. She knew this countryside the way she knew her own face. And she'd come this particular way often enough, even if not at such an hour.

He'd looked so much the same as when she'd last seen him.

Minerva pulled her hood farther over her face and let her head bend. The weight of her sadness crushed her. And the weight of what she intended to do this night.

Tonight she would put aside the last remnants of her mourning for the man she'd believed Gray Falconer to be: the champion, the guardian of her honor and safety, the love of her life—her truest friend. Tonight he had come without warning and behaved as if nothing could possibly have changed between them. Four years had passed, yet he treated her as if she were still a girl. He'd ordered her to cover herself as if she were his possession! Did he think—yes, he did think that there could be no question of her doing other than wait for him to return. Why, she could only think that he assumed she would wait until she died if necessary. That was it. He thought he *owned* her.

She didn't wish him dead, but at least if he had died she would be left with the bittersweet memories of the most perfect time in her imperfect life.

Tears were not a pleasure to her, or an indulgence she enjoyed. She cried now, and headed for their place, the place where they had always known a message left would be a message found, and where they had so often met.

Better that she had died.

A wicked thought. She was ashamed. But she had never felt such hopelessness.

Another swath of moonlight toyed with the landscape, a little longer this time, turning the dips a shady blue, then drawing up again as if a giant raised his vast lantern high, and then extinguished its flame.

Not much farther now. After the summer when she'd turned fifteen, after the naughty kiss she'd foisted upon Gray in the lane behind Ballyfog Cottage, he'd made a great show of trying to keep out of her way. But somehow she'd had little difficulty coming upon him because he seemed to choose the most obvious places to hide, such as on the other side of the wall beyond the rose garden at Willieknock. All of Ballyfog knew it was Minerva who tended that rose garden and spent so many of her spare hours there.

She could not stop her smile at the thought, not that she wanted to. Soon she would have to learn to remember only the best of her times with Gray Falconer.

Once she turned sixteen, he'd shown her the place she was going now. With supposed indifference, he'd led her over the gentle hill to the west of the village, to the very top of that hill where a copse of rowans showed their white blossoms in spring, and fed red berries to birds by autumn. They'd sat, side by side, on their mounts, Gray on his proud Thoroughbred, Minerva on Agatha. In silence they'd looked back the way they'd come until Minerva could bear the silence no longer. She'd asked why he'd brought her there.

"Because I come here often."

"I see."

She didn't.

"I wanted you to know."

"That's nice of you."

But she still hadn't understood why.

Gray had pointed downward and said, *"D'you see?"*

And Minerva had followed the direction of his steady forefinger and realized he indicated Willieknock. From that knoll there was a perfect view of the house and grounds.

"Willieknock?" she'd asked tentatively.

"Minerva," he'd responded, his voice soft and strange. *"That's where I see Minerva, even when she isn't there at all. So I come here and feel as if I'm with her. It takes some of the longing away."*

No words had come to her aid. She'd been sixteen. Gray was almost twenty-one. He seemed at once very mature and very young—and so very dear. Her heart had been his for years, but in that moment he had closed it in his fist and sealed its fate. She would never love another.

Now Agatha snorted a puff of cold air, and trudged more slowly. If she'd been able to complain in words, she'd have done so loudly, saying she'd been roused from her sleep and thought little of this nighttime trip.

Minerva looked upward and saw the naked limbs of the rowans, darker than the blue-black winter night sky. She felt a kinship with the trees. They had no choice but to stay where they were, as they were, slaves to nature and their own frailty.

She was a slave to her own frailty, too, and that frailty centered around loving a man who had changed, but whom she couldn't cease to love. Did she expect too much of him? Their time together had stopped as abruptly for him as for her. There were bound to be adjustments to make. She rubbed her cold hands together. He should know that all people change. If he were the man she'd thought him to be, he'd have come to her alone, and when she was alone, he would have spread his heart before her and explained at once what had happened to him. But he'd come as if using his friend and her cousins to shield him from frank discussion and the opportunity for them to cherish being reunited. He was a different man.

Her heart grew as cold as the snow, and the tears froze on her face.

A river of chopped snow flowed downhill, rolling and jumping on the hard-packed surface. Agatha checked her pace until Minerva urged her on.

The horse whinnied, and Minerva raised her face to the biting air and drew in a sharp, lung-chilling breath. She heard her own short cry, and felt the uncomfortable leaping of her heart.

Other plumes of vapor clouded the gloom, from another horse, this one dancing and flinging its head. Mounted on the horse that stood between Minerva and the trees, a large, unidentifiable form sat straight, looking toward the little mare and her rider.

Minerva drew Agatha to a halt and held the reins tightly, gauging whether she could turn the elderly animal and make it away with any hope of escape. Another frightened glance at the stranger's mount gave the answer. If he wanted to catch her, the task would be simple. Her throat burned, and each breath cost more pain.

"It's me," the rider said. "Gray."

Relief weakened her. *Ninny*. Why hadn't she known it

was he? Who else would come here on such a night—on any night?

Her bones turned to jelly, and she leaned to rest her face against Agatha's rough neck.

"Oh, Min. I've shocked you. I'm sorry. Hold on."

She heard concern in his voice, and she heard the crunch of his great horse's hoofs as he approached, then she felt Agatha moved sideways, complaining, as she was pulled toward the other animal and its rider.

A hand came to rest on Minerva's back. Gray did nothing more for a long time, just let his large hand remain, gentle on her spine, warm even through her heavy cloak and the simple woolen gown she wore beneath.

He touched her.

It was Gray's hand she felt—after coming to accept that he would never touch her again, he was here, breathing, living, so close. This was to have been as simple a goodbye to the past as she could find, here, on this hill where she never intended to return.

But he touched her.

"I might have known you'd come here," he said.

Of course he'd expect her to come there. Gray Falconer wouldn't be able to conceive that she'd ever want to put him from her mind. He would think that he could forever manipulate her heart and soul to his design. After all, it had been she who followed in his footsteps from the age of twelve.

"Min, I'm so sorry for hurting you as I have. Please believe that I had no choice in the matter. Can we go on from here? Nothing's really changed, has it?"

How could he think nothing had changed? Four years had passed. He'd left a twenty-one-year-old behind. A year later that girl had stopped sleeping as she waited, sick with excitement at the prospect of his return. And then had followed the months, and then the years of dwindling hope until Cadzow Falconer had come with the announcement that they must consider his nephew lost at sea. Until that point she'd visited Drumblade almost daily, asking for news, and been told there was none, but that Gray had last been seen the day he'd supposedly been about to leave the West Indies for home.

A burst of emotion straightened her spine. She pushed his arm away. "Everything's changed. How could you think otherwise?"

His face was clear enough now—too clear. If Minerva could have done so, she'd have averted her head to break the power he could cast over her with a simple look. And this look was not simple. He was bareheaded. In the glim of cloud-shrouded moon on snow, she saw the glitter of moisture in his thick, dark hair, and the flash in his eyes. The shadows needed no skill to bewitch her in their play about his arching brows, his cheekbones, the curve of his lips— which made her belly tighten—and the sharp line of his jaw.

"Has everything changed?" he asked quietly. "Can you tell me how? And why?"

When he'd left, she had still been so much the younger, more impressionable one. Gray had led the way in all things and she'd been glad to follow—or she'd thought she was then. But that had been then, and she *had* changed.

"I think everything's changed," she told him. "How? By the passage of time and the change of age and nature. Through maturity, and through disappointment."

"I never meant to disappoint—"

"No." She raised her hand to stop him. "Let me finish answering your questions."

His frown was as well wrought by the shadows as the curve of his mouth. Perhaps she would yet find something to smile about in all of this. The thought of Gray silenced by the strange occurrence of his obedient friend actually giving him an instruction wasn't without appeal.

"Why has everything changed?" she continued. "Because you have made it so."

"Min—"

"Please."

His horse danced, as it must have felt its rider's agitation, but the man didn't interrupt then.

"When you left I would have done anything you told me to do," she said. "Happily. I lived for you, and through you. And I think that was important to you, too."

"It was. More important than anything in my life."

Although she heard him, she went on as if he hadn't spoken. "That would have changed in time. Perhaps slowly. But I am not a creature of shallow intellect, or feeble spirit. Eventually I would have exerted myself—as I now do—but I think you might have adjusted with me, because the Gray Falconer I knew was a man not just of our time but of the future. You and I were dreamers together."

"I'm still a dreamer. If only you knew what a dreamer I am. Without my dreams I'd be dead."

She could not let her defenses down. Any weakness now could be the end of her. The very thought of suffering again the torment of the months after she'd come to believe him lost was unbearable.

But she would feel it anyway, just from having seen him again. "All this time you were alive. While I suffered thinking that you had died, you lived. I'm glad of that. For you, but not for **me, I** think. For me your presence now means you could put aside loving me until you were ready to forsake whatever held you elsewhere. I don't want to believe that, but since you haven't explained what happened, what else can I believe?"

"Oh, Minerva." His sigh seared her. "You don't know what you're saying. I—I missed my ship and caught another. I was shipwrecked, my love, and cast up on an island. Only good fortune allowed that I was found at last and returned home."

She pressed a hand to her throat. "But . . . But you did not tell me so, Gray. I don't know what to say." Something close to relief, relief and shame, dazed her. "I have sounded so selfish, foolish, childish. But I was afraid. I was afraid that having lost so much once, I could lose it all again. When you didn't come home I thought I would die. I'm not sure I could live through another time such as that."

"I love you."

She turned her head from his words.

"I love you, Minerva. I've never stopped loving you. If I could have come to you sooner, I would have. Trust me, please. Trust me that I'm the same man who left you, and that I want nothing more than to claim you now as I wanted to then."

"Oh, Gray, I want to."

"Then look at me."

"Give me time." Time to think. Time to be sure.

He tightened his grip on Agatha's reins, wound them around his gloved right hand and drew her to his horse's side until his booted leg pressed against Minerva's thigh. "I will not let you go again. Do you understand me?"

"You *will* not?" She did look at him direct then. "You *will* not let me go again? You didn't let me go before. You left, Gray. When you didn't return, Papa said you had met some-one else. He said that he'd always been certain you were not the man for me. But I didn't believe him. Not at first. And when your uncle told us you had been lost, probably at sea, Papa apologized and my parents mourned with me."

Gray muttered something under his breath, then said, "That is all in the past. Your life will be what it was always intended to be. You will be my wife. You will not have to think for yourself anymore, because I shall deal with every-thing for you, just as it should be."

Uncertainty swelled within her. "We cannot move too quickly, Gray. To become exactly what I was when you left is impossible. You must allow for that."

She tried to push away, but he held Agatha fast. And then, with his left hand, he held Minerva. So swiftly she didn't anticipate his intent, he took hold of her arm and all but caused her to slip from the mare's back.

"Stop it!" Struggling could only cause disaster. "Let me go at once. You were never violent, Gray. What has happened to you? What has made you so different?"

"Necessity," he said through his teeth. "And the threat of losing the only thing I care for. You. You are my heart. I cannot let you go."

"I have not asked you to let me go, only to allow me to adjust to your return. Do you expect me to throw my arms around you and say everything is just as it always was?"

"Yes. Yes, that's what I expect."

"Well, it cannot be. I have finally made some purpose for myself, and that will never change. I will never again be a silly, malleable creature who isn't whole without an overbearing man to tell her what she must do."

"Why? Is there someone else? Could it be that you've found a man who is weak enough for you to order his actions? You and your parents?"

He made no sense. "I must go back," she told him, shamed by the trembling in her voice when she so wanted to be firm.

"Oh, my love. My Minerva. My *nemesis*. You are my marvelous nemesis, because in you I have my breaking point. Nothing . . . I have not been broken by a great many things, but you could ruin me. You have been part of me since you were a child. You will always be part of me."

Snow began to fall again, lightly but steadily. "I don't know what to do," she told him, unmasked by her own honesty. "Oh, I can't think now. I must have time to think."

"There is nothing to think about but how much we love each other and that we want to be together."

"I have not stopped living while you were gone," she blurted out. "I am not the girl you left. I am a woman with a strong mind now."

"When I left, you were a girl with a strong mind. I should

be disappointed if that had changed. You will never be rid of me again. Only the death you seem to wish for me will part us now."

Jerking her face up to his, Minerva stared at him. A passionate rage welled within her. "How dare you say I wish you dead. You are more dear to me than anything. To wish you dead, I would have to wish myself dead."

"But you said you wished it."

"Yes. And you didn't understand, did you? You didn't understand that I spoke of my utter confusion. How could I make it all plain to you? When you were gone and when I was told you were dead, I did want to be dead, too. I wanted to close my eyes and go to you. I wanted to be where you were."

Very gently, he took his hand from her arm and slipped it around her shoulders. "And all the while I was gone I wished I was where you were."

He used the hand holding the reins to grip her saddle. Snow frosted his lashes and peppered his hair. And snow fell onto her upturned face—until he slowly brought his lips to hers.

Minerva tried to hold still, to make her mouth cold and unresponsive, to keep her eyes open and wait until he withdrew, puzzled and shocked as he'd undoubtedly be.

His lips were cool at first, and tasted of the night's snap and melting snow. Then the firm flesh warmed. And her eyes drifted shut. And her mouth opened, just a little.

How could she resist him when she had lived only to be with him again? Even when she'd been told he would never return, she'd continued to wait.

Now, at last, she was truthful with herself.

Gray ran his hands around her neck, inside the hood, knocking it back until she felt wind on her ears. He caressed her neck, brought the tips of his thumbs together at the point of her chin. Their mouths became as one mouth, touching, pressing, reaching to find and fuse each tiny piece of skin.

The scent of his linen, clean and soft, sharpened her awareness of him. He held her with such care, but she felt his power, his strength, and knew how vulnerable she would be in his hands were he not a gentle man. When he framed her head, ran his fingers over her ears and into her hair, her body grew hot, and languid, and filled with longing.

His tongue, passing along the slick, moist skin just inside her mouth, surprised her, and she jumped, opened her eyes. Gray raised his face just enough to look at her. He smiled and kissed her again, and this time she touched her tongue to the inside of his lips, heard him groan, and felt excitement flutter deep inside.

Once more he withdrew, and she clung to his hands, trembling so hard her teeth chattered, and she laughed with nervous happiness.

Gray rested his cheek on her brow and said, "Hush. Hush, sweet. Oh, I have dreamed of this. I've spent nights upon nights awake, just thinking of how your mouth feels." He sighed again, and his breath whispered over her face with the falling snow. "I even planned . . . Well, I will tell you more of what I planned soon."

"Tell me now."

She felt him smile. "Always the curious one. Not now. Later, when we are together as we should be."

"We shouldn't be together now?"

He laughed. "You don't understand, but you will. We're going away now, Min."

Puzzled, she grew still.

"We'll go back to Drumblade, but only to take a few things we'll need until we're well away."

"Well away?" When she pulled back until she could see him, he smiled, and touched her lips. "I don't understand. Why would we . . . ? Are you talking about running away?"

"Not running away. I have no need to run away, only to take what is mine and care for it. And to make sure no man or woman can take it away from me again."

"Do you mean *me*, Gray?" Her heart beat faster and faster. "Oh, Gray, please don't frighten me, I cannot bear it. What do you mean?"

"There's nothing to be afraid of, love. We're together now and we'll always be together. But at least for now we must go away from here. We'll be married and then, perhaps in a few months, we'll return to Drumblade, because it will be your home as it is mine."

Minerva studied his face. Could he be ill? He spoke as if he were feverish. "I should return home now."

"You want to be with me." He sounded urgent. Urgent and almost angry. "I know you want to be with me, as I want to be with you."

"I do. There are questions to be dealt with. Surely you understand that. But I do want us to be together again. Will you come to Willieknock tomorrow?"

"No. You will not return there ever. Do you hear me? Not ever."

With difficulty, she righted her seat. "Stop it, Gray. You are not yourself at all. Please come to call tomorrow. My father will want to speak with you. I know he seemed odd today, but that's only because—"

"*Never.* What I managed earlier was beyond human. Being in the same house with that man."

"Gray!"

"I had only to see him again, to hear him and listen to his pathetic affectations and the way he pretended he . . . No. I will not speak to that man again."

She had been mistaken. Gray was not at all the same. He was someone entirely different. "You are not yourself. I . . . Oh, I love you. I want to be with you."

"And you will be. *Now.* We shall leave this moment."

"I cannot."

He made a move as if to kiss her again, but she evaded him. "I shall go to my bed, Gray. Perhaps when you've slept, you'll think more clearly."

"I have never thought more clearly than at this moment. Our only hope for happiness lies in your doing as I ask. You must never see your parents again. Not as a single woman. And only as my wife if I am with you."

If he had struck her, he could not have appalled her more. Gray had released Agatha's reins, and Minerva drew the little animal away from his mount. "That's madness," she told him, and used a heel to start the mare back downhill.

"Go now and there will never be another chance for us."

She swallowed and looked over her shoulder at him. "You are ill."

"I am not ill. I am desperate."

"I cannot do what you ask. I cannot abandon my family." Expecting him to follow, she sent Agatha into a slipping, sliding course toward the valley.

"Minerva," Gray shouted. "If you love me, do as I ask. Come with me now."

She hesitated an instant, half turned in the saddle, and called, "I do love you. I always will," before continuing on toward Willieknock.

Gray didn't follow.

Chapter Five

"Your first responsibility is to your parents, Minerva." Why, Janet Arbuckle wondered, were children so *ungrateful*? "No, do not attempt to leave this room. Sit down again, and listen to what your father and I have to say to you."

"Mama," Minerva said. "I have listened. I don't understand a word you've said. Now, may I please return to my work?"

As usual, Porteous avoided a matter of grave importance by pretending a deep artistic muse. He reclined on Janet's own chaise in her dear, beautiful, pink boudoir, his eyes closed behind his silly, dark-lensed spectacles (Porteous had heard how Percy Bysshe Shelley and Lord Byron used to wear dark-lensed spectacles and had affected them ever since), and he waited for her to deal with unpleasant business.

And this entire, awful dilemma was *his* fault. He had invented the Idea in the first place, and now he thought to leave it to her to sort out.

"Mr. Arbuckle," Janet said, "kindly talk some sense into your daughter."

He laughed. *Laughed.* He turned on his side on the chaise,

drew up his knees, and chuckled until tears ran down his red cheeks.

Janet rolled her eyes. "Very well, Minerva, I shall simply have to make matters plain myself. You say you don't understand a word I've spoken. It is completely unimportant that you should. Merely say you agree, and will obey."

With a huge sigh, Minerva flopped into an armchair and closed her eyes.

Really, this was too much. "Hatch has said the McSporrans sent word to say they're on their way. They could be here at any moment. Before they arrive, I must be sure we're in agreement. *Mr. Arbuckle.* Pay attention!"

Evidently her request was cause for further hilarity.

"Papa." Minerva sat up and leaned toward her father. "I think Mama is trying to speak with you."

"No such thing," Porteous said, sobering as abruptly as he'd broken into mirth. "She is merely using me to prove a valid point. I am an artist. I cannot be expected to waste valuable creative time on the mundane. Therefore, it is of the utmost importance that you cease this foolish *inventive* nonsense, and apply your considerable intellect to keeping us out of a debtors' prison."

"Oh!" Janet could not believe the insensitivity of her own husband. "How could you mention such a thing aloud? In front of me? Why, I feel sickness upon me. Minerva, get me my salts at once."

"You aren't sick, Mama. And we are in no danger of a debtors' prison, either. Papa is making a joke, aren't you, Papa? Certainly it would be wise to curb spending. It is always wise to curb spending. But, in fact, in recent years Papa's paintings have brought in quite extraordinary sums. Every time he goes to Edinburgh or London to sell his work, I am so proud of the enormous figures he commands. Why, you must be one of the most sought-after painters in the world, Papa."

"Quite so," Porteous said.

"But, Papa," Minerva continued, "I don't understand why we must go through these outbursts when you and Mama threaten ruination. I do, as I have since I was fifteen, make certain your income is almost equal to your expenditure. With the slightest cutting back on such things as what you list in the books as 'essentials,' we would be completely sound."

"No idea what she's talking about," Porteous said, letting his arms trail to the floor. "But I am the creator in this house, not you, miss. You will use what talents God gave you in the service of your family—as God has willed you should. And you will have nothing to do with young Falconer. Do I make myself clear?"

"*Arbuckle,*" Janet wailed, assessing the effect she attained when kicking the hem of her new, mint-green and orange tartan gown behind her. The bustle could be larger. "Arbuckle, I agree that Minerva must apply herself to our affairs with fresh vigor. She has been far too preoccupied with her own *silliness* of late. But do you think it wise to, er, interfere with, er, *love*?"

Minerva rose and went to the adorable little bay casement with its leaded panes of glass, some of them in brilliant color. She took a small spyglass from somewhere concealed in her ridiculous *trousered* ensemble, and put the contraption to her eye.

"Well, of course your father is right, Minerva," Janet told her daughter. "Oh, why must you wear those unflattering *things*? And your hair, Minerva. Trailing down your back like that as if you were a peasant. You will change. There, I've spoken. And no more of your *silliness,* do you hear me? Or at least, less of it. Considerably less of it. And you should not see Gray Falconer. After all, he was dead for three years. A desirable female is bound to have made other *arrangements* in three years, dearest. If she hasn't, and she's too hasty in welcoming the departed one back the moment he decides to appear, well then, how does it look?"

Minerva grew very still, as if watching something of great interest in the distance. "Really, child," Janet said. "You are like your heartless father. You ignore me. And you live in a world of pretense, and neither of you think I see through your games."

Porteous giggled and turned completely around until his head was flat on the chaise seat, and his crossed ankles propped on the back, while he wiggled the toes of his black satin slippers.

"It's time we spoke seriously," Minerva announced without looking at her mother or father. "Several times since yesterday you've spoken of impending financial difficulty. The nature of this disaster remains vague. Is there something I don't know?"

Attempting to move with as little sound as possible, Janet went to Porteous's side. She raised her skirts and delivered a sharp kick to his shoulder.

She immediately dropped her skirts, and Porteous let out a shriek and sat up. Since Porteous frequently shrieked, and usually for no particular reason, Minerva continued to study whatever she was studying through her glass. The wretched, ungrateful girl never listened to a word said by her long-suffering parents unless they spoke direct.

Janet bent over Porteous and put her mouth to his ear. "If she gets even a hint of what you've done, she'll insist you put it right—at once. Should everything go wrong at this point, we will be ruined, Arbuckle. Ruined. Do you understand?"

This time he stopped himself from laughing. He took off his glasses and gifted her with a sly glare and a nod.

"Good. If only you had never commenced such a dangerous thing," she whispered.

"You thought it a good idea at the time. After all, as we saw yesterday, we didn't cause any real harm to him. And I don't recall that you had difficulty with the deepening of our pockets."

She placed her fingers over his lips and said, "Silence, Arbuckle. Our daughter must never know about any of this."

He shook his head.

"Very well. We are agreed that we need to keep her diverted from what must now be accomplished. Help me do this."

"How?"

"Ooh, *really*, men can be such a liability."

"You were as eager to . . . you know. You wanted to do it as much as I did."

"You intended to find a way to continue . . . well, to continue, *you know*, until you realized a really huge profit. Not that you haven't already done rather well."

Porteous narrowed his eyes further. "And you, my love? What did you intend?"

"Well"—Janet sat down beside him—"well, perhaps I more or less thought the same thing was possible. But I'm a sensible woman. I can change the way of things in a *flash*." She snapped her fingers and winced, watching for Minerva to react. Minerva didn't move.

"In a *flash*?" Porteous said. "So you say. That doesn't alter the fact that everything is about to tumble about our ears. And she"—he pointed to Minerva—"must do as she's told or she will ruin us."

"I already said as much." *Really*, he did infuriate one. "You dealt with things wrongly yesterday, though, Arbuckle. You don't understand her as I do. Push one way, and she'll go the other."

Porteous smiled, and tipped his beret forward over his brow. "I don't know that, hmm? Why do you imagine I pretended I wasn't silly with joy at seeing *him* again?"

Words failed her.

"Aha." He made circles before her nose with a stubby finger. "Surprised you, have I? I know our daughter better than you, it seems. She's likely to spurn him because she thinks he was up to . . . *thingie*, while he was supposedly dead. Dash it all, but females are unreasonable."

"We don't want her to spurn him?"

"Absolutely not, my dear. Not until he's settled the fat sum I shall request for her hand."

Why hadn't she thought of that? "Arbuckle, you clever little poppet, you. Of course. And how absolutely *fitting*. We use *him* to replenish what we've lost because of . . . *you know*."

Porteous giggled, and slapped her back so hard, she coughed. "You've got it, my rainbow. Isn't it perfect? After all, in good part it's his fault we're suddenly in this dreadful mess."

"So," Janet whispered, "we encourage her by discouraging her. Then, when she defies us by wanting him, we refuse."

Porteous brought his nose almost close enough to touch hers. "No," he said, and his eyes seemed one on top of the other. "No, my doodle-witted little rainbow. We encourage her by discouraging her. Then, when she defies us, we dash in and set the price. He pays. We keep Minerva. But, *voilà*, our losses are recouped." He gave a short, sharp cackle.

He was right, absolutely right. All was not lost after all. They would continue to live in the lovely luxury she'd become accustomed to.

The growing rumble of a deep voice in the hall caused Janet to shake her head. "Angus and Drucilla," she said. "Oh, why do they have to come today of all days?"

"They come every day," Minerva said from her vantage point over the countryside. "Why should today be any different?"

Janet and Porteous looked at each other. One could never quite be sure when Minerva was or was not listening. "We whispered," Janet told her husband softly, and he nodded.

"Aye, it's a foul wind as blows across the moors these days," Angus McSporran announced as he barged into the boudoir. "A man can't even be sure of what he's a right t'be sure of anymore. A crime is what I call it. Don't I, Drucilla? A crime."

"Minerva," Janet said, with a nervous premonition that it would be unwise for her offspring to remain in the room. "Don't you have some of your experiments to attend to?"

"Not a bit of it," Angus said, giving Janet a hard, knowing stare. "Brumby would be destroyed if he'd come all this way t'see the lass only t'have her bury hersel' with whatever it is she buries hersel' with. He'll be along soon enough. He's seein' t'the carriage. We dinna trust that lout ye employ out there."

Dressed in kilt and sporran, with many frills at his neck and at the cuffs that flowed from beneath the sleeves of his green velvet jacket, Angus went to stand beside Minerva at the window. Tall and stooped, and blessed with a luxuriant thatch of unruly gray hair, he was a man who drew every eye to him. Distinguished, they said of him, they who took him for the owner rather than the bombastic caretaker of Maudlin Manor, where he and Drucilla had held court for years.

Drucilla, a silent, pinch-mouthed priss of a woman, gave Janet her customary glance of disdain and sat in the chair Minerva had vacated. Drucilla wore nothing but black. On the one occasion when Janet had ventured to inquire why, Drucilla had said, "Some things should never be mentioned." And Janet had never again mentioned whatever thing it was that shouldn't be mentioned.

"I say, McSporran," Porteous bellowed. "Quite the fix, wouldn't you say? I suppose you've heard, of course. Quite the fix."

Janet shushed him, but he ignored her.

"We'll have to watch ourselves, wouldn't you say?" he went on. "But if we play our cards right, we could come out of this as happy men."

"I am already a happy man," Angus McSporran said.

"Never happier than when a challenge presents itself, right, Drucilla?"

"Hmph," was all his wife offered.

McSporran began his customary pacing. With his hands clasped behind his back and his kilt swinging about his knobby knees, he marched back and forth over Janet's pink and silver carpets.

Janet looked to Drucilla and raised her brows.

Drucilla elevated her thin-bridged nose with its mottling of tiny purple veins. Janet considered those veins the result of too much secret drinking. "Keeper of the purse," Drucilla pronounced in a reedy voice. "That's what McSporran means. And dear Angus does a remarkable job of keeping our purse, don't you, Angus?"

They had been regaled with the meaning of the name many times, and invariably with no more prompting than on this occasion. Janet murmured as if interested, but, as usual, Angus made no comment.

"In that case, Angus, if you're calm in the midst of tumult, then we have nothing to discuss," Porteous said, twitching the full sleeves of his smock. "Thought you'd something of importance on your mind. If you don't now, you will soon enough. But I've a model arriving momentarily. Mustn't keep genius waiting."

Angus gave Porteous his full attention, and smirked. Janet detested Angus's smirks. "A genius is she?" he said. "This model's a genius? Is that because of the way she undresses? Or what she reveals when she undresses? Or what she does with what she reveals when she undresses?"

Really, it could be so mortifying to have one's husband paint nudes if one had to keep company with Philistines who simply didn't understand the finer points of art.

"I meant," Porteous said, "my own genius. I feel particularly creative this morning and must take advantage of it."

Angus McSporran's shaggy brows waggled. "I'd say ye should. Oh, indeed, ye should. Perhaps I should come and make sure absolutely every possible advantage is taken. Of It, that is."

"*Angus.*" Drucilla raised her sharp chin. "We are confronted by disaster, and you spend time in lascivious talk."

McSporran frowned at her. His leer disappeared and he snuffled into his mustache. "Aye. Disaster. Did I tell ye about it, Porteous?"

"No," Janet said quickly. Hadn't the McSporrans just indicated that they didn't know they were all on the brink of the abyss? Really, it was too much. "No, you didn't tell any of us about it."

"Then I'd best be quick, or young Brumby will be interferin'. The worst has occurred. The unthinkable."

"We know," Janet retorted, impatience overwhelming prudence. She opened her mouth to say they'd already seen Gray Falconer with their own eyes, but remembered Minerva's presence just in time.

"Ye know?" Angus stopped in front of her. "How can that be, Janet? We only found out oursel' this mornin'."

"Well, it was yesterday when—"

"Hold your tongue," Porteous said sharply. Any affected lassitude disappeared. He stood up and approached Angus until he stood, looking up at the much taller man. "What's happened?"

"We're going t'be ruined," Angus said. "All o' us. Ruined."

Janet stood also, and made signals for Angus to be cautious.

"It'll all have t'go back. And quickly. Otherwise there are bound t'be questions." Angus was transported by the seriousness of his own concerns. "Our lives. Everythin' we've worked all these years to accomplish. Gone, I tell ye. And all because we trusted that one."

"What one?" Janet couldn't stop herself from asking.

"*Him,*" Angus said, his brown eyes wild. "The one who was never supposed to come here."

Janet grew weak with horror. Angus must be silenced.

"He'll cause us to spend everythin' we've worked for, but that's not the worst o' it."

Porteous had grown pale and silent, and no longer showed any sign of caring what Minerva might hear. "Get to it, man," he said. "We'll expire from the anticipation if you don't hurry."

"Oh," Drucilla moaned, falling back in the chair and producing an ebony fan, which she wafted before her face. "Oh, it's a terrible pass we've come to."

"Angus," Janet said. "Drucilla. *Please.* What is it?"

"Tenants," Angus said spreading his long arms, palms up, and looking toward the heavens. "We've a tenant at Maudlin Manor. After fifteen years as heirs apparent to our lovely, lovely manor, that ungrateful creature who owns the place has *leased* it."

"A tenant," Drucilla echoed. "We're ordered to act as household staff in our own home."

"Yes," Angus said, "in our own home. *Servants.*"

She was a generous woman, wasn't she? Minerva contemplated the question while she kept her glass trained on the copse of rowan trees. She'd always been considered very generous, yet she could find it in her to see more than a little justice at the thought of Angus and Drucilla McSporran having to admit that they didn't, in fact, own Maudlin Manor. She did feel sorry for poor, ineffectual, and harmless Brumby, who had to tolerate his parents' posturing and raging, but, after all, it was time he struck out on his own and showed them he was too much a man to continue to do their bidding.

Last night, after she'd returned, she'd searched out the spyglass and begun her solitary watch over the place she would hold at the center of her heart forever. There she had known bliss, and devastation. What could have driven Gray to demand that she leave her family and her home and never return unless he was with her, and then only for limited periods? Love wasn't supposed to be possessive. Gentle, and kind, and protective, yes—but not possessive.

"What sort of a tenant?" Mama asked, sounding very odd indeed. Papa and Angus had been friends since boyhood, but Mama didn't especially like the McSporrans and Minerva had always been at a loss to understand the so-called friendship between the two couples.

"A dreadful man," Drucilla said. "Could I trouble you for a wee dram of something to calm my nerves, Mr. Arbuckle?"

"Who is this dreadful man?" Papa said, and Minerva turned in time to see him take out the key to his liquor cabinet. Papa kept a very close eye on his liquor. Mama insisted he drank too much, and he said he must be certain he could always prove how much there was or wasn't in any particular bottle at any particular time.

"Tell them about Mr. Clack, Angus," Drucilla said. "Mr. Olaf Clack. Tell them that he has a strange, foreign accent we can scarcely understand, except when he orders us around. And that he's bent far over and wears a heavy gray cloak all the time, even indoors, and cannot as much as raise his face to look at a body."

"Yes," Angus said. "I should probably tell them that."

"And his hair is black and hugely curly, and reaches below his shoulders. It swings forward and is very strange. His fingernails are exceedingly long and he taps them on the silver handle of an ivory cane. And he's gold buckles on his shoes, shoes with high heels. And breeches. *Breeches,* mind you. White satin. He looks as if he were from some Frenchy court, only rough, not cultured at all. A mystery. Unless, of course, he's English, in which case there would be no mystery at all—about his being rough and uncultured, that is."

"Drucilla is—"

"And he demands food at all hours, and says he's had word that a friend of his is expected. We can only imagine what that might mean." She raised her nose even higher. "If that's the case, I shall have to leave altogether, I can tell you. I'll not be present for any goings-on."

"You leave, Drucilla," Angus said, waggling his brows again. "I'll sacrifice myself and stay for the goings-on."

"Janet," Papa said in his "pay attention" voice. "Take poor Drucilla to your rooms and have her lie down at once. Have Hatch bring her a brandy broth. And then the two of you can talk alone and you can comfort your dear friend."

Minerva could scarce control her smile at the amazed expression on Mama's face, but Mama didn't argue. She never did when Papa used his "pay attention" voice.

As soon as the door closed behind the two women, Papa looked to Minerva as if she'd been invisible before and said, "You look particularly lovely today, my child. Hmm, what do you call that garment, or garments, you're wearing?"

Intending to smother her confusion and desolation by crowding her day with creative endeavors, she'd donned another of her chiffon ensembles and gone to meet Fergus and Iona in the workroom. They had hardly begun on a new project when Minerva had been summarily called to an audience with her parents. "This?" She raised her arms to allow her sleeves to fall away, and took several giant steps to demonstrate the divided skirt. "This is an example of Minerva's Motion Unlimited. The perfect outfit for the active modern woman, the professional woman."

"*Professional* woman?" Papa and Mr. McSporran said in unison.

"Yes"—let them really be horrified—"for the professional woman set on living her life without need of any man to support her." She had nothing to lose, nothing to look forward to. Her life was over, and she might as well become eccentric. At least if she were eccentric, she would have some identity. With that, Minerva leaped upon the seat of the pink chair, pirouetted to face the two men, and hopped to place a foot on each arm to better display how the skirts separated in the center.

She wobbled dangerously at first but steadied herself, raised her head, and flung wide her arms. "See?"

The door opened and Hatch entered, hobbling even more than she had the previous evening. "More comp'ny," she said, ushering the said company from behind her. "*Mr.* Gray Falconer—again."

Chapter Six

Arbuckle would do nothing to injure him so close to home, of that Gray was certain. Paying strangers to capture and kill a man thousands of miles away was one thing, a coward's way. Doing away with a fellow on your doorstep was another matter, particularly for a coward. However, he must watch his back.

There must be no question of Arbuckle guessing he was suspected of foul doings. Gray made sure his eyes didn't linger too long in that direction before he gave his attention to the only reason he would enter this house again, the only reason he'd come to Ballyfog openly at all. If not for Minerva, he would be dosing her father with some of his own medicine. An unexpected period of imprisonment in a strange place, a distant island, say, and a threat or two would doubtless shake the truth free in considerably less than three years.

That lost three years would not be forgotten, but it must eventually be relegated to the past or it would destroy his future. Arbuckle would pay for his treachery by losing what he prized most—his daughter.

Minerva was a wild thing. A wild and wonderful thing. Gray wanted to swing her into his arms and bear her away.

But he must deal with matters exactly right, or rather than bear her away he would be deprived of her forever. That could not be.

This morning her shining brown hair was unbound and flowing over her shoulders. She wore another chiffon creation, this one in shades of blue, and gray, and purple. An extraordinary garment. He put his chin forward and endeavored to see the thing more clearly. Or was it a collection of garments? Made of scarves, perhaps? Layers of scarves?

She stood on a chair, actually on the arms of a chair. One foot on either arm of a chair.

Her skirt wasn't a skirt. As with the . . . whatever she'd worn the previous day, the bottom of her—whatever—was apparently a voluminous pair of trousers. A pair of trousers that was voluminous at the bottoms, but that draped intimately about her waist and hips. No bustle. No undergarments. At least, no sign of petticoats. How could there be petticoats when there was no skirt?

No undergarments?

"It's *him*. Oh, no, it can't be."

Gray looked into the blanched face of Angus McSporran. Evidently the man thought he was in the presence of an apparition. "Good day to you, Mr. McSporran," he said, with a degree of satisfaction at the horror he saw in the man's eyes. "I assure you that it is, indeed, *him*, if him is Gray Falconer."

"Get down, Minerva," Arbuckle said, his face without expression. "Have some modesty."

She didn't attempt to do as her father instructed. With her arms held wide and her feet braced apart, she stared at Gray. He studied all of her. Not a wispy thing at all, his Minerva.

If she wore no corset, as could certainly be the case, then . . . She definitely wore no corset or chemise. He looked at her breasts, her very charming, full breasts, and could not fail to note how their tips poked against outrageously flimsy material.

Wonderfully flimsy material.

She crossed her arms.

Gray looked at her face. And Minerva looked at his.

She wobbled, and contrived to fall into the chair quite tidily.

Arbuckle donned a pair of round, dark-lensed spectacles and crossed his arms too. He tapped a black-slippered toe, and apparently withdrew into thought.

"Good morning to you, Minerva," Gray said. "And good morning to you, gentlemen. An exceedingly fine morning it is."

"It's bloody cold," McSporran said in his heavy brogue. "We've not had snow the like o' this so early in the year for an age."

Gray went to the window and stood beside McSporran. "Delightful to see you again, McSporran. How is your lady? And Brumby?"

The man faced him and managed a ferocious expression. "Brumby's as fine a man as ever walked the face o' the earth, and he's not appreciated by some who should fall on their knees and give thanks for even a whit of his attention. If it weren't for some, he'd be the toast of the Edinburgh stage."

"The Edinburgh stage," Gray murmured.

"Aye, the Edinburgh stage. Ye'd not know it, having absented yoursel' until it pleased ye to make an appearance, but the Edinburgh stage has become exceeding fine."

"I must take advantage of the fine theater there," Gray said. "What did you see most recently, sir? I will allow myself to be guided by your advice."

The scowl deepened. McSporran hummed, then snuffled and said, "I've no head for the foolishness of such things."

Minerva had pulled her feet beneath her in the chair, and now attempted to tame her hair behind her neck. She had little success, and Gray smiled.

She caught that smile and turned pink.

"When do you propose to take yourself off again, Falconer?" Arbuckle asked rudely.

"Take myself off?" Gray puffed up his cheeks and let the air out slowly. "Take myself off? Oh, I see what you mean. Well, I might have expected you to be the one who twigged my plans—and my needs—before I'd spoken of them. After all, a man such as yourself, a man of intuition, would know I'm bound to have great plans afoot for my future."

Arbuckle's spectacles steamed up. "I would?"

"You would. And you are to be the first to have an opportunity to benefit from those plans."

"I am?"

"You are." Gray approached Minerva and extended a hand until she placed hers on his palm. "Has Minerva told you about the invitation she extended to me?"

Her very blue eyes grew huge.

"Of course she has. I know how close a family the Arbuckles are. So, Mr. Arbuckle, what do you say?"

"Yes," McSporran said, "what do you say, Porteous?"

Gray drew Minerva to her feet and turned her until her back was to her father and his companion. She lifted her brows almost to her heart-shaped hairline, then lowered them, then narrowed her eyes and mouthed a sentence from which he got only the word "What?"

"Mr. Arbuckle?" he repeated.

"Well, I hardly . . . That is . . ."

"You didn't approve?" Gray contrived to look bemused. "But we thought you would be ecstatic. After all, surely any father's deepest concern is for the safety and happiness of his offspring. Since you have only one offspring, and she is Minerva, one must assume you want the best for her."

"I do," Arbuckle blustered. "Naturally."

"Then you agree?"

"Absolutely, I agree."

Minerva tipped her head to one side and watched Gray's

eyes. There was no doubt that she had no idea what he was about.

He might be sealing his own fate, but he must take the chance. "Thank you, sir! I knew you were a man of vision. You see, Minerva, you were right. Your father is a man of vision. We must set about making plans immediately."

She frowned and tried to withdraw her hand. His duplicity would cause him further trouble with her once she realized his game.

"Hold on, there," Arbuckle said. "Let's not forget that there are some important details to be discussed. Man-to-man."

"By all means," Gray agreed, fearing his goal might be snatched from him.

"The, er, financial side of things. Much as a fella detests to bring up the subject, one does have to put things on a proper footing, what?"

Relief made it easy for Gray to smile affably. "Finances it shall be." Just as planned, the old devil assumed he was hearing an offer of marriage and grasped for the second love of his life—money. He'd already be plotting a means of getting his hands on a fat prize without actually marrying off Minerva.

Arbuckle rubbed his hands together and said, "Have you discussed this with your uncle?"

"My uncle is delighted with whatever I choose to do." In fact, Gray expected poor old Cadzow to be bemused by his actions, but he'd trust his nephew's judgment. "I'd appreciate quarters on the third floor, sir. A study. Where I can be close to the center of things, as it were."

Min's mouth dropped open.

"I thought about your invitation to come today and decided it was too good to refuse," he told her. To her father, he said, "Since Minerva and I are set on a business partnership, and since I shall be providing both technical advice and capital, you will be required to approve my coming and going from Willieknock as necessary."

A small gale of gasps swept the room.

Gray held up a hand. "No, no, don't thank me. I want to do this. For womanhood. For the future. I consider myself a fortunate man."

The unexpected crinkling of Minerva's eyes with mirth made the preposterous nature of his fabrication a delight. He should have expected the unexpected from her.

"Shall we share what we decided would make the most memorable name for our association, Minerva?"

She struggled not to laugh and said, "At once. No one should be kept in suspense a moment longer."

"We are," Gray said, thinking furiously, "Fabulous Falconer Fashions."

Min's smile might never have existed. "Astounding Arbuckle Alternatives," she returned sternly.

"Astounding Arbuckle Alternatives?" Arbuckle said faintly.

Bowing, Gray said, "As you will."

Chapter Seven

Eldora Makewell hadn't worked as hard as she had to snare Cadzow Falconer because she wished to marry the much poorer of the two Falconer males.

She was thirty-five and, if she said so herself, at the full, fascinating flowering of her womanhood. Cadzow had wanted her from the moment they met at a select Edinburgh gathering place for exceptional people of exceptional tastes. He had been hesitant, it was true, embarrassed even, because of his devout nature. *Hypocrite.* He had pursued her, wooed her, and declared his intention to care for her as she should be cared for.

After a suitable period, Eldora had accepted. She'd given up *everything* for Cadzy. True, one could agree that she'd been somewhat strapped since a quarrel with a certain married gentleman who had ungraciously withdrawn her allowance for some petty infraction. Why shouldn't a woman of robust energy enjoy an extra outlet for her appetites now and again? But that was all behind her, and she would protect what she'd earned.

Sitting before the glass in her bedroom at Drumblade, she selected pearl-and-ruby earrings and a matching necklace from the very impressive hoard of jewelry Cadzow had gifted to her in the year since they'd met.

Her rooms were beautiful, all palest of blues, and pinks, and lavenders with cavorting putti catching at real gold-leaf ribbons artfully trailed across the ceilings, and elegant floral panels on the walls. The furnishings were French. The French had such taste, such artistry, and the carved legs with brass or gold feet, the enamelwork, the marquetry, and the lacquer were perfect for a woman of Eldora's exquisite style. Her suite was discreetly separate from Cadzow's. The servants pretended respect, but, ooh, she knew they were jealous of her. If they could sully her reputation in Ballyfog, where she intended to become the most elevated female personage, they would certainly do so. And so she and Cadzow preserved an aura of respectability, or such respectability as was possible since they lived beneath the same roof.

"It is *too* much." Blinking, squeezing her eyelids together, and leaning to stare at herself in the mirror, she worked to produce tears. She did look so dramatically enticing when tears slipped from her golden eyes. Even Cadzow, who was not a man of pretty compliments, said she had golden eyes. "Too much," she repeated, raising her voice and making it break. She could have been a celebrated actress.

At last she was about to have an opportunity to persuade Cadzow of what must be done. "What I insist must be done, Cadzy," she said, well pleased with the appeal in her tone.

Max Rossmara had departed for Kirkcaldy and his family. Eldora took up the long necklace and fastened it around her neck. Mr. Rossmara wasn't a man a woman could ignore or forget. She played her fingertips over the tops of her breasts where they blossomed most satisfactorily above the low neckline of her nightgown and robe. Green-eyed men were irresistible, especially exceedingly handsome, well-made green-eyed men who made no secret of appreciating a woman's charms.

But Max had left, and Gray had set out for Willieknock Lodge.

Cadzow's rooms were below Eldora's. The staircase that rose from his dressing room to hers was their secret. Cadzy usually waited until all was quiet at night before coming to her, but today she'd told him to appear as soon as he was certain Gray had gone out.

She had *told* him, and he'd looked at her with his puppy eyes, all eager and slavish. If he were a puppy, he'd slobber. Sometimes he slobbered anyway.

A shiver ran over her body. Cadzy wasn't a beautiful man like Gray, or like young Rossmara, but he was competent for a man who denounced carnal interests in others. Yes, he was certainly very competent in what he would insist upon calling their "diddles." She regarded herself and turned the corners of her mouth down. Perhaps it was time to seek out a hobby. Yes, a hobby. One that was inventive rather than competent.

Thumping came from her dressing room and she jumped up, her heart pounding unpleasantly. What transpired between them today would be of the utmost importance. She would be especially accommodating, and, in return, he would agree to do what must be done to assure their future.

She satisfied herself that the room looked inviting. The fire had been stoked, and flames blazed up the chimney.

In the dressing room, a rug covered the trapdoor leading to the secret stairway. Eldora pulled aside the rug and lifted the trap, and whirled to run away before Cadzy could climb into the room.

She dashed to the other side of her four-poster with its peach gossamer hangings. Hiding behind a drape, she peeked out at her suitor and said, "I have been crying, Cadzy."

"Hmm?" He poured a large goblet of Madeira from the

decanter she kept full for him at all times, and drank deeply.

"I said I've been crying. Because I was afraid my Cadzy wouldn't come to me because he's bored with his Eldora."

He smacked his lips, drank more, and wiped the back of a sleeve over his mouth.

He'd discarded his cravat, waistcoat, and jacket, and his shirt was unbuttoned to the waist. She avoided looking at his portly belly, the manner in which it protruded over the waist of his trousers. A glance at those trousers confirmed another protuberance, this one quite satisfactory.

"I do believe there is only one thing you want from me, Cadzy." There was much to be said for having been an actress—well, an actress in training. One could draw upon one's dramatic experience. Eldora held the peach-colored gauze before her face and made sure her eyes were suitably doleful. "You want me only for my looks, don't you?"

Bending forward, one hand on a knee, Cadzy puffed, catching his breath from the climb up his narrow stairs followed by guzzling his drink too quickly. "I wouldn't say that, m'dear," he told her when his breathing calmed a little. "I've always told you I could enjoy those extraordinary titties of yours even if I were blind. Come here and let me show you how."

She giggled. He could be so unexpectedly crude. How fortunate she found his naughty mouth exciting—in more ways than one. "I shan't come there until you've told me you love me, and proved it without setting a hand upon me, you *carnal* man."

He advanced to brace his weight on the mattress and stare at her. Madeira slopped, but he didn't notice. "I like you in white," he said of her simply cut lawn ensemble. "Virginal. Now, there's an interesting thought. It's been some time since I had one of those."

Eldora started to pout, but was quickly distracted. "Do you want one, Cadzy? A virgin?"

Pushing out his wet, pink mouth, he frowned as if in deep thought. "Well," he said at last, "let us say that if one presented, I shouldn't shirk my duty. I'd sacrifice myself to the further education of womankind."

"Beast," she told him. "I've a good mind to send you away."

"Without a little diddle, dearest? Surely not."

She'd given up asking him not to use that preposterous word. Best get down to business. Once he'd had his "little diddle," he'd be impossible to reason with.

"Cadzy, we've got to talk."

"We'll talk. Later."

"Now, Cadzy."

"I said later, Eldora. Have you forgotten whose house this is? And who pays for your lovely clothes and jewels? And who owns you?"

Heat washed her neck. "I own myself. I can leave at any time."

"Very well. Go, if that's what you prefer. I will not force you to stay."

His indifferent tone frightened her, and the tears came effortlessly.

"I dislike it when you cry, my dear. Why don't we stop this nonsense and get on with it."

Just like that. Very well, they would "get on with it," but not in the manner that tended to suit him. He seemed to prefer that she lie passive while he labored over her, sometimes for painfully long periods, until he satisfied himself. In the process he would do a good deal of squeezing and pinching—which Eldora enjoyed—then he would require that she help him finish, pleasing herself in the process.

Not today.

"Have you really ever had a virgin, Cadzy?"

Pausing in the midst of removing his shirt, he frowned at her. "Of course I have."

"A young, beautiful virgin in white? One who, despite

her fear of you, wants your pleasure more than her own life? She is imaginative and instinctively innovative."

"Eldora, enough. Take off your clothes."

"Certainly," she told him meekly, and slipped out of the robe. She had retained her stays beneath the gown to make certain the very best was made of her large breasts. "But let me entertain you a little, dear one, just to get your juices flowing."

He hitched at his crotch and said, "Me juices are already flowin'. All I need is somewhere for them to flow to."

She would not be hurried. "Sit down, Cadzy. In that chair."

"I'll be damned if I will."

"I said *sit* down, Cadzy. You won't be sorry."

At first she thought he would come around the bed and seize her. When he was aroused he wasn't above using force to get what he wanted. Instead he grumbled, but sat in a chair on the opposite side of the bed. "Hurry up, then, Eldora. We're both too old for silly games."

"Speak for yourself," she told him, wounded. She would show him who was too old, and it wouldn't be Eldora Makewell.

Anger made her even more bold.

"Undo your trousers. I want to see the measure of my success."

"I'll be . . . Just *undo* my trousers? So that you can . . ."

"Look at you, dearest. I want to study progress so that I can time our 'little diddle' exactly right. Trust me. I'm going to make it worth every second of your time."

He crossed his legs.

Eldora climbed onto the mattress and went to all fours. "Come on. Undo them. Show me what you've got."

He turned a little pink and shook his head.

She began to enjoy herself. "You must agree to a rule. Will you do that?"

"Depends." He sounded like a petulant boy.

"If I promise you're going to be more excited than you've ever been in your life? If I tell you I'm going to do things you've never even dreamed of? Will you agree to a rule then?"

"What's the rule?"

"Don't touch me until I ask you to."

He looked directly down the front of her gown. "Tall order, that. Especially when I'm looking at those."

"Agreed, Cadzy?"

Smiling slightly, he shrugged and said, "Agreed. But get to it, Eldora."

"You're in a hurry. I like that. Undo the trousers."

"No, I . . . Oh, all right." He did as she asked, unbuttoning his trousers and laying them open to expose himself, showing that he really needed no additional preparation for his "diddle."

Eldora turned her back on him and slipped the loose neck of her gown from her shoulders and arms, letting it fall around her hips.

"Oh, lovey," Cadzow breathed. "Don't make me wait."

The gown pooled about her naked bottom, and she left it there while she faced him again, making sure he could see her belly but no lower. What he could see plainly was the white mounds of her breasts upthrust by her stays, her nipples all but hidden by the clever cups that supported her from beneath.

"Oh . . . my . . . Gawd," Cadzow muttered. "I never saw a better pair than those."

When he made to rise from the chair, Eldora said, "Ah, ah, ah. You promised. Down you go," but when she looked at his private parts, she added, "except for that beauty. That can stay up."

"Hussy," he said, turning up one side of his mouth. He reached for his Madeira again and watched her over the rim of his glass. "You have the soul of a whore. But then . . ." His smile became knowing.

He would pay for that comment, Eldora thought, and for his insinuation. But for now she had other matters to deal with. "I want to get married," she told him, and lay down on her back. She scooted around until she could let her head hang from the bed. She raised her knees and let them loll apart. "I don't want to wait any longer."

"Not now." Even upside down she could see the depth of his scowl, and the heightening of his color. His cock rose, full and dark. He clutched the arms of the chair and wriggled. "Enough of this."

Taking her time, Eldora worked her way closer to the edge of the bed. Slowly, she unlaced the stays, unlaced, and unhooked, and opened—and parted. The weight of her breasts made her gasp a little, but dearest Cadzow had a view he was never likely to forget. Pressing her arms together, she presented the poor man with a vision guaranteed to entirely undo him.

"*Eldora.*" He got unsteadily to his feet and came for her.

She caught him before he could touch her, caught him by the very part that already suffered the most. And he *howled.* Cadzow howled, and Eldora laughed, and writhed. "Naughty," she shrieked. "Naughty, Cadzow! Stand still or I shall twist off our pride and joy."

His attempts to pry loose her fingers were useless. The more he tried, the harder she squeezed, and his hips began to move.

The sound of her own panting filled the room. Abruptly she released him, and shoved him. "Stay back," she ordered, contriving to sound ferocious. Rolling to her knees again, this time she was naked. "You promised. And you will promise other things."

While he watched, his lips slack, his tongue darting in and out of his mouth, Eldora dipped her fingers between her legs, into the slick folds, over the swollen point of her need. And she fell back to support herself on one hand, and brought herself to throbbing pleasure while he stared.

Before the thrilling waves had even passed, she put the bed between them again and twirled, and twirled, setting her breasts swaying, showing him her nakedness from every angle.

Cadzow all but ripped off his trousers. He lunged around the bed, but she was quicker. A leap and she was atop the mattress once more, laughing, then on the floor on the opposite side, taunting him.

She did not evade him again. With a growl, and with more agility than he should have found possible, he vaulted onto the mattress himself, anticipated her next move, and dropped to grab her. With a mighty heave, he threw her onto the bed.

"Not good enough," she shouted, giggling deep in her throat. He was once more at her head, and she didn't waste her opportunity to grab his vulnerable rod. One tug and she had him in her mouth, had him secured between her teeth.

Wailing, he filled his hands with her breasts and moaned. Frenzy made her burn. Inflamed, Cadzow fell over her and delved between her thighs with his tongue and teeth.

He jerked mightily, and stiffened. A second, two, and his body was heavy on hers, and he was panting and writhing, and she writhed with him.

Now the time would come. He would need to be inside her. Eldora helped him climb with her to rest their heads upon the pillows, but crossed her legs when he probed to make way for himself there.

"What is it?" he asked, testy. "Open up for me, there's a good girl."

"I am a good girl," she said. "I'm a very good girl, and now I want my reward."

All but tearing her legs apart, he heaved his hips between her thighs.

Promptly, Eldora reached down and gave his rod a sharp pinch. And she smiled when he shouted, "Ouch, you bitch! You'll suffer for that."

"Such language from a holy man," she said, taking advantage of his pain to grab him again, and fastened her fingers so tightly about him that to remove her would have caused him agony. "Listen to me. Then I'll make it all better for you. I'll make it better than it's ever been."

"You're hurting me," he told her through his teeth. "I'll kill you for this."

"No you won't. You'll save your energy for other things."

"Damn it, Eldora."

"Marry me."

"I've told you I will. In time. When it's the right time." She squeezed a little tighter. "It is the right time."

"Eldora—"

"You need heirs. A son to help you with the business, and to inherit eventually."

"Heirs? *Heirs.* What bloody heirs? Why? He's the lord and master. Gray's the keeper of it all now. I get the crumbs, but they'll be enough."

"You get crumbs if that's what you decide to be satisfied with," she said very sweetly, and guided him inside her. "But you aren't going to be satisfied. *We're* not going to be satisfied. And they won't be enough."

"God, Eldora, you feel so good. Even if I will have to punish you for your nasty tricks."

He pushed deeper, then was content to remain there. But she'd had her fun and would have more. Now she would use the very considerable powers of persuasion she could exert.

The fire still burned hot, painting a sheen on her sweating lover's skin. "Gray was dead," she said. "At least, we were led to believe he was."

Cadzow squeezed his eyes shut. "We were led to believe wrong."

"If he's dead, everything is yours again."

"Move your hips."

She obliged. "All we're going to do is turn back the clock. We're going to turn it back to the time when Gray was dead. But then, when we carry on with our lives, he won't come back again."

He sat astride her thighs and bounced. "You're daft. Is that a necklace I gave you?"

"You know it is. I wear only things you give me."

"Good. Let's see what else it's good for."

"No, Cadzy! Concentrate."

"I am concentrating." He concentrated on taking off the necklace, pulling out of her, and thrusting the rubies and pearls inside instead. "You aren't the only one with imagination." His laughter cracked, and he worked and worked until Eldora writhed and made grabs at his hands.

The sensation drove her wild. Cadzow was rarely innovative, but when he was he derived enormous pleasure from contemplating his own brilliance. "Wonderful," she panted, bucking up, ensuring that her breasts bobbed before his eyes. "You deserve the best, my prince. You deserve all you've worked for these four years. You've run everything. You've made Falconer even more successful. And you shall have it for yourself."

"Speak of this no more." The last of the beads was inserted. "Now, shall we leave them there, or get them out?"

Gathering all her will, she held still and said, "Gray is with the Arbuckles."

"Not *now*. We will not speak of it now."

"We need a plan before he comes back. The sooner we act, the better."

"But not so soon that you miss your fun, hey?" He gave

the necklace an extra shove, and she yelped. "I think I shall take it out again."

"Curses, Cadzow. You promised me all this. You said it was yours and it would be mine. You told me your nephew was dead, and so he shall be. Help me and he will disappear. We'll say he was unbalanced by his terrible experiences and took his own life."

A relentless hand lifted each of her legs, and Eldora's breasts were crushed beneath her own thighs. "Stop it." She panted, struggling for breath. "Stop it now. Let me go. I know how we'll do it. In the river. We'll drown him and say he'd told us he felt drawn to the water because it had almost claimed him once. He felt drawn to it and said he was afraid he'd have to return to it one day."

"No." Placing his mouth between her legs, he fastened his lips over her and sucked.

Eldora screamed. She screamed with pleasure, and felt the beads drawn forth just the tiniest bit. "*Cadzow.* No. Oh, yes, Cadzow, yes."

He paused and grinned up at her. "You like it, hmm? Good, because when you're too tired to move, my sweet of the lovely big titties, I shall make sure you don't sleep until I'm finished with you."

"We could write a note." Desperation drove her. "Please, Cadzow, help me to do this for us. We can have it all, I tell you. All of it can be ours forever."

"Gray is my nephew. My brother's son. I have responsibilities to him. Don't raise the subject again."

"But—"

"*Don't* raise it again. You shall have everything you deserve. Do I make myself clear?"

"Well—"

"Do I make myself clear?" He gradually replaced his mouth, this time taking pearls and rubies between his teeth.

"Everything I deserve?" With each exquisite pop of a

gem from within, her bottom bobbled off the bed. "Oh! Everything, Cadzow?"

He nodded. And another bead slipped free, and another, and, slowly, another!

"Oh, Cadzy, this is . . . this is . . . oh." Pearl followed ruby. Ruby followed pearl, tugged and sucked, one by one until, with the very last one, Eldora's arms and legs flopped and she had not a jot of energy to use another muscle.

Cadzow lay on his side and indolently trailed the fabulous necklace over her breasts and belly. "You have a few moments, my treasure, then it will be time. I have saved the best for last."

She thought to protest, but thought better of it. "You will not consider my suggestion—about the other?"

"Never," he said shortly, rolling himself over her and presenting her with "the best." His eyes closed, and he labored.

Very well, Eldora thought, propping her hands behind her head, in that case she would proceed without him. Afterward he would be grateful. To accomplish her goal, she would have to offer her assistance to another who would doubtless be more than glad to aid in her scheme— once she'd explained the considerable risks of not doing so.

Chapter Eight

" The joke is over, Gray." Minerva heard the door to the workroom close as her father left them. "And it was cruel. You made fun of my father."

"I assure you that this is no joke, my love," Gray said. He gathered Minerva's hair into one hand and passed it over his lips, never taking his eyes from hers. "I am playing a very serious game."

"You pretended you were asking to marry me." Her face grew hot. "You tricked him."

Tension sprang tighter and tighter between them. "I have already asked you to marry me," he said. "Don't you remember? More than once?"

She pulled her hair from his fingers, but he caught her hand and took that to his mouth instead.

"You put conditions on that proposal, Gray."

"There are always conditions—on anything that matters a great deal."

He did with her fingers what he'd done with her hair, smoothed them with his lips. He lifted them and kissed each tip, each base, and blew, very gently, on her palm.

Minerva shuddered.

"We are meant to be together, you and I," he told her. "Help me make sure we can be."

She would not mention his preposterous demand of the previous night again.

"I don't understand why my father would accept such an absurd proposal as you made." Nor did she understand why Papa had insisted upon escorting Gray and herself to the workroom.

"No, I'm sure you don't understand." An enigmatic expression suited Gray too well. "Business is a matter for men. Your father wants something from me, and he doesn't much care how he gets it. Don't trouble your head with such a matter. Leave it to us, because we're so much better at it."

He must be funning her. "You're deliberately trying to annoy me. And succeeding. But I won't give you the pleasure of seeing me lose my temper. How you dare to come here like this after what you said last night, I can't imagine." Wretched creature that she was, she'd done exactly what she'd determined not to do.

"If you've had your pleasure, I suggest you leave."

A mighty clatter diverted her, and she whirled around.

"Sorry, Min," Fergus shouted from the far side of the room where he'd just dropped a bucket. "I'm clearing away the evidence."

Gray had befuddled her so much that she'd forgotten Iona and Fergus. "Evidence?" she said.

"Of muddy failure," he said, far too pleasantly. "You were gone a long time."

"You were, Min," Iona said. "Must have been important." Dwarfed by a too-large, mauve wool gown with tiered skirts (another of Mama's castoffs)—that did look frightful with her red hair and pale, freckled skin—she raised her brows expectantly.

Fergus and Iona were impossibly curious. They would attempt to prod her until she told them why Mama and Papa had sent their imperious morning summons to Mama's boudoir. "Mama and Papa wished to speak with me."

The twins looked disgustedly at each other.

Minerva decided she must take control of an absurd situation. "Gray is visiting—"

" 'Morning, you two," Gray said, deliberately interrupting Minerva. "Don't let me interfere with progress here. What I saw yesterday was fascinating. Thought I'd come back and see what you're up to today."

"Good morning to you, Gray," Fergus said, all hearty good cheer. "We're happy t'see you. We're not going on with the Mud—"

"Thank you, Fergus," Minerva said.

"It's Practical—"

"Gray isn't interested, Iona," she said, losing patience with the pair.

"Any notions about an alternative to the sailcloth, Gray?" Fergus-the-Unsinkable asked. "I expect you've had experience with such things."

"I might have an idea or two. I'll consult with some of our people. We're into manufacture as well as growing, of course."

Minerva fumed in silence. One would think that one's cousins, the two oldest and dearest friends one possessed, could be relied upon at a time of extreme need. Not so with Iona and Fergus. In this, Minerva's most stressful hour, they chose to be completely useless to her. Fergus was actually behaving as if Gray were a regular visitor to the workroom, and Iona showed every sign of following her twin's lead.

The Mud Thwarter Hem was under construction again. A new water-resistant medium must be located—without assistance from Gray Falconer. Today they had planned to test the invention closest to Minerva's heart—Practical Pulleys. But she could not contemplate working in Gray's presence. After what he said about her parents, telling her not to return home without him, ever—after that she could not contemplate his presence at Willieknock at all.

But there he stood, propped nonchalantly against a bookcase, his arms crossed, observing Iona's back-and-forth progress to check the weight of the prototype Practical Pulleys. Iona pretended to be quite comfortable in front of an audience.

"It is heavy," she said, making her skirts sway.

"Should we put her up on the platform?" Fergus asked. "Shouldn't think we'd need the dais." Supposedly intent on studying Minerva's sketches, he made a good job of hiding his face.

"No," Minerva told him shortly. "We have company, remember?"

"Gray?" Fergus looked at the "company" as if vastly surprised. "Oh, sorry, Min. I thought Uncle Arbuckle said he was t'be a partner in the venture."

So they had heard some of what Papa had said in leaving. The innocence in her cousin's eyes didn't amuse Minerva. "Papa is precipitate in this instance. He has forgotten that what he and Mama have been pleased to call my 'silliness' is, indeed, *my* silliness and I'm not obliged to accept a partner."

"Come, now," Gray said, and she didn't have to see his smile to know it was there, "you know you've been outfoxed. You didn't protest my suggestion that I become a partner in all this. Not to your parents. Why do so now?"

She would not allow him to play with her emotions further. "You caught me by surprise," she said, dropping her voice. "I never considered you might be serious."

"I am most often serious, Minerva."

He tucked back his black coat and pushed his hands into his pockets. His dark waistcoat fitted a solid chest and flat stomach without a wrinkle. Four years had matured a great deal about Gray Falconer.

Their perusal of each other lasted too long for comfort.

Minerva said, "Last night I was foolish. I was swept away by old memories of old emotions. Females can be like that. We are, after all, given to such foolishness as clinging to times we thought were special, or that seemed special at the time."

Gray straightened and braced his feet apart. From time to time he glanced toward the door, then up at the balcony. "Are you suggesting our times together have ever been less than special?"

She would not look at him, or respond.

"Minerva, I'm speaking to you. Do you deny that what we felt last evening was special? That our kiss was special?"

Her breath caught. He was intent upon winding her bruised senses around his probing words. It wouldn't work. "Why did you ask me to leave my family?" There, he could taste the annoyance of having his questions answered with questions.

A creak from above captured Gray's entire attention. His arms fell to his sides and he searched the shadowed balcony.

"You're nervous," Minerva told him, surprised. "Are you expecting an ambush?"

He shot out a hand and gripped her upper arm. Through the chiffon sleeve his fingers bit into her flesh.

Minerva sucked in a breath and attempted to pry him loose.

"Why would you ask such a thing?" He jerked her closer. "Tell me?"

Some women might be intimidated by him. Minerva felt a quite different emotion. "You are changed," she said, holding her head high. "The Gray Falconer I used to know would never have hurt me."

He looked at her arm and released it abruptly. "Forgive me. These have been difficult times. But I can expect you to accept that I am the man you promised to marry and, therefore, you owe me your allegiance and your understanding. Unconditional understanding."

"Pah! Only a man would ask such a thing. *Unconditional* understanding? I don't think you care a whit whether I understand or not. All you want is for me to do as you tell me to do. It's a male thing. The female is supposed to do the male's bidding without bothering to think at all." She paused to take a breath before continuing. "Well, Gray, it's possible I might have done as you asked without a word when I was twenty-one and still a silly girl, but I'm twenty-five now, and a professional woman of the world."

He looked steadily into her face. "You are not changed," he said, his voice very low, very still. "You are the girl I left behind, the girl who promised she would wait for me."

"And I waited." Stinging in her eyes warned of how desperately unsettled she was. "You didn't come when you said you would."

"As you know, I came as soon as I could." His lips came together in a hard line. "Do you doubt how much I suffered from wanting to reach you when I couldn't? If so, then I question that you ever knew me at all."

He wanted her to forget all that had gone before, and to accept his demands without demur. She needed to end this.

"Fergus." Walking backward, she made sure Gray saw he had disturbed her. She spun away. "Fergus, let's proceed. On the platform, Iona, dear. Be careful. That skirt is cumbersome. We shall have to start making our own garments soon. So they fit you. When I have a little more money again, we'll purchase materials."

"*We* have money now," Gray said from behind her.

Minerva closed her eyes briefly before continuing. "Up you go, Iona. That's the way. Now, we went over the pulleys. Do you remember what each one does?"

"Aye," Iona said. "I think so."

"She won't," Fergus said, and chuckled. "She's the memory of a chicken."

"*Fergus,*" Iona protested, but she pursed her mouth to keep from smiling.

"This will be simpler than a ball gown," Minerva remarked. "Of course, our aim must be to adapt the system for ball gowns. That is where they will be most useful."

"Wait till you see this, Gray," Fergus said, all robust enthusiasm. "It's a corker."

"Thank you, Fergus," Minerva said. "We'll start with Up Steps. Very well, Iona, *go.*"

Slipping her fingers beneath an artfully concealing shawl collar (made from a discarded bedsheet especially for the experiment), Iona frowned fiercely, moved her lips, counting silently, then tugged.

With a sound resembling parting stage curtains, the lowest tier of the dress rose several inches in front.

"I got the right pulleys," Iona exclaimed. "And it works, Min. I could climb steps unimpeded and upright. With my eyes ahead. I could *sail* up *flight* after *flight* of stairs."

Applause from the audience made Minerva first grow warm with pleasure, then cool with annoyance. He was making fun of her accomplishments. "Thank you, Gray," she said. "We have ambitious plans, but we know we have far to go."

"Will it matter that you can see everything now?" Fergus asked. "The workings?"

Minerva had been too intent on the hem. The pulleys were attached to strong twine inserted into casings sewn inside the bodice and skirt. When Iona used the pulleys, the handles showed beneath the shawl collar.

"A minor adjustment. That's all we need. Iona, *sit.*"

From behind her Minerva heard the words, "good dog," quite clearly, but she ignored the implication.

Fergus placed a small, gilt, straight-backed chair on the platform. Iona concentrated again, and with a sawing creak the back of her skirt rose from the level of the center tier. She looked triumphantly at Minerva and sank carefully to the edge of the chair. "There, you see? You've tamed the hoops, you clever thing."

More applause.

Minerva bowed her head but kept her attention on her willing assistant.

"D'you think it'll do that her fingers are turning white from holding up all the weight?" Fergus asked. His brow crinkled, and he moved nearer. "Then there's, well, the other. Um, d'you think . . .? Well, no, I don't suppose you do."

"Oh, Fergus, stop shilly-shallying around," Minerva said. "Do I think it appropriate for a lady at a ball to show the backs of her limbs all the way to the knees? And her drawers? No, I do not!"

Iona yelped, jumped up, and released the pulleys. The skirt descended with a *thwump*. She pressed her hands together. "Min, it's really coming along very well." Peeking toward Gray, she gulped and reached beneath the large collar once more. "Truly it is. Don't you feel bad for an instant. You're so clever. Look how well everything works."

To Minerva's mortification, her well-meaning cousin stared straight at her and pulled on various combinations of pulleys. Tiers of mauve wool raised and lowered in the most ungainly fashion, tipping up at a side, rising to reveal one knee in front, ruckling the entire length of the back and hauling it high like an Austrian blind for Minerva's most daring and most Practical application: For the Necessary Inconvenience.

If Gray dared to laugh . . .

He didn't, but that would earn him no accolades.

"Thank you, cousin," Minerva said, smiling warmly although she would like to run away. "You're right. We're making marvelous progress. You must be tired. I know I am. Let's stop for today."

"You do think It's progressing?" Iona asked anxiously, and accepted her brother's assistance from the platform.

"It's a wonder," Gray said, much too enthusiastically. "Such ingenuity."

"As you've heard us say," Minerva told him, "this is an early model. There are a great many modifications to be made."

"Really," he said. "But everything rises and falls so . . . interestingly."

Minerva turned around slowly.

"I'll change," Iona said, making much of passing between Minerva and Gray so that she could look at Minerva and shake her head.

"I know you think I shouldn't be made angry by unkindness, Iona," Minerva said. "You're such a peacemaker. But Gray doesn't deserve your help, and he knows it. Don't you, Gray?"

He widened his eyes and said, "You're suggesting I'm unkind?"

The door opened to admit Brumby McSporran, complete with his familiar whistling. Brumby whistled his way through life, possibly because the pretty, tuneful sound he made helped to blot out the incessant chatter of his parents.

"Haloo, Brumby," Fergus hailed. "We all missed you yesterday. And the day before."

"I was in Edinburgh," Brumby said, staring at Gray with no sign of warmth. "I had a small matter of importance to attend to there."

"Out with it, then," Fergus said. "What's her name?"

Iona nodded to Brumby and left to change from the cumbersome gown.

"I'll ignore that, Fergus Drummond." He turned his intelligent brown eyes on Minerva. "The only woman of interest t'me isn't in Edinburgh, and well ye know it."

Not quite as tall as his father, Brumby was of similar thin build with a tendency to appear indolent. He spoke slowly, strolled rather than walked, and generally took his time about whatever he did. And he rarely showed particular emotion about anything.

Brumby's last comment was out of character in its obvious meaning. And in contrast to their usual gentle expression, his eyes were sharp, his pleasant mouth with its upturned corners drawn flat against his teeth. He'd matured into a good-looking man, Minerva had noted on more than one occasion, a man who should be finding himself a wife. Once she'd made the mistake of telling him so and he'd painfully put his heart in her hands, pouring out how he had never wanted any woman but her. Somehow she'd found the words to tell him she was still in love with another man. Saying who that man was wasn't necessary, and now Gray had returned, and Brumby, who had let her know he continued to hope she would change her mind about him, showed the closest thing to hate that Minerva had ever seen in him.

"Good day to you, Brumby," Gray said, pleasantly enough although he could not possibly have missed the other man's attitude toward him. "How's life on the stage?"

Brumby colored instantly, and the intense dislike Minerva felt in him toward Gray frightened her. "I've had little chance to do what I'd like to do," he said, in a voice quite unlike his own. "*Duty,* you know. To those who need me. Duty and honor are strong enough in some of us to make us put our own selfish desires aside."

"Admirable," Gray said. Brumby's eyes might be cold, but they should melt before Gray's frigid stare. "Taxing is it, this duty that keeps you from a career?"

As vaguely untidy as usual, Brumby swept his brown curls away from his face. "What would you say if I told you I'd been trying my hand at a little fencing? Hmm? What would you say to that?"

Minerva held her breath. Gray was a master fencer whose reputation had been known throughout Scotland prior to his departure for the Indies.

He considered before saying, "I'd congratulate you on choosing a fine art to pursue. Does a great deal for a man's powers of concentration. His inner peace."

"And for his ability to demonstrate he's as good as any

man," Brumby said, blustering. His face shone with perspiration. "As a matter of fact, I've done more than try my hand. With a sword at my command I'm a man to be contended with, I can tell you."

Minerva was aware of Fergus hovering anxiously, and of her own heart beating too fast. If Brumby was really trying to provoke Gray, he was being exceedingly foolish.

"You'll have to come over to the manor," Brumby continued. "We've a fine new Thoroughbred, as fine as you'll ever see. Father bought it for me."

Minerva lowered her eyes and waited for Gray's response to that careless disclosure.

"I'll do that" was Gray's only comment. "Minerva, I promised Cadzow I'd take you back to Drumblade for a visit today. He's agitating to see relations between the families back on a firm footing."

"Minerva, could you come back to the manor with me?" Brumby said in a rush. "I expect my parents mentioned we've an old family acquaintance in residence the while. I'd appreciate your agreeing to meet him. He's a man who says he wants to rusticate, but then he complains that he's bored. You couldn't bore anyone, my dear, so you'd be doing us all a great favor."

She had never before been the object of a territorial fight between two men—and she'd never hoped to be, especially when those two men meant so much to her in different ways.

Gray began a tour of Grandpapa's massive collection of books.

In other words, Minerva thought, he would allow her to suffer while deciding how to avert disaster between himself and Brumby.

And Brumby angered her, too, with his fabrication of his relationship to the new inhabitant of Maudlin Manor.

"Well, Min," Fergus said, his brogue as beautifully soft as always, "looks as if you've become the object of all desire. You'll have them dueling over you next. If you want me as a second, either of you, you'll have to explain the ropes. I've never done that before."

Horrified, Minerva went to him and stood so close he pulled in his jaw. "That's not funny, Fergus Drummond. Dueling's against the law, in case you haven't noticed."

"Oh, Min, this is man stuff. Men have their ways of doing things that are outside the law. They always have."

"*Man* stuff? How dare you use a term like that to me. Man stuff. And you, my right hand in my experiments to free women from at least one aspect of the oppression of foolish men who can only keep us from our rightful places as their equals by their *outrageous* laws, and the devious measures they employ to make our lives as difficult as possible. Like the wretched clothes *men* design, or that pathetic, mewling, scraping women design to ingratiate themselves with men." When she closed her mouth, she must promptly open it again or expire for want of air.

Fergus stepped backward and said, "Sorry, Min," gently enough for her to believe he was at least sorry to have borne the brunt of her ire.

"I've always agreed with you, Min," Brumby said. "You're any man's equal—in many ways."

She would not persist in such a confrontation between people she cared for deeply, not, she noted, that Gray rushed to declare that he was wrongheaded.

"So," he said, "how long will it take you to be ready to leave? I brought a new gelding Cadzow acquired recently. Nice fellow. Meek. He'll be a good mount for you."

"Because I'm so hopeless in the saddle?" she flared at him.

"You must expect the arrogant to be arrogant," Brumby remarked. "Mama and Papa said you'd be glad to come with me and meet Clack."

"I didn't mean I thought you were hopeless in the saddle," Gray said. "Read me a little better, darling. My first concern has always been for your safety. I know you're an excellent horsewoman, but there's no harm in my wanting you on an animal with a steady disposition."

"Mollycoddling," Minerva muttered.

"You can ride my new Thoroughbred," Brumby told her. "I know you're up for it."

"That great, wild-eyed beast I saw in the yard?" Gray asked, and when Brumby admitted that was, indeed, the animal, said, "She will go nowhere near it. No doubt you got it for a song. Unfit for riding, if I had my best guess."

"The days when you can say what Minerva should or shouldn't do are over, Falconer." Brumby put himself far too close to Gray. "When you went away, and stayed away, you forfeited your right to decide what's right for her."

They spoke as if she were absent!

"Back away, McSporran," Gray said, but he kept anger from his voice. "Tempers are touchy today. We'd best say good day."

"Good day," Brumby said, sweeping an arm toward the door, indicating that Gray should leave. "I suggest you don't return."

Minerva all but moaned with frustration.

"That won't be possible." When pleasant as Gray was now pleasant, he became a subtly fearsome force. "Minerva and I have entered into a partnership. We'll be consulting together on Arbuckle Astounding Alternatives."

"Astounding Arbuckle Alternatives," Minerva corrected automatically.

"As I said," Gray replied without looking at her. "So I shall be spending a great deal of time here, you see."

"The devil you will." Brumby bristled. He pounded his right fist into his left palm. He rummaged through his pockets and cast about, plainly searching for something.

"What is it?" Minerva asked. "What have you lost?"

"A glove." A rhythmic twitch pulled at his left cheek. "I can't find a glove."

"Why do you want a glove, Brumby?" Fergus asked.

Minerva felt almost faint.

"To call the devil out. Can't call a devil out without a glove to throw down, can I?"

"No, you *can't*," Minerva cried. "So don't even think about it. I think you should both go—to your respective homes."

"I doubt Brumby would agree to come to mine," Gray said, visibly amused.

Brumby pounded a track around his declared adversary. "Tell the arrogant bastard to go away, Minerva."

"Language," Gray and Fergus thundered in unison.

Minerva felt sorry for Brumby, who, although intelligent, was not Gray's equal in polish and did not have his worldly experience. "I'll be happy to come to Maudlin Manor, Brumby," she told him, moving quickly to his side and holding his arm. "But not today, I'm afraid. I have a great deal to attend to here, today." Such as making sure Gray knew he wasn't a partner in her endeavors.

"I want you to come now," Brumby insisted, sounding petulant and out of character. "I told you this Clack is a bother and I need your help."

"And Minerva told you she couldn't come today," Gray said. "So why don't you run along and let us work."

Brumby recommenced his frantic search through his pockets.

"Gray," Minerva hissed. "Don't agitate Brumby, please. He's not at all like himself."

"No, he's not." Gray made no attempt to lower his own voice. "He used to be a reasonable fellow who knew his place. And he knew you belonged to me and always will belong to me. I can't think what's got into him."

"Brumby." Minerva launched herself between the two men. "You are upsetting me. You're both upsetting me. Please, Brumby, go to the manor. I very much want to see the new horse. And I want to see Mr. Clack. He sounds fascinating."

"Who is Clack?" Gray asked, quite rudely. "Are you taking in boarders these days? Not a bad way to defray expenses, I suppose."

Brumby fell back. His wounded expression cut Minerva. "I'm going," he told her. "I won't stay in the same room with *him* a moment longer. I'll come for you in the morning. Will *that* be convenient?"

How could she refuse? "Quite convenient, thank you. Shall we say ten?"

"Ten it will be." Brumby stared at Gray again. "You'd best be dealing with your rusty sword arm, Falconer. You've been away from the pursuits of civilized men for too long."

"How would you know?" Gray asked quietly.

Brumby stared, and grew even more red. "I heard you've said you were somewhere you didn't want to be, and that you couldn't do any of the things you might want to do."

"You heard that? How interesting. I didn't say any of those things."

"You must have said something similar, or we wouldn't have heard it," Brumby insisted. "Anyway, I'll be speaking with you again, or someone will speak to you on my behalf."

Minerva's heart all but stopped beating. "Brumby, put this nonsense from your mind."

"You heard me, Falconer. Be prepared to defend yourself."

"Damned strange way to call a man out," Gray murmured. "More or less: If you're not very good, old man, I'll call you out. Is that what I'm to assume you're telling me, McSporran?"

"No," Brumby said, his face paler now, and his nostrils drawn in. "No, you can take it that I'm going to be watching every move you make. And I'm prepared to fight for what I want—for what would be better in my care than yours. I'd cherish a treasure the like of the one you *ignored* for years."

To Minerva's amazement, Brumby seized her hand and kissed it fiercely, closing his eyes as he did so. Equally abruptly, he released her and marched to the door, his coat-tails flying. He paused there to send her a long, passionate look, raised a hand in a wave, and swept out.

"Grief," Fergus said, and whistled. "Our Brumby's in a state over you, our Min."

She couldn't look at him, or at Gray. Brumby could never be to her what he evidently wanted to be, but she couldn't bear for him to be so miserable. She also couldn't bear the idea of him doing something so dangerous as to call Gray out.

"Well," Fergus said, "seems like I'm not wanted around here. I think I'll go and take a look at the horses that must be milling around the yard in droves."

Minerva giggled a little at that and said, "Not quite droves, Fergus. Don't exaggerate so."

"It must be all the *passions* flying around in here. They've gone to my head. Just make sure they don't go to yours, Min. Remember, more than one woman's been caught between two men who supposedly wanted her more than their lives. Only once one of them had her, the main point of the battle was over. He'd won. Then the woman found out that for her ardent lover, the excitement had ended with the chase. I'll be leaving you now."

Chapter Nine

Alone with Gray, Minerva heard Fergus's ringing words. She did not believe them, but what *did* she believe?

How could it all be sorted out, all this tension and trouble? Wishing that for once she were more traditionally garbed, Minerva went to a dark corner of the windowless room, the only corner not stacked with roles of drawings and heaps of supplies, and sat on a small stool.

"You're angry with me," Gray said.

"Yes."

"Why?"

"You know why."

He closed the door carefully but firmly, and approached her slowly. "You're angry with me for continuing to press my suit. Not that I should have to press it. We already have an agreement. You have agreed to marry me."

"Yes. But you are perfectly aware that nothing about this situation is simple."

"No, I'm not."

"Of course it's simple. I kept my word. Apparently, you didn't."

He muddled her impossibly. "At this point we have nothing to discuss."

"We have everything to discuss. Resuming our engagement. How we shall celebrate that engagement. The events we shall plan. How long that engagement shall last—I should prefer that it be exceedingly short. And we need to design a wedding. I say design because it will be the most beautiful wedding Ballyfog has seen. I suggest we go to see Reverend Pumfrey at once."

She spun on the stool until he was confronted with her back. "And then what?" she asked him. "What have you decided will happen then?"

His hands came to rest on her shoulders. "Then," he said very softly, "it will be my pleasure to make you truly my wife."

Her eyelids lowered of their own accord. On too many occasions since his return, she had grown impossibly hot. She was impossibly hot again now. And when he bent to kiss the side of her neck, her body weakened and trembled.

"There is much to becoming a man's wife in the true sense, dearest. No doubt you have some ideas about what is entailed."

"Of course I do." She intended to sound sharp, but her voice wobbled.

"Should you like to discuss the matter with me?"

He thought to unnerve her into submission. "There's no need for discussion. I am well versed in such things, thank you."

Gray slipped his long fingers beneath the chiffon at her neck. "This is quite delightful, this little nothing you wear. I think I shall make sure you have many of them after we're married."

"Why?"

He laughed against her skin, and nipped the lobe of her ear. "You are well versed in such things. Surely you can guess."

The pressure of his mouth urged her to incline her head, and he pressed a great many short, gentle kisses to her temple and jaw, and to the tender skin just beneath her jaw, and downward to where he revealed a little of what had formerly been covered at the very edge of her shoulder.

"Before I left you, you were a complete innocent, Minerva." The kisses made a return trail. "I certainly never kissed you even like this, did I?"

"No." And it was entirely possible that she should stop him from doing so at once.

"And last night. Our kiss was a little less chaste, don't you think?"

He meant because . . . Direct, that was the way to deal with things. "You mean because you put your tongue into my mouth?"

This time he chuckled. "And if I remember correctly, my apt little student, you put your tongue into mine. Less chaste, do you agree?"

Warm, fresh breath accompanied each word, each kiss, caressing her skin until she grew weak with longing for . . . She wasn't sure what she longed for, but she did long.

"Minerva?"

"If you mean that the feelings evoked by the type of kisses we exchanged last evening were somewhat more intense than I have previously experienced, well, then, yes, I should have to agree."

His fingers glided from the skin at her shoulders to that which rested in awfully close proximity to . . . her *breasts*. Definitely she should not allow this to continue; at least she should not allow it without some sort of protest. Even if she didn't really mean it.

"If it were not for you, I should not have survived," he said, as if speaking as much to himself as to her. He found the corner of her mouth, kissed her there, and rested his cheek against hers.

And his fingertips went lower inside her bodice. And lower.

She should protest.

And lower.

"You are"—he took a breath, and she felt his touch reach the unrestrained upper fullness of each breast—"you are so beautifully made, dearest. Yet so unaware of yourself. I love that in you. I love so much in you."

Lower.

"I will do nothing to hurt or compromise you. Not ever. You do know that, don't you, Minerva?"

What did she know? That the pad of each of his middle fingers touched—*actually* touched the rims of the centers of her breasts.

And it was wonderful. Not enough, but still wonderful.

"Say something, Minerva. Please."

"Yes." Oh, that wasn't at all the thing.

"Oh, my love. I cannot wait much longer for you."

Surely there was something more, something that would feel even more intensely marvelous. She rested her head back against his stomach, and he surprised her by making what was almost a growling sound. Or perhaps a groan.

"Yes," he said. "Oh, yes. You are ready for me. But I must be strong for both of us. I have always promised myself that I would be the keeper of your purity for as long as it must be kept."

"Yes," she said. Why could she think of nothing more to actually speak aloud? She rocked her face from side to side, and his body seemed to press the harder against the back of her head.

With his nails, he brushed around the sensitive circles that were almost the very middle of her breasts. He seemed to know that she would find that . . . She found it indescribable and held the edges of the stool, thrusting her chest forward. Most surely she shouldn't do such a thing, but Gray didn't seem to mind, in fact he made more sounds that suggested he highly approved.

"Sweet Minerva," he murmured, and actually . . . he actually held the centers of her breasts, the buds that grew hard sometimes when she was chilled, held them between forefingers and thumbs and pinched slightly. "We will make up for what was taken from us," Gray said.

"I feel so . . . I like that, Gray. Oh, Gray!"

He pulled them, and it thrilled her. She wanted him to do it again, and again, and with more vigor.

"You must be mine," he told her. "And very, very soon."

"Do that some more," she told him, not caring if she should say something quite different. No wonder there were women who went astray because they spent such large amounts of their time in what Mama had denounced as "dangerous pleasures of the flesh." "Pleasure my flesh, Gray."

"Oh, certainly, miss." He laughed again, kept his thumbs where they were, but dipped the rest of his long fingers to completely support her breasts. And then he definitely groaned. She knew a real groan when she heard one. Gray groaned.

"Are you ill?" she asked.

"I have never been quite so close to complete health," he told her. "You hold the key to making me the fittest man in all Scotland. Stay, sweet one. Soon I must restrain myself, but not without one more liberty, if you will allow it."

Another liberty? "Oh, absolutely."

To her utter amazement, he drew the loose chiffon bodice completely below her breasts, made them absolutely bare, went to a knee at her side, and used his mouth as he had used his fingers and thumbs.

Minerva cried out, and took hold of a handful of his thick hair. He didn't appear to notice.

He pulled that part of her with his *mouth*. With his mouth, and ever so gently with his teeth, while he put the tip, the very tip of his tongue on the very tip of her—right *there*. The sensation was . . .

"Mmmm." He made a sound she was sure was one of pleasure.

"This is ecstasy, Gray." Looking down, she saw his dark hair against the white flesh of her left breast, and his hand, tanned by a faraway sun, holding her right breast so that it seemed very much larger than she'd noticed, didn't it?

That thought embarrassed her. But males must not mind large breasts or females wouldn't be in the habit of doing things to make those parts of them appear bigger, would they?

She grew still. He released her breast and put his hand on her leg instead, on her thigh, and moved upward.

There were other feelings, very far inside her. In the stomach area, or behind it—under it, perhaps.

And there was *moisture* in the bit between her legs.

Oh, she'd heard mutterings about all this among girls at parties and the like. She was probably quite backward about such matters, mostly because, since Gray went away she had kept a great deal to herself, and . . . Dear, oh, dear, should she be quite so enraptured by the sight of him touching her, by the dragging that went from beneath his mouth all the way through her body? To the wet bit?

No, she definitely should not.

With his free palm, he made circles on her breast. He raised his head, which she dearly wished he had not because she would like the feeling to go on and on, but he lifted his head to look at her. He looked at her breasts, and his hands upon her breasts, and she breathed deeper because she couldn't stop herself, and she actually made her breasts as large as she could, and silently urged him to keep holding them.

He said something she couldn't quite make out, and nestled his face in the middle of her chest, between . . . well, *between*.

Minerva loved him. From what must be her soul came a great surge of the most powerful emotion. She stroked his hair, and found his chin, and raised his face until she could see his eyes.

Smiling was impossible. There was too much inside her for smiles. Rather, she parted her lips and felt tears in her eyes.

Once more he glanced at her breasts, but then he covered them carefully, adjusted the neck of her bodice just as carefully, and smoothed her shoulders. He stood, and took her hands to pull her to her feet.

They kissed again, the tongue kind of kiss, only it went on longer this time and started to cause the draggy feeling in her breasts all over again. And the bit between her legs got wet some more.

"I must stop," he said, sharply, so sharply Minerva jumped, and flinched. "Don't look shocked, sweet. I'm the one who needs to be shocked, not you. You're perfect. Perfectly ready. Listen, why don't we dispense with the engagement? Naturally, there are some things to be dealt with, but what matters is for us to be together."

"Yes." He was absolutely right. "We should go to my parents at once. Is that what we should do?"

With only the smallest hesitation, Gray said, "Perhaps."

"I could not go against my parents' wishes."

"No, of course you couldn't." The warmth left his voice—and his eyes. "That's part of what I love in you, your honor. But I want all of your honor for myself. Min, I have a reason to keep the truth of what happened to me, where I have been, secret. Not for long, I hope, but will you help me?"

"If that's what you want, but—"

The briefest of knocks sounded at the door before it was opened to admit Mama. She paused, rather dramatically, Minerva thought, before sweeping toward them in her new tartan silk dress. "Brumby said I should find you here," she said with a very unkind sort of look at Gray. "Minerva, you are not a child. You know better than to be alone with a man like this."

If Mama had arrived only moments earlier, she would have been a great deal more upset. Minerva had an immediate vision of Gray's hand on her breast, of his head bowed over her other breast, and her skin prickled from head to foot.

"Minerva is betrothed to me, Mrs. Arbuckle," Gray said. "She was betrothed to me before I left England."

"Not officially."

"We had an understanding. Your husband agreed that the betrothal would take place the moment I returned. I have returned."

"Considerably later than you intimated would be the case. You assume that my daughter has had no other suitors in your absence. I assure you that is not the case."

"Mama, please."

"Speak when you're spoken to, miss," Mama ordered. Beneath the artfully applied rouge, she was paler than usual. "At first I didn't intend to come up here at all, because I couldn't conceive that you would be so foolish as to entertain the suit of a man who would desert you as Mr. Falconer has."

"I did not desert her." Gray's face showed anger deep enough to shake Minerva. "In fact . . ." His words trailed away. He looked from Mama to Minerva, and muscles in his jaw contracted to make him appear very harsh.

"This foolishness over some sort of partnership with you in your silly invention nonsense is out of the question, Minerva."

Minerva stood her ground, but she quaked inwardly, with hurt, not with fear.

"Be good enough to leave this house, Mr. Falconer."

He stared at Minerva. "I prefer not to remain where my presence is abhorrent," he said. "Will you come with me?"

She wavered, desperately searching for the answer she should give. She wanted to say, *yes, oh, yes.*

"You will remain where you are, daughter," Mama said.

"Minerva?" Gray said.

"He is not what he appears to be," Mama said. "This man is an imposter."

"No. No, Mama, he is Gray. I know Gray, how could I not?"

"Oh, he is Gray, all right, but ask him where he's been for three years since he left the Indies."

"She has asked," Gray told her, raising a single brow. "I have not chosen to tell her—yet."

"Because you don't dare." Passion lent a fullness to Mama's voice. "We've heard what you intend. You are a bounder, sir, a bounder of the worst kind. We have heard that you actually accused us. Us. My dear, incredibly talented Porteous, and my own self, I who am and have always been above reproach in any regard. You have suggested that your prolonged absence was in some way our fault. Deny that if you can."

Minerva gasped.

"Who told you that?" Gray asked.

"There, you see, Minerva?" Mama shrieked. "He doesn't deny it."

"I asked where you got such a preposterous slander."

"And I asked you to deny it."

Gray averted his gaze from Minerva's and strode rapidly toward the door. He said, "You are a clever woman, Mrs. Arbuckle, I'll grant you that. I bid you a good day, although I do not wish you one."

Chapter Ten

The dratted village came by its name honestly. Since early morning, Gray had been walking, through snow, in a fickle fog that was at once thick enough to wall a man off from the world, but then gone. And when the fog was no more, a glittering sheen drew over the leaden sky.

All beautiful, he supposed, if a man was disposed to find anything at all beautiful.

"Bally, bloody, *fog,*" he muttered, missing the step from the pathway in front of the village shops to the street, and all but tipping rear over noggin. "Enough to make a man long for island breezes." Ah, but he was a fellow with a fine sense of humor. And he was a fool in a pickle who might find himself back on a certain island if he didn't watch himself.

It wasn't over.

He wasn't safe.

And he wasn't giving up and running away, not to suit Porteous and Janet Arbuckle, or anyone else involved in their criminal schemes.

The fog thinned for a stretch, revealing cozy shop windows, lighted inside to foil the gloom.

Would he ever feel cozy or safe again? He carried a pistol tucked into the waist of his trousers. His swirling black cloak hid all evidence of what he concealed, and the weapon gave him a measure of comfort. So did the knife he'd taken to wearing in his boot.

That woman and her conniving mate had bested him by accusing him of accusing them, and by rushing in with righteous indignation. Her aim had been to warn him off. If he dared pursue them, they had their story ready. They must expect to send him scuttling away, defeated.

Not so. He had lived through hell and escaped. They would be unmasked, but not, he had decided, until he'd made their daughter his own. Then he would use her against them. If they loved a living soul, it was Minerva. With her as his wife, their fangs would be blunted. Min would find out and hate him for it, at least at first. Then, if he was fortunate, she would forgive him, but she'd have lost her family because he would not countenance his wife being on congenial terms with those who had tried to kill him.

This was driving him to madness.

He kicked at clumps of ice churned by the passage of carts plying their business between outlying farms and the village market held every Wednesday. Today was Wednesday, and folk hurried past, muffled against the cold, with baskets over their arms.

The leather satchel he carried over his shoulder was heavy. His intention, before giving in to an urge to tramp the hills, had been to leave Drumblade and go directly to the church where the Falconers had the benefit of a private chapel. He was going to the church now. There he planned to close himself away from the dreaded possibility of an intrusion by Cadzow's frightful intended—who had found three reasons to enter his suite on the previous evening.

Her voice was like a sharp nail to his inflamed nerves.

Her questions, and posing, and infernal good humor made him *sick.*

He must put diversions aside. Reacquainting himself with

the business was of the utmost importance. And if the only place he could do so was the chapel, then so be it.

Dammit, if necessary he'd do as Cadzow wanted to do: retain an army to stand watch until his enemies were too old to concern him further.

But he would have Minerva.

Mmm, he should not have done what he'd done the previous day.

Mmm, he had enjoyed every second. She was incredible. She was sweeter than any female on the face of the earth. And she had the kind of voluptuous potential, the promise of such carnal appetites as to have kept him in a state of near readiness since he'd left her.

Men were base, and he was no exception. Unfortunately, he couldn't find it in himself to regret desiring sweet Minerva.

An unexpected gust of wind whipped snow from the ground, and brushed fog before it. Wrapping his cloak about him, Gray bent his head and proceeded past the Flying Drum and Pig, Ballyfog's inn, and the single watering hole for miles around.

A coach must be recently arrived. A fresh team was being backed into the shafts, and there was much shouting and rushing about with trunks. Smells of horse sweat and dung and heated leather sullied the clean air.

Two people walked toward Gray, one a small, hunched creature of indeterminate sex and swathed in flapping layers of clothing, the other a thin, prancing fellow. The small creature half-carried, half-dragged two bulging tapestry valises. His emaciated companion, in a gaudy costume reminiscent of a Bond Street rake of more than a decade earlier, capered along unhampered by anything but an immensely long cane apparently made entirely of silver. The cane was gripped in the man's gloved left hand and carried clamped to his chest.

Gray realized he'd stared and set off again.

"I say, there! You, there! Tarry."

Gray stopped. *Tarry?* An oddly old-fashioned figure of speech. No doubt the dandy had observed Gray looking at him and was about to make an unpleasantness of the fact. Naturally. Why shouldn't one more unpleasant event occur?

"Yes, *you*," the stranger said, and Gray heard the crunch of feet behind him.

"I say," the man said, drawing near. "Don't suppose you could help a fellow, could you? Doesn't seem to be a civilized soul in the entire vicinity."

Gray wasn't in the mood to argue that Ballyfog was full of very civilized people. "What can I do for you?"

The stranger shot out his hand. "Silas Meaner." He swept off the tallest hat Gray had seen on any man's head. "Awfully good of you. This is my valet, Finish. Micky Finish. Doesn't look like much, but he's a gem, a perfect gem, I assure you."

"As you say." Gray was mesmerized by Silas Meaner's completely bald pate. The man had powdered it to a startling white. Not a hint of a hair showed there, which was a shocking contrast to his sallow face, where a wide, waxed blond mustache and full beard, together with vastly bushy brows, all but obliterated any features. Gray murmured, "You were saying you needed . . . ?"

"Directions, my good man." Meaner tottered, apparently rendered off balance by the corset that held his body in an absurd forward arch. He fumbled in a pocket of his yellow trousers and produced a gold sovereign. "This is for you if you can tell us where we'll find Olaf Clack."

Words failed Gray. Anger at such insult was out of the question. The man was a fool.

"Actually, I should have asked for the whereabouts of Maudlin Manor. Clack's there, damn his eyes. And we're going to make sure he—"

The bundle of clothes at Meaner's side trod on his foot, effectively cutting off whatever Meaner had been about to announce. Then the small person tugged on the other's red coat and pulled him down to whisper in his ear.

"Oh, oh, quite, Finish," Meaner said, quickly putting the coin away again. "Not the thing here. I see that now. I do become distracted on occasion. You see, I'm an artistic sort of man, and we artistic sorts find it difficult to concentrate on the ordinary details of life, don't y'know."

Gray hesitated. He didn't like what he felt in the presence of these two. They were obviously harmless, yet there was about them a whiff of something distasteful—or was it that they were familiar in some manner? Could they be familiar? He peered a little more closely. Couldn't be. He would definitely never forget either of them.

Too much time alone to think could make a man imagine things.

He was tempted to direct the popinjay to Willieknock Lodge, where he might find a like spirit in Porteous Arbuckle. A like *artistic* spirit. That was unlikely to aid Gray's cause at all, and his own cause was all that could concern him, at least for the moment.

"Maudlin Manor lies two miles from the village," Gray said, civilly enough. "To the north."

"*Two miles?* Two miles? But I was told the place was in Ballyfog." He staggered about, looking up at the inn sign, then in either direction along the village street. "This is Ballyfog, ain't it? After all, there's the *bally fog,* what?" He guffawed at his own small joke.

"They'll take you from the inn," Gray said, anxious to be on his way again. "Go inside and ask. There's always someone eager to earn a shilling."

Silas Meaner clutched his stick to his chest and raised both magnificent eyebrows. "I'll do as you suggest. Very wise. I'd thought I could walk there, you see, and so I should if it weren't for this inclement weather."

Gray nodded and made to walk away.

"And your name, sir? Forgive me for not asking sooner."

"Gray Falconer." He didn't remain for more pleasantries, but set off toward the church.

He did glance back once, to see the ill-assorted pair standing exactly where he'd left them. Standing, and staring at him. Once they realized he'd seen them, they turned and rushed back into the inn yard.

Shaking his head, he carried on toward the church at the far end of the village.

Another quarter of a mile and he arrived at the gates of St. Aldhelm's, and saw the reassuring figure of the Reverend Pumfrey brushing snow out of the vestibule of the ancient stone church.

Pumfrey's sharp blue eyes recognized Gray at a hundred yards, even after not having seen him for years. "Hey, there, young Falconer," the reverend called. "I heard ye were returned to the fold, and glad I am of it, very glad."

"Thank you, Reverend," Gray said. "Will you mind if I spend a quiet while in the Falconer chapel? I've a mind to contemplate."

Pumfrey's long, generous face showed amusement. "To contemplate, ye say? Och, I'll be more'n glad for ye to contemplate. About time, I'd say. The Gray Falconer who went from Ballyfog wasna' about contemplation."

Gray inclined his head, and took off his hat preparatory to entering the building. "You're right, of course. But I was considerably younger, and more foolish. If a man lives long enough, he learns some wisdom."

"Does he, now? Well, I'd say some do and some don't, but I always knew ye'd grow t'be a wise one. Go along inside with ye, and welcome. God'll be pleased wi' your comp'ny."

Reverend Pumfrey had been born in Ballyfog, been educated by a former minister at St. Aldhelm's, and sent away to school by that good man with the understanding he'd return to take over care of the souls thereabouts. And Pumfrey had done just that, bringing Pamela, his twittery little wren of a wife, with him.

Gray entered the dignified old building with its narrow nave and incredibly beautiful stained-glass window behind the altar, and made his way past pews of wood turned to black by the ages. Needlepoint kneelers, many faded and pale, all lovingly made by the hands of wives and mothers and daughters, marked the designated spots of particular parishioners.

The Falconer chapel with its gilded screens occupied a corner at the back of the church, beside a vaguely pagan-looking baptismal font carved from the trunk of a fallen oak long before the time of anyone living.

With a rush of gratitude, a sense of having reached a safe sanctuary, Gray used the little key he'd taken from Drumblade and let himself into the chapel.

It was just as he remembered. Rather than pews, Falconers gone by had chosen to provide themselves with wooden armchairs. Cracks webbed the brown leather seats and backs.

Gray closed himself in and sank into the chair that had been his father's. It felt right. Today he needed his father's clear head and sensible reasoning.

He unpacked the satchel, heaped books and papers on the cold flagstones beside him. His cloak kept him warm enough. A little chilliness was a small price to pay for the peace and safety he felt here.

When next he looked at his watch, several hours had passed. He no longer felt at peace.

What in . . . not here, he would even watch the words he thought here. But what in *hell* had Cadzow done with all that money?

Large sums. Large sums, at more or less regular intervals, had been taken from Gray's personal accounts, the accounts over which Cadzow had been given control until Gray was twenty-five, which he had been by the time he set out to return to England.

Gambling? Surely not. But what? Could Cadzow have been in financial trouble and felt he would be safe taking Gray's money since he was never expected to return?

Cadzow was a changed man, but he'd already been a good man; he would be unlikely to turn into a thief. There had to be another reason for the discrepancies. If they were discrepancies. For all Gray knew, the sums had been necessary expenditures. But they were listed merely as "miscellaneous." In God's name . . . He massaged his temples. What miscellany could possibly cost so much? So much, so often?

Memory played the sounds of voices far away. Raucous and slurred from too much drink. Raised in a careless frenzy that reached him in snatches. They'd cried out about Mr. No-name, called him the fool who paid for nothing and who would go on paying for nothing.

Gray stared unseeingly ahead. Visions came of faceless creatures cavorting through flickering light from their fire on the beach. A night when the ship had returned and the band's celebration continued until dawn. Always he'd waited for them to go mad enough to come for him, to kill him. He would forever believe that, in time, they would have done away with him. God had not been ready to allow him to leave the earth quite yet.

Mr. No-name.

He stamped his feet and blew on his hands, and returned to studying the figures. So engrossed was he that he was unaware of another visitor to the chapel until a voice said, "There you are. You worried me out of my mind," and, startled, he looked up to see Cadzow closing the door behind him. "You didn't tell a soul where you were going, and none of the staff saw you leave."

Gray spread his hands over the pages before him and hoped his uncle wouldn't know exactly what he was doing. Had Cadzow tried to get rid of him?

"Fortunately a very odd pair, who were trudging through the lanes looking damnably cold, told me they'd talked to a chap like you outside the Flying Drum and Pig."

"Sorry," Gray said, distracted by his thoughts, and by what he held on his lap. Then he considered what Cadzow had said. "A tall man in outmoded clothes, and a little fellow wearing—"

"The same," Cadzow said. "Good thing they came across my path, I can tell you. Put them in the carriage and took them to Maudlin Manor. They might be frozen statues by now otherwise."

"They were walking in the direction of Drumblade?" Gray said. "Odd. That's west. I told them Maudlin Manor was north."

Cadzow grunted.

"And I told them to hire a conveyance."

"Don't think they had the blunt," Cadzow said. "Anyway, no matter. I know what you're up to, my boy, and I must come clean before you think the worst of me."

Gray recalled Silas Meaner's readily produced sovereign. Certainly money enough to secure conveyance to Maudlin Manor. But it was, as Cadzow had already said, of no importance. Gray glanced down at the pages beneath his fingers, and when he raised his eyes he found Cadzow looking at those pages too.

"You've found me out." Glum resignation settled about the other man's plump features. "But it's not the way it looks, my boy, it truly isn't. I was in a queer way and didn't have any choice but to use your blunt, don't y'know."

"Actually, Cadzow, I don't know." Gray tried for a light enough tone.

With much clearing of the throat, and humming, and scuffling of his boots, Cadzow showed himself to be uncertain how to deal with his difficulty.

"You're telling me you were short of the ready. So you borrowed from me. Is that correct?"

"In a manner of speaking."

"Either it is, or it isn't."

"It is."

"Just so."

"But only because of certain events."

Gray sighed. "You have a handsome allowance from the estate, Cadzow. And that's over and above your share of profits from the business—which are substantial by any man's standards."

"Well, hmm, my expenses have been exceptionally large of late. I met Eldora and you know how a fella needs to impress a beautiful woman if he's going to snag her."

This was not an appropriate moment to tell Cadzow what he thought of Eldora Makewell. There never would be an appropriate time, unless Cadzow came to his senses and broke with the creature.

"But that wasn't what I used your money on, Gray. Honestly not. No, I used my own for those, hmm, trifles, and that was the problem that put me in such a pickle. I'd much have preferred to pay up with my funds rather than yours, but it just wasn't on, because I couldn't keep everything running, the way your dear father could—with such ease. I have always found it near impossible to be clever with money, don't you see. My interests have always been—well, I don't need to tell you again that I don't care for business. But I absolutely had to come up with the blunt, and I had to come up with it when it was asked for, didn't I?"

Confusion left Gray with his mouth open. He closed it at once. Was the man actually going to confess his sins outright?

"Didn't I?" Cadzow repeated. "After all, there was too much at stake to take the risk of not paying. I know I could have gambled on it all being ruse. I was fairly sure it was, in fact, but I couldn't do it, Gray. I just couldn't. So I paid with your money. There. Now you know. And I beg you to forgive me. I'm sorry. I shall do my best to pay it all back, even though it wasn't for me, because—"

"*Cadzow.*" Gray ran his fingers through his hair. "Stop babbling, man, I beg of you. Whatever has happened . . . well, we'll have to work it out, I suppose. You'd decided I wasn't coming back anyway. Of course you had—that goes without saying. You used my funds because you expected them to become your funds anyway. It doesn't make me a happy man, but I suppose I can learn to understand." He was bemused and undone, and doubted he could learn any such thing.

"That wasn't how it was." Tears, actual tears, filmed Cadzow's blue eyes. He gulped and looked away, embarrassed, no doubt.

Embarrassed himself, Gray rose and put the book on his chair. He went to Cadzow and said, "You'd better come clean, old man. Always the best way."

"I suppose so." Cadzow sniffed, and bowed his head, and smoothed his gloves over the backs of his hands. "I'm undone by this, Gray. Ewan would have handled it all so much better, and I owed it to him to do just as well. I panicked, I suppose. Almost fell apart, if the truth were told."

Gray patted his uncle's shoulder. "Tell it slowly, and calmly. We'll get through this together."

"You're too good to me." When Cadzow raised his face, tears streaked his cheeks and dripped from his chin. He wiped them away. "Damned mortifyin', this. Not at all the manly thing."

Cast adrift in unfamiliar waters, Gray drew Cadzow into an embrace and thumped his back. "Out with it. The quicker the better, hmm?" This was his only relative, his dead father's brother. Forgiveness was the better part here.

"I had to pay up, you see." Loud sniffs followed, and Gray had a thought for his cloak. "They said—that is, the messages they sent told me to pay, or else. So what could I do but pay? I ask you, Gray, what could I do?"

"Who sent you messages?" he asked, clinging to his patience. "About what?"

"Oh, I didn't say, did I? Well, I was told that you were still alive."

Gray held quite still. Cadzow continued to lean on his shoulder and Gray stared past him at the gilt screens and waited.

"They said I had to pay to keep you alive. Now, I had no means of knowing if you were alive or dead, had I? After all, at first it seemed you must be dead, and later, I was certain you were."

"Go on," Gray said softly.

"Yes, well, anyway, I couldn't risk it. As long as they kept insisting they'd keep you alive as long as I sent the money, well, then, I sent the money. I had to do anything I could to get you back, don't you see?"

The emotion that swelled in Gray's breast came close to making him light-headed. "I . . . I don't know what to say."

"They sent messages by a man who arrived in Ballyfog on a coach, and left that way afterward. He took back the note each time, and the money along with it. I kept wanting to track the bounder, but I was *terrified*. He said I was being watched and if I tried to unmask him, you'd die. I'd have paid anything to get you back. But I felt so helpless."

"It was ransom, Gray." Wiping the back of a hand over his eyes, Cadzow stepped away. "They kept saying they'd return you, but they didn't. Time went by and there were more hopes, and more hopes dashed again. I only became more desperate to get you back, and more desolate at the thought that I'd never let you know how dear you were to me. After all, I never had children of my own."

Gray turned away. He couldn't speak. What would Cadzow think if he knew his neighbors had been behind the kidnapping—and Gray was now certain the Arbuckles were those who arranged the whole thing. *Damn*, it all became clearer by the moment. They'd probably come up with this scheme Cadzow spoke of to keep him paying in hopes of keeping Gray alive. Little wonder they were horrified at the sight of their prize pigeon returned to cut off their endless supply of blunt.

He swung back to Cadzow. "Uncle . . ." If he told him, there might be some interference in his plans to have Minerva.

"Yes, Gray?"

"Nothing, nothing." Also, he must not only be sure of the Arbuckles' crimes, but able to prove them. He smiled. "Thank you. I'll never be able to thank you enough."

"It wasn't through me that you were saved. You saved yourself."

Cadzow was a truly honorable man. "Nevertheless, I thank you for your faith. And I thank you for loving me enough to keep that faith alive, rather than giving up on me. I am humbled."

The other man's sigh pained Gray.

"If I were a better manager, I should have paid those sums from my own pocket as I wished to. I've tried hard, but, oh, you know. There's plenty in the business, but I hesitated to have others discover what was going on in case they—those people found out and . . . *killed* you. As of now, I have depleted my fortunes dreadfully. From now on I must make myself a new man in every way. I will learn to manage my affairs better."

"I'll arrange a substantial transfer to your personal account today," Gray told him. "Let me assist you . . . That is, would you pay me the honor of allowing me to advise you in matters of commerce and the management of your affairs? Your financial affairs, that is."

"You're too good." Pressing a fist to his mouth, Cadzow backed away. "Thank you, Gray. You are your father's son. He would be so proud of you. Thank you, thank you. I accept."

Moments later, the outer door of the church clanged shut

and Gray was alone again, alone with more thoughts than he would choose to embrace.

He'd been right to keep his own counsel about the Arbuckles, but that matter only became stickier.

Cadzow had brought him low, brought his trust in his own judgment of a man low. With luck he would learn from his own mistakes and give others more leeway to prove themselves in the future.

Gad, the sums that must have been frittered on La Makewell. He had given more than a glance to the heavy rope of rubies and pearls she favored. They were incredible and must have cost Cadzow a fortune, but how many more fabulous baubles had he showered on the creature?

His uncle had championed him, and he was grateful, but there was little doubt that the man had squandered a fortune. At least he'd agreed to some help in that area, but Gray would have to keep a close eye on him in the future. It was fortunate for the Falconer empire that with Gray's return, Cadzow would play only a minor part in its destiny.

He prayed Cadzow had been completely honest when he'd said he hadn't touched company funds. If Cadzow had contrived to meddle there, where others were involved, Gray might not find it a simple task to save the man's public reputation.

Chapter Eleven

Someone turned the ring handle on the outer door to the church again. The grinding sound echoed into the cavernous ceilings of the building.

He must be ever vigilant.

Drawing back into a draped corner, Gray watched light slide through the opening door—and felt a fresh rush of cold air. A cloaked female with a hood drawn over her head entered the building, peering around as she came.

No cloak could disguise his Minerva. She did not appear sure of herself when she closed the door again and tiptoed forward. At the sight of her, Gray felt watchful, alive. She crept as if she feared making a sound in a holy place.

And her huddled form suggested she was anxious. He could not bear to see her disquieted and not do what he could to comfort her, but if he shouted, she might faint from shock.

At the center aisle, she paused and searched all about her and whispered, "Gray? Are you here?"

He expelled the breath he'd been holding and whispered back, "Yes, dear one. Stay there, I'm coming."

She met him beside the baptismal font. The cold had whipped color into her face, bright light into her eyes.

"How did you come here?" Words, the right words, were not easy to find. "Are you alone?"

"Of course I'm alone," she told him tersely. "And I came on foot."

"In this weather? You are not made for such excursions."

"I am probably made to milk cows and collect eggs at dawn. I am, sir, a female of sturdy build and fine constitution, not at all the fainting waif you seem to consider me."

She was abrupt and forceful. Her agitation showed in the manner in which she rose to her toes and bobbed.

"As you say." The better part often rested in being able to judge a woman's mood. Minerva was not herself today. She might be in that certain time of the month that was said to render women quite beyond reason. Yes, that must be it. She glared at him. Actually *glared at him.*

"Is that all you have to say to me?" she asked.

"About what?"

Her eyes fixed on his, she took a step toward him, and so fierce was the set of her beloved face that Gray, in turn, took a backward step.

Minerva advanced again.

Gray retreated again. "What is it, dearest? You need my help, don't you? Talk to me. Tell me what is in your heart."

She looked about her. "This is God's house."

Poor darling, her mind was quite unsettled. "Indeed, it is. A good place to be."

"Not a good place to speak what is in my heart, I assure you, Gray Falconer. I'll thank you to accompany me outside. At once."

"I beg your pardon."

"I pardon you nothing. I'll await you outside."

While he recovered something of his composure, she flung away and marched back the way she'd come. He barely remembered to gather the books and papers from the chapel floor and stuff them into his satchel before dashing from the church in a manner sadly lacking in the decorum required by his surroundings.

"Minerva!" He burst from the vestibule onto the outside path, where fresh snow had piled. More swirled from skies that were one with the softened land. "Minerva, where are you?" There was no sign of her dark-green-clad figure.

"I am here."

He whirled around to discover he had passed her. She sat on one of the stone benches that lined the vestibule.

He hurried to sit beside her.

As quickly, she rose and left that place, setting out across the graveyard.

"I say, dear one," he puffed, catching up. "I must insist—"

"You are in no position to insist upon anything. I'm not at all sure I can even speak to you. And if I can speak to you, I'm definitely not sure why that should be."

"Because you love me," he said promptly.

"Pah!"

"You adore me, as I adore you."

"Pah!"

He jogged sideways, keeping her face in view while she continued he knew not where. "Since you were a girl—a child—of twelve you have known your place was with me."

"Arrogant to boot," she muttered.

He felt heated, and not only from exertion in heavy clothing. "Not a bit of it. Factual, damn it—I mean, well, just factual."

"I have heard such language before, I'll thank you to remember. I may not care for it, but I'd prefer not to be treated like the *child* you seem determined to consider me."

"Let us love, not fight, my darling."

She checked her stride. "Oh, such poetry." Her eyes rolled heavenward. "I may become sick."

Gray felt the instant when the emotion that drove him began to change. "Minerva," he said, "such waspishness is not becoming."

"Oh"—she tilted her head, and her smile was wickedly derisive—"not becoming. Oh, I am undone. I am beside myself. I am destroyed to think that you don't find my behavior becoming. Can you imagine such a thing? Minerva Arbuckle, *unbecomingly waspish.* Pah." She clomped onward, her feet squidging through snow that grew deeper by the minute.

For several seconds Gray watched her purposeful progress. He adjusted the satchel on his shoulder and planted his fists on his hips. "Damnable females," he said, loud enough for any to hear—if the snow were not damping all sound.

"Min! Minerva!" Drat her. Just where did she think she was going, anyway? "Minerva, stop!" He loped after her, silently cursing the beautiful handicap that was the snow.

When he drew abreast of her again, she kept her head down and made to angle away from him.

Gray strode to cut her off, and she reversed direction.

He corrected again, and met her, face-to-face, between two tombs made vast beneath their white mantles. "Stop," he ordered. "This minute. Do you hear me, Min? Stop at once."

She did stop. Her breath made steamy puffs. With her head down, he couldn't see her face, but the attitude of her shoulders suggested that some of the ire had gone out of her.

Praise the Lord.

Minerva raised her head and studied him.

Gray went to touch her, but knew his mistake in time to draw back. "Oh, Minerva. You are . . . Surely nothing can come between us, nothing that would tear at you so. You're crying, dear one."

"I—am not." She sniffed and tipped her face to the sky. "The snow is melting on my cheeks."

"You are crying."

"I never cry."

"You are crying."

"I can cry if I want to."

"There is no arguing with females. Especially at such times."

"Such times?" She glared at him. "What exactly do you mean by that?"

He shrugged, cast adrift by a subject he wasn't sure how to broach. "*Female* times, I suppose. Yes, female times. Since male persons don't have such times, that would appear an appropriate term. Men know that females are not stable during their, er, *times,* as it were. Most unstable, some of them, so I've heard."

Her eyes grew wider, and fixed.

"Now, now, don't upset yourself. Does this always happen, my dear? Has it perhaps become more intense with age?"

"With—*age?*" Minerva narrowed her eyes now, and pressed her lips together. And, to Gray's absolute horror, the tears she denied welled along her bottom eyelids. "I am five and twenty, sir. Hardly a fresh young thing, but hardly an aged crone, either. And, since the niceties of life seem unknown to you, it is completely inappropriate for you to speak of such things as you refer to as, oh, *female times.*"

Abashed, he widened his stance and frowned. "How should a man deal with these things, then? If he's to be sympathetic when a woman's in her . . . Oh, dash it all."

"You dare to suggest that because I am angry beyond any anger I have ever known it must be because I am somehow *indisposed* by *female times?* How insensitive. How insulting. How utterly beyond all. How *thickheaded.*" Planting her small feet as wide apart as his own, she fixed him with her deep blue eyes and said, "How male."

He no longer knew the time, but this day had already been entirely too long. Matters must be taken in hand. From now on, he would decide how things should be handled. "Listen, Minerva. We have both been through extremely difficult events. If I'm clumsy, and I know I am sometimes very clumsy, I apologize. Extraordinary events may dull some of our skills—such as social skills. Please accept that I only sought to be understanding of something I clearly don't understand at all. After all, my experience of female—"

"Stop," she ordered, raising a gloved hand. "Don't return to that subject, please. And, for your instruction, I am not in the, er, condition you allude to."

"Oh."

Her very pink face attested to his having blundered in mentioning the subject at all.

"It is extremely cold, Minerva. I am concerned for your health. Should—"

"Do not be concerned for my health. As I have already told you, I am as healthy as any farm girl. I have never coddled myself, and I shall not start now."

"*I'm* cold, then," he declared, his own temper thinning. "And I don't wish to continue this conversation in a churchyard."

"Why not? What better place? At least we don't have to concern ourselves with who may be listening."

Gray pondered that a moment before smiling. "You always were a quick wit, my girl. Too quick for your own good sometimes. I suggest we retire—"

"Do you think that an appropriate suggestion under the circumstances?"

"If you would let me finish. I suggest we retire somewhere more comfortable. Then you can do what you obviously came to do. You can berate me at your leisure without danger of either of us expiring from exposure."

"I want to be alone with you, Gray."

"Well—"

"Absolutely alone for as long as it takes to get to the bottom of all this."

Casting about, Gray reminded himself that she had not just extended an invitation for him to join her in secret to enjoy the pleasures of the flesh. A pity.

"I see you have no immediate suggestion for where we might go to accomplish this. Perhaps that should please me."

There were, and always had been, moments when her meaning escaped him.

"Oh, Gray, really, you can be such an innocent. Or is it that you think I'm too much of an innocent to think of such things? I meant that since you have no ready solution for where we may go to be alone, it's possible that you are not as accustomed to private trysts with females as most gentlemen are purported to be."

"Dash it all, Min. You're remarkably personal on occasion."

"You say *I'm* personal."

"I do. And may I make it clear that the reason I didn't consider taking you to any private place that might come immediately to mind is that I think of you quite differently from the manner in which I think of any other . . ."

"Quite so," she said, lowering her eyes in a demure manner that didn't convince him of her naïveté. "I, on the other hand, do have a private place in mind. I go there quite often—to think without the babel of empty voices driven by empty minds. Should you care to go there with me?"

"Yes." What else could he say? What else might he *want* to say? "Should I get you inside somewhere and go for a carriage?"

"We have very little distance to go. Just let me lead the way."

He did so without further comment, longing to touch her in some way, to take her arm perhaps, but restraining himself and walking behind her stalwart, upright little figure instead.

Through the graveyard they progressed, to a gate leading to Reverend and Mrs. Pumfrey's house. Minerva opened the gate and left it open behind her.

Gray followed and closed the gate behind him. "Minerva," he said uncertainly. "This is—"

"I know where I am. Just for once would you allow me to guide you?" She glanced back at him. "Would you trust me—just once?"

Before he could respond, she continued along the path and around the pretty Tudor house with its dark, crooked cross beams and white wattle walls, to the back of the building.

Gray carried a picture of her face in his mind, her face looking back at him. She was grown ever more beautiful. Some said she was stolid, ordinary. They did not really see her. Minerva Arbuckle was the most beautiful of women.

She rapped on the kitchen door. It was quickly opened by Pamela Pumfrey, her light hair restrained by a white cap, a frilled white apron all but covering a simple gray dress. She saw Minerva and broke into chuckles. "Ye came. Och, look at ye. Blue wi' the cold. Inside wi' ye." She looked past Minerva at Gray. "And ye, too, young Gray Falconer. In wi' ye, afore ye freeze."

Once inside kitchens that radiated heat and assaulted the nostrils with the scents of baking delicacies, Gray became uncertain of how to proceed. "Good day to you, Mrs. Pumfrey," he said, trying for a formal tone. "Very civil of you to invite us in, I must say. But—"

"Gray is always on his best, formal behavior Mrs. P.," Minerva said. "He hasn't given me an opportunity to tell him we were coming here, so he's confused, you see."

"Och, not a bit o' it," Pamela Pumfrey said. Exceedingly small, with tiny bones, her manner of moving was so rapid she barely seemed to touch the floor. "Minerva's nervous, Gray. Same as y'sel'. Don't ye believe otherwise. She told me she might need to talk to ye alone, so, o' course, that would have t'be here." The last was delivered in a matter-of-fact manner.

"Would it indeed be here, *o' course*?" Gray asked Minerva quietly. "And when did you arrange this, miss? And, by the way, how did you find me at the church?"

"Min comes to us often," Mrs. Pumfrey said quickly, leading the way from the kitchens into a narrow hall and up crooked stairs, all smelling of the lavender wax used on beautiful old wood. "She visited yesterday, and she was in a state, I can tell ye. The pickles ye younguns do get into. She said she needed to talk t'ye alone, and we agreed we should aid ye. Pumfrey and mysel', that is. We agreed. We had quite the struggle oursel' y'know, when we were young and wantin' to be together. We understand these things."

"We just need a place to talk," Minerva said. "It's simple enough. We are not discussing, er—well, we're not dealing with the more . . . *personal* sorts of things you and the reverend dealt with."

"Aren't ye?" Mrs. Pumfrey said, starting up another set of stairs, this one from the entry hall. "Well, I'm sure ye'll decide what ye are discussin' when ye've time all by yoursel'. As t'the other, Gray, I canna tell ye how Minerva knew where ye were. Here ye are, then. This place is yours for as long as ye need it. Ye willna be interrupted."

They entered a room where a cradle stood empty and handmade animals and dolls lined a deep window seat. A rocking chair stood to one side of a fireplace where a fire had been lighted. Mrs. Pumfrey walked to a door beside that fireplace and opened it. "If ye need more room to move around, there's this, too. I'll not tell anyone ye're here."

With that, she left them alone.

Minerva went to the window seat and picked up a monkey fashioned from scraps of chintz material.

"How did you find me?" Gray said, uncomfortable in his surroundings.

"The Pumfreys have a daughter. Did you know that?"

"Of course I know that. Morag. She's married."

"Mmm. They keep this room for when she and her husband visit with their little boy."

"Ah-hah." He nodded. Sometimes a man must just allow a woman to make her own way to the subject nearest to her heart—by whatever route she chooses.

"I envy Morag," Minerva said.

Gray dropped the satchel to the floor. He took off his cloak, set it on a small cedar chest, then placed his hat and gloves on top.

"Morag is a dear. But she's very lucky. She's always known she could speak to her parents and they'd listen, and they wouldn't be waiting for the briefest of pauses so that they could change the subject."

He looked at his wet boots, remembered the pistol, and made certain his jacket covered the handle. "The Pumfreys are special people." He'd never really considered that Minerva might feel a sense of loss at having parents too involved in their own affairs to consider hers.

"Yes, well." She swung off her own cloak and shook melted snow from the green wool. Then she thrust her gloves in a pocket. Today she wore a dress of a dark green similar to the cloak's. The close-fitting, high-necked bodice buttoned the length of the front and finished in a dashing little peplum edged with gold braid. Narrow gold lace edged the neck, the bottoms of short oversleeves, and the ends of long, tight sleeves beneath.

Her body was a delight. He now knew that so well. . . . Such thoughts must be put aside, at least for now. But she filled the bodice of her gown to perfection, and her waist wasn't tiny, as was the fashion, but of a size to make her exceedingly well proportioned.

Dash it all, what was he shilly-shallying around about? Minerva Arbuckle was absolutely perfect, and he wanted to bear her away immediately.

"Kindly stop staring at me as if you'd like to take off my clothes."

Gray jumped. "I bed—I mean, I beg your pardon."

She untied the pretty matching bonnet she wore and

removed it, shaking it as she'd shaken the cloak, and smoothing moisture from the jaunty green feather that curved over the brim.

Folding her hands before her, she said, "You study me most intimately, Gray Falconer. I'm not at all sure it's appropriate for a man to look at a woman in such a manner."

He had to smile. She was such a miss. "I have," he said, closing the space between them slowly, "done considerably more than look at you."

She tossed her head but had the grace to smile a little, even if she did blush. "A gentleman would not mention such things."

"Then I am no gentleman, because I take pleasure in mentioning such things. Shall I chronicle for you exactly what I saw when we were together yesterday?"

"If you do, I shall leave at once and never speak to you again."

"Hmm. In that case, perhaps we should proceed with this meeting according to your rules."

"Very wise."

"May I at least ask one more time how you knew I was at the church? Oh, of course, Reverend Pumfrey must have told you."

"He did not. Olaf Clack did."

Gray frowned. "Olaf . . . Olaf Clack? The boarder at the McSporrans'?"

"The tenant at Maudlin Manor. The McSporrans do not own the manor. They care for it in the absence of the owner. I only tell you this because I believe in honesty and I think it better for all concerned if such fabrications are abandoned. They always create unnecessary problems."

"I am well aware of the true situation there. So you went to the manor?"

"I did. With Brumby, as I promised."

"I don't want you to see Brumby alone." That numskull

had actually come close to calling him out. "Never alone again, do you understand me? He has designs on you."

"Don't tell me what to do."

"You are my fiancée."

"At this moment, I am not a fiancée at all—to any man. I kept my word and went to Maudlin Manor with Brumby. I went even though I wanted to meet with you and make sure we understand each other clearly."

Not a comforting sound to that. "You could have sent word. I'd have come to you at once."

"We both know it would be impossible for us to speak in private at Willieknock."

He contained the urge to tell her that her parents were responsible for that state of affairs, and a great deal more.

"I met Olaf Clack."

"I trust that was enjoyable."

"It was extraordinary, but no matter as to that. It was from two others who came to visit him that I learned you had been seen in the village."

"Mr. Meaner and Mr. Finish?"

"I believe those were the names. Finding you once I got into Ballyfog was simple enough. What happened between you and Cadzow in the church? He appeared in a great ill humor when he left you."

Ill humor. "You misunderstand my uncle. We had a most meaningful exchange. We are closer than we have ever been. I'm sure he was as moved by our encounter as I was. That's what you witnessed." He could not discuss that matter further.

Looking unbearably pretty in her soft dress, and with her hair, as usual, managing to sneak from its looped braids, Minerva trailed away into the other room.

Gray followed and found that they were beneath a sloping section of roof where the ceiling met the deep casement of a wide dormer window. Plump cushions covered with rose-strewn material heaped the window seat. Draperies on a four-poster were of matching material. A fire blazed in this room also. Minerva's pleasure in the gentle surroundings was obvious.

"So," Gray said when Minerva showed no sign of continuing. "Those men told you they'd seen me."

"Not me. They told Mr. Clack."

Gray was puzzled. "Told him? Why? I mean, what prompted them?"

She moved so quickly, he didn't guess her intention until she seized his hand and dragged him to the window. There she pushed him to the seat and sat beside him. "There is a great deal afoot that troubles me. And, odd as it may seem, your lack of subtlety, your rudeness, your presumptuousness and inappropriate behavior toward me, are not all that troubles me."

"Good," Gray said, uncertain if he was expected to be amused or severely chastened. "I'd hate to think little sins such as those could cast you down so entirely."

"Do not meddle with my emotions further, Gray."

Severely chastened. "Forgive my flippancy."

Minerva caught at her skirts. Her brow puckered. "No, no, Gray, I am snappish. It is I who should ask for forgiveness from you. My only defense is that the past three years have been unspeakable."

"I blame you for nothing," he told her, heartened by the softening he felt in her.

"I cannot continue as I am. You have asked me to keep my own counsel about your having been shipwrecked and I shall do so, although I don't understand why."

Of course she didn't, yet he must not risk drawing her further into the intrigue yet, and certainly not in light of the shock that might be ahead for her when he'd discovered solid evidence of her parents' involvement. "Thank you, Min. Thank you for agreeing to do as I ask."

"If I love you, I must, and I do love you," she said. "But there is something exceedingly odd going on. Possibly something dangerous. Please tell me all that you know. Then I will tell you what I have learned at Maudlin Manor. Not, of course, that I was intended to learn anything at all. I overheard."

Caution must remain his beacon. Collecting his thoughts, he took her hands in his. Gray looked to the leaded windows with their collection of bowed and crooked panes. Outside the daylight failed, but deep reds, greens, blues, and ambers reflected warmly in the firelight.

Minerva's stern face troubled him. "You are lovely, Min. I admire you in every way. It undoes me to see you so unhappy."

"I am more than unhappy. I am afraid—for you. And I believe I will become afraid for myself very soon."

"Why—"

"Please allow me to finish." She looked, unblinking, into his eyes. "I need to know what happened while you were missing. I do not believe you were simply shipwrecked. Yes, that happened, but there is more, much more, or you would not be so loath to speak of it, so secretive."

Words failed him.

"Hah. I see I have spoken truth. Why are you hiding these things from me? Do you think that by telling me the whole truth you would place yourself in even greater danger than you may already be in?"

"I shall never be able to hide anything from you for long, Min." In this case, knowledge could prove dangerous—possibly to her, and that he would never allow. "Don't trouble your pretty head with—"

"*Enough.* Stop it, Gray. We have moved beyond convention here. You cannot continue to treat me as an empty-headed woman to be protected from the world. I never was an empty-headed woman, but no matter about that now. I will make myself very clear."

When she paused and swallowed, he found himself balanced on the edge of the most intense anxiety he'd experienced since his escape.

"Gray," she said, looking at him again, leaning toward him. "I heard mention of the importance of making sure you never found out the truth of what was done to you."

He held his breath, then let it out slowly, through his mouth. "They spoke of that?"

"They did. They said you were a danger to them. They said that it could never have been expected that you would return, and that you could ruin everything they'd worked for."

"Go on."

"They said that if the truth of it—that was the way they put it—if the truth of it became known to certain parties, they might have to buy their safety by paying back everything they'd worked for. They said that to save themselves, they must finish what had been begun."

Gray regarded her solemnly. "I never wished you to be any part of this, Minerva."

"And that makes me so *angry* with you." She made fists and brought them down on his knees. "You say I am your love, the light of your life, yet you do not confide in me."

"I want to keep you safe. To do so, I must protect you from such ugliness."

"And will I feel safe, and protected, if I do not have you?" Her lips remained parted, and her brow puckered. "Do you think that on the day your uncle informed me that I should regard you as lost, I forgot you and looked for another?"

"Minerva, my darling. You cannot blame me for trying to keep you safely removed from so harsh a reality. But we must finish this. How did they say things should be . . . finished?"

"They didn't, but I suspect what their perfectly detestable notion might be. They would feel better if you were dead." She covered her mouth. "Oh, Gray, why has all this happened? I don't understand."

He wasn't sure he still understood himself.

"I do know that I shall stand at your side through whatever is to come," Minerva continued. "It may be that our alliance should be secret. Perhaps that will allow me to be the most help. But we shall overcome this menace together. And you will never, ever, keep secrets from me again. Do you promise?"

"Well—"

"You promise, Gray?"

"I shall do my utmost. Do not press me further than that. No man knows exactly what life will bring."

She closed her eyes and said, "Very well. Good enough for now. You must begin by telling me the whole story. The story of the three years when I heard nothing from you."

He did not believe she ought to have such information. What she did not know could not put her in the way of making a careless comment.

"Gray, please."

"It is so important that I keep my own counsel in certain aspects of this. At least for the present."

"Your counsel is my counsel."

She would never settle for less than the whole story. Gray saw with utter clarity that any attempt on his part to hide some elements would be evident to his beloved girl's sharp intellect. "Very well," he said. "I shall tell you all of it. But it is long, Minerva, and very strange."

"Mrs. P. has said we shall not be disturbed for as long as we wish to remain here."

An odd decision to be made by the wife of a minister of the church, Gray thought. Evidently he was considered a man of iron will and irreproachable moral standards. Hmm, the most discerning of souls could make mistakes.

"Where shall I start?" He asked himself, not Minerva. "At the beginning, I suppose, but first, would you tell me a little more about the exchanges you overheard between this man Clack and his preposterous friends?"

She scrutinized him carefully. "You misunderstood. Those men told Clack they had seen you in the village. They mentioned you by name, which I thought strange."

"Yes. I did understand that."

"It was not Clack and his friends that I overheard discussing what should become of you, and what a danger you are to them. It was Angus and Drucilla McSporran."

Chapter Twelve

Women were called upon to suffer, Janet Arbuckle thought. To suffer, and to bear the responsibility for preserving those things of utmost importance: the image one presented to the world, the good opinions of others toward oneself and one's family, and keeping those of lesser station firmly in their place.

Arbuckle had never appreciated the flair with which Janet had executed her duties as his wife and as the mistress of Willieknock. Oh, and as the mother of his child, even if that child was only a daughter.

"What can this fella, Clack, want with us?" Arbuckle grumbled. He'd invaded her boudoir once more and claimed her chaise. She would swear he reclined there for no other reason than to annoy her.

"*Janet!*"

She jumped up from her chair and shouted, "What?"

"This fella Hatch is bringin' up. What does he want?"

"We can hope to discover the answer to that question after he tells us, don't you think?"

Arbuckle flipped a wrist. "Couldn't care less. We'll send him away the instant he comes in. Now, tell me again what you said to young Falconer. Stupid woman. When will you learn to consult me before you throw years of work to the dogs?"

"If," Janet said, careful to keep her voice low, "if you would only think before you speak, Mr. Arbuckle, you'd know how foolish you sound. You just suggested I *planned* to ruin us. If any ruin has been accomplished, I assure you we have only yourself to blame. Not, of course, that I should dream of blaming you for anything, my love. You are beyond reproach. An exemplary being of incredible artistic acumen, a prince among men, a blessing on our house, a gift to us from the gods—" She paused, expecting him to stop her, and when he didn't, said, "A royal pain in one's noble nether regions."

His closed eyes remained closed. And he continued to smile as if vastly pleased with something she couldn't see.

He was a *curse.* "Arbuckle, what are you grinning about?"

"I am not grinning. I am contemplating the composition of my next work. Most intriguing. Most taxing. But without challenge there can be no ultimate satisfaction for a man who commands such a uniquely powerful technique."

So the ruination of the Arbuckles was forgotten. For this small mercy she was grateful.

"If Falconer twigs what you were gabbling about earlier, he'll come roaring in here threatening all sorts of nastiness. He's no fool. He could begin to ask questions we don't ever want asked."

"He'll never twig—realize what I meant."

"Aha!" Arbuckle stood up and pointed rudely at Janet. "Aha, a confession. You confess you spoke unwisely, that you gave intelligence to the enemy." He laughed, paused, laughed his way up his incredible scale. "How can we be certain the enemy won't stumble toward the truth? Or whatever? Why shouldn't he begin to suspect we have benefited from his suffering?"

"He left this house, didn't he?" Janet said. "And he didn't

know what I meant, I tell you. He just had the good sense to know he wasn't welcome here."

"What if he asks questions, hmm, tell me that? What if he starts making inquiries about us, about possible improvements in our fortunes since his unfortunate failure to return—when he was supposed to return, that is?"

Really, he exhausted one. "Arbuckle, will you please stop inventing these dreadful possibilities. How could he possibly see any connection? Everybody knows about your trips to London and Edinburgh. They know about your marvelous success as a *painter.*"

Arbuckle's glare afforded Janet considerable pleasure. How suitable that he should suffer discomfort for a change.

Hatch opened the door without knocking and puffed in, her hair awry. "I canna fathom why ye will insist on entertainin' up here."

"We like it up here, Hatch. This is a beautiful room. And where we choose to entertain is no affair of yours. It is, by the way, *my* room." She eyed Arbuckle, who studied a pointed toe. "You said we had company, Hatch," Janet said.

"Ye do. *When* he manages to climb the stairs. That means ye may not have comp'ny."

Sighs and moans wafted from some lower region, gradually growing closer. An occasional grunt punctuated a litany of the sounds of suffering.

Hatch put a hand on one hip and watched the visitor's approach. "Don't ye hurry yoursel'," she said. "Take your time. Well, well, ye decided t'come after all. Ye can be sure o' a fittin' welcome." She took two steps into the room and bobbed a curtsy. "Mr. Olaf Clack of Maudlin Manor. Come to pay his respects to those elevated *parsonages,* the Arbuckles. His words, not mine."

She backed around the visitor, colliding with him in the process. Her squeal, and flustered "Oh, ye devil. Takin' such liberties," suggested Mr. Clack might be considerably swifter with his white-gloved fingers than with his feet.

"Oh, dear," Janet said, and instantly clamped a hand over her mouth, not that the newcomer would know she'd done so. He couldn't see her. She looked at Arbuckle, who rubbed at his dark spectacles with a sleeve, and peered more closely at the man.

"Olaf Clack," the fellow said, speaking into his chest since his head was doubled over from the neck. "Belated to meet you, I'm sure, Mr. and Mrs. Arbuckle. In fact, I'd say my pleasure is 'uge in its proportions to any pleasure I've ever 'ad before."

For once Arbuckle had no ready remark.

"Thank you, Mr., er, Clack," Janet said. "Won't you come in and take a seat? Perhaps by the fire. It's certainly a most inclement day."

"As you says, missus, a nasty sort of day."

Really, who had sent the creature into their midst? Certainly no suitable connection of the Arbuckles.

Clack had undoubtedly been a cripple all his life. The grotesque, bent, and twisted angle of his spine rendered him curved almost in half, and he leaned heavily on a mahogany cane with an incongruous handle in the shape of a gentleman's boot. As the McSporrans had reported, he was possessed of a great quantity of very black, very curly, very long hair that draped over his back and fell forward to create a cavernous shadow where his face must be.

With a sudden burst of energy and, no doubt, the recollection of his duty as master of the house, Arbuckle surged toward the visitor. "Mr. Olaf Clack, didn't you say? *The* Mr. Olaf Clack, no doubt."

"Wouldn't know about *the.* Just Mr. Olaf Clack. In residue at Maudlin Manor for a hindefinite period."

Janet and Arbuckle looked at each other. *Indefinite* was the word of deepest concern. With the McSporrans, they'd agreed that their fortunes might depend upon making certain Clack didn't decide to stay long.

"Gotta stool, 'ave you? I don't dwell, of course, but I ham

by way of 'aving a slight infirmity. Not that you would notice if I didn't point it out. Old war wound suffered in Hinja."

Janet screwed up her face in question, and Arbuckle whispered, "India."

She mouthed, *Oh.*

"I hasked if you 'ave a stool. Hallows me to spread out, make a broader base, hif you see what I mean."

"A stool," Janet said, bobbing and turning about. "Arbuckle? A stool?"

"A stool," Arbuckle said, raising a single finger. "Yes. *There.* A stool." Balanced on the balls of his feet, he reached beneath Janet's gilt demilune table and produced a small, red velvet hassock he'd forgotten she owned. "Not exactly a stool, old man, but close enough, I'll warrant. Get yourself comfortable on that."

Arbuckle slid the hassock against the white silk stocking-clad calves of Clack's bent legs. Promptly the man plopped to sit with his knees splayed wide, showing off puce satin breeches. Layers of fine lace ruffles cascaded from the neck of his shirt. He grunted, and sighed, and wiggled his skinny nether quarters. His left hand he extended; his right clutched the cane. More ruffles dripped from cuffs that extended from the sleeves of a silver brocade coat of very old-fashioned cut.

"Drucilla said he always wore a cloak," Janet said, quite forgetting herself. She recovered quickly enough to add, "Drucilla mentioned your beautiful cloaks, Mr. Clack."

"Too 'ot in 'ere," he said, still wiggling to settle his crab-like balance firmly. Finally satisfied, he sniffed and slowly brought his left hand to his knee. "There. Very nice, I'm sure. I 'ope you'll forgive me for hintruding, but I've uncertained that the Arbuckles are the first family of Ballyfog. Naturally, I couldn't rest until I'd paid my suspects, like."

He might muddle his words somewhat, but at least he had the wit to recognize quality when he encountered it. Janet preened. Only a very little. Never let it be said that she was less than humble. "Very nice of you, I'm sure, Mr. Clack."

"Where are you from?" Arbuckle said, with his customary lack of finesse.

Mr. Clack raised his behind an inch or so, made sure the tails of his coat were quite free, and sat again. "I'm from Hinja. I thought I told you I was hinjured there."

"Yes, but—"

"Decided it was time to find a new camp after that. Took me a few years to decline on Scotland. 'Ad to see the world first. Been all over, I can tell you. Not much these eyes 'aven't seen." He pointed into the dark wedge between curtains of hair. "But now I don't know my mind. It's Scotland for me. Maudlin Manor. Ah, yes. That's for me, too. On disapproval it is, at the present, but I'm going to approve of it, I already know as much. " 'Ow about you. Where are you from?"

"Scotland," Janet and Arbuckle announced together.

He could not stay at Maudlin, he simply could not. Janet laced her fingers together and twisted them. She glared at Arbuckle, wordlessly ordering him to do something.

"In the bones, is it, Mr. Clack?" Arbuckle said. "I understand these war wounds tend to settle in the bones."

"Indeed. In the bones," Clack agreed. "There are times when it's a feast of courage to keep myself in the pink, but a man 'as to show 'is best face to the world, doesn't 'e?"

"He does indeed," Janet agreed, wondering if this was what Mr. Clack considered his "best face."

Clack lifted his cane, pounded it down hard in front of him, and plunked both hands on the carved boot. "Got to start off on the best foot. Show the locals my colors. Set the tune."

"Mmm," Janet said, gesturing for Arbuckle to do his share.

Starting, her husband said, "Drink? Like a drink, would you?"

" 'Andsome of you. They said you was a prince among men, and they was right!" He slapped a knee, wobbled, and threw out his arm to maintain balance. "I'll 'ave whiskey. Make it a good measure. I'm feeling the cold in my old war hinjury."

Arbuckle produced the key to his liquor cabinet and trotted obediently to produce the whiskey.

"Well, Mr. Clack," Janet said, filling her voice with warmth. "And is there a *Mrs.* Clack?"

"Oh, no!" Clack tittered. "Afraid not. I'm too shy. Makes it 'ard to, well, you know, to— No, no, there isn't a Mrs. Clack. Yet."

"*Yet?*" Janet leaned forward.

Arbuckle brought the whiskey and held the glass where one would expect Clack to see it. He did. He took it, leaned farther over, and made a loud, sucking noise. Janet saw the level of the whiskey lower.

Clack smacked his knee and emitted rasping breaths. "Hah, fair sits a man up. Good stuff, that, Arbuckle. You're an officer and a gentleman."

Arbuckle had never been any kind of an officer, and the question of his status as a gentleman wasn't clear as far as Janet was concerned.

"We certainly thank you for taking time from your busy day to pay your respects," Janet said when Clack became so engrossed in his whiskey as to apparently forget his hosts' presence. "We do hope you'll come again. We'll find an occasion when we can *invite* you."

A white-gloved finger shot out. "A woman of *vision*. Invite. Exactly. That's why I'm 'ere. I was in England before, you know, before I was in Hinja. I'm an Englishman in my bowels, missus. Once an Englishman, always an Englishman."

"Unfortunately," Arbuckle muttered.

"But I've decided it's Scotland for me. I've been away from civilization too long, far too long. Now I'm ready to henjoy the 'igher pleasures of gentle life, like."

A pause followed, while Clack *hmm*ed, and Arbuckle showed signs of losing consciousness.

"Very commendable, I'm sure," Janet announced loudly. "Don't you think that's very commendable, Mr. Arbuckle?"

"If you say so, my love."

"I've decided to entertain at the manor."

Janet felt sick. She was sure she must look deathly ill. Arbuckle had certainly lost color rapidly, too.

"I'm 'aving a saloon. All the trimmings, mind. Lots of grub and drink. A piano player. Game or two. You'll know what I mean by that, Mr. Arbuckle."

Grub. A piano player. A saloon! "Sounds . . . charming," Janet said faintly.

"I knew you'd like it! Women, too, of course. Lots of women, Arbuckle. But only the 'ighest quality. We'll bring 'em in from London."

"What's wrong with Edinburgh?" Janet snapped, then said, "I mean . . ." and couldn't think what she had meant.

"There, too," Clack agreed. "So, what wouldn't you say? Are you in?"

"In?" Janet paced nervously to the window and back. "What does . . . Arbuckle?"

"Naturally we're in, old chap," Arbuckle said, winking at Janet as he hadn't winked in years. "We'll be honored."

"Can't believe me luck, then. *The* Arbuckles. At Olaf Clack's first saloon. Reckon it'll make the papers, don't you? Society stuff. Prob'ly in Hinja."

"Shouldn't be surprised."

Janet breathed a little more easily. She could kiss Arbuckle. He had such a way of making dreadful things seem less dreadful.

Clack sucked more whiskey. "Well, then," he said, "that brings me to the reason I 'ad to come 'ere first. To see you. Being as 'ow you're the most elevated parsonages in Bally-fog—and who knows where not. I know on account of I've been told by all the most unimportant people I've met 'ere."

"Oh, well." Janet opened her fan and fluttered it rapidly.

"That being the case, I've got to make sure to hold my saloon when you aren't otherwise engaged."

"Oh, no," Janet said quickly. "Not at all. Of course, we shall be *devastated* if we can't attend, but we won't hear of you ordering your plans to suit us."

"And I won't 'ere of doing anything else. No. If you can't attend there'll be no saloon. Simple as that."

Janet jiggled, and shot silent appeals at Arbuckle.

"Not a problem," he said. "We're rarely not free. Pick the day, old man, I'm sure it'll be a good one."

"Friday of the coming week, then? It'll be by way of an early Michaelmas celebration, too."

"Friday of the coming week?" Janet pursed her lips and frowned. She hummed thoughtfully. "A mere six days away. Oh, dear, I do believe—"

"Exactly, Janet," Arbuckle said. "We'll all be free. The whole clan. Will that trouble you, Mr. Clack? We are five when we're all free, you see. I'm sure Janet's concerned that we'll be presuming too much."

"Not a bit of it. Honored I'll be. Good. So it'll be a week from Friday. The best of everything, mind. I've promised. And you'll bring that lovely daughter of yours?"

"We will," Arbuckle said, laughing.

Janet waved her arms, but Arbuckle ignored her. The fool.

Arbuckle said, "And our niece and nephew will be with us. My wife's sister's droppings. Orphans, you know. Very sad. But we've done well by them. They don't want for anything, do they, Janet?"

"I should think not." *Really,* men could be utterly useless. How could Arbuckle countenance accepting an invitation to this dreadful person's *saloon*.

"Now," Clack said. "Oh, I shouldn't ask. I've already predicted too much."

"Yes—"

"Not at all," Arbuckle said, smiling sweetly at Janet.

"We're delighted. Predict away, Mr. Clack. I haven't looked forward to anything so much since I don't know when. Wine, women, and song, eh? Ah, yes, can't remember when."

Trembling, clinging to his cane, Clack rose from the hassock to stand in what reminded Janet of croquet hoop fashion. He coughed, and cleared his throat loudly.

"Sick, are you?" Arbuckle asked, and Janet heard concern that could only be on account of his anxiety that there might be no "wine, women, and song." He should pay for that later.

"Not sick." Clack coughed some more. "Missus, I 'ave to ask you to do me the greatest humor by hadvising me on the matter of unsuitable parsonages. Unsuitable parsonages I should hinvite to my saloon."

She would faint. She knew she would. There could be absolutely no question of her being associated with someone so beyond the pale. Turning away, she closed her eyes. Such a disaster would make her the laughingstock of Ballyfog—and probably parts more distant.

"I haven't asked enough," Clack said behind her. "I've delighted you and you insist on more. You will send out the hinvitations? Yes, of course you'll want to send them. Only to the best, mind you. 'Elp me impress myself to all of them. The biggest saloon they've 'ad the pleasure of, mind. I can leave it to you?"

"Oh, I don't—"

"Absolutely, Clack," Arbuckle said, clapping the man on the back with near-cataclysmic results. Clack's knees buckled almost to the floor, and Arbuckle had to ease him gently back to his former position. "Sorry, old chap. You've got me so enthusiastic I was carried away there for a moment. Of course Mrs. Arbuckle will send out your invitations. Overwhelmed, we are, aren't we, Mrs. Arbuckle?"

"Oh."

"There, you see? So overwhelmed, she can't speak. And

since there isn't a Mrs. Clack, we insist on your allowing Mrs. Arbuckle to act as your hostess. No, no," he held up a hand Clack had no chance of seeing, "no, we insist."

Janet said, "Oh," very quietly, and sat on the chaise. "My salts, Arbuckle."

"Out of sorts?" Clack bellowed. "Your missus is out of sorts, did she say, Arbuckle?"

"No. Tough as an old shoe, my wife. She was talking about the sorts of guests she'll invite."

"Ah." Clack delved into the deep pockets in his brocade coat. "Nothing but the best guests, mind. Hah. You didn't know I was a poet, did you? Best guests. Hah! Best guests. Costumes, too, hmm?"

"Why don't I show you out," Arbuckle said. "It'll take you a fair amount of time to get back to the manor in this weather."

Clack worked a handful of something red from his left coat pocket. "Got to do this first. This is for you, missus. A small token of my gratitude." He shook out his gift.

Janet fell against the pillows on her chaise. She rested the back of a hand on her brow and panted. She would faint. She *wanted* to faint.

"The best, this is. Come by with intentions, I can tell you. Taken from The Lady of France. No, no, I mean, a lady from France. *Ballocks,* this tongue of mine gets all cocked up."

"Arbuckle?" Janet whispered, but her disgracefully neglectful husband was too engaged to hear her. Too engaged in appreciation of the gift the Clack person waved before her like a flag.

"I got 'em from a French piece—*damnation.* They're French. There. Take 'em. Wear 'em in good 'ealth. Too drafty if you're out of sorts."

The pair of divided, red silk bloomers he held drifted into Janet's lap.

Chapter Thirteen

"I wasn't shipwrecked."

"*Not* shipwrecked?" Min plunked her hands on her hips. "You lied about such a thing?"

"Yes. No—not completely. Yes, I more or less lied. But the story is short and unpleasant. I had thought to save you from the details, but I should have known you would never allow such a thing."

"If not shipwrecked, then where were you?" She would not complain about his falsehood. Clearly he suffered with every word he spoke.

"I embarked upon the appointed ship. On the first night out, while I stood on deck, ruffians—pirates—boarded silently and captured me. They took me by rowboat to their own ship, and from there to an island where I was imprisoned behind a fence—not that there was any immediate means of escape across the sea."

Minerva reached for him, but he shook his head and she dropped her arms.

"For three years I slowly made the roof of my hut into a seaworthy raft. Eventually the raft was ready, and there was a suitable time for my getaway. And God smiled on me. I was picked up by a ship bound for England and brought home."

She couldn't form the words that needed to be said. All feeling left her hands and feet.

"You will have more questions, and since I already know them, I shall answer. I believe someone wanted to be rid of me. Those pirates were paid to take me from the ship and kill me."

"No!" She could not stop herself from shaking.

Gray bowed his head. "I would rather not tell you this, but you will never rest unless I do. Rather than kill me, they continued to extort money from my enemies. They threatened to reveal the whole plot unless their demands for payment were met. There, now you have it. Except that I think it possible—probable—that my life is still at grave risk."

"Oh, Gray, and I have been so difficult. My poor, dear—"

"Please." He shook his head, and pain crossed his features. Gray didn't want her pity.

Very tall, very straight-backed before the windows, he stared into the darkness, his profile showing nothing but austere withdrawal.

Men were handicapped.

Minerva had pulled off her damp half-boots and she curled her stocking-clad toes against worn green carpet.

Men were handicapped by the ridiculous limits they placed upon their emotions. Stiff upper lip, never let the side down, do the done thing, stronger of the species. *Piffle.* No wonder there were so many widows. No doubt the male populace would laugh uproariously at such a suggestion, but she wouldn't be surprised if a woman's ability to have a rousing good cry when the need arose was jolly healthy. Imagine stuffing down all that *male* pride on top of pain and hurt and never feeling free to let it out.

"*Ridiculous.*"

"Hmm? What did you say, Min?"

He was inside himself with his anger and couldn't even allow himself to reach out and accept the help she so wanted to give him. "I said I am so angry at what has happened to you that I think I may fly into a rage and do something quite extraordinary."

"And what would that accomplish?"

They simply didn't understand, poor things. "It would make me feel better, Gray."

"It wouldn't change anything."

How very sane. "Aha, but once my anger was spent, I should become focused, and when I become focused I am a force to be reckoned with."

"You are always a force to be reckoned with."

She disliked the distant quality in his voice. He had told her the most horrifying story, and she knew, with her very considerable talent for assessing such things, that this man she adored spoke the truth. "We are going to stand shoulder to shoulder and discover who was behind this outrage against you."

"No such thing," he said, looking at her sharply. "Promise me this instant that you will do absolutely nothing in the matter. This is a man's affair and will be dealt with by men."

"Men?"

He glanced to the windows again, where only the occasional snowflake glittered against the panes. "Yes, men. My uncle knows what occurred and is determined to help me get to the bottom of the crime. And Max Rossmara is only a few miles distant. We have an arrangement by which a messenger would go for him if necessary."

"I was not remarking on the fact that you are but one man, Gray. I was reacting to your assumption that only men are equipped to deal with intrigue and evil. It is not so, and I will not allow you to close me out of this. The crime against you was also a crime against me. You were taken from me, and I will fight back."

He studied her, his expression so solemn as to make her

long to go to him, to hold him and make him vent his frustration.

"They took three years of your life!"

"Minerva, you would never have allowed me to rest unless I confided in you, so I told you all of it. What happens now is up to me, and I shall, I assure you, exact my vengeance."

"But you find no peace in knowing this."

The downward turn of his mouth erased any gentleness from his features. "There will be time enough for peace—to hope for peace—when those responsible have been brought to justice."

"And you think you can expect me to put all this from my mind?"

"I think I can rely on you to give me my part. I am the man. I am also the one who was wronged. It is my place."

She must tread with care. But she must also be ever vigilant, because she would help him, regardless of his warning, she would be there for him, and share the burden. "What of the investigations in the Indies?"

"In the Indies, Min?"

"Perhaps I misunderstand matters. Did your trunks, the possessions you must have put aboard the ship for your return—did they arrive?"

"No. Cadzow tells me the ship's captain, to whom he spoke, said I had not been noted aboard at all."

"But you did board? And with luggage?"

"Of course."

"So the captain and his crew were villains and part of the plot. Unless your possessions have been found."

"They have not." Drawing a deep breath, he took off his jacket and set it aside. "Will you be missed at home? You've been absent a long time."

"They think I'm working."

"I'm grateful for that. I need you with me."

Her throat grew so tight, it hurt. "And I need to be with

you," she told him quietly, but she judged he was not ready for her to try to touch him.

"It is possible the captain was involved to some degree—but not necessarily. Although the ship seems to have disappeared, and we assume its registry and name may have been changed. My view of that is that the captain was afraid of being blamed for my disappearance. Cadzow agrees."

"If it were not for . . ." This was so difficult. "Had I not overheard the McSporrans speaking of their need to be rid of you, I might have said we should look to your life in the Indies for our answer."

Gray extended a hand to her and smiled a little. "How shall I ever keep up with you? Come, let me take your hand in mine. I draw strength from you."

He lifted her heart with that smile, and with his simple declaration. She held his hand and they stood, side by side, looking out into the gathering darkness.

"There were too many hints—that I heard on that wretched island—that pointed back to Scotland, to their 'little pots of Scottish gold.' No, the answer lies here, and with every hour I expect some move to be made against me."

So did Minerva. Fear dried her mouth, and he struggled to remain calm. "Where would the McSporrans get the money to do such a thing, Gray?"

"*Damn* it!" He squeezed her hand, pressed the bones together. "Of course. I wager that's it."

"Gray?" She looked up at him. "You have thought of an answer. Tell me."

"Not"—he glanced at her and shook his head—"not an answer exactly. An idea. But nothing new, really. Let me think about it."

Pushing Gray at once would not gain her what she wanted. "Mr. McSporran came from a genteel family of reduced means and cannot be more than modestly comfortable himself. He and my father have known each other since they were boys in school. Mr. McSporran was a charity pupil, I believe, although that is never mentioned. Mama doesn't care for Drucilla, but Brumby is a good man."

"Brumby—"

"Ah, ah," she touched his lips, "Brumby *is* a good man. I pray he will meet someone else to fall in love with. His affection for me is doubtless the result of there being too few eligible women to pursue in Ballyfog."

A small jerk, and Gray had her so close her nose bumped the pin in his cravat. "His affection—and I dislike even to mention it—but his affection is absolutely understandable. No man could be in your company and not want you."

"You are turned to a flatterer." She pushed against his chest.

Gray looped his arms around her waist and made certain she couldn't get away from him. "I have never been a flatterer. I am an honest man. And a lucky one."

"It's important to make certain they don't know we suspect them," Minerva said. "That means we should make sure I have plenty of opportunities to observe their activities."

"You will stay away from them."

She ignored him. "They have annoyed me with their repeated requests for my company at Maudlin Manor. Now I shall give them their wish."

"*No.*"

"You don't have the right to tell me what I may not do. Kindly remember that. As I was saying, I shall spend time at Maudlin Manor, where I may attempt to gather intelligence on their activities. There is danger for you here, and I intend to protect you from that danger."

"Damn it!" His grip tightened, but he released her instantly and stepped back, his face stark. "What must I do to impress upon you that this is no game? Abduct you? Lock you away?"

But for the grim set of his features, she might have laughed. "I think not," she said.

"Stay away from that house, and from those people."

She bowed her head and went to the window seat, where she caught up her skirts and knelt with her hands flattened against the panes.

"Minerva. I wish to resume our engagement. In private, if that would be easier at present, but I must know that there is an understanding between us."

"I have told you—"

"Not good enough."

"You underestimate my parents. We should go to them at once. The only reason I have not already told them what I overheard is that I wanted to tell you first."

He said, "My God," softly, but so intensely she looked over her shoulder at him. He turned away and stared into the fire.

"What are you keeping from me?" she asked him. "You say you have now been honest with me, but I feel how you still hold part of yourself secret."

"Leave me be, woman. You don't understand these things. Why must you press me? Why don't you accept that I know what's best?"

His tone shook her, and she caught her breath. Trembling, she rested her brow on the cool window and willed her heart to be steady. He had never spoken to her so harshly.

Beyond the Pumfreys' garden wall, gravestones cast shadows upon the snow. The church was a silhouette.

Below, in the Pumfreys' frozen garden, a dark shadow down there passed over the ground, a creature with outstretched, flapping wings, and . . . Minerva pressed closer to the glass. She hadn't been considering what she saw. No winged creature, but a human figure that reached the gate, paused to look back—and upward toward the window where she knelt—before fleeing through the gate and disappearing among the gravestones.

"Gray! Gray, look."

He joined her at once, said, "Look? Where?"

"It . . . Someone was down there. They ran through the garden, then out into the graveyard."

"I don't see anyone."

"He's gone. But he was there. I saw him clearly. At first I thought he was a bird. The shadow of a bird . . ." She faltered, kept her gaze on the world outside, and waited for Gray's response.

"The shadow of a bird?"

"But it wasn't." How addlepated she sounded. "I mean—meant—that I had the impression of a bird because of the light. But then I realized it was not. He stopped at the gate and looked up here before running away."

"Perhaps you only thought this person looked at this window."

"No! No, he did, I tell you."

"Very well. But I doubt it is of any significance. He—if it was a he—turned back and his attention was caught by a light in the window. Probably nothing more. Is that not possible?"

Minerva thought about it, then said, "Possible. Yes."

"People come and go here all the time," Gray observed. "They always have. It is understood that the Pumfreys are happy for people to cut through their garden on the way to St. Aldhelm's."

All true. "You're right." She would put it from her mind. "I'm just so troubled, Gray."

"You would be abnormal if you weren't. Take heart. This is not a large community. It is not a wide and distant ocean where the loss of a man may go almost unnoticed. I take comfort from that. There is some measure of control—or I feel that there is. We have good friends, friends who will aid us. We will win this battle in the end."

Would they? Before Gray returned she had mourned him, as she'd mourned him for three years, but she had not been aware of the presence of great evil—as she was now. If only she and Gray need never leave this room again. "I would die here with you," she murmured to herself.

"Don't say such things! Minerva, you are my life, do you understand me? You pour out your feelings. You want me to tell you all is well or that all is simple, and I cannot. Not yet. Please, let us not argue this further."

She sat on the window seat with a thud and crossed her arms tightly.

"Forgive me," Gray said, moving away from her again. "I was careless in what I said before. I want to push it all away, too. And I am confused, my love. More confused than you can possibly know."

"Why did you ask me to leave my parents without a word and go with you?"

"Because . . ." She heard him take a poker to the fire and strike at the coals with force. "Because I want you to myself. I don't know who is friend and who is foe here—you must see that now—and I am tempted to separate myself from Ballyfog entirely. But I cannot do that if you will not come with me."

The cold that had crept into her fled. "I will not allow you to do so without me."

He continued to poke the fire.

"We need help. We need to ensure your safety. If the McSporrans— No, I cannot believe they actually intend you bodily harm, but what they said means that you are of some threat to them. I cannot imagine why."

"Of course you can't."

"With your uncle and my parents to help us, we could mount some defense against—"

"No."

"A constable—"

"No, Minerva. You are bound by the convention of your experience. We are not dealing with what you understand here. There are no pirates in Ballyfog, no pirate ships or islands inhabited by pirates. I shall deal with this my way.

My uncle and I shall deal with it. We have already decided that we must proceed with extreme caution."

She saw it then, what she should have noticed at once. "You have a pistol." The knowledge made her weak. "Surely there is no need to carry such a dangerous thing."

"Oh, no need at all." He laughed, and took it into his hand. "Why should a man seek to protect his life and the lives of those he loves?"

"I do not really believe anyone intended to *kill* you, do you? After all, they didn't, although they had plenty of chances. They didn't have to keep you alive to pretend that they had, did they?"

The poker clattered to the blue-tiled hearth. "What did you say?"

"Those villains could have killed you and kept on asking for money with the excuse that you lived still and could be produced. How would anyone have known whether you were dead or alive? They must have had a reason for wanting you alive. Perhaps they even wanted you to escape and come back to Scotland."

They might have helped him get away, or at least turned a blind eye to what he was doing.

"Min?" His hand on her shoulder made her jump this time. "It could be, couldn't it?"

"I think so."

"What possible reason could the McSporrans have for going to such lengths to be rid of me? Other than wanting their son to step into my shoes with you?"

She could think of none, and shook her head.

"Yet they are in a stew about my return." He frowned deeply, and rubbed her shoulder. "Min . . . Dash it, but this is awkward. You've already alluded to the McSporrans having pretty shallow pockets?"

In a manner of speaking, she had, but she'd never really considered the subject. "They always seem fairly—well—I don't think they are too poor. They have lived a pretense for so long that everyone hereabouts thinks they own Maudlin Manor. That will change now that the Olaf Clack person and his friends are in residence. But, no, I don't suppose they're especially wealthy."

"Whereas your own family is . . . ?" A series of odd expressions crossed Gray's face before he puffed up his cheeks, and expelled the air again. "Your family is certainly considerably better fixed than the McSporrans. The death of his godfather brought your father an enviable inheritance, didn't it? And I understand his paintings are fetching huge sums."

"True, but who told you?"

"Actually, it's all over Ballyfog. I heard it at the Flying Drum and Pig when I stopped there the other day."

Minerva didn't especially approve of gossip, especially about the inheritance, but she wasn't displeased that her father was receiving attention after so long. "I don't think I see the connection, Gray."

"It's far-fetched," he said. "But if the McSporrans had planned their future around Brumby marrying you and your bringing a handsome dowry with you, well, then, they would hardly mourn my death, and my return wouldn't be at all a pleasant surprise, would it? Particularly in the latter case, if they'd paid to be rid of me in the first place."

"As you say, it's—"

"Far-fetched. Yes. I can think of only one way to discover the truth."

Minerva was afraid she knew what that might be. "To confront them?"

"Yes. But not now. Not until I have all the pieces of the puzzle, or I may overlook the most dangerous part. Every plan begins with a single thought, from a single mind. It is my task to find that single mind while I keep you safe, and myself alive."

"It isn't your task alone," she told him anxiously.

"Trust me not to be foolish." He turned the full force of

his gray eyes upon her. "I have been wrong. I have judged you as a woman."

He had judged her as a woman? "I *am* a woman."

"I have been unfair. It's little wonder your parents depend upon you so for advice in their affairs. Yet because of your sex I have not given you credit for being quite extraordinary."

The pickle he was creating for himself should not bring her so much pleasure. "You mean you have wronged me by not judging me against men?"

"Yes. At least, I rather think that's the case."

She must remember that he was only a man. "I believe it must be a matter of your thinking I am weaker than men."

"That is true, because it is true."

"Is it?" She placed a finger on her chin and raised her eyebrows. "Because a man is *physically* stronger than a woman?"

"Minerva! There is no doubt that conventional wisdom considers women to have less, er, strength of *wit*. After all, women do not have to play the parts that men play in the world, do they? They are not involved in matters of state. They do not fight for their countries. They do not perform tasks that put them in grave danger. They—"

"Because men, through exerting their superior *brute* strength, have managed to push women into subservient positions. But the brain, the *mind,* is not, as far as I know, a muscle. Of course, if you believe that muscles are what rule the intelligent world, then you are correct, men are the greater force. But if you believe that intellect is the ultimate power, then"—she spread her hands—"then you should not presume to make any final judgment on the issue."

"Damn it all." He blustered. There was no other term for it. Cool, self-assured Gray Falconer had been bested in an argument, and now he blustered. "I'm dashed, all I've been trying to do is compliment you."

"By apologizing for not judging me against men, rather than women? Oh, well, then I do thank you most humbly."

"I give up."

Of course he did, poor lamb.

"No, I don't. Stop hiding behind your clever tongue, miss, and deal with me as a man—a woman, I mean."

She swallowed a laugh, but Gray laughed aloud and said, "You have an infuriating habit of twisting me up and making the fool. I don't think I care for that at all. But you're right to chastise me. I put things badly. By any standards you have the quickest mind I know, and I count myself fortunate that you tolerate a thick oaf like me at all."

"Oh, Gray." She got to her feet and poked his stomach. "Now I am supposed to do the *done* thing and insist you are mistaken, and that you are the sharpest wit, the most acute mind."

Gritting his teeth at the assault of her sharp fingertip on his middle, he backed away, and she wondered if he had any idea that he held the pistol aloft as if in submission. He said, sounding wounded, "That might be pleasant."

"In fact," she said, "I do consider you the most forward-thinking man of my acquaintance."

"You do?" His obvious delight amused her. Clearly, he had not perceived the irony in her comment. "Why, that's awfully good of you, Min."

"I most certainly do. Of course, the fact that my acquaintances are rather small in number might detract from that statement, but have hope, I'm persuaded you'd hold up tolerably well in any group."

"That's it." Capturing her hand, he held it against his chest and changed the direction of their passage. He backed her across the room.

A rap sounded at the outer door, the door to the nursery, and Mrs. P.'s voice called, "Minerva? Gray? I'd not be doin' me duty if I didna at least give a shout. Ye've been chatterin' up here for hours."

Minerva wrinkled her nose and said, "We're in here, Mrs. P. And we're still arguing. I mean *discussing* matters." She made wide eyes at Gray, pointed to the pistol, and skipped into the other room, just in time to see Mrs. P. slide a tray onto the table before the fire. The table creaked beneath the weight of bread and cheese, apples, a wedge of fruit pie, tea, a bottle of homemade wine, and a glass.

"Ye look a sight happier," Mrs. Pumfrey said, looking past Minerva at Gray, who had joined them—with no pistol evident. "Pumfrey and I always say there's little as canna be made t'sound silly if ye say it for long enough."

Gray's laugh lightened Minerva's heart, and she laughed with him. "You didn't have to feed us. You've already been too kind."

Mrs. P. waved Minerva's demur aside. "Get away wi' ye. It's past suppertime. Ye're young growin' things. The wine's Pumfrey's own and prob'ly not what ye're accustomed to, Gray, but it'll warm ye. Eat up, and blither some more until ye can laugh the way home. It's past time for ye two younguns t'be together. We'd thought t'be seein' your weddin' long afore now."

"So had I," Gray announced, so heartily that Mrs. P. laughed afresh, and kept laughing until she'd descended the stairs and gone from their hearing.

"A trusting woman, that," Gray remarked, his smile gone.

"They're both very dear." Soon she and Gray must leave. Minerva didn't relish being separated from him.

"They're wise people," Gray commented.

Minerva turned to study his face. "Of course they are."

He picked up the wine bottle and the glass, shut the door, and took her by the arm. "I meant they're wise because they've decided, correctly, that I won't take advantage of you in their house."

"Gray!"

His response was to lean and kiss her soundly until she grew weak enough to cling to him. "There," he said, keeping an arm around her but raising his head. "That is to demonstrate the superior strength of the male."

"Superior strength? Pah! I could have stopped you if I'd wanted to."

He kissed her again.

Minerva clung again.

"No contest," he said when their lips parted once more.

"There was a point I intended to make earlier in our discussion, Gray. You were suggesting, wrongly, that in order to prove herself equal to a man, a woman must become like a man."

If he was thinking at all, it was about her mouth—or other things. She would persevere. "Not so, sir. Women can stand on their own merits." This was not an appropriate time to point out the valuable part her inventions would play in helping to prove her theory.

"Their own merits," Gray said.

Hopeless. "I had better get home," she told him, turning her face to avoid another kiss. "Sooner or later someone will look for me. Then Iona and Fergus will think they have to make up stories to protect me. That's not fair."

"Not fair at all."

Feeling wicked, and loving it, she framed his face with her hands and made the next kiss her own. Tentative at first, she quickly got into the mood of the moment. One of his tongue kisses wasn't so difficult, and she enjoyed it very much. So, evidently, did Gray, for he almost dropped the bottle and glass in his attempts to take a firmer hold on her.

From his face, she trailed her fingers down his neck, over his shoulders, and back to his chest, his very hard and broad chest. He had become such a large man, which was just as well, because she might not be very tall but she certainly was not a small woman.

"Gray?" Gasping, she leaned far enough away to see his eyes. "I am not what most men like, am I?"

"What?" His remarkable eyes weren't as clear as usual.

"Me. I'm not a slender, sylphlike creature such as is the fashion. In fact, I am quite . . . substantial. There, now I've said it. I, Minerva Arbuckle, am *substantial*. You, on the other hand—"

"I am not substantial?"

"Oh, you know perfectly well that it is extremely desirable for a man to be tall, with broad shoulders and a deep chest, and well-muscled arms, and fine, strong legs. And if, as is the case with you, he also happens to be so . . . well, so exactly the way I want you to look, because I love your eyes and the way they see everything, and your sharp bones, and your mouth. Your mouth is very talented, you know. It moves mine as I didn't think it could move. When I'm alone, I can feel how your mouth feels on mine. I can see you absolutely clearly. Sometimes—" She would finish what she had begun. She would. "Sometimes I imagine you are beside me when I sleep. I can almost touch you. I'm sure that is inappropriate, but I believe in speaking the truth."

Evidently she had displeased him. He frowned, and stared at her as if there was a great deal he'd like to say but he was doing his utmost not to.

Minerva lowered her eyes. "I'm sorry."

"We'd better leave."

Her stomach felt horrid. "Yes, I suppose we should."

"We'll wrap some of the food in a handkerchief."

"So that we don't hurt Mrs. P.'s feelings?"

"Exactly."

"You are thoughtful."

"I'm desperate."

She made to step away from him, but he jerked her closer. "What is it?" Glancing up at him, she found it hard to keep her voice even. "I am too forward, aren't I? Too direct in my manner of expressing myself. I have shocked you with my unladylike behavior. What are you doing?"

With the bottle and glass in one hand, he spread the other over her back and pressed her against him. He moved just the slightest bit, so that he rubbed her breasts enough to make her gasp and grab handfuls of his shirtsleeves.

"You weren't listening," he told her, his expression ever more grim. "You told me how you see me, and how you feel about me."

Rising to her toes, she kissed his jaw, his cheek, and then his mouth. And he made that sound, that groaning, in his throat. "I cannot help how I am with you, Gray."

"And I cannot help how I am with you—or I shall not be able to help it for much longer." With a great surge, he put her from him and produced a handkerchief. The wine was quickly opened and a glass poured, and swallowed. He poured tea and pushed the cup into Minerva's hands. "Drink. Now."

Tipping the cooling brew to her lips, she tried to take a sip, but shook so badly she feared she would spill it.

Bread, cheese, and the pie were rapidly gathered into the handkerchief and pressed inside Gray's waistcoat. Next the apples disappeared into his pockets.

Astonished, Minerva gaped at him.

A dash to the other room and he returned, pulling on his jacket. He went to one knee and held first one of her boots, then the other, while she pushed in her feet.

For one tiny, incredible instant, he slipped his fingertips upward, over her calf. In another instant, he bent and pressed his mouth to her ankle.

Minerva closed her eyes and ran her fingers through his hair.

He gathered her to him, buried his face against her stomach. He did not behave as if he found her words or actions other than to his liking.

On his feet again, looking into her eyes again, he drew her cloak around her and turned away only long enough to don his own.

"You confuse me," she told him. "You say you must be with me. Then you look so angry. And then you say you are desperate and you show how much you want to be gone from me. And *then* . . . Gray, then you touch me so . . ." She could not finish.

Holding her hand, he led her toward the door. "Have you forgotten what I told you about the Pumfreys?"

"They are wise?"

"What else?"

"Trusting?"

He opened the door. "Yes, and more. I said they knew I would not take advantage of you in their house."

"Yes. You said that."

"And then we touched. Oh, Minerva, how we do touch. No woman could do with a great deal of worldly wiles what you do to me with a simple look, a guileless touch."

"And then we touched," she repeated. Every word he spoke had a form, a sound other than its meaning. "How we touch."

"And I told you I was desperate."

Minerva frowned. "Yes, you said that."

"Because I *am* desperate. Desperate to be elsewhere than in this house—where I can touch you."

Chapter Fourteen

"Mr. and Mrs. Arbuckle, I have been remiss." Eldora bustled into the most frightful pink boudoir she had ever had the misfortune to encounter. "Charming room, Mrs. Arbuckle. May I call you Janet? Such rich, rosy tones, such clever use of silver, and plush. Oh, and that chaise. Why, I do believe I shall ask Cadzow to find me one exactly like it.

"I should have visited *long* ago. And now that we are to be related, as it were, I must rush to correct my frightful carelessness by making sure we are intimately acquainted."

"Miss Eldora Makewell," the lard-faced housekeeper said from behind her. "Will there be anythin' else ye'll be needin' before I go t'me bed?"

The Arbuckles observed Eldora as if she were an exotic, a priceless and exotic work of art. She raised her chin and smiled at the woman, then, for a lingering while, she gave her attention to Arbuckle himself. Frightful little fop. "Porteous," she said, stretching his name, then sucking her bottom lip between her teeth and lowering her eyelashes as if she'd curtsied, which, of course, she most definitely had not. "May I call you Porteous? I am Eldora."

"So I told 'em," the servant said.

"Take yourself off," Eldora told her, then remembered herself and smiled as sweetly as she knew how—which was exceedingly sweet, and said, "Thank you for showing me up."

Janet Arbuckle inhaled abruptly and deeply.

With his eyes on Eldora's bosom, Arbuckle took a breath to match his wife's. "You heard the lady, Hatch. Take yourself off."

The door slammed so hard that Eldora's ears rang. Doing her utmost to behave as if she'd noticed nothing of the servant's appalling behavior, she smoothed the off-the-shoulder bodice of the feather-trimmed, white satin evening gown she'd chosen especially for the occasion. "Mr. Falconer and I have another engagement later this evening. Important company." She allowed the impression of how important the company must be to settle in the Arbuckles' imaginations. "Please forgive me for coming to you unsuitably attired, but I preferred to spend as much time with you as you would permit, rather than be forced to rush away and change."

"Not unsuitable as far as I can see," Arbuckle said. He strutted from his place before the fire and settled a hand on the back of a low wing chair. "A woman like yourself should always be shown off to advantage. She should be the center of her landscape, so to speak, not merely one of the details. Sit here, my dear Eldora."

Mrs. Arbuckle shifted irritably on her ugly chaise, and Eldora said, "How that chaise does suit you, Janet. Definitely a stage that shows *you* off to advantage." The woman's complexion and woolen afternoon dress blended very nicely with the violently pink brocade upon which she reclined. Eldora arranged herself in the chair she'd been offered. "Thank you, Porteous. I admit I'm a little fatigued today. So much on one's mind of late."

"Do make yourself comfortable, my dear," Arbuckle

said, leaning over her. Apparently his study of the female breast was ongoing.

Inclining her head and neck just so, and with the slightest twist of her shoulders, Eldora did her best to assist his perusal of her.

"What exactly did you want, Miss Makewell?" the Arbuckle woman demanded. "We wouldn't want to hurry you, but Arbuckle and I do have another engagement."

Eldora waited in hope that Arbuckle would contradict his wife's announcement. Evidently he was otherwise engrossed, so Eldora said, "Oh, Janet, I don't blame you for being *snippy* with me."

"I am never *snippy*."

"Forgive me. I meant I don't blame you for being somewhat uncertain as to how you should respond to my charitable and selfless offering of myself in friendship. But I have hesitated to intrude upon your unhappiness, the unhappiness you must have suffered during the time when you assumed the pigeon—I mean, while you thought Gray was lost to us all."

"Magnificent," Arbuckle murmured, and Eldora looked up at him. He looked down the front of her dress. Then he glanced at her face and said, "Such magnificent thoughtfulness and daring."

"Daring?" his wife said. "How so, Arbuckle?"

He pulled a blue beret from his head, revealing thin, sandy hair. "Throwing herself on our kindness, my dear. Daring thing to do for one with such obviously tender sensibilities."

"It's you who are kind," Eldora said, making sure her smile included Janet Arbuckle. "You and I understand the difficulties of being women, don't we, Janet? Women with gentle feelings in a harsh world. But I thought that with Gray's return, you might be disposed to welcome my friendship. We should certainly do our utmost to become much closer."

"Much closer," Arbuckle said. "Oh, yes, much closer."

Janet Arbuckle's face grew a more intense shade of pink, and she pressed her lips together.

"You must be so proud of your husband," Eldora said. "To be married to an *artist*. Especially an artist of such enormous repute."

Arbuckle made little humming noises.

"My husband is exceedingly successful," Janet said. "I like to think I have played at least a small part in that success by ensuring he need never worry about any detail in life other than his art."

"Commendable," Eldora said, gazing at the woman.

"Ever modeled, have you?" Arbuckle asked.

Eldora giggled, and flipped open the feather fan she carried. "Why, no, of course not, Porteous. Why, I wouldn't be at all a suitable model."

"My dear, I am an expert in these matters. Your beauty on canvas would be as breathtaking as a perfect sunrise on snowy peaks."

"She said she isn't a model, Arbuckle," Janet said.

"I did want to be an actress," Eldora said, running the tips of her fan feathers down her neck and bringing them to rest on her bosom. "A *classical* actress. But, naturally, I had to bow before my family's superior judgment. In short, I turned my back on my obvious talent in favor of being the lady I was born to be."

She heard Janet Arbuckle mutter, "Very *obvious* talent, indeed," but pretended not to. "Isn't it exciting that Minerva and I are both to be married? Who could have hoped that such a dreadful situation as Gray's disappearance would turn out so well for everyone?"

Neither Porteous nor Janet replied.

Eldora wafted her fan and made certain the diamond drop on her gold necklace was precisely placed—placed to its best advantage. She smiled to herself. The diamond was, in fact, a landscape detail designed to enhance the "center" of the picture.

She allowed an extensive pause before saying, "There was one personal matter I wanted to discuss with you before we continue with those things we share. I'm hoping you'll help me with my plan to give Cadzow a wedding gift that will delight him forever."

Janet said, "Porteous, ring for Hatch, would you? I need my salts."

"We would be delighted to assist you," Porteous said. With one satin-slippered foot, he hooked a red hassock close to Eldora's limbs and sat down. "Only ask, my dear."

"Well, it's rather funny really, given our discussion, but do you take actual commissions, Porteous? I mean, do you paint to order, as it were?"

"No, he does not," Janet said. "He doesn't have to. He can sell whatever he paints for vast sums, can't you, Arbuckle?"

"Mrs. Arbuckle and I are breathless with anticipation," Porteous said. "What is your plan?"

"In the light of what's already been said, I hardly dare voice it," Eldora said.

"But we insist, don't we, Mrs. Arbuckle?"

A reluctant "We insist" followed. Janet wasn't about to find herself in a position opposing that of her husband and another woman.

"Oh, if you insist, then I will tell you. I'd like to give my darling Cadzow a painting. A portrait. Of myself." She lowered her eyes demurely. "He has said so often that he would like to have me painted so that he can look at me whenever he pleases."

"Arbuckle only paints—nudes." Janet Arbuckle stared at her husband's back.

Arbuckle stared at Eldora.

"I know," she said. "I realize I may not be the measure of those professional models you choose, but would you be able to make an exception just this once? I'm prepared to pay a large commission, a huge commission, in fact."

"*Well,*" Janet said, sitting up on the chaise. "Well . . . How huge?"

"For you, my dear Eldora, the fee would be—"

"*Huge,*" Arbuckle's wife interrupted him. "Let's consider your starting offer."

The woman's reaction pleased Eldora far more than the husband's. "We will. I do have a price in mind. Porteous—Janet, I hesitate to ask this, but my conscience insists that I must. Would I be correct in thinking that you may not be as ecstatic at Gray Falconer's return as some might expect you to be?"

Janet Arbuckle's lips parted.

Porteous Arbuckle's concentration wavered from his scrutiny of a potentially lucrative subject. He said, "Eh?"

"Gray Falconer? Are you less than pleased at his return?"

"Well, I'm damned," Porteous said, popping to his feet. "Dashed queer question."

Eldora shrugged eloquently. "But only a question, surely. I'm a friend. *Your* friend, or I hope you will allow me to be. Nothing you say will go beyond these ears." She closed her fan and tapped each of her diamond earrings. "But, naturally, I will not push the subject. However, I would definitely understand if you were—well, dismayed, even, at the thought of your darling daughter marrying Gray."

"Arbuckle! What can she mean? Why would she say such a thing to us?"

"More importantly," Arbuckle said to his wife, "why does she feel safe in saying such a thing to us?"

Aha, so there was something here that could save the day, Eldora thought. The enormous risk she'd taken would land her the fortune she'd been promised, and without help from that pious hypocrite she'd have to marry regardless.

"Miss Makewell?" Porteous crammed the beret back on

his head, produced spectacles with small, dark lenses, and donned them also. "We want to know what you know. Or rather what you think you know."

The first would do very nicely. She quelled a smile of triumph. The failure of the Arbuckles to pay a triumphant visit to Drumblade, chortling about Gray's reappearance and an imminent joining of the families—with an aside about their future son-in-law's position being superior to his uncle's—had convinced her to take this step.

Eldora rose and stood looking down upon Arbuckle. "I think we understand each other quite well. Regardless of the reasons, we might all prefer that your daughter not marry Gray. Or should I say that you are not pleased with the prospect because it represents a threat to you."

Janet cringed on the couch. Arbuckle might think his spectacles made him appear mysterious and more authoritative. Eldora found them ridiculous. "I don't care about your little intrigues, do you understand?"

They both nodded slowly.

"Good. I propose that we get rid of our joint annoyance. What do you say?"

Arbuckle turned to his wife, who said, "Oh, dear," then, "Why would we do such a thing?"

"I," said Eldora, "intended to marry a man with an extensive fortune. An extensive fortune tied to international business dealings in which he held the majority share. I did not intend to marry a man with—albeit a sizable portion—with the secondary share. No, that will not do, even if that man is pious and above reproach in the eyes of the world. A *humble* man. One cannot wear humility!"

When no response was forthcoming from her gaping audience, she continued, "And I have a responsibility. I must protect the man I love from himself."

Janet Arbuckle swallowed, and Eldora heard how dry the woman's throat must be. "Quite . . . that is to say, very commendable, Eldora. True love, selfless love, is a beautiful thing."

The proximity of victory warmed Eldora's blood. "I'm so glad we agree. And, since we do, we shall enter into a most lucrative arrangement—for both of us."

"One moment." Arbuckle jiggled on his toes and grinned slyly. "I think we should be the ones making any arrangements here. After all, as you point out, our daughter would be marrying the possessor of the largest share. Why shouldn't we wish our daughter to marry him?"

"*Arbuckle,*" Janet hissed.

"Your wife has answered your question. You already know that you will gain little from the marriage. You know Gray doesn't like you—either of you."

The Arbuckles gasped.

"I heard him tell his uncle as much." A lie, but it would work. "Cadzow, as he would, of course—being pious, and above reproach in the eyes of the world, and humble—tried to dissuade him from the course he has chosen, but . . ." She let her words hang there.

The Arbuckles leaned toward her.

"Gray would not be moved. He hates you." She granted the statement its just moment for their reflection. "I hadn't come with the intention of revealing all this, but now I'm so glad I have. It was my duty."

Janet rose from the chaise and tottered a few steps toward Eldora. "Go on," she whispered. "What did he propose to Cadzow?"

"Propose? Nothing. He told him. Informed him. And remember that on their marriage, it would be Minerva who gained access to the Falconer fortune, not you."

"Yes, but—"

"*But,* Janet? No, no, once she becomes his wife there is no redeeming element here. If she became his wife, he will bestow all that wealth upon her. She will be mistress of the estates—here, and in the north, and in the Indies, of countless servants, fabulous collections of furniture, china, silver, carriages, livestock, *jewels,* money without end, and—"

"Tell us what he said!" Janet made fists and drummed her feet. "Now. At once. Do you hear me?"

"Oh, certainly. He said that the moment they marry, he will remove Minerva from you forever. She will never see you again and you will not gain a whit in recognition through the connection, nor see a penny of Falconer money by any means you may have thought you might."

"Oh!" Janet dropped her hands to her sides. "Arbuckle? Did you hear that? The ungrateful hound. After all we've done for him."

"Ungrateful," Porteous said.

"Actually," Eldora said conversationally, "I suppose one could say you'd gain very little in comparison to Minerva anyway. So it would seem to make sense for you to enter into an agreement with me that would assure us of what we want."

Porteous surprised her by taking off his spectacles and regarding her steadily. "I think that's enough shilly-shallying around, madam."

"Miss," she said out of habit.

"There are those who know you otherwise, I'll wager," Arbuckle said. "What do you intend?"

"I've told you. That we remove the impediment to our happiness."

"We agree," he said promptly. "Don't we, my love?"

"Yes," Janet said, her voice high and thin. "What do we have to do?"

Eldora smiled, flicked her fan beneath Arbuckle's chin, and started toward the door. "I must get back to Drumblade. Cadzow will wonder where I am, and, as I've said, we're expecting important company. We'll talk more about my sittings for Cadzow's wedding gift later."

"But the other, the—"

"We have to have some reason for me to pay you that

huge sum. That huge sop to compensate you for watching your ungrateful daughter run off with the fortune you deserve to share. *You* will need to explain such a sum, don't you think? It will be the fee for my portrait." Not that she had any intention of paying them a farthing.

"Yes, but how will we do it?" Janet asked. "You know, the deed."

They wanted Gray dead so badly, Eldora longed to laugh. She would get what she wanted, and all because she had the courage to take a fantastic chance.

"It will be simple," she said. "Minerva will do it for us."

Chapter Fifteen

G ray had worried about how he would return Minerva to Willieknock. Although it lay but a mile from the village, he would not countenance taking her there on foot. But the Pumfreys had insisted he use their Stanhope gig, of which they were inordinately proud. "Och, we'll not need it till the mornin'," Reverend Pumfrey had assured him, and of their treasured bay cob, he said, "We dinna drive poor Tilly oft enough."

"You must leave me at the gates," Minerva said. She huddled deep in her cloak, with the hood pulled so far forward it hid her face. "If we drive closer we'll be heard by those inside the house, and then there would be too many questions."

He would not argue, but neither would he allow her to walk down the heavily tree-lined driveway alone, and in darkness.

"You didn't believe I really saw someone until we found the footsteps, did you?"

"I believed you," Gray said, driving slowly through deep ruts in the lane leading to Willieknock. "I told you people have always passed through the Pumfreys' garden on their way to the church."

"But he wasn't going to the church."

They had already discussed the figure she'd seen in the Pumfreys' gardens, at length, and Minerva's repeated chatter on the subject was evidence of her nervousness. "We'll never know exactly where he came from, or where he went, except from an icy trail behind the house to the street in front of the church. He was there, Min, I grant you that, but do not imagine his presence had anything to do with us."

She turned her head and looked at him. Gray had raised the hood over the seat of the gig to close out as much chill as possible. The interior was dim, and a single lamp swinging from one of the shafts barely illuminated Minerva's features. He could, however, see uncertainty in her eyes.

"Min—"

"There are the gates," she said, facing forward again. "Let me down now."

"No, Minerva. Please let me decide what's best here. Dash it all! Hold on to me!" He barely managed to draw Tilly far enough onto a verge to avoid a carriage and pair that swung from the entrance to Willieknock and bowled toward them at far too rapid a pace. "Whoa, Tilly. Good girl. Whoa!" He dragged on the reins.

Urged on by the coachman, the other horses strained, gaining speed despite the ice and snow.

"Bloody fool!" Gray shouted, then recognized the landau that passed.

Snorting, and pawing the frozen ground, Tilly threw up her head, sending streams of white vapor into the air. The sounds of the departing landau at first filled the night, then gradually faded.

Minerva had done as Gray instructed: She'd taken a grip on him, on his cloak, and held tightly. She held him still and said, "Coming from Willieknock at this hour? There must be something wrong. No visitors come so late, or almost never."

"There may be something wrong," Gray told her, gently

disengaging her fingers, "but not of the variety you fear. Come, let us find out what's happened here, and why—or as much of it as we can. I'll take the gig inside the gates and among the trees where it won't be seen. Then I will ask you to do a service for me."

"You knew who that was? In the coach?"

He drove between stone gateposts and set off into a stand of pines, grateful that the Pumfreys' gig was small enough to present little difficulty in the hiding.

"Gray?"

"I want to get as close to the house as possible, so that you won't have far to come when you return." He found her hand and held it while he leaned forward to get a better view of what lay ahead. "That was a Falconer landau. Its occupant was Eldora Makewell, my uncle Cadzow's fiancée."

"Here?" Minerva bounced at his side. "That's the woman they talk . . . There has been some mention of her being in residence at Drumblade for some time."

"The very one," Gray said grimly. "What possible reason she could have for coming here I cannot imagine. I want you to go inside and find out. You will have to be careful to pose your questions well. You cannot say you saw her driving away. Perhaps—"

"Gray, I am not a ninny who needs her words to be chosen for her. Kindly leave all of this to me. We'll have our answers soon enough. There! Pull up over there and extinguish the lamp. You will have a perfect view of the house, but the gig should be invisible from below."

With a small rise before the gig, he jumped out, hitched the reins to a low branch on a venerable beech tree, and went around to hand Minerva down. But he did not immediately release her or stand back. Rather, he made little space for her between himself and the wheel of the gig.

She tried to bow her head, but her forehead bumped his chest instead, and she rested it there, rested her hands there, also.

"I shall watch you," he told her. "Every step of the way. And I shall wait for your return."

"Yes," she said.

"I'm not sure I can bear to be parted from you again."

"There is no choice."

"There is always a choice, Minerva." He eased back her hood and nestled his mouth in her hair. Such sweetness. "Go now. And come back quickly. Can you do that without bringing attention to yourself?"

She nodded, and said, "I will speak with Mama and Papa as if I am about to retire." Her sigh was not a happy one. "I detest deception, but there is no choice, is there?"

"No choice," he assured her. "But this will end, and we shall be free of it all."

"Gray," she tucked her hands inside his cloak, inside his jacket, and smoothed his chest, "we have had precious little time to talk of things closest to our hearts. I feel there will never be enough time to make up for the years we've lost."

"There will be time."

"Will there?" Her face, raised to his, was purely in shades of shadow now. "We intended to spend our lives together. We were to have courted and planned, and had the time a man and woman need to become more accustomed to each other."

He could not stop himself from laughing a little. "I hope I will not offend you if I tell you I think I know you rather well. You are honest and true, witty, and entirely too intelligent—for my good—and your capacity for loving thrills me. Be grateful that I must have some of my uncle's pious tendencies—somewhere. Surely they will keep me from sinking to a place where pleasures of the flesh, yours and mine, consume me. Don't you think?"

With her face turned up to his, she was silent.

Gray cleared his throat. "I have confused you. Forgive me, please."

"Confused me? How dare you. I am merely formulating

my response, and now I have it. I'm not at all sure I'm grateful if you have some of your uncle's pious tendencies—particularly if you intend to quote biblical passages whenever we are about to sink to that place where the pleasures of the flesh consume us. What a bore. What a shocking interruption."

He laughed, then smothered that laugh. "Incorrigible miss."

"You shall discover just how incorrigible."

She slid her hands as far around him as she could reach, but whispered, "I must go."

Gray rubbed her back lightly. "You must indeed."

"I will return as soon as I can." With her thumbs, she located his nipples through the fine stuff of his shirt, and he jumped. "Aha! So you do feel what I feel there."

The quickening in his groin was no surprise; it was instant and impossible to ignore. "I feel a great deal," he told her. "Evidently you have not forgotten what you feel."

"Never," she said, shaking her head so vehemently that her hood slipped to her shoulders. "I am afraid, Gray."

"I cannot tell you not to be afraid. But I can say that as long as I have life, you will be my first concern. I will protect you as best I can and I believe that means you will be safe. Go. I shall be waiting for you." By which time he would manage to compose himself—only to lose that composure again, no doubt.

"I must also be certain that Fergus and Iona are not concerned for me. Very often we spend evenings discussing my inventions."

"Ah, yes, your inventions."

She kissed him so quickly that but for the sensation that remained on his lips he might doubt she had done so at all. "And what was that for, miss?" he asked.

"To tell you that despite your amusement at my endeavors, I may still find it in my heart to care for you." She tossed her head and turned from him.

Gray made to pull her back into his arms, but restrained himself. "Hurry. If you don't return within what feels a reasonable time, don't think I shall leave like an unwanted dog. I'll enter by the front door and bear you away."

"In that case," she said, looking back over her shoulder, "I shall not even consider returning unaided."

Minerva ran as best she could, lifting high each foot before it sank into the snow again.

Within minutes he saw her enter Willieknock by a door in the side of the house nearest his hiding place. At first he thought she might stand in the light and wave, but then he shook his head at his own stupidity. She would not make such a mistake and risk drawing attention to him, as well as to herself.

Half an hour passed.

Lights in the lodge went on, or went out.

An owl hooted in the trees to Gray's left, and the sound brought a smile of pleasure to his lips. He was reminded of other nights in these woods, nights long ago, when he had come to meet Minerva. There were few spots in the region of Willieknock, or Drumblade, or indeed all of Ballyfog, that did not hold the imprints of their young love.

He wanted to make those imprints again.

The smile was lost to the flaring of his nostrils, the tightening of his lips. It could be that he would have to remove his Minerva from this place they both loved—if things went as expected with her parents.

Tilly nickered and he went to her, smoothed her and adjusted the blanket he'd thrown over her broad back. The animal shifted fretfully. "Good girl," he told her gently. "Fine girl." She brought her head around, and he saw the whites of her eyes. Even the horse seemed anxious to be gone from here.

Gray decided to climb into the gig. He'd have a good view of the approach to the house from there, and be somewhat warmer.

Faint cracking sounded in the trees. A small animal or two skittered here or there. Clouds gradually slipped away from the moon, leaving its blue-white light upon the eerie scene.

He strained to make out the time once more. More than an hour now.

What could take this long?

Tilly blew, and whinnied, and the rig moved. Gray gave a firm tug on the reins to calm the horse.

A meagerly lighted window opened in the area of the kitchens, very near the door where Min had entered. Gray knew it opened because he saw someone push wide the casement. The figure pushed it wide, climbed out, and took the time to close it again.

Exclaiming under his breath, Gray was on his feet in the gig and straining to see. If it was Minerva leaving in such a way, then something was definitely amiss.

At first the figure did run in his direction, but soon it veered slightly to his right. And he saw this was a taller person than Min, much taller, and swathed in dark garb from head to foot.

Careful to be silent, Gray climbed from the gig and positioned himself by Tilly's head where he could stroke her nose, whisper quietly to her and try to keep her silent.

Partway up the slope to the trees, the fugitive turned back and stared at the house, and Gray remembered what Minerva had said about her faceless intruder at the Pumfreys'. She said he had stopped and looked at the house, at the window where she was, she'd thought.

Gray snapped his attention to the house again, to the second floor, and the window he knew to be Minerva's. A light showed there now, and he saw silhouettes moving within.

The watcher was utterly still, gazing in the direction of that window. Then he threw up long arms, waving something in one hand, and ran on, his night-shaded clothes billowing behind him. He ran into the trees not more than a few hundred yards from where Gray stood.

He could capture the bounder.

Crouched, Gray made his way in the direction the other had taken. The owl hooted again, stopping Gray as he waited to see if his quarry would also pause at the otherworldly sound.

The next noises he heard were of branches weighted with snow and swaying together. An occasional twig snapped, and then, incongruously, a voice softly sang words to a single note like those that might be heard sometimes in a church. A priest's high mass monotone.

Gray's skin prickled. Hair rose on the back of his neck.

"Dance, dance, dance, dance," the voice sang forth. *"Shadows on the wall."*

Very clearly came the whinny of a horse, the clink of tack, and, through the trees, he saw a rider swing into the saddle of what appeared to be a fine, but flighty, Thoroughbred. Little wonder Tilly had been restless. Gray cursed himself for not noticing some sound the other animal might have made. Had he done so, he would not have sent Minerva on alone.

Gray shrank back. If he tried to follow the horse and rider, he would risk Min's returning only to find him gone. She would be at a loss to know what had made him leave, and what she should do next. And in a gig, and driving a bay cob gone plump from an easy life, he would have no chance of catching the Thoroughbred.

Obviously unaware that he was observed, and feeling secure in his hiding place, the man, and Gray was certain it was a man, reined in his mount and turned it in a tight circle, keeping his eyes on Minerva's window.

"Capering on the wall."

A shape did move within that room.

"My marionette. A twitch here, a tug there. Take from you what you most desire. A twitch here, a tug there. See how you weep."

Easing forward, Gray tried to get closer, to see some distinguishing feature.

"*A twitch here, a tug there. See how you die!*"

The rider whirled his horse once more and set off. A clearly accomplished horseman, he threaded a path rapidly through the trees and was gone. Soon Gray heard only a faint crackling, the pound of a hoof on a patch of ice. Then, at last, nothing.

Gray followed a way to look for anything the intruder might have dropped, any clue to his identity. The cold night chilled his flesh now, but the echo of the man's voice chilled it more. That creature seemed to intone his message to Minerva—or was Gray's own imagination as capricious as hers?

Her imagination?

Imagination had been no part of what either of them had seen.

Chapter Sixteen

All about Gray an emptiness settled, an emptiness filled with the indefinable seething quality of things unknown.

A bleakness descended upon him. Perhaps he should be grateful that there had been overt signs that all was not well in Ballyfog, that he need no longer suffer occasional doubts as to his own sanity. He could not be other than devastated that Minerva was being pulled into the center of whatever was afoot.

He reversed his path to the gig, in time to see another figure, this one a great deal smaller, toiling uphill toward him.

Breathless, her cloak thrown back from her shoulders, she arrived panting, and leaned upon him while she caught her breath. And she struggled when he tried to gather the cloak around her once more. "Too hot," she said. "Please, too hot."

He allowed her a few moments more, then ignored her batting hands and covered her anyway. "You will take a chill, and I will not have you ill because of me. I will not have you ill at all, do you understand me?"

Her failure to respond quickly enough earned her a kiss that rendered her akin to a cloth doll in his arms, except that her mouth had forgotten nothing of the lessons he had taught. She kissed him also, using her lips and tongue in a manner that caused him to remind himself that he was a strong and an honorable man who did not throw young virgins into the snow and ravage them.

More was the pity.

He hauled her against him and hid her face beneath his chin where she could not see his wry grimace.

"Now, into the gig with you. And you shall tell me all you've discovered." But he would say nothing of the intruder, not unless some event in the future made the revelation inevitable. Ignoring her protests, he swung her into his arms and walked to deposit her on the leather seat before climbing up beside her. A fur throw of somewhat questionable origins had been supplied by the Pumfreys, and Gray spread this over them both, tucking it to Minerva's chin. Her shivers did not please him.

He let her silence go on, embracing her closely all the while and breathing her in, her scents of the cool night, and whatever subtle floral water she used in her toilette. Could he dare to hope that there would come days, months, years when he could hold her with the assurance that no danger lurked, waiting to crush their happiness?

"Oh." She shuddered and huddled closer. "I'm quite sure it's absolutely shocking of me, but I think I could be very happy to stay just so for a very long time."

He smiled to himself. "My thought exactly. And we shall do such things before too long. When you are my wife."

"But not always in a bed?"

Would she always have the power to steal his composure? "Well, I suppose if you want—"

"I do. I mean, I will. I will want to be like this, exactly like this, in the snow at night, in a gig. Beneath a fur throw." She snuggled closer. "With *no* clothes on."

"*Minerva!*"

"Oh, *Minerva,* how dare you say such wicked things," she

said. "Only men should say such things. Women shouldn't even *think* them, any more than they should wear sleeves that allow them to move their arms more than a few inches from their sides."

He failed to make the connection, but no matter, she was a treasure with her unexpected announcements. "We really shouldn't discuss such things until we are married, my love. If you had more guidance from a female relative, you would know this."

"Now you chastise me." She sounded hurt.

Gray laughed. "If I truly chastised you, I should be a fool. In fact, you excite me with every word you speak, every move you make. I am only trying to be responsible, and it's very hard."

"You mean you would like us to be without clothes also?"

Grant him strength. "We won't discuss this further. Not right now, because we do have other matters to attend. What did you discover, dearest?"

She grumbled to herself, but said, "Something extraordinary. Fergus and Iona are in bed."

"And that's extraordinary?"

"No, no! I merely mentioned that as an aside because I told you I would check on them. They are in bed, but they were worried about me. I must find a way to put their minds at rest."

"Tell them nothing."

She twisted in his arms. "Don't tell me what to say and do, please, Gray. You are not my husband yet, and may never be. And if you are, please do not tell me what to say and do then, either."

"A man is the head of his wife, Minerva, my dear, the head of his household. It must be so."

She tipped her face up to his, and he could see her frown. "I would not, of course, presume to say that a man should not do his utmost to be a guide to his wife and family, but not in a superior manner. Not in a manner that suggests he thinks his wife less responsible than himself. And if she is—at least at first—why, then, he should want to help her grow in all ways so that she may be not just the partner of his heart, but of his whole life."

The lump that formed in his throat was wholly unexpected. He swallowed and looked down at her, a tenderness welling up with such force as to all but undo him. "I shall bear your advice in mind, Miss Arbuckle. But I do believe you are already extremely wise."

"Sometimes," she said, her voice strangely small and remote. "Sometimes I feel quite lost within myself and I wish I knew a great deal more."

He brushed her top lip with the pad of a thumb and chose not to answer. After all, a fellow must maintain some control in these things.

"That man Clack, Mr. Olaf Clack, has visited here. He came to see Mama and Papa."

"Who else should he come to see?" Gray said, more sharply than he knew he should. But Clack didn't interest him, Eldora Makewell did.

Minerva averted her head and said, "Well, if you *will*, be unpleasant."

"I will if it's necessary. Please carry on."

A coolness crept between them. She said, "He is dreadful, you know. Like a clown or something. All garish costume and hair, as if he were some character in a play. And he postures and is quite doubled over. He used a cane with a handle shaped like a boot."

"Yes," Gray said, more and more impatient.

"And he speaks strangely, as if he were completely without education but pretending otherwise. Papa said he *fawned* upon them. How sickening. Can you imagine?"

"Oh, indeed." And he could imagine how much the Arbuckles would enjoy the event. The sooner the story of Clack was finished, the sooner they could move on to Eldora—he hoped. "What did Clack want?"

"According to Mama and Papa, to become friends with us!" She laughed. Gray loved her abandoned laughter. "I am not at all uppity about who our friends should be, but why would a man who is apparently wealthy enough to lease a property like Maudlin Manor, and retain the services of the McSporrans, and plan great parties, need to scrape to Mama and Papa? He called them the most elevated *parsonages* in the neighborhood, and mixed up his words in a ridiculous fashion. It would take too long to tell it all."

"Then do not bother," Gray said, hoping he didn't sound too impatient. "I doubt he'll bother your parents again."

"Oh, but he *will*. He has enlisted their help with an important salon, er, *saloon* as he called it, an important *saloon* he intends to hold at the manor a week from Friday. Mama is to make up the guest list and send invitations to only the most suitable people. Actually, he said, the most *unsuitable parsonages*."

Gray laughed shortly. "Poor fellow. He's to be pitied. New money, no doubt. If we encounter him, we must attempt to be kind."

"Poor fellow? Poor Mama, you mean. Papa was so enamored of Clack's flamboyant behavior that he told him that since he has no wife, Mama would be his hostess."

"Then"—this time Gray was careful not to laugh—"then it is your father who has my sympathy, and your mother, of course. Now, Eldora—"

"*That* is even more extraordinary, Gray. You are simply not going to believe it."

"Ooh, let me try." He opened his cloak and managed to ease Minerva against him again. "This will keep you warmer," he told her.

"Eldora came to say how happy she is that our two families are to be united," she said.

"Really." Gray raised his eyebrows. What did the wretched woman think she was about? "Just that?"

"Nooo. She wanted to talk about a certain wedding gift she wishes to give to her fiancé."

"What in God's . . . Why would Eldora Makewell come here to talk about such a thing?"

Minerva giggled, actually giggled, and she was not a woman given to such girlishness.

He kissed the tip of her nose, and contrived to *accidentally* sweep a hand over her breast. Her gasp brought him considerable satisfaction, of which he allowed no sign to show. "Come, you can tell me, dearest."

"She wants Papa to paint her portrait for Mr. Falconer." The prim countenance she achieved seemed quite fragile. "Evidently she will be coming for sittings very soon."

Gray thought about Eldora sitting for Porteous Arbuckle. Then he thought about the paintings adorning the walls inside Willieknock Lodge. "Doesn't your father paint exclusively nudes?"

"Oh, yes." She had her composure under complete control now.

Gray didn't. He laughed explosively, tried to choke the laughter back, and failed miserably. Rolling against the back of the seat, he pulled the fur throw over his mouth to muffle the sound before someone heard and decided to investigate.

Minerva punched him, none too gently, in the side. "Gather yourself together at once," she told him. "Such an ungentlemanly outburst. What can have come over you?"

"Far more than will be coming over Eldora most of the time she's sitting for your father, I'll wager. Gad, Cadzow will burst a vein. He'll have apoplexy on the spot."

She began to chuckle. "I did wonder. After all, do pious gentlemen appreciate such things as nude portraits of their wives-to-be?"

"Dashed if I know. Maybe she hopes to hurry the nuptials along. After all, poor old Cadzow does seem to be dragging his heels. Probably deathly afraid of what she'll do to him on the wedding . . ." He managed to close his lips at the last safe moment.

"Why would her portrait hurry the nuptials?"

He waved a hand. "Don't know. I was just speculating. Loosen him up, I expect that's what I meant."

Even if he couldn't exactly see her frown, he could feel it. "Will he like the painting, do you think?" she asked. "Or will it make him angry with her?"

"Oh, I should think he'd be well pleased that she's making the sacrifice."

"Sacrifice?"

"Taking her clothes off for a stranger—all for him."

"But Papa's a painter. He paints naked women all the time. I know, I've seen him."

"You have." Gray didn't like the idea. "I'm amazed he'd allow such a thing. Very unsuitable for a young—"

"Oh, he didn't know I saw."

"Ah." Gray didn't think he'd press her for more details. "Well, well, a portrait of Eldora in the nude. What a thought."

He felt Minerva grow quite still and rolled his head toward her. "Something wrong, dearest?"

"Are you thinking about how Eldora looks without her clothes?"

"Well—"

"You are! How perfectly horrid of you." In a flurry, she started to push the throw aside.

"You will stop right there," Gray told her, exerting just enough strength to enforce the order. "I am not ready to move yet. That means you will not move either."

"I shall move if I want to. I shall go home at once."

"No. No, I don't think so. I think it's time I made sure you understand that you are mine, and mine alone. And why that is so."

"And if I don't feel like discussing the matter now?"

"We won't talk about it. I'll persuade you without any words at all."

"How will you—"

He pulled her over him, maneuvered her charming bottom onto his lap, and kissed her to silence. And while he kissed her he set about unbuttoning the annoyingly small buttons that closed her bodice all the way to her waist and several inches below.

Without attempting to remove her mouth from his, she did clamp her hand on top of his as if to stop his progress. She was no match for him.

He should wait to do this in a more leisurely manner—rather than out in a snow-blanketed forest on a freezing night, with the lights of the girl's own home shining below. He shouldn't do this at all until they were man and wife.

He pressed hard and determinedly against her female parts. He knew how little separated his salient parts from her salient parts, and the result was predictable.

"Gray," she gasped when their mouths parted at last. "I'm sure this is wrong."

"You're right." Her bodice was entirely unbuttoned, and he parted it, shielding her from the cold by pulling the throw over her shoulders. How impossible it was to stop himself from spreading his fingers over the full tops of her breasts. "Should we stop?"

She undid his cravat, then began to deal with his shirt buttons.

Gray loosened the ribbon at the low neck of her chemise. "Should we stop, Minerva?" He was unfair. He led the way. How could she decide what they should do?

Still quietly absorbed, she opened his shirt and pulled it from his trousers. With the tips of her fingers, she explored the hair on his chest, the way it swirled around his nipples, the skin over his ribs, and then more hair where it followed a line to his trousers. Her forefinger, probing his navel, brought his knees jackknifing beneath her, and she gave a small cry.

"It's all right," he told her. "I wasn't expecting you to do that." He hadn't expected her to do anything in particular, except to allow him to further her education.

"You feel so different from me."

"Thank God."

"What?"

"I said, I'm glad we're very different. That's what it's all about, how different we are. Your body and mine are like two halves, Min. Put them together and they make a whole." *Oh, very smooth, Falconer.* Praise be he wasn't overheard.

"Will I like that? Don't think I'm completely unaware of what you mean. I'm a mature woman, and I know a great deal. But I don't know how much the event will please me."

The event? She made it sound like a three-legged race, or a game of croquet, perhaps. "You may not like it immediately, but very soon you will want to do it all the time, I promise you."

"Hmm."

Let her think about that while he helped show her he told the truth. He'd completely loosened the ribbon through the neck of her chemise. Now he folded the garment down and lifted her breasts into his hands.

"Gray," she said, and he sensed some apprehension.

For a few moments he played the pads of his thumbs over her hardened nipples, and felt victory when she moaned, and pressed closer. Obligingly, he used his mouth to replace first one, then the other thumb. Minerva's urging body turned wilder. She twisted on his lap, pushed her fingers into his hair, and held him to her.

She was the loveliest thing, the most desirable thing.

Gray desired her. He *lusted* for her. If he weren't throbbing against her buttocks, his penis seeking its rightful place inside her, he might feel shame at his lust, but he could not feel shame.

She sought to touch all of him that she could reach. When she pushed the fingers of one hand inside his trousers and played with the coarse hair that was dangerously close to the base of his engorged manhood, he feared for his self-control. He feared he might lose himself entirely, and shock her beyond his own redemption.

Her nails scraped his most sensitive skin, and he sucked air through his teeth.

She withdrew her hand quickly. "What? What is it? Does that hurt?"

"It doesn't hurt," he told her, bending to suckle her again in hopes of diverting some of her attention from more southerly points. "How does this feel?"

"Delightful." Her voice was breathless, husky. "This is all part of what we shall do all the time when we're married. I know this."

"Oh, surely, my love, surely." And with that he found the hem of her woolen dress, slid a hand beneath, and slowly smoothed the inside of a limb. "How does this feel? My hand upon your leg like this?"

"You touched my leg before."

Drat her confoundedly logical mind. "Yes, sweet, but not exactly like this." He reached the place above her knee where a garter held up her stocking. There he made fleeting passes over the satin-soft skin, and he smiled when she jumped. "This is different. Am I right?"

"Oh, quite right."

She breathed in very deeply, and even in the gloom beneath the throw, Gray was afforded a vision of expanding white flesh enough to drive away any man's reason. Shadowed at the tips of that flesh were her nipples, stiff buds that brought whimpers of delight with even the lightest of his touches. She needed no stays, no artful devices to enhance the fullness of her woman's body. Her breasts were more than his hands could cover, but the effort to do so caused a violent pumping between his legs and he was too gladly frail of spirit to fear the consequences anymore.

"Touch me there," Minerva whispered. She held his hands to her breasts, pushing them together.

"There?" he asked, scarcely able to breathe. "Where?"

"The place that throbs. Do you know there is a place on a woman that throbs at times like—"

"I know you sometimes talk too much." And he kissed her quickly, sucked her bottom lip gently between his teeth and nibbled. Her head arched back, and he loved her abandon.

Knowing what throbbing drove her to need his touch, he smoothed higher up her thighs, smoothed inch by inch, slowly, allowing her to writhe in her attempt to make him satisfy her faster. She would learn these things, the way they were accomplished, the many ways, but not too quickly. And all she would learn now would be enough to make her yearn for him day and night. The easier to make her do his bidding.

As soon as the thought was made, he pushed it aside. He would not deal with the future tonight. Tonight was only for them, the beginning of their future together, and he would take great care of this treasure of his.

Her writhing became wilder. If he didn't keep the throw about them, and the cloaks, she would gladly be naked and care nothing for the elements.

At last he reached into her drawers, smiling afresh at the dampness of fine lawn, and held apart the folds that hid that which demanded something she didn't yet know.

Then he touched it.

She screamed, and threw herself against him, and drove his hand so hard into her moist flesh that he dare not move at once.

"Let me do this, love," he told her softly. "Relax. It is new, and wonderful. You will be amazed by it. Put your arms around my neck and let me please you."

Slowly, panting as she did so, Minerva did as he asked,

and almost before she had laced her fingers behind his neck, he brought her the amazement he'd promised.

She was too new, too unspoiled, to ask for more, or even to ask if there was more. For a very long time she clung to him, crying, and he let her cry because he understood that the tears were of joy and the thrill of discovery. She now knew more about her own body, her own body as it could be with his. Soon he would have to take her farther on that journey.

"Hush," he told her, and squeezed his eyes shut against the violent urge to set aside his finer feelings and take her now. Holding her so tight he ought to fear hurting her, he smoothed her hair, her face, her neck, her breasts, over and over again.

"I don't care if it's wrong," she said at last. "I know I want to do it again. If you do."

Gray was too uncomfortable to laugh. "I do want to, but we must get you home soon. We have to make plans, and make them quickly, because I will not be without you for long."

"Nor will I be without you," she told him, utterly earnest. "Can we speak with my parents and proceed?"

"We will do what must be done," he said. "You know there is some danger here."

"Gray—"

"No, sweet, just listen to me." He began straightening her clothes. "There is danger, and it may . . . it *will* become worse if I don't act to stop it."

"You frighten me."

"That's as well. If you're frightened, you will listen carefully and do as I ask. I am not frightened." Not for himself. "You spoke of going to Maudlin Manor and watching the McSporrans. I argued. I'm not arguing anymore. You will go, but I will go with you."

"Brumby won't like it."

"To hell with Brumby!" He must hold himself back. "I'm

sorry. I liked Brumby well enough once. I can like him again. You and I will go to the manor, and I will impress upon Brumby that I wish to renew our old friendship."

"He's angry with you."

"I'll be persuasive."

She sighed, and finished buttoning her dress and arranging her skirts. "As you say, then. I will do what you think is best."

"Thank you, Min. Nothing is final. If what I propose doesn't appear to serve our purposes, then we'll change course. Now, are you ready? I'll walk some of the way with you, just until you're close enough to get inside without being intercepted."

"There's no one here but us."

There had been. "No, but I will feel more assured. Here, pull this cloak on properly, and find your gloves."

He donned his own cloak and got down from the gig. When he went to lift Minerva to the ground, she fumbled to pull her gloves from her pocket and something white fell to the floorboards. Gray picked it up and held it out to her.

Minerva took the small, white-wrapped square and looked at it. "Not mine," she said.

"It was in your pocket, love."

She shrugged and unfolded the paper. "A pretty sugar confection," she said, holding it on the palm of her hand beneath the faint moonlight. "It's beautiful, but I didn't put it in my pocket."

"Oh, you must have," he said, reaching for her.

"I . . . Oh, Gray Falconer, you teaser. I was in such a hurry, I forgot the box of sweetmeats left in my room. When did you manage to deliver them there?"

He smiled, but said nothing.

"You must have put this in my pocket at the Pumfreys'. You are so sly, but so dear. Do you want to fatten me up? Am I too scrawny for you?"

He recognized something of the coquette in her tone but

had no time to enjoy it. He opened his mouth to tell her he knew nothing of the sweets, when she raised her hand toward her mouth, watching him while she prepared to eat the thing off her palm.

So abruptly that Minerva gasped, he swept the sugared square off her hand and into his own.

"What's the matter with you?" she said, drawing away from him.

Gray opened his hand to find it filled with crumbled sugar. Evidently grown damp from being carried too long in Minerva's cloak, it fell apart.

"Now look what you've done," she said, sounding aggrieved. "How nasty of you. I don't understand you, Gray. Didn't you want me to find this until you were gone? I've got the whole box you sent me in my room."

Not caring who saw, Gray relit the lamp on the gig shaft and held his hand where he could see clearly what rested there. He poked about among the crystals, and the tiny pink flower made of some finer sugar concoction. Nothing. As she'd said, just a sweet. He felt absurd. "I'm sorry. It's just that I'm not the admirer who brought the gift, my dear."

"Your name is on the card."

"I didn't send you a gift." He looked at the destroyed pieces again. "You're sure you didn't take this from the box?"

"Absolutely sure. And it wasn't there when I left home this morning. The only time it could have got into my pocket was when my cloak was in the nursery while we were in the other room at the Pumfreys'."

And a figure had run through the gardens, just as a figure had left Willieknock through a window while Gray watched.

He narrowed his eyes and realized what should have been clear earlier. If that person was part of all that had happened to him in the Indies, and if the Arbuckles were the masters of that plot, there should be no need for coming and going through windows, or hiding horses in the forest.

Could he be entirely wrong about the Arbuckles?

"A mystery," Gray said, speaking of far more than a few candies. He peered more closely at the sugar again, and poked the pink flower. At its center was a dark blue blob, no doubt the product of the clever confectioner's skill. The blob fell away and he scoured it with a fingernail. Promptly, it broke in half, revealing a tiny quantity of a smooth, thick, creamy substance. "My God," he said quietly. "Bumwallow? Here?"

"Gray?"

He shook his head and bent to sniff, very carefully, at what was no blob of sugar from any confectioner's cloth. Rapidly Gray took the paper from Minerva and scooped the fragments inside. He twisted it shut and thrust it into his own pocket. Then he grabbed Minerva's hands and plunged them into the snow.

"Stop it!" she cried. "Gray, stop it. You're really frightening me."

"Wash your hands with the snow. Like this." He showed her how. "Under your nails, too. And as soon as you're inside the house, take that box and wrap it tightly in paper. Tie it with string and hide it where no one is likely to touch it until you can get it to me. You will not open the box again. Do you understand me?"

"Yes," she said, and bent to wash her hands with vigor. "What's happening?"

He didn't want to terrify her, yet if he was going to have her cooperation in keeping her safe, he must. "Someone intended to poison you with that sweet."

Her mouth fell open.

"The small round thing in the center isn't sugar. It's a seed. Known in the West Indies as the bumwallow. It's grown in very small quantities by nefarious people and sold to other nefarious people for purposes I don't want you to think about."

"Bumwallow seeds? I've never heard of them. They're poisonous?"

"Known as Dancing Death. Eat one tiny seed, and after a few minutes of writhing agony, you die."

"Dance, dance, dance, dance," the priestly monotone had urged.

Gray pulled Minerva forcefully into his arms and hugged her until she fought for breath.

Chapter Seventeen

"Dash it all, Gray," Max Rossmara said, still clinging to the piece of toast he'd snatched from his plate when Gray dragged him out of the breakfast room at Drumblade. "What the devil are you up to?"

The instant Eldora and Cadzow had left, because Eldora was fretful at being ignored and pleaded indisposition, Gray had seized the moment to get Max alone.

"Where are we going?" Max demanded, striding along beside Gray, who led him to the billiard room and closed the door firmly behind them. Max looked at the table. "Hate the bloody things. Ella, my sister Ella, could always beat me. Mortifying. Won't play, and that's that."

Despite the gravity of the moment, Gray smiled and took his hand from his friend's arm. "If you hadn't arrived in the middle of breakfast, I wouldn't have been reduced to near idiocy because all I could think of was speaking to you without wretched Eldora in attendance."

Max raised his expressive brows, leaned against the end of the billiard table, and crossed his ankles. "I might point out that you were breakfasting exceedingly late. But do tell all." He took a large bite of toast that left little more than a morsel of crust in his fingers.

"What are you doing here?"

"Doing here?" Max said, muffled by the mouthful of toast. "Whadyoumean?"

Gray glanced at the door and selected a cue. "You heard me. You made no mention of coming back this way unless you heard from me." He racked the balls and broke them. Then he stuffed another cue into Max's free hand.

"Told you I wasn't interested in playing—"

"Appearances," Gray said. "In case the enemy arrives."

"Really?" Max definitely looked more interested. "So you've made good progress? You've got a definite identification of the scoundrels?"

"I'm more confused than ever," Gray told him, downcast at hearing the probable truth spoken aloud. "Or I am in some ways. In others, perhaps not. There is a definite connection to the West Indies. Why did you come?"

"I was in the vicinity. How could there not be a connection to the West Indies?"

"In the vicinity why?"

"Because I couldn't stand not knowing what was happening with you. There, now you have the truth of it."

"I already knew the truth of it." He slapped the other's back. "But I'm damn glad to see you. I was considering asking you to come anyway. Look, I want to tell you a story."

"Goody," Max said, grinning, and hauling himself to sit on the table. "Always was fond of a story. It isn't scary, is it?"

"Be serious," Gray told him. "There are strange things in this world, y'know."

Max's grin gradually dissolved. "You do amaze me. One day, when you're really bored and we've a week or two to spare, I'll share a strange thing or two of my own with you. They'll wait. Today it's your turn."

"Yes," Gray agreed. Max had always been somewhat of an enigma, an enigma with a charming sense of humor, a wicked way with the ladies, and a penchant for wild tales of his own, and wild behavior—or he had been.

"Go *on*," Max pressed. "Something strange?"

"This happened when I was in the Indies. After I'd learned the ropes at the Falconer plantations and I was more or less overseeing things. A fellow came to see me. Unholy sort of chap, if you know what I mean. Made me wonder what would happen if I closed my eyes. Would he be there when I opened them."

"Or would you be alive to open them again?" Max suggested.

Gray stared at him, at his slanted green eyes that could appear so guileless if you didn't know him. "What made you say that?" Gray asked.

"Sorry. Something told me that's what you were about to say yourself."

"More or less," Gray admitted, still feeling uncomfortably as if his mind had been ransacked. "Anyway, this fellow was very dark. Swarthy. Beard, mustache, bronze skin. I thought he might have been injured. Kept an arm tight against his side. Wore a white turban and long white robes. Thought he was some sort of Indian from India, but I'm not sure."

"And he came to see you at the plantations."

"Yes. Spoke English very well. Cultured. Made it impossible to come to any decisions about his origins. Not that any of that matters. At least, I don't suppose it does. Or will. Unless I come across him again."

"Are you likely to?"

"No." Gray thought about it. "But his visit allowed me to save Minerva's life last night."

Max dropped his remnant of toast and took the end of the billiard cue to his mouth. He looked at it without recognition and slowly lowered it. "The devil you say," he murmured. "Don't keep a fellow in suspense, then. What happened?"

"Back to the chap in the turban first. He was selling something. Or trying to sell it." Neither was exactly the right explanation. "No, he was offering to pay me to take something."

Max shook his head, and light caught at dark red glints in his hair. "I won't say I understand, but you'll get there. Take it slowly. Minerva's all right, isn't she?"

"Yes." He'd detested leaving her at Willieknock, and didn't intend to be without her for much longer. "The man wanted me to ship something to England for him. Hidden in a cargo of our sugar."

Footsteps sounded in the passageway outside and Cadzow opened the door. When he saw Gray and Max he joined them, closing the door again. "Wondered where the two of you had gone," he said. "I hope poor Eldora's little turn didn't put you off your food."

Gray restrained himself from saying that if anything about Eldora were to put him off his food it would be the lady herself, not her "little turn." He could not abide the woman, and, without being certain why, he did not trust her. "Not at all," he said, looking at Max. "Actually, I'm glad Eldora . . . That is, I'm not glad Eldora's indisposed, but I am glad we finally have an opportunity to speak in private. Doesn't do to parade one's problems in front of the fairer sex, don't you agree?"

"Absolutely," Cadzow said, frowning deeply. "What is it, my boy? How may I help you?"

Why did any quiet conversation with his uncle always seem like a prelude to a confession? Gray flexed his shoulders and pushed such thoughts away. "If I hadn't returned so late last night, I'd have spoken to you of this then. This morning your lady was already in attendance, so I had to wait. I was just talking to Max about it, but Max being Max, I haven't got far."

"I say," Max said, almost managing to sound aggrieved. "You'll give a man a bad reputation as a listener."

Gray shook his head and quickly told his story to the point he'd reached when Cadzow arrived.

"You mean he offered to pay you for some sort of additional cargo?" Cadzow asked. "We've never had a policy against filling tonnage if we had any to spare, have we?"

"No." What Gray hadn't yet repeated was the exact nature of the deadly threat to Minerva. "The man spoke as if he'd had a prior arrangement with someone at Falconer, and as if he expected the new request to be merely a formality."

Cadzow nodded. "That might well be so. Of course, when I was there I wasn't involved with such things. But I do recall the plantation manager being proud of maximizing every load that shipped out. I seem to remember silk from somewhere or other. Trinkets."

"I don't suppose they'd have asked you to help with what my gentleman had in mind. It wasn't silk or trinkets, Uncle. It was bumwallow seeds. He wanted to pay me to ship them out with a Falconer cargo."

A bewildered expression left Cadzow's face as quickly as it appeared. "*Bumwallow?* Dancing Death, Gray? Oh, surely not."

"You know of it, then?" Even the corroboration of the seeds' existence was some relief.

"As you know, I went out there to spread the good word," Cadzow said. "Unfortunately, my efforts took me into some unsavory situations. Yes, I know of that wretched devil's crop. Never mind how. Suffice to say I did my best to persuade some men that they were in danger of losing their souls.

"Anyway, dear boy, the most important thing is that you let this person know that the name of Falconer would never be associated with such—" He took a step backward. "Why do you choose to discuss this now? Here? And in private?"

"Last night some villain attempted to poison Minerva with a bumwallow seed. It was on top of a sugared confection."

Cadzow's eyes popped. He fell back several more steps, felt behind him until he touched the arm of a leather chair, and fell into it. "Here?" he asked, his face white. "But . . . Gray, you must be mistaken."

"No mistake. I saw the seeds because that man I've spoken of showed me his little shipment of a thousand deaths as calmly as if they had been peppercorns. Had they not been blue and shiny, I might have thought that's what they were."

"And they are always deadly?" Max asked.

"Always," Gray told him. "The truly damnable thing about them is that they taste extremely good. Anyone who has one will have more if they can, at once. And even as they're putting them in their mouths they will begin to tingle all over. Then they lose the use of their limbs. The process is so rapid—a matter of minutes to total paralysis—that the victim doesn't know death is imminent until he's writhing on the ground, helpless, and racked with pain. There is complete loss of control of all bodily function, and—"

"Stop!" Cadzow pleaded. Sweat had broken out on his smooth brow. He saw Gray studying him and said, "I cannot bear it. After all these years of trying to do the Lord's work, such evil still has the power to cast me so low, Gray, so very low. Is there no hope for the salvation of men's souls?"

Max cleared his throat and slid to stand on the floor again. "I have an uncle, Calum—he's the Duke of Franchot. Calum is frequently cast down by the evil men can do. But he invariably rallies to inform us that if the nature of men were not fragile there would be no need of God."

"So we should be grateful Minerva came close to death last night?" Cadzow asked, somewhat out of character, Gray thought.

"If that's what was intended," Max said.

Gray watched him for a moment before saying, "Ah, I hadn't thought of that. You mean that the entire affair may have been intended as a warning? To me?"

"It could be so. It could have been anticipated that you would see the danger and stop it."

"But an entire box of the things was delivered to her room. The sugar sweets, I mean. With a card bearing my supposed signature, by the way."

"Yet the plan cannot have been to make her death look as if you had caused it," Cadzow said thoughtfully. "No ordinary Scottish country physician would have any notion of the existence of bumwallow."

"What if others ate some of the sweets and also died?" Gray asked. "Wouldn't that at least raise some bright fellow's curiosity?"

Max aimed a finger at Gray. "You've got a point there. What did you do with that thing you stopped Minerva from eating?"

"I have it in a safe place. We must make no impetuous moves, like drawing attention to what we think we know, until we've more information. The last thing we must risk is causing the bounder to flee. He'll stick around as long as he thinks he's anonymous."

"He is," Max pointed out.

Gray ignored him. "And he'll stay while he has a mission. To prove to me that I'm dangerous to be around, evidently."

"By killing people, if necessary," Cadzow said somberly. "We must work together, and with great care. Any mistake could be disastrous. Can you think of any reason why someone would want to get rid of you, Gray? I know the question seems a bit late in the asking, but that is what it's all about, isn't it?"

"Yes," Gray said. He wasn't ready to parade his theories yet. "I'm not sure why, but I will be. I'm a grave threat to someone—possibly several people."

"Which means," Max said, "that you're the one in danger. Perhaps you're too vulnerable here. You could always go somewhere and hide out until—"

"That's what they want." Gray felt deeply cold. "That's

exactly what they want. To make me run. They want me where it'll be easy to get at me."

A light tap sounded, and Ratley poked his pointed nose into the room. "Some young people t'see Mr. Gray." Disapproval hung on the words "young people."

"Who are they?" Gray asked, in no mood to be interrupted.

"The orphan pair from Willieknock, sir. Ragtag sorts, if ye remember. Charity cases."

There were frequently times when Gray wanted to tell Ratley he was a snob with a mean turn of mind, but the man was a good butler and would never change his view of the world, or his place in it. "Fergus and Iona Drummond," Gray said. "Show them in then, Ratley."

"I'd be glad t'send them away, sir."

"No such thing."

"Oh, I'd tell Miss Arbuckle she was welcome, o' course. But the other two, well—"

"Minerva's here?" Gray started forward. "For God's sake, man. Why didn't you say so?"

"Well, I'm sure I dinna mean t'put anythin' wrong."

Gray strode into the passageway just in time to see Minerva arrive at the other end. He held his hands out to her, and she ran toward him in typical abandoned Minerva fashion. Her braids slipped free to trail behind her and her eyes shone with delight. Her cloak, the same one she'd worn the previous night, flapped open to reveal what Gray was afraid might be a divided skirt, but at least it was made of some heavy blue material rather than almost transparent chiffon.

"Gray!" She reached him and buried her face in his chest. "I cannot stand a moment without you anymore."

"Nor I without you," he said quietly against the top of her head. Then he put his mouth close to her ear and said, "We are not alone here. We are among friends, but I should not like the servants to know anything was amiss, nor Eldora, should she decide to join us again. You have the box of sweets safe?"

Minerva raised her face, and Gray saw how she glowed. There was no other suitable word to describe her. "I'll be discreet." She raised her shoulders, and wrinkled her nose, and pressed her fingers to his cheeks. "And I have the box. I have made a decision, a most important decision."

"I say, Gray," Cadzow called from the billiard room. "I hear you out there. What is it? What do the children want?"

The "children" in question hovered at the end of the passageway, watching Gray and Minerva while trying to appear uninterested.

"My love," Gray said, covering Minerva's hands on his face. "Let us find a way to be together. Alone together. We will deal with all this crush of people and meet later."

"How much later?" She showed signs of preparing to kiss him.

Gray glanced at the audience and kissed Minerva himself, very firmly, but fleetingly. "Leave it all to me. I feel things are going to become clearer. Even as I thought I was unutterably beset, I began to feel fortunate. My enemies have started to reveal themselves. My job is to draw them out entirely."

"*Our* job," she told him. "Whatever is your affair is my affair."

"Not so. You will—"

"We must examine every element. What of the McSporrans? What of their fear? They were afraid of you, or so it seemed. Or perhaps angered by you." She raised her shoulders and frowned. "There is so much that is strange."

"Yes, yes," he had to agree. "But please allow me to consider what is to be done next."

"I am the one who almost ate the Death Dance."

"Dancing Death. *Minerva.* Hush, please." He waved Fergus and Iona toward them and said heartily, "Come along you two. Into the light of day. Stop skulking back there."

The twins approached rapidly, their faces so alike despite

Iona's being the feminine version of her brother's strongly masculine set of features.

Reluctantly, Gray set Minerva from him. He bowed slightly and knew that his heart was as much in his eyes as Minerva's was in hers. "Come, sweet, let's deal with the inevitable. Max Rossmara is here. Remember? He is an old friend."

They went into the billiard room with the Drummond twins behind them. Ratley stood by with a pained expression. His red brows drawn together, he held his head to one side on his stooped shoulders.

"It's all right, Ratley," Gray told him heartily. "We'll manage from here. Iona and Fergus are Minerva's cousins. Minerva, as you may remember, is my fiancée."

"A wedding!" Iona squealed and covered her mouth.

Fergus blushed so hard at his sister's outburst that Gray pitied the young man.

"As ye say, Mr. Gray," Ratley said, glaring at the Drummonds. But he had the sense to say no more before taking the visitors' cloaks and bowing out of the room.

"He doesn't care for orphans," Iona said, her sweet voice without malice. "It's not unusual, you know. Some think orphans are the fault of their parents, especially twin orphans. They say twin orphans are left because their parents are to be punished for giving them birth."

"No such thing," Minerva said sternly. "Where have you come by such a piece of fiction?"

"Hatch," Fergus said, while his sister attempted to shush him. "Iona will listen to everything the beastie dowd tells her. Do you know that woman thinks like a savage? She thinks that if a woman is delivered of twins, she must have—"

"Er, Fergus," Gray said, appalled at the direction in which the boy might be going. "I don't think—"

"Don't worry. I wasn't going to spell out how she said our mother must have been a gay one, as she put it. I put it t'her, that she'd have been a good deal the better for having been a gay one hersel'. She hasn't spoken t'me since, which makes me happy. Ye'll not speak t'her either, Iona."

Iona said, "Fergus was only going to say that Hatch thinks the mother of twins has done whatever one has to do to have children twice. Now, what do you think of that?"

"Come and sit here, Miss Drummond," Max said, surprising Gray, who thought of his friend as a careless blade.

Iona looked at Max and moved toward the chair he indicated as if she walked in her sleep. The girl's freckled face had the lovely transparent quality so delightful in some Scottish females, and her hair was a pale red that was almost the color of pink-tinged honey. Dressed in light green with lace at her neck and cuffs, and wide lace flounces on her skirt, she made a slender charmer.

Gray groaned to himself and decided he must warn Max not to turn the heads of young girls in whom he had no interest, especially if they were related to Minerva.

"Welcome, Minerva," Cadzow said, already on his feet and bowing to her. "It's been too long, my dear. After I came with the dreadful news . . . Well, we should not dwell on that now. God smiled upon us and brought Gray home. But I am ashamed that I had not the courage to try to bring you more solace in difficult times."

Minerva let him take her hand to his mouth, then, as only this dear impulsive girl would, she bobbed up and kissed Cadzow's cheek. "You have had your own terribly difficult times. So much thrust upon you that you never wanted. We must celebrate our joy now, not mourn what is past."

Cadzow turned his face away and said indistinctly, "Such wisdom from one so young. I shall endeavor to learn from you, my dear." He walked to a window overlooking the snow-covered driveway outside.

"I'm sorry," Minerva said softly, and pressed her hands together. "I didn't mean to upset anyone."

"You haven't," Gray said. "How could you ever do such a thing?"

She put a hand on his arm and frowned.

"What?" he asked softly.

She frowned even more deeply, and glanced at the twins.

"Our aunt sent us," Fergus said in a rush. "We're to deliver an invitation by hand, Mr. Falconer. Mr. Cadzow Falconer."

"I decided to come with them," Minerva said, never looking away from Gray.

She made him weak, a strange feeling for a strong man. Her gown did, indeed, have a divided skirt that didn't cover her ankles. The bodice had a nautical air, with a sailor's collar and brass buttons. She looked *dashing,* he thought with pleasure, dashingly feminine.

Cadzow turned back from the window. "Minerva's parents are inviting me? For what purpose?"

"No, no," Fergus said. "Explain, Iona."

Iona gazed up at Max with the most open admiration Gray had ever seen on another's face. And Max, damn his liver and lights, smiled at the girl so charmingly that she was bound to be rendered a gibbering moonling before long.

"Iona!" Fergus repeated. "Say what it is we're to give the invitation for."

"Oh." Her face prettily pink, she turned to the rest and said, "To a salon at Maudlin Manor. A salon presented five evenings this evening, that's Friday next, by Mr. Olaf Clack."

Then Fergus presented an envelope that must contain the said invitation, and Gray quelled an urge to ask why the Drummonds hadn't saved themselves the irritation of a verbal explanation.

"It's to be a splendid affair," Iona said. She looked to Max again. "Mr. Clack is bound to want you there once he knows you're in residence here."

"Whereas he clearly does not want *me* there," Gray said.

An awkward pause followed before Minerva said, "No such thing. Why, I know he specifically said he wanted both of the Mr. Falconers present. Mama has made a mistake."

Cadzow looked up. "Your mama is issuing invitations on behalf of this Clack fella?"

"He's new to the area," Minerva said, sounding flustered. "He came and threw himself upon her mercy, pleading the lack of a wife and his desire to give an important event that would allow him to make the acquaintance of all the neighborhood. Papa and Mama kindly agreed to assist him."

"Minerva's mother will be Mr. Clack's hostess," Gray said. "At Mr. Arbuckle's insistence, of course. Generous man, Mr. Arbuckle." He caught Max's eye.

"There's never been the like of it in Ballyfog," Iona said, still blushing and sparkling. "Fergus and I are t'go, aren't we, Fergus?"

Fergus shrugged, showing little enthusiasm.

More footsteps sounded in the passage—a number of pairs of footsteps, to be precise—and Ratley, his appearance more disturbed than Gray recalled on any previous occasion, wedged himself into the opening of the door.

"What is it?" Cadzow said. "For goodness' sake, man, what is it now? People coming and going. Mostly coming. And our butler, who should be the calm keeper of our castle, popping in and out in a most annoying manner."

"Sorry, Mr. Falconer," Ratley said, his lips thin against his teeth. "But there are some very *unusual* persons here. And they insist you will want to see them. One of them insists you will want to see him. The others are by way of accompanying him, I believe."

"Well, then," Cadzow said, sounding exceedingly short-tempered. "Well, then, *who* is this person?"

Ratley stretched his scrawny neck, managing only to make himself appear even shorter. "A, er, Mr. Olaf Clack, sir. He says he's o' Maudlin Manor, but we know that canna be true."

Cadzow produced a handkerchief and mopped his brow. "I am not accustomed to so much activity."

"Mr. Clack does live at the manor," Minerva said, going to Cadzow and threading a hand beneath his elbow. "I apologize for such a large and boisterous intrusion. Perhaps we should leave now so you may speak with Mr. Clack in a more peaceful manner."

"Nonsense." The benevolent smile Cadzow bestowed upon Minerva left Gray in no doubt that his uncle was captivated by her. "I want you to stay right here where you belong. After all, this is to be your home. Send the gentleman in, Ratley. And thank you for doing your duty so industriously."

All expression left Ratley's face, but he straightened considerably and said, "Should I request that the other two wait in the kitchens? I could have cook give them a cup of tea."

The door burst wide open, all but depositing Ratley on the floor. Gray barely missed being hit by the door himself. Even from the back he recognized Olaf Clack from Minerva's description of him. The two men with him were Silas Meaner and Micky Finish.

His balance recovered, if not his pride, Ratley looked to Cadzow for an answer to his question.

"We'll be staying," Meaner announced. "We are very old friends of Mr. Clack, Mr. Falconer. Very old. Known each other since we were all—"

"Boys," Clack said from the recesses behind his flowing black hair. "Recently and happily reunited."

"Thank you, Ratley," Cadzow said, staring at the newcomers as if transfixed. "We'll call if we need anything."

"We'll call," Clack repeated as Ratley sailed from the room. "But we won't need anything, will we, Mr. Falconer?"

From his position behind the newcomers, Gray observed how Cadzow blinked, and glanced from one of the group to the next, and the next.

"I see as 'ow the pleasure of our disporting ourselves to you 'as overexcited you," Clack said. "You think of it, my good man. The pleasure isn't ours."

The man was a buffoon. A joke. Or he was joking. Gray was moved to laugh, but thought better of the idea.

"Nice of you to visit," Cadzow said finally, sounding undone rather than pleased at all. "Understand this is an invitation." He wiggled the envelope Fergus had given him.

"A *saloon*," Clack roared. "By way of an early Christmas liberation. Mrs. Arbuckle—fine female that—insisted on helping. Glad she's doing the 'orrors prompt, like."

"She didn't send one for Max," Iona said.

Gray crossed his arms and rubbed his jaw, noting that Max avoided looking him in the eye.

"Max," Clack said. "Max?"

"Max Rossmara," Iona said, her voice very small. "This is Max Rossmara, from Castle Kirkcaldy, we're told. His father's a viscount."

Clack made his shuffling, cane-stomping way across the room toward Max and said, "I'll be dishonored to have you at my 'ouse. An hinvitation will be delivered forthworth."

"There wasn't one for Gray, either," Iona went on, smiling now, and evidently gathering courage. "Mr. Gray Falconer. That's him there."

Olaf Clack stood still, as if listening. "Gray Falconer?" he said, and dropped his head even lower. Slowly, he pivoted about and reared up until a gap—but no discernible features—showed between wings of hair. "Well, I did not see you there, sir. Of course you must come, too."

Silas Meaner and Micky Finish also turned to observe Gray. Neither spoke to him, but Silas said to Micky, "Cold times remembered, what? More to come, perhaps? Soon."

Micky nodded his head. Thick, shaggy hair flopped over his face and the upturned collar of his baggy, floor-length coat.

Gray thought himself tired of obscure comments and more obscure actions.

"You'll be with us, of course, dear thing," Silas Meaner said to Iona. He went to her and sat on the arm of her chair as if they were the most intimate of acquaintances. "It's to be a masquerade, I think. Or it can be. I see you as one of those Arabian damsels. Or some sort of goddess, anyway."

"Who are they?" Fergus asked, his expression thunderous. "These goddesses?"

Clack laughed, and staggered about. "Probably some bawds out of them myths. Didn't take to clothes much, if I have my guess. Good idea. Cheap outfits."

"Why," Fergus said, actually raising his fists at the bestriped and beflowered Meaner with his powdered pate and dandyish frills. "I shall fight you for such a suggestion about my sister."

"No need," Max said, a deal less pleasant than before. "I'd appreciate your removing yourself from Miss Drummond's chair, sir. She is visiting me."

Holding his silver stick to his chest, Meaner lolled back. "No need to take offense, laddie. Just being friendly." He waved his free hand in the air. "Always a friendly chap just looking for ways to work together with others."

"No doubt," Max said. "But I would appreciate your showing more respect to my friend just the same."

Gray longed for peace. Minerva alone, and peace. He knew Max was only being a gentleman in coming to the aid of a young lady, but he doubted Iona would fail to place more emphasis on his behavior.

"Everyone 'appy, then," Clack inquired. "All hinvited to my saloon? Costumes inquired."

"A costume *saloon*," Max remarked, his gaze firmly centered on Meaner, who got languidly to his feet and bowed to Iona. "I don't think I ever heard of such a thing before."

"Eunuch!" Clack announced with gusto. "That's me. Once eunuch, always eunuch, and proud to display it. Fine place you got, Falconer. Came to pay my suspects, and glad I disported myself here for the purpose. Things in common, us, Falconer. Things to impair."

Cadzow stirred himself. "Yes, well, we're glad you came, too. Why don't I show you around a bit before you have to leave—soon, I'm sure."

Once more Gray wanted to groan. Poor Cadzow mistakenly thought he was dealing with people who might hear a hint in his words.

"Charming of you, sir," Meaner said, still observing Iona from head to foot. "I'm sure we'd all enjoy looking over the place, wouldn't we, Mickey?"

All but obscured by his layers of shapelessness, Mickey Finish bobbed his disheveled head again.

"There, you see?" Meaner looped an arm around Cadzow's shoulders and walked him toward the door. "We're all eager for the tour, old friend. Can't tell you how glad we are to—"

"Good enough." Cadzow's stiff stance showed that his temper had thinned to breaking point. "Let's get on with it, then."

When the foursome had straggled away, Gray said, "Poor old Cadzow. He deserves a medal."

"He's very kind," Minerva said. "He didn't want that nasty Mr. Meaner . . . well, you know."

"Yes, I do know," Fergus said angrily. "But I can take care of my sister myself."

"Of course you can," Minerva said. "But so much the better to avoid real unpleasantness."

"Gray," Max said. "Hadn't we better get on?"

"Does he know?" Fergus asked Gray, his face quite red as he indicated Max, at whom he looked without a great deal of affection. "About, you know, the *dancing* thing? Min told us. We made her."

The thought of the twins being involved didn't comfort Gray, but he supposed he could understand Minerva taking them into her confidence. "Max knows," he said. "Max and I have shared a good deal."

"Someone tried to poison Minerva," Iona said. "We're not going to eat anything we don't make ourselves, are we, Fergus? Are we, Minerva?"

"We're going to have to make a pact to keep all this absolutely private," Gray said. "Even the smallest slip—one word spoken in the wrong place—could be dangerous."

"Deadly," Iona whispered.

Max didn't cover his smile quickly enough. He caught Gray's eye and managed a sober expression instantly. "We'll work out a plan. No one's going to die because of a carelessly spoken word."

"Will you excuse Gray and me for just a moment?" Minerva said, her voice more strident than usual. "And please don't think me rude, but there's something I absolutely have to tell him in private."

Max's "But of *course*" sank low under the weight of innuendo.

With two pairs of eyes on them—Iona's were on Max—Gray and Minerva left the room. As soon as they were alone, she took him by the hand, looked in each direction, and set off to the right. Gray presumed she chose the right because the left led back to the foyer and the possibility of encountering Cadzow and the vile visitors.

Gray let her lead him to the end of the passageway, then pulled her to a halt and took her by the shoulders. "Out with it, my love," he said, not allowing himself to regard her mouth or the soft skin on her neck where a pulse . . . He must not be distracted by her now.

"Kiss me, Gray." She closed her eyes.

He stood straight, hardened the muscles in his thighs, and lightly touched his lips to her brow.

Her eyes popped open. For an instant he thought she would protest his poor effort, but then she nodded and smiled, and said, "I'm sorry. I am a selfish creature and we must concentrate. Not one word we've spoken about danger is too strong."

"No, Min, it isn't. I believe I am a lure to terrible disaster." And he intended to make sure that if he couldn't avert that disaster, it would touch no one else.

"Partly right," Minerva said. "Perhaps entirely right. I have thought it all through. Everything you've told me and everything that's happened. It is you they want to get rid of. Whoever they are. But they decided they could use me against you."

He would not try to comfort her with denials. "Yes. And I know what I must do, at least for the present. I must leave Ballyfog. As long as I'm near you, you are at terrible risk."

"No, Gray."

"Yes!" He embraced her fiercely. "My God, I could have lost you last night. I could have cost you your life."

Her arms went around him. "And if you go away, go away and find some safe refuge while you seek out your enemies, well, then we cannot be certain they will not find a way to use me against you again."

Hiding truth from his silver-witted girl would never be easy. "Min, don't even think such a thing."

"Even though you're thinking it? There is only one answer, Gray. You and I must go away together."

Chapter Eighteen

"Gray? You do agree?" Minerva couldn't stand still. She took hold of his hands and tugged insistently. "Say you agree. We must go away."

He looked at her, yet didn't look at her.

He looked at her, and . . . saw something else?

"You wanted us to leave Ballyfog together—or you wanted us to marry at once, anyway, which is the same thing, since we could not have done so here."

His demeanor, the intensity in his eyes, frightened her. "Gray, what is it? What are you thinking?"

He started, and she saw the instant he focused on her again. "I'm going to tell you something that will amaze you. Disgust you at first, no doubt. But you will understand. Yes, when I explain you will understand how I could come to certain conclusions."

There was fire in him now. He squeezed her hands so tightly, she flinched.

"Min"—his hesitation was slight, yet heavy with struggle—"Min, this is not the place to discuss this. Not at all the place, given that we cannot be certain of privacy."

"I don't think there is time to waste," she told him. "Until we know the truth of it all, we must assume that the enemy is everywhere."

His frown drew his dark brows together. He released her and paced a few steps, pushing back his coat with one hand and breathing into the other fist. Then he stopped and stared at her. "Can your cousins be trusted?"

She had never felt such dread.

Resolution set Gray's features. "Minerva? Your cousins?"

She rallied and nodded, yes. "Fergus and Iona are the dearest souls. Honest and good."

"They will also need to be patient, for I shall ask them to go back to Willieknock and say nothing, behave as if they know nothing, and have seen nothing."

But Gray knew something. He had come to a conclusion he wanted to share with her. "They will complain, but they will do it. Why can't you tell me what you've decided?"

He returned and held her arms. He held them, and she felt how strong he was. "What would you think of a man who persuaded himself of something when he didn't have proof other than a remark spoken in anger?" he asked. "Certainly not sufficient proof? And what if he could have come to his conclusions in some part because he harbored dislike for certain individuals?"

Minerva hesitated, then said, "That would depend upon the man, and—in most cases—of what it was that he persuaded himself. You refer to yourself, of course. I could never think less of you."

"Couldn't you? I wonder."

So abruptly did he gather her in his arms, so harshly did his mouth descend over hers, that she could only hold him as fiercely—to retain her balance, and kiss him with as much desperation—because she wanted to.

He kept on kissing her, even when she heard footsteps and was sure he must also have heard them.

He kissed her when a masculine voice said, "Gray, Gray!" in a hoarse whisper.

Minerva softened against him. Through the smooth stuff of his coat she felt heavy muscles move. Before he'd left

Ballyfog, she'd thought him as much a man as any could ever be, but he'd become more so. In the heat on that strange, distant island, he'd become what Gray Falconer was today: an irresistible force.

"Damn it, Gray, this is . . . *Gray.*"

He raised his head and looked down at her.

Min managed to extract an arm and point past his shoulder. She'd been afire from those kisses, but she grew hotter, if that was possible.

Gray's lips thinned and he breathed deeply. "Yes, Max?"

"I've got to talk to you."

"Now?"

"Now."

"Right now?"

"This second, Gray."

Visibly gathering himself, Gray slipped an arm around Minerva's shoulders and faced his friend. "Yes?"

Minerva wished she didn't blush so predictably—especially when she'd already been blushing.

"Look," Max said. "I'm sorry to barge in on you like this, but I've been thinking. I could be absolutely wrong, but I may not be."

"Code," Gray said. "Another bloody code to unravel, as if my life weren't already enough of a bloody indecipherable code."

"Gray," Minerva murmured, and immediately wished she hadn't.

"Sorry," he said. "Damn mouth . . . Sorry."

"You don't have to be. We're in such a mess. Max, I want Gray to come away with me."

Gray turned to stare at her. "That's between us."

She shrugged helplessly. "I don't know what to say or do to make you agree. But I know I must."

"It might be better if Iona and Fergus—"

"I know," Gray interrupted Max. "Min and I have decided it would be as well to dispatch them home."

Max turned on his heel. "Then we'll send them at once. I've important things to discuss with you."

Still holding Minerva, Gray was at the other man's heels when they went back into the billiard room, where the twins stood close together.

"Listen, you two," Gray said, settling a hand on Fergus's shoulder. "You already know there's something extraordinary going on."

"We'll do anythin' we can t'help," Fergus said.

Iona drew her fine red brows together. "We're very nervous. For Minerva. Tell us what we can do."

"Go home," Gray said, his voice firm but kind.

"But—"

"Please," he insisted, interrupting Fergus. "We need you there. Watch for anyone coming or going, but don't do anything to intercede. Understand?"

Iona took Minerva's hands in her own. "I don't want t'leave you, Min. I'm afraid."

"So am I," Min admitted. "But we're not alone."

"Hush!" Gray held up a hand and listened. "Someone's coming, I think. Very quietly."

Before he could drop his hand again, the door opened a crack, then a few inches, and Silas Meaner's sallow, blond-bewhiskered face appeared. He grinned, trotted inside, and stood with his corseted body thrust forward. "Thought I'd left something," he said, and proceeded to make a tour of the room, looking behind chairs and under cushions.

"Something we might be able to help you find?" Gray asked.

The man was a toad, a despicable creature, Minerva thought, and was taken aback at her reaction. She didn't even know the creature, yet she detested him.

"Doubt it," Meaner said, pausing beside Minerva and using his silver stick to scratch his bald head. A fine rain of white powder sprayed down to settle on the shoulders of his red coat. "You're Minerva?"

"Yes. We met at Maudlin Manor, if you remember."

"Bad memory. Have had for years. You're the Arbuckles' girl?"

She distinctly recalled him paying her considerable attention when they'd met at the manor. "Porteous and Janet Arbuckle. Yes, I'm their only daughter."

"Feeling all right, are you?" Meaner asked.

Minerva looked past him to Gray and said, "Very well, thank you. Why?"

He clutched the stick as a small child might a favorite doll, very tightly in his gloved hand. Not as confident a man as he would have one think. "We heard there'd been some commotion at Willieknock last night. One of the servants mentioned it. Said you'd had a spot of bother. Suffered some sort of . . . hmm. Well, don't see what I was looking for."

He slipped out again, leaving the door open.

Max closed it.

Iona said, "What servants? Surely Brumby's parents aren't confiding in that man."

"Don't concern yourself," Max said, giving her a brilliant smile. "Go home with Fergus. I promise you I'll make it my personal mission to keep you informed of anything that happens."

Minerva saw how Iona looked at Max, and almost groaned aloud. The man was charming and undoubtedly sought only to reassure Iona. Iona, on the other hand, showed every sign of becoming too enamored of Mr. Max Rossmara.

More silently than before, Silas Meaner entered. This time he nodded, said nothing, and made another round of the room until he stood close to Gray.

"Back again?" Gray said, showing teeth without smiling.

"Clack's slow. Good man, but slow to get about. You can see what I mean, can't you? Cripple. Sad. Hmm."

"Very sad," Minerva said.

"Cold again today," Meaner remarked, rising to his toes

as if he couldn't see through the floor-to-ceiling windows if he didn't. "Even colder than yesterday, I should say. Warm enough, are you, Mr. Falconer?"

"Quite, thank you."

"Hmm." Meaner clasped his hands beneath his coattails and rocked backward to peer behind Gray and across the room. "Wouldn't want to be outside without enough to keep me warm, would you?"

"No," Gray said. "What's your point, Meaner?"

"Oh, nothing. Just making conversation. Being polite, and so on. Better get back." With that he exited once more, closing the door himself this time.

"He's so strange," Minerva said. "He makes my skin feel odd."

"He makes me feel as if little things were creeping over mine," Iona said, shivering. "Come, Fergus, we'd best be on our way."

"I'm stating the obvious," Gray said, "but I don't like that man. He may be no more than a gossipmonger, but I don't want him in my house."

"Make sure he isn't admitted again," Max said. "Then put him out of your mind. We've more important matters to attend to."

Gray rang for Ratley, and they met him in the beautiful hall where a great fire blazed in a massive fireplace at one end.

"Mr. and Miss Drummond are leaving," Gray told the butler, who left to retrieve cloaks.

They waited, aware of having much to say yet daring to say nothing that might be overheard.

Firelight gave off pleasant warmth, and burnished suits of standing armor and the huge stone flags.

"What's keeping your butler?" Max said, bending before the fire and rubbing his hands.

"Not so quick as he was," Gray said. "Happens to us all."

"If we live long enough," Max said.

Minerva shivered this time.

"Och, I'll turn ye t'blood puddin', see if I dinna!" Ratley could be heard shouting from a room off the hall. "I knew ye were up t'no good t'minute I set eyes on ye."

Gray strode across the stones, his heels clipping sharply, and went in the direction of Ratley's fury.

"Found the little beggar in here, I did, sir," Ratley cried. "An' will ye look at that? He's a thief. I wouldna' be surprised if they were all thieves. A ring. Y'know the way they talk about rings? In Edinburgh, so I'm told. It's a ring, I tell ye."

"Get up," Gray said sharply.

Shaking his head, Max went after Gray. So did Minerva and the twins, into a small-paneled compartment that smelled of polish and damp wool. The latter was no doubt attributable to the quantity of outer garments scattered on the floor.

On the floor?

Gray stood over the object of Ratley's ire and suspicion.

The person called Micky Finish sat amid the cloaks and coats, his head hanging forward, his hands hidden in the sleeves of his own coat.

"Into the pockets, he was," Ratley announced. "Shouldn't be surprised, anyhow. Searchin', and droppin' everythin' down the while. Thief, that's what he is. I say we search him."

Finish contrived to curl himself into a ball.

"Oh, there you are, Micky." Mr. Olaf Clack stomped in. "Wondered where you'd got off to, m'boy. Well, now, what's this, then?" Crouching low, his hair trailed over Finish's head, but the boy didn't move.

"I'm afraid he was found meddling with the coats and so forth," Gray said. "Making all this mess, too."

"What's the trouble, then, Micky?" Clack poked the accused with his cane and Micky shook his head. "Oh, I'm appraised of all. He's upset! He never gets upset unless he's

. . . Did you actually accuse him of something? Trying to pinch something? Micky? Micky, pinch? Never. Honest as he's long, I can tell you. Sorry old chap. Willing he is, always. Feel a bit chilly, meself. Chilled, like. Cold. Asked Micky here to get my coat."

"You arrived in that cape you're wearing," Ratley muttered. "You didn't have a coat."

Undeterred, Clack continued, "Ah, yes, I see you were lookin' for my coat, Micky, but they thought you were trying to steal. I understand with compunction now."

"You got all that from one shake of his head?" Gray asked, sounding mild but with iron in his eyes.

"Great deal you don't understand," Clack said, using the carved boot on his cane to hook Micky's collar. He stood back and hauled him up as if he were a particularly resistant fish. "A bond we have. No words, just a bond. Yes, 'course you want to leave, Micky. We'll go at once. Wouldn't . . . No, absently not. Wouldn't persist on you staying. Off we go, then."

Making his way through the path Minerva, Gray and the others made for them, Clack continued to skewer Micky's collar with the cane and push him along.

"My uncle didn't return with you?" Gray said to Clack.

"Good old Cadzow. Not a bit of it. Wouldn't allow for it. Tired. Gone to bed."

"Don't leave without Mr. Meaner," Minerva said, no longer caring if she sounded rude. "Where is he?"

"Gone," Clack said, clomping along with his splay-footed gait. "Had to leave us. Sweet sorrow, and so forth. Ta ta. See you for goddesses."

"Good Lord," Max said distinctly when the madness had departed. "They aren't *real*, are they? I mean, they're from some circus, perhaps?"

"I wish they were," Gray said. "And I wish they'd go back."

Iona assisted Ratley in picking up the fallen garments.

She assisted until not one was left, and said, "Where's my cloak?"

"Ye've missed it, lassie," Fergus told her, puffing with annoyance. "Och, it's a'ways somethin'. Here, let me look."

A very few minutes and Fergus also pronounced the cloak missing.

Her heart dropping, Minerva glanced at Gray, who made fists on his hips.

"I'm going to take the two of you home," Max said, waving aside Fergus's protests that they'd walked to Drumblade and they'd walk back to Willieknock. With his own cloak around Iona's shoulders, he told the twins to go out by the fire while he borrowed another cloak.

The instant he was alone with Gray and Minerva, he dropped his voice and said, "Well?"

"Someone took Iona's cloak," Minerva said.

"Meaner asked some damned strange questions," Max said, "then he was gone."

"With Iona's cloak," Gray said, crossing his arms. "Took it by mistake, thinking it was Minerva's. Since they know she found the sweet, they want to try to remove any evidence remaining in the pocket, I'd bet on it."

Max said, "I must get out there before Iona and Fergus come looking for me. They'll be as aware as we are that Meaner probably took the cloak, but not why. We've got to try to keep them out of this. It's too dangerous, and they're somewhat too enthusiastic."

"I agree," Gray said, and turned questioning eyes on Minerva, who nodded.

"What I wanted to say to you privately, Gray," Max said, "was that I wonder exactly who the bumwallow was meant for."

Gray let his head bow.

"You could have been the intended victim, couldn't you?" Max pressed.

"Of course I could." Gray raised his face again. "And I

probably was. Easy enough mistake. Fellow was in a hurry. Put the thing in the wrong pocket. The two cloaks were in a heap at the Pumfreys'. Both dark cloth and heavy. He put it in Minerva's instead of mine."

"But you were likely to recognize it," Minerva reminded him. "The seed."

"They'd have no way of knowing I'd seen the things before. Your gloves were wet and in the same pocket, so the sweet crumbled. Maybe I wouldn't have seen the seed at all if it hadn't."

"Look the other way, please," Minerva said matter-of-factly. Then she lifted one half of her divided skirt to reveal a pouch strapped to her leg. "This will be a very popular item. A safe place to carry valuables that will be entirely hidden."

"Don't keep us in suspense," Gray said, and she saw him peek but pretended not to.

She removed the paper and string-wrapped box of confections from the pouch, then straightened her clothes again. "This is what proves you're wrong, Max. And you, Gray. The poison was intended for me." Proving this point would bring no particular jubilation. "If you were right, and it was you they intended to kill, why would they have left a whole box of these terrible things in my rooms?"

"Ah, yes."

The two men looked at each other, and Gray took the box. He pulled off the string Minerva had tied in place, and ripped away the paper. When the top of the box was removed, neat rows of pretty sugar shapes were revealed, each with a colored flower iced on top.

A space showed where one sweet had been removed.

Max took up a sugared morsel and deliberately crushed it, looked at it in his palm, and dropped it back into the box. He repeated the performance with another, and another. Gray joined him, and the two continued until they had destroyed every piece.

"What does it mean?" Minerva said.

"That I was right," Max said, gripping Gray's arm.

Not a single seed lay in the jumble of battered sugar.

He insisted they ride out, out and away from Drumblade or any place that could hide a listener.

The man she loved led the way to the place overlooking Willieknock. Their horses moved gamely through the snow, but the going became labored. They entered the trees at the top of the hill just as snow began to fall again.

Cold poked Minerva's nose and cheeks, and her eyes watered, but she held her peace, sensing Gray's inner tumult and his need for both her presence and her acceptance of whatever he intended to say. And he did intend to say something. She'd felt a declaration brewing since they'd left Drumblade.

He reached for her mount's bridle and urged the animal alongside his own. With absent attention, he then pulled Minerva's hood farther forward and tucked her cloak together over her gloved hands.

That done, he stared out over the land, over the hills and valleys, and the white ribbon of the River Tay as it unfurled and curved along its gentle way.

"I do think they—whoever they are—intended it to be you," she said. "Then, if the question ever arose about what you might have been eating before you died, and the presence of sugar crystals, they would have said I had given you one of the sweets you had given me. Then it would be decided that it was obviously harmless because the rest were."

"Exactly. And if you denied giving me anything, it wouldn't matter in the end. And I would be neatly dead."

"But *why*?"

He gave a short laugh. "Why. Ah, yes, why. Should you like to hear the reason for everything that's happened to me—the reason I intended to prove upon my return to Ballyfog?"

Such strangeness in his voice, Minerva thought.

"We must mount a close watch on Maudlin Manor," Gray said.

"Yes."

"The McSporrans are part of it."

She pressed her hands against her middle. "So it would seem."

"So it *is*." Quiet vehemence made him more cutting than had he raised his voice.

"I am not the enemy, Gray. I'm—"

"Forgive me. I'm sharp because I'm angry—but not with you. You are the love of my life. I have wronged you through ignorance. When I should have been recognizing you for the woman you have become, and allowing for the independence you will always need, I was trying to tie you to conventions into which you will never fit. In that I intend to change. But above all, I have to hurt you. Against my will, but hurt you nevertheless."

"Hurt me?" Aghast, she pushed back her hood, not caring that snow peppered her hair. "You have never done anything to harm me. Nothing. You never would."

"I hope you will repeat that when I finish saying what must be said. I will start by telling you that I may be wrong, but I don't think so. Not now, although I wish I were, because the truth may cost me you."

"You are frightening me, Gray."

"Look at me."

She did so. "You are—desperate."

"You read me well. First I will give you some reasons for the conclusions I have drawn. This afternoon I decided that no parent would risk losing a child. Do you agree?"

"Of course."

"Especially if that child were highly prized, and the rock on which the family's security stood? Such situations exist, where a child becomes the one looked to for guidance, even as he or she is repeatedly reminded of their subservience."

"A child is a child, no matter the rest," Minerva said. "But I suppose one child may be more favored than another."

He tried to raise her hood again, but she stopped him. "Very well," he said. "You are willful, but so be it. I do believe I grow to like your willfulness—at least a little. Do you think it possible that a parent could need a child so much that they would not want that child to leave them, even in marriage?"

Minerva thought about his question. "A selfish parent, perhaps. But they would do this in the mistaken belief that it was out of love."

"Just so. Selfish. Selfishness can lead to great harm. A parent might even take drastic steps to intervene in any relationship that would remove the child from their control. After all, if the so-called child is the keeper of the family accounts, the savior of the family fortunes, as it were, because she is *brilliant*, and the parents are irresponsible, they might be terrified to lose her assistance—especially if there could be certain aspects of their affairs they would not be prepared to reveal to a stranger's eyes. Add to this a deep possessiveness toward the offspring in question and the parent could lose all reason, could they not?"

Icy water dripped inside the neck of her cloak. "I don't know what you mean by that."

"You do if you think about it."

She didn't want to think about it.

"Perhaps it would seem a good solution to try to arrange a marriage with someone who could also be controlled. Someone malleable. Someone who had already shown an inability to separate from their own parents' domination. These parents might be good friends of the first parents. They might spend a great deal of time together—forcing their children together. Especially once the threat, the threat of the one who might have taken the darling child away— once *he* was gone."

"Gray," she whispered. "You can't mean this."

"Then, of course, it would be such a bitter disappointment if everything they thought had been so perfectly managed— even if the substitute marriage hadn't been pulled off— but if they believed they were rid of the threat and then he came back. What would they feel? Anger? Would they—or even one of them—pretend not to know this man who returned from the dead? Would the doting parent speak of there never having been an understanding about marriage, even though he himself persuaded the young couple to wait for an official betrothal until the young man returned from a journey he was forced to make?"

"Stop this at once!"

"I told you you would hate me. And, of course, there was that comment that the father of the young woman in question made, that he would see the man dead before he'd see him married to the daughter. Even though you heard your own mother accuse me of what I had not, at that point, done. She accused me of suggesting she and your father had something to do with what happened to me in the West Indies. But I honestly hadn't made that accusation, Min. She was rushing in because she was desperate. She thought that she could call my bluff and make sure no one would ever believe my story."

Minerva wanted to rest her head on the horse's soaked neck. She wanted to wrap her arms around it and slip away from consciousness. When she awoke, this would all have been a nightmare.

"You yourself told me about the McSporrans. They spoke of having to get rid of me. If I remained, I would ruin them. Why? Because they expected to benefit from the marriage, too. Their son would be a docile mate for you, agree to live at Willieknock, no doubt, and allow you to continue as your parents' right hand? And your parents, now that their pockets are so deep, would make sure the McSporrans never wanted for anything either."

"You don't *know* any of this. And it's not true."

"Of course you don't want to believe it. But you may have to in time."

"You think my parents tried to have you murdered in the West Indies?"

"Probably."

"And then tried again with that *seed* you say you saw on a sweet?"

"I did see it. I still have it in a safe place. And, yes, that's what I think."

She attempted to wheel her horse away. Gray held it fast.

"How could they do such things? *Think*, Gray. How?"

"Connections they made for the purpose."

Tears ran into the melted snow on her face. Her vision blurred. She didn't care. And she didn't care that her throat burned. "What connections?"

"Your father goes away, doesn't he? Regularly?"

"To sell paintings. He has shows and sells paintings. He's very famous."

"Is he? Well, we'll not pursue that. I think he used one of his trips to meet someone who would help him."

"Who?"

"The men who are now at Maudlin Manor. The men who so wanted to get their hands on your cloak today but took Iona's by mistake. They'd heard something about last night and wanted to make sure no part of that damnable piece of sugared poison was still in your pocket."

"A fantastic story."

"Fantastic indeed. I was meant to die last night. *Again.* I thank God I saved you. I cannot tell you yet what is exactly the story about Clack and his friends, but they are some part of it."

"Perhaps they are." They could be. They were strange and had no reason to be here at all. "Mama and Papa also think them strange, Gray. They have said as much."

"I'm sure they would say just that."

"You will not hear me. You have made up your mind.

When I told them about the poison, and how you had saved me, they . . ."

Gray held his head high and stared into her eyes. "You told your parents?"

She swallowed with great difficulty. "They were horrified. And grateful to you."

"Were they really? Grateful to me, I mean?"

"Yes. Yes! Papa said he must thank you personally."

"Yet I don't recall that he rushed to do so. But Clack and Meaner rushed to Drumblade, didn't they?"

"No."

"They did rush—"

"No, I will not believe that after I told my parents you saved my life, they went to those men."

"You will not believe it." His laugh was mirthless.

"No. My parents were distraught by it all. Mama was afraid she would have to take to her bed. Papa even asked if you had taken any of the poison at all—and if you were safe."

"*Did* he?"

"*Yes.* Mama almost fainted."

"After she knew I wasn't dead?"

It couldn't be true. "She was overwhelmed, I tell you. And Papa said he would deal with the impossible . . . fools." She trembled and felt weak.

"Just so," Gray said, his nostrils narrowed.

Every word she spoke could be twisted. Gray sat astride his mount, his eyes colder than the ice spicules that assaulted her skin as he found her parents guilty of trying to murder him.

"You are wrong," Minerva told him.

He adjusted his gloves and looked to the layers of low clouds. "You won't believe it."

"I cannot." She loved him, but she could not betray her family. "They are my parents."

Gray's arm snaked out, and he gripped the back of her neck. Fight as she might, Minerva could not stop him from kissing her. His kiss, hard, cruel even, pressed her lips to her teeth. Snow mixed with ice pricked her face and melted to mingle with her tears, and with the taste of Gray.

"Come away with me now," he gasped when he could no longer continue to kiss her and breathe. "I agree that I am at grave risk here, so leave with me. You said that's what you wished to do."

He framed her face and studied her mouth. When their eyes met, the harshly fervent glitter in his made Minerva cry, "Gray! Please, you are wrong about this. How can I go with you when you are so wrong about my family?"

The glitter softened, but not the almost demonic fervor she saw in him. "Once we are married, it may be safe to return eventually," he told her. "They will not dare to try to hurt us then."

"You're asking me to . . ." A thundering pounded in her ears with such force as to make her almost deaf.

She raised her crop, and would have struck him had he not caught her wrist.

"We are meant to be together, Minerva," he said, working the crop from her clenched fingers. "Nothing can change that. Fate brought us together. Fate saved me when I should have died. Not once, but twice. It's time for me to make you my wife."

Gasping, too cold to feel anything but the despair with which she must somehow make peace, she pulled on her horse's rein, made the animal dance sideways before it turned downhill.

"Minerva," Gray shouted. "Don't try to leave me. You'll never be able to do it. You will be my wife."

"Never." The horse plunged downhill toward Willieknock. "Not unless your heart softens. Until then, stay away from me, Gray Falconer."

Chapter Nineteen

Porteous Arbuckle's cluttered studio delighted Eldora. Here, as in no other part of Willieknock she had yet seen, was an atmosphere that hinted at something deep, and dark, and luscious. This, Eldora thought, was where the true nature of Porteous Arbuckle must dwell. Even if one did wonder why there was quite such an abundance of furnishings.

"Beautiful," she said, looking down on him from her considerably greater height. Really, why must all the men she had to deal with be short? "Your superior taste shines in this place. It's magnificent. Such colors. Such *undercurrents*, Porteous. You are a voluptuary, my dear, aren't you, a lover of exquisite pleasure?"

The pompous little man literally swelled with delight. "Ah, my dear Eldora. *You* are a woman of superior taste. *You* are magnificent." His lips grew moist, and she saw his eyes survey her from the shadow of his affected dark spectacles. "We shall make something spectacular together, you and I."

Arbuckle laughed, and his laugh soared higher, and higher.

Eldora pretended to be engrossed in a vast chinoiserie wall hanging on one vast wall. She inclined her head and pointed to a face peeping from a temple door. "She seems to be watching for someone. A lover, perhaps? But in a temple?"

Porteous Arbuckle laughed again, and Eldora glanced covertly at him. Over his arm trailed a length of fine silk the color of ripe peaches. This silk he fingered, and occasionally rubbed against his cheek.

"Very few are admitted to this room," he said, and his brows rose above the spectacles. "Almost no one, in fact."

"Oh, all of your models, surely."

He shook his head, no, and his disquieting laugh fluted upward once more. "Not at all. Absolutely not, in fact. See through here. Come along, come along." He waved her forward. He lifted a corner of the hanging to reveal a door. "There. You look through there and you'll see where they come. They don't even know of the existence of this haven. Ha, ha!"

The place he indicated was a peephole, and Eldora obediently took a peek. She looked through the door into a small cubicle on the other side. Large enough to contain only a chaise, a dressing table, and a full-length mirror, she saw no sign of painting equipment. Frowning, she turned to Porteous—and found him standing so close, she jumped. "You can't possibly paint in there," she told him. "There's no room."

Once more his cackle pealed out. "No, no, no. That's where I study my subjects. As they prepare for me, I prepare to make the best of them. Much the best to observe without being observed. That way they are natural and I get some idea of the way they move. Movement is so important in the piece. I achieve my extraordinary sense of movement because I have had the opportunity to observe *unobserved*."

Eldora looked again. "This is where your models change, isn't it?"

He giggled and, when she glanced at him, clasped his hands together and nodded enthusiastically. "Yes, yes, exactly. From this vantage point, when they are unconscious of my presence and therefore *natural*, I gain the priceless gift of knowing how flesh moves over muscle and bone, of catching those small, infinitely erotic nuances when a woman looks at herself and appreciates her sexuality. Those are the moments when she is most naked, most vulnerable. From these elements I gain the *essence* of my subject."

The old lecher was a Peeping Tom in disguise. A very thin disguise. Eldora smiled and nodded.

Warmed to his topic, Porteous continued, "Then I do preliminary work with them in a studio outside that little room."

Eldora stepped back. "Then why do you also need all this?" This room—in fact, all of Porteous's domain—was in a wing of the house that seemed closed off. Here he was surrounded by fabulous furnishings crowded so close together one wondered why he didn't choose to display at least some pieces to better advantage elsewhere.

Porteous pouted. He actually pouted.

"I've offended you?" Eldora asked, amused.

"No, no, no. Not at all." He flipped a wrist. "How could you know that I derive great inspiration from being surrounded with those things I hold most precious. I could not possibly waste such exquisiteness on . . . Well, need I be more direct? You have met my family."

She must tread carefully. Success might rest in giving him the impression that she agreed with every word he spoke without actually agreeing at all. "You didn't answer my question about the temple girl."

"A coquette," he said simply. "She has chosen to hide inside the temple. To hide from a pursuer, but she wants to be found. In that she is no different from any woman. They are all deceitful. They all use their bodies to get what they want. That is my task, to reveal to the world the true nature of the female behind her mincing and fluttering, her downcast eyes."

"And what of me? How will you portray me?"

"You." He made a circle around her, his steps exaggerated. "You I will ask to disrobe where I cannot see you. This is because I believe I know a great deal about you, about what you want from life. And most particularly, from *men*."

She pressed her lips together and waited.

"You want a great deal from men, don't you, Eldora? You have so much to offer, but the price is high. Am I to discover exactly how high?"

He was more astute than she had guessed, which could prove a problem. She untied the ribbons that secured her pink tulle bonnet and removed it, setting it aside. "It is true that I believe you and I should enter into an arrangement, Porteous. A mutually beneficial arrangement." She lowered her eyes to his. "We both have a great deal to gain . . . or a great deal to lose." The import of what she'd suggested hovered between them, and she felt no doubt but that she was taking a risk that must be taken by drawing him into a conspiracy.

Porteous buried his face in the peach-colored silk, and when he raised his head, his spectacles slipped to the end of his nose and his eyes were closed as if in transporting ecstasy. "Please put this on," he said, his voice suddenly sharp. "Nothing but this. And take your hair down. Then you will sit . . . here." He patted the saddle of an old wooden rocking horse, its once-bright paint cracked.

"You're the artist," Eldora said, looking for a place to change.

"Over there," Porteous said. "Behind the armoire."

"It's beautiful," Eldora said of the piece, looking more closely. "Fabulous, in fact."

"Boulle Marquetry," Porteous said, his chest expanding with pride. "Brass and tortoiseshell. See the scrolled foliage, the geometric borders. Priceless."

"No doubt," Eldora said, her curiosity piqued. "Tell me

about that cabinet. The one with all the drawers and the mother-of-pearl."

A crafty expression came over Porteous's undistinguished face. "You must promise to forget you ever saw any of these treasures of mine. There are those who would seek to take them from me, but I will protect them at all costs."

"I promise." He was, she understood, the son of a gardener. He'd happened to meet and marry Janet, the then heiress to a Glasgow merchant who owned Willieknock. In other words, Porteous had come into his marriage with little or nothing, and Janet could hardly have been fabulously wealthy, certainly not wealthy enough to have a collection such as this.

Porteous was opening and closing the small drawers Eldora had mentioned. "Case furniture," he remarked. "Very opulent. This one was probably made by Pierre Golle. It is ebony and gilt. Then there is the tortoiseshell, of course, and the mother-of-pearl you spoke of. Some ivory. Note the ebony legs on which the cabinet stands. The details about the feet are gold." He clasped his hands before him and hummed.

"So lovely," Eldora said, careful not to break his trance while she surveyed the large, high-ceilinged room with its crush of obviously precious furniture that seemed entirely out of place. Like a storehouse, she decided, surprised at the thought. A storehouse for the purpose of hiding these things.

"I know what you're thinking."

His words startled her. He'd removed the spectacles, and his small, bright eyes stared hard into hers.

Eldora giggled and inclined her head. "You only think you do because you consider all women transparent. I, Porteous Arbuckle, am a very complicated woman."

"Indeed you are. A complicated woman with a complicated agenda. We shall do exceedingly well together. And, in exchange for my silence, I will be assured of yours?"

She considered him and said slowly, "I doubt I'll have

any choice. But you didn't have to bring me here to your treasure house, where there is obviously something that makes you vulnerable."

"No!" He twirled on the toes of his satin slippers. "Nothing that makes me vulnerable. All of this is mine. Bought and paid for. It is not I who am in a pretty fix about such matters. Put them from your head, though, because I have told you to. And take off your clothes as you've been told. We have work to do." Immediately he turned to preparing a canvas and arranging the tools of his art.

Trembling with anticipation, Eldora swept behind the armoire and did as he asked. The man did not appeal to her as anything but a male who showed the promise of ingenuity. And she was bored with Cadzy, and angry with the potential destruction of her plans. A diversion would not go amiss.

She spared more than a few thoughts for the priceless treasures surrounding her. What could they mean? And who was in what Porteous termed "a pretty fix" because of them?

The silk was the thinnest she had ever held in her hands. It had the quality of gossamer, and she judged it to have come from India perhaps. A sheen almost of gold caught the light as she lifted what was a long, sleeveless tunic over her head.

A mirror would have pleased her.

Looking down at herself, she noted how the fabric settled on her nipples and how the large openings for her arms—the garment was little more than two pieces of material stitched at the shoulders and sides and with a deep V descending between her breasts—the large openings for her arms moved easily to show more than would cause Porteous to strain his imagination. Stitching at the sides barely reached the tops of her limbs, but the creation was voluminous and she could, with care, cover herself adequately—as long as she decided she wished to do so.

Unbraiding her hair as she went, Eldora left the shield of

the armoire and walked, barefoot, toward the large rocking horse. "How will I climb on it?" she asked.

Porteous turned from his paints and brushes, and his smile left her in no doubt that what he saw pleased him greatly. "Use this," he said, pulling forward a black lacquer stool.

"May I have a mirror?" she asked, avoiding his eyes. "Just so I may see that I'm doing as you wish."

Wordlessly, he shifted a pier glass framed with jade and ebony in front of the horse's head.

What she saw excited Eldora—although she thought she would be more provocative without clothes, of course. "Should I take this off first?" She plucked at the tunic.

He shook his head. "Not now."

Eldora stepped onto the stool and arranged herself, sitting sideways, on the horse. She was grateful that its back was broad or she would have been at considerable difficulty to find any degree of comfort and safety. "Like this?" she asked, feeling less than graceful.

"Astride," he said shortly, turning to his paints.

She frowned at his back, opened her mouth to protest, but decided against saying anything at all. Rather she contrived to do as he asked. A small thrill ran through her. He had something special in mind, this odd little sensualist.

"Cadzow still doesn't know you intend to give him such a gift?" Porteous asked.

"Oh, no!" She laughed and tossed back her hair, reveling in how it fell, long and thick and wavy to her waist. "Absolutely not. It will be a complete surprise."

"On, or before, the wedding night?"

What was he suggesting? "That is yet to be decided."

"Depending on how quickly you can persuade him to the altar?"

For a second she didn't answer. Then anger flared. "He will go to the altar whenever I'm ready," she told him. "That is my decision, not his."

"So you say."

"So it is."

"*So* you say."

He looked at her, approached her and lifted a handful of her hair. He put it to his face as he had the silk, and breathed in with closed eyes.

And while he breathed in, he covered one of her breasts, on top of the silk, covered and weighted it, and sighed, and pinched the nipple.

Eldora let out a little shriek of surprise. To keep her skin from the wood, she'd made certain some of the silk covered the horse's saddle. And, to her shocked amazement, that silk had grown instantly wet.

"Is this how I should sit?" she asked, breathless and strangely disturbed.

"Be silent."

She closed her mouth and watched him, fascinated. He continued to rub her hair over his face, and to fondle first one, then her other breast, always keeping the silk between them and his hand.

"Let me take it off," she whispered, tension and desire mounting in her flesh. "It will make it easier."

"What will it make easier? How could you possibly know the working of an artist's mind? You will do as I tell you. Silence. Until I give you permission to speak."

Silence while he molested her in the name of art, Eldora thought, smiling secretly.

"You have a plan," he said, then, "Do not answer. I am merely speaking my thoughts aloud. Your breasts will be spectacular on my canvas. I will make of them even more than they are."

"You won't need to," she snapped.

His eyes opened, and there was no sign that he had been too swept away to know his mind. "I will make these even more than they are," he said sonorously, and squeezed.

Eldora gasped, but said nothing.

"Slide back somewhat and lie over the horse's neck. Loop

your arms around his head. Cover his eyes. After all, we would not want him to see you in the mirror."

She stared at him but did her best to obey. The result was not at all comfortable, but at least she knew he must now be looking at some of the flesh he had yet to see uncovered.

He didn't touch the exposed side of her breast. His hand went instead to her bottom, where he smoothed each rounded cheek, lingered on the cleft between.

Minutes later, when Eldora began to feel bruised from the hard angles of the wooden horse, she shifted irritably. The man had touched every part of her—as long as it was covered by silk. "What's the matter with you?" she asked, unable to keep silent any longer. "What do you think you're doing?"

"I am," he told her, "imprinting the shape of you on my mind so that, as I work, I will know exactly how you look."

"Let me take off this thing, and you'll *see* exactly how I look. That, I assure you, is a sight you will never forget."

"Sidesaddle now," he told her. "A hat? I wonder. One moment. Arrange yourself, please."

Grumbling, Eldora heaved herself to sit sidesaddle, raising the inner knee to an exaggerated height as if the wooden horse did indeed sport a lady's saddle.

Porteous returned with a toque of vast proportion and placed it on her head. Fashioned of huge puffs of stiffened red satin topped with curling red feathers and loops of red gauze ribbon that trailed over her left shoulder, she knew it must make her ridiculous, and she said so.

"You are wrong," he told her. "When I paint you, it will be without the tunic. The fabulous hat will lend an air of wickedness, of flaunting all convention. It will be as if you arrived at a formal ball naked, except for this creation on your head—and with your hair trailing."

Yet he did not want her naked while he painted her?

"I am almost ready to begin my sketch," he said. "And

while I sketch, I shall ask you questions and you will answer. Nothing more."

"I shall bloody well say whatever I please," she told him, tired of his charade.

"Really? And what if I go to Cadzow Falconer and tell him you forced your way in here and tried to make me make love to you?"

She stared at him until her eyes watered. "He would never believe you."

With great deliberation, he approached until, with his arm extended, he could slip his brush beneath the hem of the tunic.

Eldora's mouth fell open, and she couldn't make a sound.

Porteous Arbuckle proceeded to work the bristles of his brush into her most sensitive folds, and while he did so, he kept his attention on her face. He brushed her *there* with unerring certainty, flicking the bristles back and forth until she panted and made a grab for the brush.

Instantly he withdrew it.

"No," she gasped. "No, don't stop, please."

"You like it?" He laughed suddenly, searingly, the sounds warbling wildly higher and higher. "You *like* it! So I shall do what you like, of course. It will give me more to put upon my canvas."

Assuming a fencer's position, once more he found the spot with his brush and used more and more pressure until Eldora bounced on the wooden saddle.

"Wonderful," Porteous shrieked. "Better than I could have hoped for. What a seat. What rhythm. Oh, oh, careful, we wouldn't want to break my brush, little flower. Hold still a moment, and I shall please you more."

Her bosom heaving, Eldora forced herself to sit still, but when Porteous inserted a less slender brush, and its handle, far inside her, and made up for in motion what the object lacked in size, she all but fell to the floor.

"Aha," he squealed. "And aha. And aha!" And with each

"aha" he made an elegant thrust, then withdrew to finish his performance where he knew it could now be easily accomplished.

Eldora screamed, and bucked on her sturdy mount. "Marvelous," she panted. "Oh, Porteous, can't we lie down somewhere? Anywhere." But then she was swept to the peak of all feeling and couldn't speak anymore, and when she slumped forward, he promptly removed the brush and went to his blank canvas.

The pulse quivered into her center and she held fast to the tattered bridle, and caught sight of herself in the glass: the grotesque red hat on her wild hair, the paint streaked on her face, the frightful clash of almost orange silk with the crimson headpiece. And there was no doubt that her reflection showed her to be a woman in the throes of sexual satisfaction—near satisfaction.

"It wouldn't take long," she told Porteous, wheedling, taking off the hat. "You would never forget it, I assure it."

"Let us begin the sketch. And our business."

"I shall complain to Cadzow."

"Of what?"

"That you molested me. That you agreed to paint a portrait for me to give him, then took advantage of me."

"Oh, I don't think you will do that. Especially since Janet is present to be my witness. Given the exceedingly delicate possibilities with these things, she is always present."

"Janet?"

"My wife. Janet, dear, I think I need you to protect my virtue."

To Eldora's complete mortification, Janet Arbuckle, dressed in demure gray gros de Naples with a simple, lightly ribboned white lawn cap on her hair, came from behind a chinoiserie screen, glanced at Eldora, and sat primly on a beautiful little gilt-and-brocade chair.

"Ooh, you're hateful," Eldora said through her teeth,

plopping herself more securely on the horse and making certain her breasts, and every other part of her, were covered.

"Only careful, we assure you," Janet said. "Now, let's begin with our arrangements, my dear. I know you have certain things you wish to accomplish. And so do we."

Eldora raised her chin and wouldn't say a word.

"Very well," Janet said conversationally. "You have already told us you are dissatisfied with your lot. You planned to marry the heir to the Falconer empire. Now, with the inconvenient return of Gray, you see your dreams slipping away. Am I correct?"

Really, this was more than embarrassing. "I shall not waste time on pretty speeches," Eldora declared. "Gray Falconer must be disposed of."

"Oho, so direct," Porteous said. He set down his brush and returned to stand before her. He looked closely at her breasts. "Starting to sag. That is unfortunate, but such immense size does tend to cause that problem. I can correct it."

"Well!" Eldora placed her hands on her hips and thrust her breasts high. "I hardly think there is much to correct."

Porteous giggled. "You are too modest. There is a great deal to correct."

The wretched Janet sat with her hands demurely clasped in her lap and her eyes lowered, and said not a word.

"Tell us what you have in mind?" Porteous said.

She disliked feeling that they could govern her. "It's a simple matter, but it will benefit all of us. I have already explained the way payment will work. You will receive a vast sum for this portrait."

"It will be worth a vast sum."

"Yes, well, that remains to be seen."

"What you did not explain," Janet said, speaking softly, "was how we should remove Gray from the picture."

"There is something I wish to request from you first," Porteous said. "Some time ago, Cadzow and I had a disagreement. A small disagreement, it's true, but I have always regretted it. Could I ask you to intercede on my behalf?"

The request genuinely surprised her. "Why?"

"Because I want it so," he shouted, slashing at the canvas. "That is all you need to know. Go to him and ask him to let the past go. Tell him it is forgotten by me, and I would consider it a great favor if he would also put it behind him."

"What happened?"

"Do *not* question me on this. Understand that if any of this plan of yours is to succeed, it is imperative that Cadzow get past his anger with me."

"He's never mentioned being angry with you."

"He wouldn't. He has his own reasons not to. Do as I ask."

She fidgeted. "Tell him you wish to let the past die? To go forward as friends?"

"*Exactly.* I could not have put it better myself, my dear. Can you do that?"

"Yes," she said hesitantly. "If that is important to you."

"It is. It's also important that he should get my assurance that I am prepared to forget every unpleasantness from the past if he is. Will you remember that?"

"I am not an idiot."

"Very well, then, it would seem we are on our way to salvation."

Eldora stared at him again, then at Janet Arbuckle. The anxiety she heard in Porteous's voice was mirrored in his face, and in Janet's, who said, "Shall we be able to deal with the other, do you think?"

"Hush," Porteous said. "That is a separate matter and quite safe from all this, I assure you."

"Even if they do something foolish again and—"

"*Hush,* I tell you. Not another word."

"No, Porteous," Janet said, looking at her hands in her lap once more.

Eldora had no idea what they were talking about, and she

didn't care. "Are we secure here?" she asked, looking around and wondering how many more listeners were secreted behind pieces of furniture. "There is no one else?"

"No one else," Porteous said. "You have my word."

As if his word would comfort her. "Very well, then. You already know what is of the utmost importance—to you and to me."

The Arbuckles looked at each other, and Janet nodded.

"It would be worth a great deal to you if Gray Falconer were no longer in a position to take over the family fortunes, as it were."

Eldora tried to seat herself more comfortably, and to ignore the damp silk upon which she sat. "It would be worth a great deal to both of us. We need not go into the reasons again. What must be discussed is how this is to be accomplished."

"We will listen to your ideas," Porteous said, and began to apply rapid lines to the canvas without as much as glancing in her direction.

Eldora was accustomed to having people take notice of her wishes and follow them. This offhand treatment did not at all please her. "Tell me about those savages at Maudlin Manor," she said, hoping to disquiet the Arbuckles. "What are they doing here?"

"Doing here?" Porteous frowned at her. "Why would I have any idea? Clack has leased the property from the owner for an indefinite period. Seems to have exceedingly deep pockets and to be intent on ingratiating himself with the local populace. There, that's all I know."

She didn't believe him, but the subject could wait. Cadzow had clearly been disturbed by Clack and his henchmen, but that could well be because Cadzow-the-holy felt himself in the presence of some evil, foreign element that might present danger to his soul if he didn't tame and save it.

"It would seem to me that this ridiculous salon Clack's

holding will provide a perfect opportunity for us to carry out our plan."

"Plan?" Janet said suddenly. "What plan? We have no plan. All we have are silly, empty promises from you that if we help you dispose of Gray Falconer, you will pay us a fortune. And you have said that somehow our Minerva will help accomplish this feat."

"Well, then," Eldora said, feeling much more sure of herself again, "so we do understand each other. As far as we have gone, anyway. The rest will be details, nothing but details. Those two are besotted with each other, so this is my idea. We will contrive to have Gray and Minerva *elope*—"

"Oh, Arbuckle!" Janet jumped up from her chair. "What can she mean? Elope? The shame of it."

"Yes," Eldora said, glaring at the woman. "Elope. And to accomplish this it must seem that there is resistance to any idea of a marriage. Then the notion must be planted that the salon will be the perfect cover for them to make their getaway."

"I don't want my daughter to elope," Janet moaned. "Oh, the shame of it, the shame of it."

"I believe you mentioned that before, my love," Porteous said mildly. "Several times, in fact. How do you intend that this should be accomplished, Eldora?"

She had given the matter a great deal of thought. "We persuade Gray that for Minerva to remain would be dangerous." She smiled at her own brilliance. "After all, from what I've heard about this silly bumwallow nonsense, that shouldn't be difficult to impress upon him. You would only have to speak—desperately—about how you perceive her to be in grave danger, then state that you will not hear of her marrying him because he obviously has some connection to whatever criminal did the deed, and you won't have to do more. They will be looking for a means to escape together."

"Speculation," Janet said. "You cannot be certain. My

daughter is very principled and would not wish to upset her mother."

"Porteous," Eldora said. "I have an idea that I was loath to mention, but I think I'd best do so."

He continued to scatter lines on the canvas in an almost frenzied manner.

"Go to Gray and tell him you fear your wife will try to find a way to stop the marriage."

"Porteous!" Janet was on her feet at once. "Don't you dare do such a thing."

Undeterred, Eldora continued. "Tell him that you think he is Minerva's salvation, that she can never be happy without him, and that you will aid in their escape."

"Don't want to," he said.

Eldora ground her teeth. "But you must, or all will be lost."

"All *is* lost," Janet whined. "Porteous, I believe we are lost."

"Hold your tongue, woman. If I tell young Falconer this, why should he believe me when I've already made it clear I don't want to lose my . . . that I don't want my daughter to marry him."

"That you don't want to lose your daughter," Eldora said softly. "That's it, isn't it? You need her too much. Cadzy told me how she keeps you from financial ruin with her steady head. No matter. That is no business of mine. You will not lose her anyway."

"You won't forget to mention the little matter of allowing bygones to be bygones?" Porteous said. "To Cadzow?"

"You have my word."

"And I am to talk Gray into an elopement stating that concern for my daughter's safety is the reason?"

"Exactly."

"Oh, Porteous," beastly Janet wailed. "There must be another way."

"Name it," her husband said. "We are within a whisker of ruin."

"How can you be certain that even if everything goes as planned, we will be able to deal with all that money and—"

"We will deal with it if it becomes necessary, which it may not."

Janet rocked in an agitated manner and said, "You never would confront the truth, Arbuckle. In a matter of days, we *will* have to confront it."

"How much do you owe?" Eldora asked, not expecting an answer.

"Twenty thousand guineas," Porteous said, stopping to look at her. "That's what we need, and not a penny less will do."

"Twenty thousand guineas." Eldora looked away and repeated the sum to herself. Of course, Cadzow had that and a great deal more. With Gray out of the way, such a sum would be nothing, but how to get him to give it to her? She swallowed. "You shall have it."

Janet gave a cry and clapped her hands over her mouth.

Porteous cast her a triumphant stare and said, "There, there, my dear. All will be well."

"Indeed," Eldora agreed, finally so uncomfortable that she slid from the back of the rocking horse and walked stiffly between the pieces of furniture. "We have only a few days to finalize our plans. For this to work, you two must pretend to be at odds. You, Porteous, will pretend to disagree with Janet's hardness in the matter."

"Why shouldn't it be me who has softened?" Janet said. "Far more believable."

"Not at all," Porteous said.

Eldora considered before saying, "She's right. It is you who so desperately wants your daughter to continue as slave to your fortunes. You have allowed her to run matters for you since she was old enough to do so. Cadzow informed me of this."

"None of his damned business," Porteous said, but he didn't say he wouldn't acquiesce to the idea of Janet being the one to implement the escape.

"So," Janet said. "I will go to Minerva as her mother and friend and tell her I understand love. Which I do. And I shall tell her the only way around her father's implacable decision to stop the marriage is for them to elope."

"Precisely," Eldora agreed.

"And then I will suggest that during all the revelry of Clack's salon will be the perfect time to make their getaway."

"Yes. They will be allowed to get well away from Ballyfog. No doubt they will make for some convenient spot, find the necessary witnesses, and marry."

"We could stop them and have Falconer arrested for abducting her," Porteous said. "Why shouldn't that be sufficient?"

"Because," Eldora said, trying for a patience she didn't feel, "he would still be alive and would eventually return. We don't want him to return. Ever. We want him dead, and so he shall be. Did you try to poison him?"

"With *bumwallow* seeds?" Porteous asked, apparently shocked. "How would I know of such things? If such things exist."

"Gray says they do."

"And perhaps Gray was inventing some reason to make Minerva so grateful she would do whatever he suggested."

"Perhaps," Eldora said, although she did not think so, and the notion that there were forces at work in Ballyfog about which none of them knew anything of substance bothered her considerably.

"I will help Gray and Minerva run away from the salon," Janet said, looking a deal paler than when she had first appeared. "Then what will happen?"

"Then they will be followed. An opportunity will be found to separate Minerva from Gray and she will be told it has been learned that he has no intention of marrying her, only ruining her reputation because he hates her parents."

"This is dreadful," Janet said, evidently entering entirely into the spirit of the tale. "My poor daughter."

"Quite. And while she is diverted, Gray will be captured and killed. The apparent victim of robbers. Simple as that No possible connection to any of us."

Both Arbuckles looked at her.

"It's what has to happen if we are all to get our just rewards," she said.

"Killed," Janet said.

"Killed," Porteous echoed.

"Drastic," Janet said.

"Drastic," Porteous agreed.

"Can either of you think of an alternative?"

"Why did he have to come back?" Janet said.

She eyed them disgustedly. "The fact is that he has come back. Thanks to some sort of carelessness somewhere. But I don't imagine you want me to delve too deeply into that subject."

Porteous took her by the arm and yanked her close. "What do you mean by that?"

She swallowed. "Nothing really. Only that I find it strange that as long as he was supposedly disposed of thousands of miles from Ballyfog, you had no difficulty with the concept. But you become squeamish about doing the job here instead."

"Are you suggesting you think we had something to do with what happened to Gray out there?"

Eldora knew when to back away from a difficult topic. "Not at all. I was merely making a point about the difference between events that occur out of sight, out of mind, as it were, and those that are close by."

"It won't be too close by, will it, Porteous?" Janet asked.

He looked at Eldora and said, "I don't think I recall your

telling me exactly how the final stage of this plan of yours was to be accomplished."

She contrived to appear innocent—not an easy feat—and shook her head as if she had no idea what he might mean.

"How?" he persisted.

Janet went to her husband's side and threaded an arm beneath his elbow. "Yes, kindly tell us how this shall be done."

"I told you," Eldora said. "At Clack's silly salon. His masquerade *saloon*. You will advise Minerva and Gray on the best time for them to effect their escape. Provide them with transportation. Decide how and where best to intercept them. I should think that might be best once they have stopped for the night, which they must probably do before they're able to find someone to marry them. Especially if they leave Maudlin Manor late, and you will have to ensure that that is the case."

"*We* will have to ensure?" Janet said. "Porteous, she has told us what must be done. Now she expects *us* to be entirely responsible, and all for her benefit."

"For the benefit of us all." This wasn't working as well as she'd hoped. "Surely the matter of engaging someone to shoot Gray will be simple."

Janet's hands flew to her mouth. "*Shoot* Gray. Oh, dear. Oh, no, I absolutely cannot have any part in such a thing."

"Even if it means saving everything you hold dear?" Eldora asked mildly.

"We are not . . . well, I assure you we have no experience of actually killing anyone firsthand."

"Only secondhand." She made her voice sweet, and smiled just as sweetly.

"Have a care what you say." Janet stood tall.

"But you are happy to put Gray in the way of having someone else kill him?"

The Arbuckles looked at each other.

"What of the McSporrans?"

"What of them?" Porteous said. "What do you mean by that question?"

"Oh," she shrugged, "I wondered if they might feel less squeamish. After all, didn't I hear mention that there was hope that Brumby, not Gray, might become Minerva's husband?"

"Very suitable," Janet said with tears in her eyes. "Brumby understands a parent's needs."

"Just so. And could it be that you and the McSporrans had gone so far as to plan such a match before Gray had the ill grace to come back?"

"Yes," Porteous said—roared, in fact. "That is exactly what we had planned. And very suitable, too. Everything was going exactly according to plan."

"Good," she told them softly. "And it can again now that we have our answer."

"What answer, you stupid female?"

She restrained a retort. "Brumby loves her, doesn't he?"

"Adores her." Tears dripped down Janet's plump cheeks. "He would never get over the loss of her."

"So there you have it, then. Brumby will be the savior of Minerva's honor. Why, that delightful Mrs. Hatch mentioned to me that she'd overheard a dreadful argument between Gray and Brumby in which Brumby called Gray out."

"Hatch is too free with her mouth," Janet said. "I shall have to speak to her."

"She was only repeating what she heard those orphans talking about. You're awfully good to tolerate such an inconvenience as two extra mouths to feed, by the way. Very inconvenient."

"My sister's children," Janet said stiffly. "I couldn't do less."

"Yes, well." No advantage was to be gained there, evidently. "As I was saying, Brumby called Gray out, or as good as called him out, but was put off by Minerva. Obviously the boy is passionate about her. He's the answer. Take him aside and tell him you've learned of Gray's plan to run off with Minerva. Say you have reason to believe he doesn't intend to do right by her, and send Brumby on his way—with a pistol. Just to protect himself, of course."

"Could work," Porteous said. "Brumby's always been a soft sort, though."

"Nice boy," Janet said, sounding defensive. "Nicer than one could expect of Drucilla McSporran's child."

"He'd be protecting the honor of a wronged young woman," Eldora pointed out. "Should be an easy enough matter to get around any unpleasantness. Cadzow could come forward as the grieving uncle still willing to plead for Brumby to be let off. We'd all talk about his fine character and how he'd saved poor, indecisive Minerva."

"My daughter's got a will of iron," Porteous said.

"No woman has a will of iron when she's swept off her feet," Eldora said, thinking at the same time that she'd never come close to being swept anywhere she didn't want to go. "So are we agreed?"

The Arbuckles stood close together and whispered. They took so long that Eldora began to fear she'd have more persuasion ahead of her, but then Porteous said, "Agreed." And Janet said, "We'll have to start setting our plan in motion at once. We'll deal with Brumby when we meet."

"From what I saw of Minerva and Gray together, your task there should be an easy one. Where's Minerva now?"

"Probably in her workroom," Porteous said. "She came back some time ago, but we don't see much of her if she's into an invention."

"One of her pieces of silliness," Janet added, taking a deep breath. "If I don't make a move, I shall lose my nerve."

"Make a move, then," Eldora urged her. "Go along and break it to her that you intend to help her and Gray. Then hurry back and tell us how it goes." She eyed the brush in Porteous's hand and calculated how long Janet might be gone. "I understand your anxiety, Janet dear. Take your time with your lovely daughter, convince her of your sympathy for her plight."

Janet drew herself up, straightened her shoulders, and said, "I shall do it at once, before I can weaken." She raised her chin and swished from the room.

Eldora hauled herself up onto the wooden horse's back again and hooked up a knee. "We should use our time well, Porteous. After all, I do need to have something to give Cadzow when I ask for all that money." All that money that she had no intention of requesting, since Cadzow would consider such a sum outrageous. But as long as the Arbuckles thought they would be paid, she'd get what she wanted.

"I think I have made a good start," Porteous told her.

"We have time for a little something, surely." She lowered her face and looked up at him. "A little more brushwork, perhaps." Why shouldn't she enjoy herself where she might?

Cadzow would give some money, but she would tell Porteous and Janet that he'd refused entirely. Then she'd keep the windfall. After all, the Arbuckles could hardly complain that they hadn't been paid for arranging a murder.

Porteous was regarding her so steadily that she felt uneasy. "Come along," she told him. "And bring that lovely brush. Or something else if you're tired of not having any fun yourself."

"I think not," he said. "I believe we should concentrate on the very serious decisions we've made. Come, we'll watch Janet's progress."

Without ceremony he hauled her from the rocking horse and pulled her behind him to the corridor outside the room. He led her what felt like an extremely long distance through many passageways while she grew cold and anxious in the thin, revealing piece of silk.

"Be absolutely silent," he told her when they arrived outside a door. He extinguished the light in the passage. "Not a sound."

"I can't go anywhere dressed like this. What would people think?"

"No one is going to see you."

He opened the door, and dim light showed inside. Very quickly he pushed her before him onto a gallery high above some other room, and closed the door again. Instantly he pulled her to sit on the floor, and he eased forward until he could peek downward.

"What—"

His hand, slapped over her mouth, stole her breath and she tasted blood on her tongue.

"Be silent," he whispered in her ear. "Or you will ruin everything. You will ruin yourself."

She nodded, afraid he would hurt her more if she did anything further to annoy him.

Following his lead, she pressed close to the floor and edged forward until she could see into a circular area below. All around them in the gallery were books. Books in bookcases, and stacked on tables, and heaped on the floor. And more books lined the lower walls, thousands of books.

At one side of the room into which she stared, Eldora saw Minerva Arbuckle and her mother. Minerva had her back to her parent and appeared to be fussing with rectangles of some thick, dark stuff. From a distance it resembled shiny, black wood.

"Minerva," Janet's voice rose to them. "Kindly leave that silliness alone and give me your attention."

"I'm tired, Mama," Minerva said. "I came here to clear my mind of everything. Can your discussion wait until tomorrow when I may be rested and more at peace?"

"Why aren't you at peace presently?" Janet asked. "Tell me at once. What has happened to upset you? Not that ridiculous poison nonsense, surely? That's all over."

"Please leave me alone, Mama."

"Very well. But first I must tell you what I want to do. I want to help you, darling."

"Very affecting," Porteous whispered. "Janet was always good at just the right touch at the right time."

Eldora wasn't interested in odes to Janet Arbuckle.

"Your father and I haven't been as sympathetic as we should have been. To you and Gray, that is."

"Not *now*," Minerva said, arranging her nasty-looking pieces of whatever in an overlapping row.

"I don't blame you for not trusting me. Oh, dearest, please find it in your heart to forgive me. I only want what's best for you, and frankly, perhaps I am not such a natural mother as I always thought. Perhaps I am too selfish in wanting to keep you for myself."

"We don't ever have to discuss this."

Eldora grew still. She didn't like the finality in Minerva's tone. "What's the matter with her?" she whispered to Porteous, who didn't answer.

"You love Gray Falconer. He loves you. We've been wrong not to help you be together and happy."

"Mother—"

"No, no, listen to me. Blame it on our fear for you. There has been so much about his absence and then his reappearance that has disturbed us. But we were less than supportive. I apologize. The thing that must be done is to assist the two of you to get away from here."

"Please, Mama, let me speak—"

"Not until I am finished. This poisoning thing is very frightening. Someone is evidently determined to get rid of him. How perfectly dreadful."

The sound of sobbing, Minerva sobbing, startled Eldora. She gasped, and Porteous put a hand over her mouth again.

"Oh, my darling," Janet said, clutching her daughter to her. "How we must have made you suffer. But that is all behind us. I am going to help the pair of you. In all the confusion of Clack's salon, you and Gray will have the perfect opportunity to get away. You will be long gone before anyone even notices. Your father will come around when I explain my reasons for helping you. Then, later, when your father and I have helped dear Cadzow get to the bottom of these dreadful events that have threatened Gray's life, you can come back to Ballyfog. Won't that be wonderful?"

Minerva's sobs became wails. She threw her arms around her mother and buried her face in her shoulder. It took minutes for Janet to calm the girl and say, "What is it, darling? Tell me at once. Are you just overwhelmed with relief?"

"You are so good," Minerva cried. "You are the best mother in the world, and I don't deserve you."

"Of course you do. You're the best daughter."

"I'm going to try to be."

"Of course you are. Go to Gray and tell him you've worked out a plan for Friday evening. Don't mention me. Not until it's all over, because I don't think he trusts me a great deal."

"Oh, Mama," Minerva cried afresh. "Dear, dear, Mama."

"She has always loved me best," Porteous whispered.

Eldora rolled her eyes and said, "Why doesn't Janet get on with it, and get it over with."

"We will make sure there are horses to hand," Janet said, "and plan the best moment for your departure."

Minerva stepped away from her mother. She sniffed, and found a handkerchief with which to mop her face. Then she said, "Mama, I shall not be going away with Gray Falconer. Not ever."

Porteous said, "Gad."

Eldora thought she'd misheard the little fool.

"Of course you will, dear. I've just told you you will. You love him, and I insist you be together."

"I do love him. More than my life."

"Well, then? Everything will be as you want it."

"I love him, Mama, but he's a pigheaded, hard-hearted, blind, thoughtless, infuriating—"

"He's done something to upset you?"

"Brilliant," Eldora muttered.

Porteous said, "Hush."

"To upset me? *Pah.* You have no idea, and please God you never will."

"Darling, be sensible. You love him. He loves you. For his safety, he needs to leave Ballyfog and go somewhere while we determine what exactly is the problem. What has occurred to bring such evil in his wake."

"Probably his evil, suspicious mind," Minerva said.

"Leave everything to us, dear one," Janet said. "Trust me to do this and you will be away and alone on Friday evening. From then on, your lives will change. You will have a wonderful new future before you."

"You are not listening to me, Mama," Minerva insisted. "If I am to have a wonderful new future, then you'd better find me someone wonderful to marry. I will never, ever consent to marry Gray Falconer."

Chapter Twenty

Maudlin Manor reeked of a certain glamorous decay. Gray had not been there since boyhood when he'd come home from school for the holidays and often had too much time on nimble hands. On more than one occasion he'd found his way into the rambling grounds, grounds that, even overgrown as they now were, retained hints of former glory.

"Someone ought to buy this place," Max said, walking about a room of huge proportions. "Damn shame. Going to ruin for want of care."

"If we keep our voices down, perhaps they'll forget we're here," Gray said. "That is, supposing our silent little doorkeeper remembers to tell them we arrived in the first place."

"Let's give it a few minutes, and hope he hasn't," Max agreed. "If no one comes, we can conduct our own reconnaissance until they catch up with us."

The rumpled creature, Micky Finish, had admitted them and brought them to this beautifully designed space, which might be a ballroom, or a large music room, or perhaps a gallery minus paintings—minus any furnishings at all, in fact.

Max stared upward and said, "Remember Rome?" knowing neither of them would forget a great many things about their visit to Italy, one of them being noble St. Peter's.

"Whoever painted these ceilings was also there," Gray remarked. "Magnificent. And the arches. Amazing it's all in relatively good condition, considering."

"You were never inside the manor before, then?"

Gray smiled a little. "Oh, yes, I was inside. Got in through the conservatory and crept about, but I wasn't as much into the finer things in those days. Although it was different then. The previous owner was still alive. On the Continent most of the time, I think. Yes, there was a piano at the end there, and pretty French chairs along the walls. Big, gilded demilunes between the windows, a great deal of porcelain and crystal, and so on. The snow makes it harder to see, but there's a fine terrace outside those doors, and steps down to lawns and gardens. The original house must have been built a couple of hundred years back."

"Alone, were you?"

"You, Max Rossmara, have a one-track mind. If you think I'm going to answer that, you're mistaken. Let's just say that I was diverted."

Max examined fine floral moldings in alcoves along the walls. The moldings were etched with gold leaf against stark white relief, and the walls were a deep rose color. "All right," he said, and made a purposeful stand in front of Gray, "do you suppose you could give me a hint about why we had to rush over here at such an ungodly hour? Other than to see who we might catch watering the bumwallow plants?"

Gray was already questioning his decision of the previous day to tell Max all, the whole fantastic and unedited story of what had happened in the West Indies, and his own theories about the how and why of those events. A change of topic might be in order. "The present owner is a niece or something of the former owner. Old chap died with no offspring of his own, I gather, and his bequest wasn't warmly enough greeted to warrant as much as a visit. Apart from the

McSporrans, it's been empty until this lot descended—Clack and his entourage, that is."

"Only house of any consequence available in the area, isn't it?"

Gray nodded. "Which I suppose is why Clack chose it, although why he chose Ballyfog itself defies the imagination, doesn't it?" He gave Max a hard look.

"Does it?" Max said, very softly. "I rather thought you'd decided he chose Ballyfog for a very good reason. You. You think Clack is in cahoots with the Arbuckles?"

Hearing the words spoken aloud lent them a certain ridiculousness. "Evidently you can answer your own questions, so I won't bother," Gray said.

"You're thoroughly bloody, Falconer. You do know that, don't you? Bloody, and probably a fool to boot."

Gray rounded on him. "Damn you. I . . . Forget it."

"It's Minerva, isn't it? When you were spilling all, there was something you didn't tell me about your loved one."

Of course it was Minerva. For two days he'd made repeated treks to that cold and haunted spot among the trees above Willieknock, praying that she'd be drawn there, too, even as he'd been certain she would not come.

"You may regret finally telling me the whole story—or as much as you know—but you did," Max said, still keeping his voice down, "and now that I know, I've got to urge you to leave Ballyfog, Gray. Someone here wants you dead."

"Silence," Gray said, and regretted his autocratic response. "Please, my friend, this is definitely a time when we have to assume the walls *do* have ears."

Max beckoned him close.

He could not, Gray told himself, countenance life without Minerva.

"Come here, Gray, would you?"

"Yes, surely." He went to Max and stood shoulder to shoulder with him, regarding his own boots. "Minerva and I had a disagreement."

"I knew it. What about?"

"I hardly think that an appropriate question."

"If it's likely to cost my friend his life, it's appropriate."

"She says she will not have me. I think she hates me."

Max looked sideways at him. "Minerva loves the air you breathe."

He thought about that. "Love and hate are remarkable companions, don't you think?"

"Not as remarkable as love and pride."

This time it was Gray who stared, but he knew his friend was not likely to elucidate further.

"You didn't, by any chance," Max said, "tell Minerva your theory about her parents wanting you dead?"

Gray sank his hands into his pockets.

"You did? Yes, of course you did. And you can't be sure she hasn't gone to them direct?"

"I don't believe she would." But he could not, in honesty, be certain.

"In heaven's name, Gray, why are you still here? I want you to leave Ballyfog at once. Today."

"No."

"Yes. We'll finish this call, because it can be made to look as if you are entrenched here in Ballyfog with no intention of leaving at all. The master of the most prime estate in the area come to visit tenants here. Jolly. Looking forward to the *saloon,* and all that. Of course, we'll keep our eyes and ears open as planned. But then we wait for nightfall and go."

"No."

"Damn it all, man," Max said through his teeth. "Don't you feel it possible that time is running out? Don't you think it could be that, as we speak, plans are being made to get rid of you? Someone paid for, and someone was paid to do, the job. A rash course such as only rash men would take. They will not stop until it is done."

"You're correct."

"The longer you stay . . . I'm correct? You agree, then?"

"I'm nobody's fool. I'm the one who escaped that island. The reason they didn't kill me then was that they were greedy. They kept me alive in case they ever wanted to prove that someone ought to continue paying for silence on the matter of my disappearance. Now I'm a danger to both parties—both those who paid and those who were paid."

"If you agree," Max said, bringing his green eyes near, "why aren't you doing what you should be doing? Putting as much distance between yourself and this place as possible? It's obvious that those who wish you dead are among those you look at somewhere here. Look at. Speak to. *Touch,* even. They must be terrified you'll find out who they are and go after them."

Gray grasped Max's shoulder and narrowed his own eyes. "First, I will not be driven from my home. Second, without Minerva, I will never leave."

Looking at Gray's hand on his sleeve, Max said, "If you're dead, you will lose any say in where you will or will not be."

"Without her, I might as well be dead."

Max turned forcefully from Gray. "A madman's words. No woman is worth a man's life."

Gray reached him in a single stride and spun him around. "You are wrong. Minerva is, and always will be, worth my life. I cannot go to Willieknock, but I can come here. And my purpose is to gauge whether Min has kept her counsel entirely—about our situation. I think Brumby and his parents should be a good measure of that, don't you? And I expect to encounter them here in due course."

Max squeezed Gray's arm. "Hear that?"

Whispering. In the fantastic foyer that rose through all three stories of the manor.

"I hear it," Gray said. "Let's spread out and admire the ceiling."

They were both gazing upward when Gray sensed they were no longer alone.

"I say," Max called. "Enough to make a man sick, isn't it?"

"Sick?"

"Wandering around with your neck half snapping."

Gray said, "Beautiful, though. Must have cost a mint."

"I assure you," said Silas Meaner's unmistakable nasal drawl, "that those murals are priceless. Too bad there's so little of substance around here that's of equal value."

Gray looked at the man. "Good morning to you. Max and I decided to come and pay our respects to Mr. Clack. We did give our cards to—"

"Micky," Meaner said. Today his coat was the yellow of lemons and his breeches black. Black dots scattered his white waistcoat. If he were a plumper man, Gray decided, there might be about him something of the bumblebee.

Clack, dressed exactly as he had been for his visit to Drumblade several days earlier, tottered back and forth, muttering incoherently.

"Not a good day," Meaner said, glaring, and thumping his silver stick against his chest. "Big party, y'know. Great deal t'do."

Clack reared up a few inches and said, "Arbuckle woman," and continued his unsteady progress before adding, "said she'd do. When do she do, that's the gist of it? Hinvitations out, damn 'n blast it. Time flew."

"Clack's in a bit of a state," Meaner said, superfluously. "I say, Clack, I told you it will all be done, didn't I?"

Once more the black mane rose and a cackle followed. " 'Ave I told you about Silas, then, gents? 'Ave I?"

"Well—"

"No need," Silas Meaner said, cutting Gray off. "Sorry we can't be more hospitable, gentlemen. Do enjoy the gardens as you leave."

"Ah, ha! Silas is my right 'and, 'e is." Clack slapped his knees and all but collapsed on the black-and-white marble floor. " 'E—'e's my right 'and. Just as well, eh? Can't be me left, 'cause 'e don't 'ave one." Clack snorted, while Meaner glowered.

"Too bad for you," Gray said. "Nasty accident, I suppose."

"Never did have a left hand," Silas said, his mouth thin between blond mustache and beard. He raised his chin and listened. "Born without it. One compensates. I hear more visitors, Clack."

Gray noted that Max had positioned himself slightly to his own rear, as if on guard.

Next to enter the big chamber were Micky Finish, holding Brumby's sleeve, and Minerva.

Gray felt himself stop breathing but was helpless to do anything about it.

"What's he doing here?" Brumby asked in surly tones, looking at Gray. "Get out now."

"Good morning to you," Max said. "I don't think we've been introduced. I'm Max Rossmara of Castle Kirkcaldy."

Brumby took his churlish frown from Gray for a brief instant. "If you're with him, I suggest you get yourself back there."

"Oh, Brumby," Minerva said, her voice faint. "Please don't."

"Hardly the way to treat a gentleman and a neighbor, what?" Meaner said, curling his upper lip to disclose long, narrow teeth. "Clack, you've got to do something about the servants. They're out of hand."

Clack was too occupied with peering at Minerva.

"I'm no servant," Brumby said, "and neither are my parents."

"What are you, then?" Meaner asked.

"We'd be obliged if you'd continue your domestic discussions at another time," Max said. "We only came to pay our respects. So—"

"My mother sent me," Minerva said clearly.

Gray couldn't look anywhere but at her. In the pale light

of a sunny, early-December morning, she appeared transparent. Thinner, he realized, gripped with remorse, then, as rapidly, with anxiety. She could be ill. That illness could have nothing to do with him, or with . . . She suffered, just as he did, and had lost interest in food and sleep. Dark marks underscored her deep blue eyes. Beneath the flower-trimmed brim of her blue bonnet, her brown hair shone. Gray's glance automatically swept downward. Today he glimpsed the hem of a very proper, blue cashmere dress.

He realized others had spoken, but had no idea what had been said.

He didn't care.

Minerva stared back at him with such sadness in her eyes that anger tinged his need for her. He was angry that the interference of malign forces had come between them.

". . . 'ave to 'ave chairs."

Gray heard Clack finish speaking and looked at the man.

" 'Eard me, did you, McSporran?" Clack said, apparently to Brumby. "*Chairs.* Can't hinvite nobility to sit on hair."

"You'll have to speak with my parents," Brumby said, with eyes only for Minerva. "Why don't you tell them what your mother wants to know, Min? Then we can get out of here." He finished with another evil glance in Gray's direction.

Had Minerva taken Brumby into her confidence?

She said, "Yes, yes. Hmm, my mother has asked me to approach you about certain matters relating to your gathering on Friday, Mr. Clack."

"Whatever, whatever. Do what she likes, she can. Everyone not coming, aren't they? Hmm?"

"Quite the reverse," poor Minerva said, her eyes wide. "Because of the lack of notice, Mama had doubts, but the response has been overwhelming. The only regret so far has come from Mrs. Goddard. And that's only a provisional regret. She hopes to find herself in better health by Friday, in which case she will be here."

"A hundred years old, if she's a day," Brumby said. "Probably afraid she'll have to turn down too many dance partners."

"Chairs," Clack said.

"You'll get your bloody chairs," Brumby told him, and bent to Micky, who tugged repeatedly on his sleeve and pointed toward the door.

"You get over here, Micky," Silas Meaner snapped. "Over here."

To Gray's astonishment, the small bundle of raggedness made mangled sounds that were primarily squeaks and jumped up and down. With his cuffs held in grimy fingers, he shook his arms in the air.

"All *right*," Meaner said, visibly subdued. "Run along, then. But I don't see why you want to show *him* the pony."

More stamping and hopping ensued until Meaner waved Micky away and he left, beckoning for Brumby to follow.

"You go," Minerva said when Brumby raised his brows in her direction. "I can conduct Mama's business here."

Since no attempt was made to take the company to more comfortable surroundings, Minerva stood where she was and made notes in a small book she produced from her blue satin reticule.

Blue became her.

But then, gray became her.

Green became her.

Anything in chiffon became her.

She couldn't wear a single color or material that would not please him, Gray decided.

"Flowers?" Clack said. "It's almost Christmas. No flowers now."

"Oh, certainly," Minerva said. "There will be flowers, I assure you. We will use holly, too. Many boughs and berries. And Mama tells me Miss Eldora Makewell has offered blooms from the hothouse at Drumblade."

Gray sought her eyes, and she didn't avoid his. Miss

Eldora Makewell, hmm? Making grand gestures with the blooms in *his* hothouse.

"Shall you mind that, Gray?" Minerva asked.

"Of course not," he heard himself say. "Why not let me see what I can arrange to have brought in from Edinburgh? I do have connections and—"

"Would 'ear of it, indeed," Clack announced. "Put yourself out. Very good."

Minerva made no comment.

He would give her all the flowers he could find, if only she might take them. Emotion welled within him until he felt he must sweep her into his arms and bear her away.

Max's hand descended upon his shoulder, and his friend's voice said, "Steady, old man," very quietly.

Damn it, was he so transparent? "Since I'm newly returned to Ballyfog, Clack, why not let me play some part in this affair of yours? Bit of a homecoming offering from me. I'd be honored if you'd allow me to assist Miss Arbuckle and her mother with supplies and so forth. After all, you being new to the area, it might be a relief to put a deal of this into the hands of someone who knows everyone. What do you say?"

"You've gone berserk," Max whispered, squeezing Gray's shoulder now. "Abso-bloody-lutely mad."

"No, don't thank me," Gray said clearly, although no thanks had yet been forthcoming, "I'm a man who makes a point of knowing what he's doing, and why." The closer he got to the center of things, the more likely he was to find out something useful. And Max could consider that *abso-bloody-lutely mad* if he chose.

"That's very generous of you, Falconer," Meaner said. Clack had grown still and seemed to have nothing to say. "I'm sure Clack thinks so too, don't you, Clack?"

Clack nodded.

"Well, there are details to be covered about the menu and

so forth," Minerva said. "The details Mama seems to have acquired as duties. Now it falls to me to help also."

"And our generous neighbor shall cover them with you," Meaner responded. "I say, Clack, we had that other matter to attend. You know the one."

The audacious stroke would seem the one to take now, Gray decided. "Good idea," he said with alacrity. "I don't recall ever seeing the inside of the manor before, Clack—Meaner. If Miss Arbuckle is to help plan your—that is, our—grand event, it would seem that we should both see more of the place. Any objection to our going on a little self-conducted tour, as it were?"

Meaner sniffed, and contrived to look down his nose at Gray.

Clack didn't react.

"Naturally, I mean the reception rooms and so on." Gray laughed. "We won't be poking around—I mean, we won't intrude inappropriately."

" 'Course not," Meaner said, too quickly, Gray thought. "Can't think why not, can you, Clack?"

Gray felt Max move restlessly behind him before he said, "We're expected back at Drumblade. Luncheon. We'd better get back, or Eldora will never forgive us."

"Oh, Eldora will understand when you tell her I remained behind to help with plans for the salon." Gray didn't trust himself to look at Max. "You go on back, there's a good chap. This gathering of yours has the whole district in a flutter, Clack, not the least my uncle's fiancée, I can tell you. Cadzow's threatening dire recourse to whatever costumes she's hatching."

Clack guffawed, and hammered the tip of his cane on marble. "Fancy undress, I should wonder," he sputtered. " 'Er, not 'im. Hah!"

"Quite," Gray said. "Feel free to get about more important matters, then, gentlemen. Miss Arbuckle and I will assess matters here. Consider her fine mother's concerns and so forth. Tell Cadzow and Eldora I'll see them this evening, will you, Max?"

Minerva's face had grown tense. No doubt she was disturbed at the prospect of being alone with him.

"You're sure about this?" Max asked, and his tone left little doubt that he considered Gray good asylum fodder.

"Of course he's sure," Meaner said. "I'll show you out myself, Rossmara. Very kind of you to come. You'll be with us on Friday, of course?"

After a brief hesitation while he studied Gray, Max said, "Of course," in a manner suggestive of surrender.

Leaving Gray and Minerva facing each other, the other three set off, but as soon as they had entered the foyer, Meaner darted back and said, "What do you think of a treasure hunt, hmm? Could incite the guests to quite a frenzy." He wiggled his pale brows. "A prize worth any price? What do you say? All those lovely creatures running hither and yon in search of something precious? Possible situations one might come upon fire the imagination, what?"

"Fire it, indeed," Gray said.

"There's a wheel staircase. From back before the fire, I understand. You did know there was a fire at some time? Destroyed a great deal, we're told."

"There was frequently a fire that destroyed a great deal in houses of any consequence," Gray said with absolute honesty. "Friends of my father's hold Lanhydrock in Cornwall. Terrible fire there."

"Very interesting," Meaner said, looking bored. "Anyway, the wheel staircase. Extraordinary. Narrower as it goes up. There's a little room at the top. View for miles. Could have clues and whatnot, what? Anyway. Take a look at that, why don't you?"

Gray prepared to plead that he didn't know where the staircase was and suggest a visit on another occasion, when Minerva, her lashes lowered, confounded him by saying, "It's in the west tower. I'll be glad to lead the way there."

Chapter Twenty-one

At last the inevitable moment arrived and Minerva faced Gray, alone, and uncertain whether she wanted to stay or flee.

"You surprise me," he said. "I didn't think you'd want to spend even a moment in my company again."

"I am not easily intimidated," she announced, raising her chin. "So if you expect me to flutter and twitter, you will be disappointed. Nothing has changed, Gray. Unless it is that I am more certain than ever that you are wrong."

"Of course I don't expect you to flutter and twitter. Why should you suddenly become something you have never been? But we do need to talk, Min. We cannot, you and I, we cannot put all that has been between us into the past. All that still is between us."

The instant before she looked at her notebook, she saw a speculative gleam in his pewter-colored eyes. For herself, she felt the unwelcome prick of tears that must remain hidden. She would not appreciate his sympathizing with her because she'd come close to crying.

"A beautiful salon can be held here," he said. "I suppose it's a ballroom."

"It is."

"What do you think of the idea of a treasure hunt?"

"I don't know."

"Bit like a children's party, do you think?"

"Depends upon the treasure, I suppose."

"As always, Min, you are the pragmatist. I'd be interested to see Meaner's staircase, but I can't lead the way."

"I know the way well. I've seen much of the house. It must once have been really beautiful."

"Hmm." Gray rocked to his toes and back, apparently searching for words. "Sunshine. Very generous of it to appear. Nothing like sun on snow. But I admit I'm ready for a thaw. Longest cold snap I recall."

"I should rather like to see snow for Christmastide," Minerva said. Fiddle, she sounded breathless.

Gray didn't respond to that.

Time passed. She felt it ticking away toward . . . Who knew exactly what lay ahead, but she couldn't bear to accept that it could be merely a crowded salon for guests in costume, and treasure hunt. She also couldn't bear to contemplate dread danger closing in on Gray, as she was sure it must be.

She could not stand there worrying for one more moment. "I will show you the staircase," she said, turning about in a flurry of skirts and all but running from the ballroom.

Gray strode after her, and they climbed the wide stairs from the foyer to a three-sided balcony on the next floor. From there Minerva set off into a dark corridor that ran roughly to the west. Positioning herself in the center of the passage, she gave him no encouragement to walk at her side or to converse. So he remained behind her—in silence.

The corridor was but dimly illuminated by sconces at considerable intervals. A total absence of paintings or furnishings gave the place a barren, uninviting air.

Maudlin was an exceptionally large house, larger, in fact, than the Falconers' Drumblade, and huge in comparison to Willieknock. Much of the building could not have been used in more years than any living person would remember. They passed doors that stood open to empty rooms, rooms where the wintry sunlight shone through windows thick with dust.

Minerva took many turns, and Gray said finally, "I marvel at your memory, and your sense of direction. Unless, of course, you've come here on a number of occasions—with Brumby McSporran, perhaps?"

So her self-assured Gray was capable of jealousy after all. She didn't revel in hearing the evidence. He would detest his own weakness in revealing such feelings.

"I've been here with Brumby," she said without inflection.

The part of the house they entered now was older than the rest. Gray stone walls met gray stone floors that dipped slightly where ages of footsteps had worn a path. Heavy glass formed rude windows in small cuts through the thick walls.

Then they were at the bottom of the wheel staircase, the widest part but still not wide. As it rose it became so narrow that a rotund person would find it difficult to negotiate.

Minerva slipped rapidly upward and around, and around, her feet flying, the lace edges on her petticoats flipping about her ankles.

The sounds were of her soft boots, and Gray's very solid ones, and her shallow breathing—and, more deep and regular, Gray's. The scent of dust surrounded them, but she smelled Gray's distinctive soap and fresh linen.

She *felt* Gray.

The stairs wound upward in a tower with no purpose other than to provide a vantage point over the countryside from its top. Minerva arrived there a step before Gray and went immediately to one of the stone ledges hewn into the walls beneath windows that were much larger than those in the passageway below. She knelt there with her arms crossed on the narrow sill, and used the side of a fist to clear a spy hole on filthy glass.

"So you and Brumby have been here often," he said.

Minerva turned to look at him, and he smiled faintly.

She faced the glass again and bent close. "I've been here. If I hadn't I wouldn't know how to get here. I have known Brumby since I was a child, just as I have known you. The difference is that I never loved him as more than a friend."

She heard his next intake of breath, and its slow expulsion.

"Do you remember what a pest I was as a child?" she asked.

"You were never a pest."

"Oh, Gray," she didn't trust herself to look at him now, "you know you thought I was frightful. I followed you everywhere."

"I remember the garden party you came to at Drumblade when you were twelve. You wore pink, and a chip bonnet with pink rosebuds under the brim."

Rather than the frosty scene outside, Minerva saw the grounds at Drumblade in summer, with roses frothing in myriad shades and the perennial gardens behind the house ablaze with orange and purple, yellow and red. And she saw herself in that pink dress of which she'd been inordinately proud because it was her first quite grown-up dress. "The bonnet made me hot," she murmured. "It felt too close to my head."

"I know," Gray said softly. "When you followed me into the conservatory, you told me it was because you were too hot outside, and that you were too hot because of your bonnet."

He remembered it all, just as she did.

"What did I say to you? I expect you've forgotten."

"I have not." Now she did look at him. "You asked if it wouldn't have been easier to go beneath a tree, in the shade, and take off my bonnet, rather than go into the conservatory. And I knew you knew I'd followed you. And I blushed."

"Redder than the most red rose in the garden."

"You took my hand and led me to a little wrought-iron chair and bade me sit. I tried to untie my bonnet, but I was embarrassed and couldn't make my fingers work, so you untied it for me. And you went to the garden and returned with a glass of lemonade. You stood before me with your feet apart, looking at me with that same somber look you have now, only you have perfected it rather a lot, you know."

He gave a short laugh. "I've had many years to do so since then."

"Gray, if you thought for one moment that you cooled my young infatuation with your behavior, you were so wrong."

"I soon began to note that you continued to hold me in some regard."

She stared at the snowy hills once more. "Before, when I first noticed you, it was with that first flush of awareness—a girl's first awareness of feelings for a boy, or young man, whichever. Then, when you were so gentlemanly and you saved my wobbly feelings by treating me with kindness, well, then I fell in love."

"You did not, Min Arbuckle. You were only twelve."

"I did too. That's why I chased you everywhere from then on."

He didn't answer immediately, and when he did his voice fell very low. "I was flattered. Any boy would protest otherwise, but he would be lying. You fascinated me, Min. You were a free spirit and not at all the shrinking type. I have never cared for shrinking women, too ready with the moue and the fluttering lash."

Minerva giggled. "You mean the coquette, the consummate flirt? Dear me, I didn't learn those skills well, did I?"

"You were real, and I loved you for that."

She longed for him to continue, but he fell silent.

"But for you I should not have felt feminine at all," she told him. "As I grew up, I watched you grow taller and stronger, and when you decided it was appropriate, you made me part of your life. If I am confident, it is because you encouraged me to be so. Oh, you were always the gentleman—almost always—and you behaved as such—most of the time—but you let me be myself and told me that was as it should be."

"You make me sound like a saint."

"No!" She drew on the windowpane. "You were a rascal, and there's still a rascal inside you, I warrant. I recall how many times you hid just for the pleasure of jumping out and startling me."

"I did no such thing."

"Yes you did. And once you found you enjoyed kissing me, there were a good many kisses."

He cleared his throat.

Minerva blinked rapidly. The memories were sweet, but today they were also painful. "I suppose we should get on."

"I wish we need never *get on*."

If she said she wished it, too, and they went into each other's arms, what then? She let her eyes close and said, "Why did you offer to help Clack with his salon?"

"To have an excuse to be with you."

"I only asked the question to hear you say that. I'm pathetic, aren't I?"

He sighed. "Not as pathetic as I am, Minerva."

"Those people are . . . well, frightful."

"Totally."

"I cannot imagine why Papa and Mama agreed to have any part in this affair. Once they had said they would give some help, the demands grew and grew until Clack announced they would deal with everything."

Would he break this fragile truce with another accusation against her parents?

"Possibly your parents could not think of a graceful way to refuse."

Now she sighed. "Thank you for saying that anyway." He must wish their differences over as much as she did, but he also must know, as she did, that there was little chance of that. "You have made a terrible mistake, Gray."

She heard him walk to and fro, to and fro.

"Gray?"

Still he paced and didn't answer her. "It doesn't matter," she said. "This is all a waste of time. I can never forgive you for what you thought."

"You mean for what I *think*?"

Minerva slid to sit on the ledge, half facing the wall, her legs tucked beneath her. "My mother is concerned for your safety."

He laughed, actually *laughed*.

She rested her forehead on rough, cold stone. "You are so uncompromising. Do you know— Of course you don't. Mama came to me and apologized because she and Papa haven't been as supportive of us—you and me—as they feel they should have been."

"How touching."

"You can be so unyielding." She pressed closer to the stone. "Mama said she knows I love you. And that you love me."

"Hardly news."

Why couldn't she make him see that he was wrong? "She told me that her failure to welcome you as she should have, and Papa's, was because they were afraid for me. There was a great deal about your disappearance, and then the way you came back, that worried them."

"No doubt," Gray muttered.

She would press on. "They apologize. They have been deeply shaken by the poisoning attempt."

"I should hope so. You almost died."

"Gray, will you open your heart? They didn't have to tell me they were horrified that something might have happened to you. They are afraid for you now. They think you should go away."

"Preferably forever."

Minerva looked over her shoulder at him. "Intractable as ever. Help the pair of us, that's what Mama wants to do."

"Didn't I hear you tell me . . ." He met her eyes briefly and looked away, but not before she saw his pain. "You said you would have no part of me, Minerva. You want no part of me, remember?"

It would serve him right if she repeated those words. "That's how I should feel, don't you think?"

"Because your parents may have had some part in a plot against me, you should hate me?"

"You are *wrong*. And you wrong my family. Mama told me I should not tell you yet, but she is so concerned for your safety—and so desperate to make up for failing to welcome you home—that she wants to help us to elope. She accepts that I will go wherever you go, and so she will do all she can for us. And Papa will come around in time. Now tell me that they are against you."

He approached until he stood over her. She saw his large, well-made hand clenched at his side, his white linen cuff stark against that tanned hand. And she saw his flat stomach beneath his black waistcoat, and a hard thigh braced.

Minerva felt emotion in Gray like a great wave drawing back, ready to crash upon rocks.

"Mama thinks," she said tremulously, "that we should leave during the salon, when everyone is engaged in revelry. There would be horses made ready, and supplies enough to get us well away."

She did not expect him to reach for the ribbons that secured her bonnet, and to remove it entirely, but he did. Drawing her cape around her, she huddled smaller.

"Are you cold?" he asked.

"No. Sturdy women like myself don't feel the cold."

"Sturdy, hmm. Minerva, you appear thinner. And pale."

"My health is not under discussion here." To prove her point, she undid her cape and removed it, rolled and set it on the ledge beside her. Gray put her bonnet on top.

"If not your parents—that is to say, if your parents aren't behind everything, then who is?"

She'd lied. She'd been cold, and now she was colder. Allowing her teeth to chatter would be an embarrassment.

"Minerva? Who?"

"I don't know. But what about your uncle? What about Cadzow, who stood to gain the most if you never returned from the Indies?"

"*Most* is subjective, Minerva. How do you or I know who really stood to gain the most?"

"You are arrogant. And you have no concern for my feelings. If you did, you would be extremely careful before suggesting the horrible things you've suggested."

Gently, he removed her cape and bonnet to another ledge, and sat beside her in very confined quarters. Not touching was an impossibility.

"I do know," he said, "that you and I have already lost a great deal, but that I wish, more than I wish to live, that we might put it all back together again."

To allow him to lull her would be so simple. To slowly lean toward him until he took her in his arms would be the most natural thing in the world.

He stroked her cheek, cupped her jaw, and raised her face until she looked at him. The air seemed to grow thin. Gray looked into her eyes, then his gaze shifted to her mouth. He rested his thumb on the spot in her neck where her pulse beat too hard. "You don't stop me from touching you," he said.

"No. Because I'm too weak to bring myself to give up the pleasure of your touch. To say otherwise would be to lie."

The rough edge of his thumb moved back and forth over her lower lip. Minerva closed her eyes and swallowed. Low inside her stomach, things clenched, but not in an unpleasant manner.

"Why would Cadzow scheme against me when he has everything he wants?" Gray's own lips parted, revealing his very white teeth. Even when he was serious, the dimples beside his mouth were visible.

"I used to think you'd been left by gypsies," she said, and stopped, horrified at such a careless comment.

Gray only grinned, very widely, turning his flamboyant features to a vaguely satanic cast—all flare and angle.

"Sorry," she said.

"Not at all. You never told me this before. Why gypsies?"

She pressed her lips together but could not contain her own smile. "I am still incorrigible. I cannot control my errant tongue. Dark curly hair that was always too long, and skin that captured the sun with ease, and eyes that matched your name in a hundred shades, and your sharp bones and the way you laugh—and your mouth. And you are strong and were always very quick, and rode so well."

"And I shall soon become quite intolerable from such compliments."

"Compliments? Characteristics of a wild gypsy prince?"

"Oh, I do think so. I think your girlish heart used to beat at such thoughts."

"Gray Falconer! You are impossible."

"The way my boyish heart used to beat at the very sight of you. From looking at your pale, smooth skin and blue eyes—such very dark, enigmatic eyes. And the softest, most enticing lips I ever saw. Your face is gentle and sweet, yet there is such intelligence in those blue eyes of yours."

"And you had the fine, lithe figure of a creature of the moors," Minerva continued, warming to her subject. "Broad of shoulder, narrow of hip, strong of leg. A fine figure of a man such as we do not often see in these parts."

"How can you question my love for you, Minerva Arbuckle? You are a seductress."

"A seductress who is interested in seducing only one . . ." Enough, she had said enough.

He dipped his head to look at her, took a teasing knuckle

to the corner of her mouth and brushed it there until she smiled at him.

"I would have you do nothing but smile for the rest of our lives. And I would have them be exceedingly long lives."

"But we cannot simply think of such things, can we?" she reminded him.

"As I said, Min, why would Cadzow scheme against me when he has everything he wants? You don't know him, or you'd never make such a suggestion."

"Because he is your uncle and you love him, and you are furious that I would say such a dastardly thing about him?"

Gray hesitated, then said, "Point taken. We both have reasons for our suspicions, don't we?"

"Yes." Unable to simply sit passive while he touched her, not for an instant longer, she took his hand in both of hers. She kissed each fingertip slowly, lingeringly. First the tip, then the base, then, spreading them, she kissed between. She kissed his palms and trailed her tongue to his wrists. When he jumped, he surprised her.

"You are a natural seductress," he told her, "and I can hardly wait until it is time for you to practice the full potential of your natural wonders. I have waited long enough."

"I have also waited long enough." With her mouth pressed to the heel of his right hand, she raised her eyes to his and saw lines of stark strain there. "If we trust each other, perhaps we may be together one day after all."

"Yes, Minerva, oh, yes." She had no chance of resisting when he removed his hands from hers, took hold of her face, and kissed her fully, deeply.

She rose to her knees and his arm went around her, urging her closer. And he pressed his cheek to her breasts through the heavy cashmere of her dress. The thickness of the stuff made little difference. At once her nipples ached, and she responded to him in those ways she had come to expect. With fingers that were clumsy, he unbuttoned her bodice from its high neck to the waist, and slipped his hands inside, and inside her fine lawn chemise to fondle her breasts.

Minerva said, "Gray," but couldn't seem to think of anything more. Rather, she used her concentration to unbutton his waistcoat and his shirt. Her fingers made contact with the pistol he evidently carried at all times.

"Try not to touch it," he told her, his voice thick. "But as far as anything else goes, be my guest, love."

"The feelings I have are wonderful, and they are dreadful. They make me want so much."

"Then they match mine." He lifted her to sit astride his big thighs and leaned to ensure that her skirts fanned free, leaving her most vulnerable parts firmly settled on his hard flesh.

Minerva reached beneath her skirts to find that part of Gray she'd taken a great deal of notice of on previous occasions. She found and covered it, and watched his face very closely. So many expressions, and one would think he suffered great pain.

"I have made it a project to examine as many male statues as I've been able to encounter," she told him. "And I've spent time among my grandfather's books in what is now my workroom. This part of you is certainly not particularly elegant."

Minerva squeezed his not-particularly-elegant part more firmly and heard the breath leave him in a hiss.

"I assure you," he said in hoarse tones, "that the part in question is both functional and functions extremely well. I am persuaded that should all go according to the plan I've carried in my mind for longer than should have been necessary, you will discover that you find it functional. In fact, I wouldn't be surprised if, within time, you come to consider it elegant in its own way."

Minerva pulled her upper lip between her teeth, frowned, and used both hands to assess the length, breadth, and particular shape of the Part. "Not elegant, I shouldn't think," she said finally. "But powerful, certainly. It appears to have a life of its own. See how it responds to me." She poked it with a single fingertip, and nodded with satisfaction when it pulsed in response. Then she squeezed, felt the answering leap, and breathed out a long, gratified breath through her nose. "You're right. Very functional. And I don't believe it can be unpleasant for it to be inserted inside a female. If it was, why would so many ladies be so anxious to secure gentlemen to make sure they may experience just that on a regular basis?"

"*Minerva!*"

"*Pah!* I am five and twenty and I know what I know. In fact, it would seem to me high time for us to set about the business of trying this out. For all I know, a woman cannot manage such things at all if she doesn't start doing so by a certain age and I am getting quite senior."

"You, my dear, are getting impossible."

"What you did to me that other time, Gray. I'm sure it wasn't right—in the true sense of the word—but I did enjoy it. And I'm not ashamed to say so."

"Neither should you be. Would you like me to do it again now?"

"I've become very diverted, haven't I?"

"We both have," he said, and bent his head to her breasts. They rested in his hands, overflowed his hands. Really, she was very sturdy. "You are wonderful to kiss—in every way. I don't think I can wait much longer to claim all of you."

"We *are* diverted, Gray." She could scarcely think at all. He continued to kiss her.

"Gray?"

"We have already agreed that we are diverted. Let us remain diverted. Let us stay in this wonderful tower and never return."

Catching hold of his ears very firmly, she endeavored to stop herself from rocking on his thighs, but it did feel so exciting, particularly when she could feel his Part pressing against her.

"My . . . ears," he gasped.

"We have to concentrate. Your Part is becoming very large."

"It tends to do that."

"Often?"

"Oh, *really*. Yes, if you are near me, very often."

"Oh. How nice."

"We're supposed to be talking about treasure hunts and whatnot, aren't we?"

"Yes," Minerva said, rocking again, and panting in time with her self-induced sensations. "We'll arrange one. There. We've discussed it. What should be the prize?"

"Depends on who wins."

"No, it doesn't. There's just one prize."

"Unless we win. If we win, the prize is that we get to come here and do this again."

She was too transported to manage a smile.

Gray fastened his teeth on one of her nipples, freeing a hand to find its way between her legs to that very ready flesh, and to do what she'd so longed for him to do again. She spread her legs wider, making the way easier for him, but, at the same time, opened his trousers.

"No, Min." He sounded desperate and clasped her wrist. "Not now, sweet. No, not now. You understand a great deal, but not quite everything."

"I understand that your Part needs something, and I also understand what it is. It can be quite easily accomplished, can't it? I mean," she contrived to free it from his trousers and was momentarily speechless when it proceeded to pop straight up between her thighs, "I—I mean, it's evident that it would not be strategically difficult to place the Part in the appropriate place. In fact, I should think it might be frightfully exciting."

He moaned, and rested his brow on her forehead.

"You have a pain? Is it because of the strain this causes?" She held the rigid protuberance and found it remarkably smooth. The end was quite like velvet; also, it seemed to grow somewhat clammy, or slick, or sticky, she couldn't decide exactly which best described the condition. Very carefully, she rubbed his Part with slow, gentle, but firm strokes. She would endeavor to soothe it, but, as she'd been taught, little was ever achieved by the timid. A firm hand in all things, that was the ticket.

"Min." Gray sounded even weaker.

She stroked with extra vigor. It grew even more. Heavens, how difficult this must become sometimes. Why his trousers would be unlikely to contain it in its present condition.

"Oh, Min," he whispered, and she feared he was close to becoming unconscious.

"Bear *up*," she exhorted him. "Trust me, and you'll rise to the occasion."

"Think I've already risen," he muttered. "Oh, Min, don't stop, you angel. Don't stop."

She beamed. He actually appreciated her efforts. "I certainly won't. I've always been told I can be relied upon to finish what I start. I'm going to make it better, I promise you. Perhaps I should kiss it."

"*No.* Er, no, not quite now, dearest. You're doing splendidly. Ah. Splendidly. Aaah. Yes, yes."

"I think my arm is growing tired."

"Change hands."

"Why didn't I think of that." She did as he suggested, but stopped almost as soon as she'd begun. "Oh, what's that?"

Gray tipped his head back against the stones. "*Yesss.*" His eyes were squeezed shut, his teeth gritted. He pulled her forward on his lap until his Part was propped between the place where her thighs came together. And he returned to fondling her breasts. And a *smile* spread over his face, a soft, satisfied smile.

Something quite extraordinary had happened. His Part

had pumped quite madly for a few moments, then, when he'd cried out, she'd felt a warm wetness surge against her—it came from the Part, of that she was certain. The stuff offspring were made of, no doubt. Would she have a child now? "Gray, shall I, er, that is, are we likely to add a small person to the world? Since you have . . . you know?"

His eyes opened lazily. "Not unless something works quite differently from the way I've always thought it does. Isn't there something you'd like, my love?"

She wiggled a little, and managed to feel his flesh against the place she knew could bring quite marvelous sensations. "I would, but it doesn't matter. You mean that sensation, don't you?" She really should just presume. "Of course you do. But—"

He raised his hips, and hers with them, and bounced her. With a squeal, she grappled for his shoulders. His part had grown hard again and it jarred against her, and the fiery ache began again, and built so quickly she gasped. And when she gasped, Gray kissed her lips, a tongue kind of kiss, then kissed her neck, and her breasts, and he put his fingers beneath her skirt once more. And then it happened.

She curled forward over him, seeking to hold him against her, to enfold and make him one with her. Her center convulsed, and pulsed, and stole the last shreds of her reason, and she didn't care. Feeling this was all, it was everything.

Chapter Twenty-two

Minerva was his. He would have her no matter the odds, and woe to anyone who tried to stop him. She wasn't asleep, but she'd been quiet for all of half an hour while they'd remained as they were, silent but for the occasional soft kiss and murmur of endearment.

Gray had turned her sideways on his lap and rebuttoned her bodice. He would not take further risk that they might be encountered in such a compromising condition.

There had to be a way out of what had trapped them, consigned them to face the destruction of all they'd planned.

"Gray," Min said in a small voice, "you are in danger. Perhaps we are both in danger."

"What are you suggesting? That we both stand together in this?"

"Yes," she told him, "I want us to stand together against whatever comes."

"If we were to elope," he told her, "and we made a point of letting everyone know we intended to, by making it a joke in a way, we would be sure to draw my enemies after us."

"Yes. Let's do it, then."

She didn't know what she was saying. He hugged her

fiercely. Then she shifted until she could see him, and they stared at each other.

"I know what you're thinking," Min said. "You think it could be my parents who will come after us."

He managed a smile and said, "And you think it could be my uncle."

"And we both think it's possible the McSporrans are involved."

"Clack and Meaner," Gray said. "What part do you suppose they play?"

She frowned, but gradually her lips parted in a smile, and then she began to laugh. And when she laughed, he had to laugh. Within moments they laughed together, clung together laughing and crying and shaking their heads.

Gray was the first to control himself enough to say, "We may be crushed beneath the crowd."

Minerva laughed even harder.

"But then," Gray said, warming to the idea, "they could very well crush each other and leave us unscathed."

She shifted on his lap and placed a hand on each of his shoulders. Her expression was deeply serious again. "Surely someone must want their money back. Because the job wasn't done properly. Because you're still alive, that is." She grimaced. "It's ugly even to talk about, but it must be true."

"My thought exactly," he told her. "Someone, somewhere, has paid for what they have not got. Whoever they are, they will want their money back. Or satisfaction. Or probably both, since they'll feel very misused. And we'll have all our suspects together in one place on Friday evening. All those whom we suspect may have paid a great deal to avoid seeing me again. And in the middle of all the fuss and jostle, the running about, what better time to snaffle a man and arrange for him to disappear? Really disappear this time."

"You think this person will do it himself? You think he'll actually try to kill you himself?"

Gray permitted himself the liberty of stroking her limbs beneath her skirts. "You have the most desirable legs, Min."

"Keep your mind on what's important, please."

"Legs that make it very difficult to concentrate on anything else."

"Gray," she said, holding his face in her hands, "your mind should be on important things."

He smiled. "And it is. Your legs, to be precise."

"Don't joke."

"I'm extremely serious, I assure you. Your legs are—"

"*Gray.* I think I must insist that you separate carnal urges from reality. And if you say carnal urges are reality, I shall be angry with you. I'm telling you that although what we experienced here today was very pleasant—"

"*Pleasant?*"

"Enjoyable, then."

The miss should not get away with understatements on this matter. "Enjoyable as a row on the river in summer is enjoyable? Or as stroking a kitten is enjoyable?"

"You are trying to divert me by being silly. It doesn't become you. And I am not diverted one bit. Listen. This is how we will go about things. As soon as we leave here, we will return to being cool with each other, is that clear?"

"I will hear you out." He would agree to nothing unless it assured her safety and, as best as could be hoped, his own.

Eluding him, she scrambled to her feet. "At the salon we will keep our distance from each other and I will watch closely to see how each guest regards you."

The excitement in her face troubled him. This was the Minerva of old, all agitated readiness to pursue her quarry. "A poor idea," he said. "I can't imagine what it would accomplish."

"I am a very perceptive woman. I will know who it is. And what will be accomplished by the exercise is that I shall be able to tell you the identity of the villain and we shall draw him away from the rest, and corner him, and . . ."

"And? And then what, Minerva?"

"We'll expose him," she announced. "Bring him up before the law. That is, if we don't have to—umm—kill him ourselves."

Only with difficulty did Gray hold back laughter. Minerva's fists pumped in the air and she managed a most ferocious expression. But she was on his side, bless her. Would she be for him, he asked himself, were she not convinced of her parents' innocence?

Abruptly she grew still, frowned even more deeply, and pointed a finger at him. "You've already seen the flaw, haven't you." She slapped the heel of a hand to her brow. "Of course you have."

The last thing he wished to do was put even the slightest dent in her self-confidence. "It's still a good idea."

"Hah! You haven't seen the flaw after all. You're just shamming. I can follow whomever I please and leap out, and accuse them of heinous crime, but what proof will I have? I can hardly say, 'I saw you looking at Gray in a suspicious manner, therefore I know you have conspired to kill him,' can I?"

"Shouldn't think so," he agreed obligingly.

"No." Stroking her chin, she walked back and forth. "So this is what I shall do. I shall force the demon's hands."

She would force the demon's hands. "You really have become remarkably independent, Min."

"I was always independent."

That, he could not deny. "It is for me to protect myself, not you, my dear. Although I thank you for wanting to."

"I want to clear my parents' names," she said shortly, but would not meet his eyes.

"Almost as worthy a cause as taking care of the man you love."

"We're still enemies, you know," she said. "Don't imagine that a stolen kiss or two has changed that."

"Oh, do come on, Minerva. A stolen *kiss* or two. Shall I explain, in particular detail, the nature of what has passed between us here?"

"You're a gentleman. You wouldn't dare."

"Try me."

She ignored him and went to look out over the frozen countryside.

"I have an idea, if you'd care to hear it," he told her, and immediately continued. "Your cousins are good-hearted souls. I like them a great deal."

"So do I. The river is still frozen."

"And will be for some time, unless I miss my mark. I should like to ask Iona and Fergus to do me a great favor. Do you suppose they might?"

She braced a hand on either side of a window. The bodice of her gown fit so well as to accentuate her womanly shapeliness. "They would do anything for me," she said, then looked back at him, "Or for you. They think you're wonderful."

"They have good taste." He smiled.

Minerva did not smile.

"It's my notion to give the news to all concerned that I plan to make a getaway from the salon. Rather than watch them with no particular plan in mind, why not give each a piece of information that will make them watch me if I am of particular interest to them?"

"And you want Iona and Fergus to spread the rumor?"

"It would seem they'd have the easiest time getting to all concerned. A word here. A confidence there. They tell Brumby, who tells his parents. One of them mentions it to your mother and says how disconcerted they are."

"And Iona takes a basket of fresh-baked bread to Drumblade, perhaps, and drops a hint to Eldora, which would doubtless go immediately to Cadzow."

"Touché, my dear. But, of course that's how it should be done."

"Then, if one of them makes a particular effort to follow you, we will know, Gray, but we still won't be able to do anything in particular, not unless they make some overt move."

"You are wise. But the plan is good enough as a start, I think."

She turned back from the window and offered him her hand. When he took hold of it and carried it to his lips, she took his free hand to her cheek and nuzzled him. "I have another idea," she told him. "You could leave before Friday. Tomorrow would be your last chance, really. Give no notice and get well away before you are missed."

"And what would that accomplish?" He began to feel angry, yet anger had no place here.

"It would accomplish your safety, Gray."

A bare, cold little space began to hem him in. "You wish me to go somewhere and hide? And for how long? Should I ever be able to come out again?"

"Well, I hadn't exactly—"

"No, you hadn't exactly thought it through. In the midst of this ridiculous mess, I am fighting not just for my actual life, but for the way I intend to live it. As a free man and in the place where I belong."

"You could come back in time."

"Perhaps. But you have forgotten something else. I will never leave this place without you again. Do you hear me, Minerva? *Never.*"

All color drained from her face. Her eyes were huge and unblinking, and her lips were the same pallid shade as her cheeks.

"And—since we are dealing with what must be—you are not to be present at this infernal salon. Not at all. Is that understood?"

Her mouth trembled, but he saw muscles flicker in her cheeks and prepared himself for some onslaught.

"Do I hear you?" she said. *"Is that understood?* Listen to yourself. You are woefully arrogant, and yet I do love you." Her long sigh seemed to drain her.

"And you will do as I tell you?"

"Oh, no."

Gray bent over to clamp his hands above his knees, and let his head hang forward. "You try me. Oh, how you try me. I will tell you again. You are not to attend the salon. I have a feeling something dangerous may occur here, and I will not have you involved."

"Pah," she said loudly. "You cannot tell me what to do."

"I can, and I am."

"You may need me," she said.

"I want you safe."

"I *know.* And"—her next thought made her feel shy—"and I do like to feel protected by you. Just a little, of course. But what if nothing happpens because I am not there?"

Gray pushed upright and studied her carefully. "What does that mean?"

"It means that rather than simply making a getaway, you will be taking advantage of my parents' kind offer. You will be eloping with me. *That* is the word we shall put about."

"No. No, absolutely not. Minerva, I forbid it."

"You cannot forbid me to do anything, Gray."

"Then I appeal to your gentleness, your caring for me. The way you *used* to care for me when I was in your favor. I cannot bear to place you in harm's way."

"You will know exactly how I am." She caught up her cape and swung it around her shoulders. "You will know because I shall be with you."

"But you are angry with me, Min. You believe I have vilified your family. This is not the stuff marriages are built on."

She clapped her bonnet onto her head and tied its ribbons with fierce purpose. "Who said anything about marriage? All we're going to do is elope." There was a teasing light in her eyes.

Her bravado didn't deceive him. She had chosen a path designed to shock him into submission. Well, he would not fall for it. "You imagine I would allow you to ruin your reputation in such a manner?"

"I'm an old maid now. On the shelf. A wallflower. Very little harm can be done to my reputation beyond a few titters about my imagining a man like you might actually marry me. They'll all pity me. But no matter. If I am with you, I doubt any of your suspects will risk hurting me by ambushing you as we make our getaway. Later, when you are in a place of safety, I'll leave you in peace."

"Leave me in *peace*? *Titters* because you should imagine a man like me marrying you? Saints preserve us. Our marriage is expected, and has been expected. And you know only too well that I live for the moment when I make you wholly my own."

"The moment when that Part of you enters the place that will make it entirely, blissfully happy, you mean?"

He covered his eyes.

"I thought so," she said. "Fear not. I didn't say I saw any reason not to attend to those matters, only that there doesn't have to be any marriage."

"*I want to marry you,*" he roared, closing in on her but afraid to touch her in case he inadvertently snapped off some part of her. "And you are to cease talking about such matters in such a way. It isn't seemly."

"And I will never be *seemly*. I will always be an embarrassment to you. That's why we must have an arrangement. Isn't that what they call those things, *arrangements*? But this isn't the time to finalize that. What are you wearing for the salon?"

"Damn and blast the bloody salon."

"That might be an interesting idea. Clear up a lot of problems. But what are you wearing?" She tapped her mouth, then pointed in that way that made Gray dread whatever was to come. "I've got it. How absolutely perfect. You will come as a pirate. Hah! You will come as a pirate, and I shall come as a pirate also. Let's see what reactions that causes."

She was clever, he had to give her that. "Well . . . Yes, I rather like it. At least for myself. I shall come as a pirate. You will be Bo Peep, or a shepherd girl, of course."

The blank expression in her eyes troubled him. So did her quiet words: "Of course, Gray, a shepherd girl. What a splendidly original idea. We'd better get on with making some arrangements or Mama will have a good deal to say. She expects me to make up a menu and place the necessary orders. I shall have to send to Edinburgh for certain items. Then, of course, I must see what's to be done about staff, and just *hands*. We need pairs of hands. This place is so empty. I hadn't realized how empty. Usually I'm only in the drawing room where the McSporrans receive, and it's pretty in its way. But the rest of this place. Really, it will take a willing army to transform it in two days. We may have to borrow necessitites from Willieknock—and Drumblade."

Gray understood little about such things, but he did see that the task was enormous. "We have a good staff at Drumblade. They'll be placed at your disposal. And any necessary furnishings will be transported, of course."

"Yes. Yes, thank you. I'd best get on with it. Will you assist me by taking me to the village?"

"Of course I will," he told her, smiling despite the circumstances. "I will take you anywhere."

"Including away from here on Friday night," she said, in her no-nonsense, do-as-I-tell-you voice.

"May we save further discussion of that topic?"

"If that's what you prefer. But we will elope on Friday— or I suppose I should say, we'll run away together." She started for the staircase, but presented him with another of her deeply concerned expressions. "This is rather delicate, but I think we can say anything to each other, can't we?"

"I'm sure you will say whatever you want to say."

"I'd like it if you'd tell me you won't be shocked by whatever I say."

But he probably would. "I won't be shocked."

"Well, I read about certain, well, *contraptions* that can be employed on a man's Part, to avoid, I think it said, disease and other unwanted occurrences. By those occurrences, did they mean babies?"

Oh, he was beyond this, at least now and here. "I believe that would be the meaning, yes."

"Gray," she came closer and pursed her lips, "you said the product of your Part was harmless since it wasn't inside me. But I wonder—it wouldn't happen that a female would become with child on the very first time a Part entered her, would it?"

He forced himself to look her steadily in the eye. "It could happen, I believe."

"Oh."

"That troubles you?"

She twirled a bonnet ribbon around her fingers. "Not really. Except that it would certainly be inconvenient to find oneself in an interesting condition when one wasn't married. I mean, I know it happens, of course. There have been distressing instances that I've witnessed. But I had hoped that there might be a sort of building process. You know, layer on layer until there was enough of That," she touched her skirts, and he realized she must bear evidence of his carelessness on her underclothing, "until there was enough of it to do what must be done to achieve the, er, state."

Gray felt ashamed of himself, of his weakness. "No, my love. Not so. I will explain it all much more clearly when we can sit quietly." Or be together in their own bed, in each other's arms, discussing the desirability of a child to seal their love. "But I assure you that once can be enough."

"Without the device?"

The idea of nasty, hard pieces of sheepskin rudely stitched together did not please Gray. "There is that," he said, non-committal.

"Well, then, we must be prepared before Friday, because I've heard that great excitement can raise a man's need for such things. Excitement and danger. It makes his juices run strong and hot." With that, she turned away.

"Now, do you think cucumber sandwiches would be well received? They're not substantial, but they are light, and there will be so much that is rich."

Disoriented, Gray tried to concentrate.

"A variety of syllabubs, of course. And, although I hesitate to mention it, something spectacular built of sugar, maybe several somethings. I rather like the idea of a large castle. Also ice sculptures. For that someone must come from Edinburgh. Whole fish. They are always so festive. And cheeses. Fruit, whatever is the best we can obtain at this time of year. Venison pâté. My first task, after placing orders, must be to beg more members of the surrounding gentry to part with members of their staff for the actual event. We shall require an army to serve."

From his juices running strong and hot, to cucumber sandwiches and ice sculptures. She made his head whirl.

"Come," she said. "We must find the McSporrans and tell them they need gather sufficient chairs and so on. And tables for the supper. I'll tell them they can go to our house, or to Drumblade, for them. And we must decide on clues for the treasure hunt. That is a good idea; I like it. And a prize, of course."

"I shall provide the prize," Gray said, having had no intention of offering any such thing. "A valuable prize to be kept secret."

Her smile made her eyes sparkle. "You are so kind, Gray. You hide behind your formidable demeanor when it suits you, but you are the kindest of men. Thank you. Now I'm going to hunt down our disgruntled caretakers."

She started down the steps, but Gray stopped her and pulled her back. "I demand a kiss before you go."

"There isn't time."

"We will make time. I spent four years waiting to kiss you. Now I intend to make the best of every possible opportunity."

"Does your Part respond to kisses, too?"

A man of the world he might be, but his face burned. "What do you mean?"

"Does it feel something during kisses?"

Surely she couldn't mean . . . Surely she could. "It is a very sensitive area, Min. A kiss tends to have rather extreme results. Just the sensation of a tender mouth on that skin is—"

"Oh! Oh, what can you think of me? I put myself badly. I didn't mean actual kisses on the Part, of course. Oh, Gray, I am not completely base. I meant that when we kiss—the tongue kind—do you get feelings there?"

He was grateful she would think his blush was the result of her comments rather than his own feelings of foolishness. "I do, yes. But why do you ask?"

"Because I get feelings there, too. In the place where the Part goes, eventually that is, and sort of deep in here." She pressed on her stomach, very low down. "Achy, but demanding, if that sounds at all sensible."

"Very sensible." He would die anyway if he couldn't have this girl soon. "Could I still have one kiss, though?"

Standing below him, she closed her eyes, parted her lips, and held the tip of her tongue between her teeth.

Gray delicately met her tongue with the tip of his own and slowly drew her into his mouth. The kiss went on and on, and moved their heads forcefully, and made him lift her back up to stand toe-to-toe with him where she could reach to put her arms around his neck, and he could press her to him so firmly he felt every part of her.

When he lifted his face to breathe, her lips were red and swollen and her hair was escaping its braids—as usual. Very carefully, almost reverently, she put her hand between his legs and held him gently while she looked into his eyes.

"We'd better go," he said through his teeth.

"I am beginning to understand things more. If this did not become so stiff, it would be quite difficult to put in its place, wouldn't it?"

About two more words and his knees would buckle. "Yes. Let's go immediately, please."

She grinned, a little wickedly he thought, and turned from him.

"Be careful," he told her, putting her behind him. "Those skirts were never made for climbing this type of staircase."

"Of course they weren't. And when my creations are all the rage, no woman will be so encumbered."

"As you say," Gray agreed, clattering rapidly downward.

Minerva ran behind him. He heard her quickened breathing, smelled her sweet scent of woodruff and lavender, and gloried in it. He gloried in her. She was everything he could ever want.

The damn stairs were ridiculously narrow.

He had no warning.

Encased in fine leather boots, his ankles met an obstacle he could not have anticipated. "Minerva! Get back." He flailed. "Stand still. Don't come near me. Sit down on a . . . Ahhh! Damn it all."

Throwing out his arms, he grabbed at the stone walls, seeking a purchase, any purchase, and fell sideways. His shoulder hit with shuddering force. His head snapped to the side, slammed his brow on the jagged corner of a slab.

"Gray! Gray!" He felt her grab at his coat, and futile rage burgeoned.

Her grip on him was as if she were a butterfly attempting to stop the fall of an eagle.

Forward he pitched, over whatever had started his fall. The closeness of the walls made of him a tall, heavy, angular ball to be bounced from side to side.

He spun. The stairwell spun. Shapes whirled. He was like a stone sinking in water. Helpless.

Minerva screamed, and once more her fingers dug into his back. She caught at his collar and succeeded only in jerking his head back.

The world went into slow motion. From wall to wall, his heels catching the edge of a step, only to shoot out again, he buffeted downward, unable to stop the horror of the crippling damage his body received.

"Stop!" Imperious, demanding, Minerva's voice pierced his aching brain. "At once—do you hear me?—or you will kill yourself. Stop this now."

Swinging around yet another corner, his legs folded and he saw the steps rise toward him.

And then a flying thing in voluminous blue was upon him, clinging to his neck like some not very substantial beast.

Minerva.

She knocked him sideways, and their combined weight hammered him straight down to land on a hip with his legs folded painfully beneath him.

He stopped falling.

They stopped falling.

Minerva had saved him without managing to kill herself. At least, he hoped she had.

He grabbed her and held her so close, she gasped. He didn't care if she gasped, he would hold her anyway. "My God, my dearest friend, you are reckless."

"And you are clumsy."

Thundering in his chest stole what breath was left to him.

He managed to say, "You shouldn't have done that. You could have died."

"If you can't watch where you're going, I shall have to be constantly on alert."

"Had I fallen directly on top of you on this stone, I think I should have crushed you to death."

She snorted. "I am made of sturdy stuff, remember?"

Gingerly, Gray made a finger inventory of his head, his face, his body. Bumps and bruises abounded, and a fair amount of blood. He frowned at Minerva. "You must be hurt. Where? Tell me at once."

"I didn't have time to get hurt!" She eased away a little, wincing as she did so. "Well, somewhat hurt, perhaps, but nothing serious. You, on the other hand, are in a fearsome way. I must get you somewhere and tend you."

"You've hit your forehead." He picked up her hands. "And look at your knuckles."

"Oh, dear," Minerva said, giving a mock look of horror, "I shall not be able to do my embroidery this afternoon."

He grinned, but immediately shifted to relieve pressure on his hip.

"You must have broken bones, Gray. What shall we do now? You cannot travel like that, yet we must travel. I don't want you to stay here."

"On Friday—ah—on Friday I shall take you away from here. We will not be gone long, just long enough to draw my enemies after me, and for us to marry. Then we shall return to our home—to Drumblade—and to marital harmony."

She turned the corners of her mouth down. "Sounds dull."

"Really?" He drew in a hissing breath through his teeth. "Sorry you think so."

"I shall continue my work, of course."

He visualized skirts rising and falling in the most undignified manner, but made no comment.

Sickness gripped him, and he closed his eyes. There was no time for this.

"Let's see if you can stand," Minerva said.

Obligingly, he got cautiously to his feet, testing each limb as he did so. "Nothing broken," he said, overwhelmingly grateful to discover he could stand. "Now I want to see what I tripped on. We can't have guests rushing up here on Friday, only to tumble to their deaths afterward."

Minerva shuddered. "Absolutely not."

He allowed her to put a steadying hand under his elbow and to guide him up the steps.

"Gray?"

"Hush. I see it." He saw it, but didn't believe it. What sane man could believe such a willful attempt to harm another? "How is it secured?"

"Iron pegs," she said promptly. "But we would have heard the holes being made if they'd done it while we were here. No, they were ready beforehand. Whoever did this hoped to kill."

"How could they have been certain I'd come here at all—to the manor?" Gray said.

"They couldn't, but they could be sure I would. I was expected."

Gray picked up the two ends of a broken piece of fine, strong twine and followed each one to where it had been tied to an eye in a metal peg driven into crevices between stones. They'd been driven in at just the right height so that a cord stretched between would foul a man's ankles.

"The twine was put there while we were in the tower," he said, more to himself than to Minerva. "So whoever did this could have heard some of what was said."

"They could have thought I'd go down first," Minerva said, her face the color of chalk. "That would mean I was the one intended to take a terrible fall, Gray."

"Why should they expect such a break from convention? Of course they knew I would be first. And they may have hoped to injure both of us. Makes perfect sense. I don't think they care what they do, or to whom, as long as they stop us from making any plans that may unmask them."

"Now they know what we decided to do." Minerva slid to sit down on the step immediately behind her. She rested her brow on her knees, and her back rose and fell regularly.

"Darling one, please don't cry," Gray said. His mangled hands left blood on everything he touched, but he needed to touch her anyway. He stroked her hair. "It'll be all right. We'll come through with flying colors."

"You mean we'll *fly* through with flying colors, don't you?" Her voice was strangled. "You seemed to leave the ground entirely when you fell."

Hysteria mustn't be allowed to get out of hand. "Quite," he said, the corners of his mouth tugging upward. "Or leap through in a colorful manner, perhaps."

Minerva's laughter rang out. "Meaner did this. He . . . he . . . insisted we should come up here. He's part of it."

"Yes, I think so. And if I can put my mind to it, I may just remember where I've seen him. Possibly in some club in London. That silver stick is familiar. But I ought to remember his face. I don't."

"Gray! Our villains, all of them . . ." She covered her mouth.

"Yes, dear."

"They're the most unlucky v-villains in the world. They must be. Nothing goes right for them."

Gray's chuckles joined Minerva's laughter.

"Shush," he said. "We don't want to attract company."

"Don't care," she gasped between convulsive waves of laughter. "Let 'em come, I'll offer lessons in being sneaky. They'll probably accept. They are *so* unlucky."

"Unlucky," Gray agreed, flopping back against the wall and holding up his bloody hands. "Or inept."

"Or both. If it is only you they're after, I certainly do seem to get in the way of their efforts."

"Absolutely, Min. I rest my case. You do see that I can't

go anywhere without you, don't you? I certainly couldn't elope without you, even supposing that a fellow would be likely to elope alone."

"What are you trying to say, Gray? You sound fuddled. You've hit your head."

"Not a thing wrong with my head. You are my talisman. I can't be out of your sight. If I am, they will contrive to poison me, or break my neck, or who knows what awful thing they'll come up with next?" He leaned to whisper in her ear, "Let us go up again. There may not be another opportunity to deal with this, and I must tell you what I think we should do."

She was on her feet at once and, holding his wrist, climbed to the lookout once more. "So," she said, drawing him to the ledge farthest from the staircase. "Tell me your idea."

Sitting beside her, Gray kept his voice very low. "We know we must have been overheard. That means they will expect us to change our plans."

She nodded slowly and examined the mangled palm of his right hand.

"They'll expect us to make a move either before or after the salon. So we won't change our plans—not really. We shall go ahead as we'd designed, with Iona and Fergus putting out little comments here and there. Only, I shall also arrange a something that will suggest we are duping them, that we do, in fact, plan to remain until after the salon."

"How—"

"Hush, Min," he told her. "I will do it. Leave this much to me. You have quite enough to do. Max will help me do what must be done. On Friday evening we leave together, my darling. By the time the guilty ones track us down, I will be ready for them."

"And what shall I do to prepare?" Min asked.

"Put a few things together and have them ready. That's

all. But there's going to be nothing for it, Min. You're going to have to make the supreme sacrifice."

"I will if I can."

"Oh, you can. You can be with me, dearest. Morning, noon, and night. Never out of my sight, or me out of yours."

"Well, there are certain moments when that might be a little difficult."

"Doesn't matter." He shook his head emphatically. "If you're talking about mundane matters like taking baths, we'll simply have to take them together."

"Gray. You're delirious."

"I know. Lovely feeling."

"Well, I wasn't thinking about baths exactly."

"Oh, that. Well, we're grown up. I'll sing to cover any noise. If you remember, I sing quite well."

"Deranged," Minerva muttered.

Chapter Twenty-three

Gray and Minerva entered the green drawing room at Drumblade. Deep in conversation, Eldora and Max barely acknowledged their arrival. Actually, Eldora didn't appear to notice them at all. Max raised his brows significantly in Gray's direction, but nothing more.

Eldora's mouth hung slightly open, and she dabbed a handkerchief repeatedly to first one palm and then the other.

"They are not always fatal," Max said to her. Eldora wore the garb of an Egyptian queen, complete with straight, black wig and heavy kohl around her eyes. Max continued, "I should clarify that statement. Sometimes their victims die from other causes before the repeated burrowing of the worms completely undermines bodily structure."

"How horrible," Eldora said, finally turning her great cat's eyes—frightened eyes now—on Gray and Minerva. "And these—*worms*—have been seen here in Scotland. Is that what you're saying, Max?"

Max sighed hugely and seemed to require the support of a table.

"What is he talking about?" Minerva asked, leaning closer to Gray. "What worms? Eldora's scared."

"Doubtless," Gray said. "When Max decides to spin one

of his outrageous tales—not a frequent occurrence these days—you may depend that the recipient will likely be terrified. She must have done something to make him contemptuous of her."

"Contemptuous?"

"Disgusted. We'll learn what it was soon enough. Max is a brilliant man and doesn't suffer fools—or opportunists." He looked at her significantly. "Remind me of this when there's a more appropriate time. Max is famous for his stories."

"Gray," Eldora said, her raucous voice almost a shriek, "make Max explain himself properly."

"Perhaps I shouldn't have told you at all," Max said. "To this point there have only been two cases diagnosed in Scotland."

"Yourself and . . ."

"Hardly matters," Max responded. "She's dead."

"Oh," Eldora murmured. *"She?"*

"This is too painful."

"Yes, yes, but *who* was she?"

Running his fingers through his hair, Max said, "I can't bring myself to speak her name. Suffice to say she was a close friend. A very close friend. And I blame myself for what happened. The entry wounds, if they are sucked quickly enough, may drag the little parasites into the light of day, where they die before they can do their dastardly work. But my . . . to save my feelings, she did not mention what had happened until it was too late."

"The worms killed her," Eldora whispered, clutching her throat.

"I'm afraid so." Swathed in rough black fabric banded about his head with gold rope, Max appeared to be in the role of some Eastern potentate, or desert warrior of high rank, perhaps, Minerva wasn't certain which. "Got into her brain," he said. "Ghastly."

When Max paused, Eldora said, "Go on."

"If you insist. The main problem with the fleet festerer is that it's so fleet, it is rarely seen at all. It fixes its minute but viciously poisonous jaws into the flesh of his victim and begins to suck. Then it swells, and swells, and as it swells, a crater forms inside the victim's body."

"Max," Gray said, glancing at his watch, "what are you doing in costume for the big event already? We've got hours yet."

"Eldora wanted me to show her mine. Said if I would, she'd show me hers. So I showed her."

"Ah," Gray said, "I see."

"Gray," Eldora said, "did you know Max had actually been attacked by one of these fleet thingies?"

"Fleet festerer," Max told her obligingly. "Otherwise known, one supposes jokingly, as the lodger who stays, because once one of the things are in residence, so to speak, well, they're in residence. The best one can do is treat the symptoms and pray they don't eat too much too quickly."

"I say, Max," Gray said. "Any messages for me, by any chance?"

"No. For some reason, I thought everyone knew about my condition. My sad condition."

"Oh, mercy!" Eldora's hands flew to her face, and shimmering gold satin, finely pleated and of far too small a quantity, trembled all over her. "They *kill* you?"

Max sighed and poured himself a brandy. "In time. The end, of course, is horrible. That's when the convulsions take over."

"Should be fun finding out what provoked this," Gray murmured to Minerva. "Can't remember the last time I heard Max spin a good tale. Feels like old times."

"I say," Max said, standing tall and appearing remarkably fit to Minerva. "Sorry, Gray, I forgot this. Reverend Pumfrey was kind enough to bring it along when he was doing some visiting at some of the outlying farms. Special delivery from

Edinburgh. Chap delivering it got lost and went to the Rectory."

Max smiled, charmingly Minerva thought, and looked expectantly at Gray.

"Very good of Pumfrey," Gray said. "So, what did he bring?"

"Oh, dash it all." Max patted his person, feeling around in his black garb. "I know it's here somewhere, because I was wearing this when Pumfrey came. He said he wasn't sure if it was appropriate for him to be in costume tonight. I told him we'd all be very disappointed if he wasn't. What have I done with those papers?"

The patting, and peering among folds, continued.

"I didn't see Reverend Pumfrey," Eldora said.

"No. I was on my way downstairs when he got here. That was before you went up to get ready to show me yours. Gray, I know I've got them. Must say you're a sly dog. Off to America within the month. When were you going to tell us all?"

Max finally produced a fat envelope, and Gray swept it from his fingers. "Opening my post?" he said, his frown thunderous. "I've always thought better of you."

"I didn't open your bloody post, Falconer. Pumfrey said the chap who made the delivery was from the shipping company. He talked about it. I told you it was a special delivery."

"I don't care to discuss this. I'd consider it a great favor if you'd all forget you heard anything about it."

"America?" Eldora said. "But . . . what will that mean? Of course, it's none of my business, but as far as your position here goes—your business concerns? Would you—well—give them up?"

Minerva studied the woman and decided Cadzow had not chosen quite the foolish mate everyone seemed to assume Eldora to be.

"Not a bit of it," Gray said. "I can watch my affairs perfectly well from America. I've been thinking about the importance of tending to further expansion in that direction. And I'll make regular visits here. *We'll* make regular visits. Our honeymoon will be quite the adventure, won't it, darling?" He hugged Minerva.

"Quite," she said. He'd cut things fine. There wasn't that much time before the evening's festivities at Maudlin Manor, and she hoped all interested parties would be informed of the "adventurous honeymoon" by then.

"Evidently Cadzow's feeling a bit under the weather," Max said. "Eldora says he may be a late arrival this evening—if he can get there at all."

Minerva lowered her eyelids. Unless she was much mistaken, as soon as Eldora ran to tell him the news about Gray leaving for America, Cadzow would decide he must keep a close watch on his nephew at all times. Oh, what a frenzy there would be. If Gray couldn't be alive in the West Indies or in England, well, then he couldn't be allowed to be alive in America, either, could he?

Surely Gray's plan had bought them at least a little time. No one would have any reason to expect them to leave Ballyfog before there had been a wedding, and before it was time to depart Scotland.

"Eldora was hoping I might be able to take her along to Maudlin Manor, but I felt I had to let her know about my condition." Max put a forefinger into his left ear and wiggled it hard. "After all, if she did happen to be a prime host for the fleet festerer, well, then . . . Ouch, I think I feel . . . Eldora, would you mind looking into my ear, just in case? Sometimes it burrows out and then back in—very fast, of course—and one needs to cleanse the wound."

Eldora clapped her hands and said, "I declare, I would forget my very head if it were not . . . Yes, well, please excuse me. I've just remembered what I absolutely have to do before the salon."

Within seconds Gray and Minerva were alone with Max,

who assumed an innocent expression, took his brandy to a deep chair, and sat down.

"What prompted that little display?" Gray asked as soon as the door closed behind Eldora.

"The lady had it in mind to have us create a drama. I didn't care for the piece."

"Not up to the fair Eldora, hmm?" Gray said.

"I'm not up to anything," Max replied. "I took the opportunity to make certain I hadn't lost my storytelling skills, that's all. It's been too long since I was moved to *entertain*, and it seemed like the perfect opportunity. Did I do all right with the America thing?"

"Perfectly."

"Good. That's all of them, then. Mission accomplished—with Iona's and Fergus's help. The whole bunch thinks you plan to leave for America in a month. Now all we have to do is go to a jolly party and have a jolly good time."

Minerva scrunched up her face. "I shall be desperately worried until we make it away, but I do think Gray's notion is a clever one."

"Occasionally he has a passable notion," Max said. "Pirate tonight for you, hey, Gray? Too bad you can't be a black sheikh, like me. Very romantic, black sheikhs." He took part of his headdress and draped it over the lower part of his face.

"I noticed," Gray said. "Evidently you made quite the impression on Eldora. Poor Cadzow will have to watch over his property more carefully."

"Fleet festerers," Minerva added. "Where were you when you became infested?"

"Right there," Max said, pointing to the spot where Minerva stood. "Right there listening to Eldora Makewell offering to show me things."

Flaming torches driven into the snow-covered earth along the length of the driveway turned Maudlin Manor into a scene more sinister than the desired fairyland effect. Despite the cold, the front doors were thrown open, because it had been decided that the expected crush of bodies would more than compensate for the loss of heat.

Seated beside Minerva in a Falconer coach, Gray took her hand to his thigh and chafed her cold fingers. "Relax, my love. Our plan is flawless."

"Nothing is flawless," she said.

She was ever the realist, but he wouldn't have her any other way. Well, perhaps a little less the realist might be acceptable when a man was faced with a night when every move must happen at exactly the right moment and in exactly the right manner.

"You are secretive about your costume, miss," he told her. "Could I not have one tiny peek at this creation of yours?"

"No." Her hood had been pulled well forward when he'd picked her up from Willieknock, where he discovered that her parents had already left. He wondered if they had particular tasks to attend to for which they needed extra time at the manor. Or, more likely, if they'd left the lodge in order to discuss the revelation about America where no one was likely to overhear. And would their discussion include Silas Meaner? Or the McSporrans?

The line of coaches and carts, and some guests on horseback, moved slowly up the driveway. He opened the window an inch, and the sounds of laughter and music came from a distance. Nearer to the coaches, one or two hardy souls shrieked while they skated by torchlight on the frozen pool around the still fountains.

"It's all rather eerie," Gray said. "Or perhaps I should say ethereal, not quite real."

"I'm very afraid," Minerva said. "I know we have done all that we could do, but there is so much danger and so much we don't know and cannot control."

"We would be fools if we didn't fear at least some minor

impediment to our plan, but I expect to accomplish our escape, my love."

"Oh, I need your strength tonight. I'm glad you are both honest and sure." She looked up at him from the shadow of her hood. "You make a most intriguing pirate. Enough hair to tie a queue? I declare, we'd best take the shears to that very soon."

Gray smiled. He felt each passing yard beneath the coach, and with their progress, his tension and determination mounted. Tonight was the beginning of a new life for both of them. Tonight he would take Minerva away—a bold course that would declare her his—and he would prepare to wait, ever vigilant, for the arrival of his foe, or foes.

"Where is this contraption you intend to use as a diversion?" he asked Minerva.

"It is exactly where it should be," she said shortly. "I believe everything will work admirably. I have to believe that."

The coach swung in front of the steps and halted. In due time, the coachman opened the door and put down steps before handing Minerva out. Gray followed and took her arm as they climbed to the front door.

From inside the manor came the glad sounds of a Christmas carol played on fiddles, piano, flute, and harp. The entry hall, formerly dowdy and more than a little dusty, gleamed and was trimmed with evergreen boughs threaded through with strings of holly berries. The scent of pine was heady.

"Good Lord," Gray muttered. "Incredible. How was it all done?"

"With a great deal of hard work from a great many people," she told him. "Christmas is almost upon us, and we decided to start the celebrations tonight. After all, it's special that so many of those who live in and around Ballyfog should be together like this."

Gray inclined his head and adjusted his black mask, shielding his voice as he did so. "I should like them together at our wedding," he said softly, as they reached the top step. "At St. Aldhelm's, if I had my choice. And afterward, at Drumblade to drink to our health."

"Not for us, the traditional celebration, I think," Minerva said, and Gray heard her regret. But she added, "However, I have never been traditional."

The continuation of their conversation must wait. Already they were swept deep into the masked throng in the entry hall.

"My goodness," Minerva cried, clapping her hands. "Mrs. Pumfrey! Who do you suppose she is?"

Evidently Mrs. Pumfrey had sharp ears. Holding her white-feathered mask by its ivory stick, she squeezed close, smiled up at Gray and Minerva, and said, "I'm Caroline of Brunswick." And her heavily rouged cheeks and lowcut, bright-pink dress, together with a powdered white wig, did indeed give a suitably wanton appearance. She pointed to a large, black, heart-shaped patch affixed to one cheek. "Beauty mark. I feel completely outrageous. Reverend Pumfrey says St. Peter won't even interview me. Hah!" She trotted off and disappeared in the crowd.

"How long must we wait?" Minerva asked.

"A little while, my love," he told her. "I thought we'd allow things to become somewhat jolly—if you understand my meaning—then insist loudly that they begin the treasure hunt. And then we proceed with our plans."

"Things are already jolly," Minerva pointed out.

Gray sensed the depth of her nervousness. He must give her the strength to be patient. "Let's make our way to the ballroom. I must say, I had no idea there were this many people in the entire area."

"People aren't generally terribly social here, do you think? I don't. I believe curiosity has brought them out."

"Curiosity?"

"The first affair at Maudlin Manor in anyone's memory.

Presided over by strangers everyone wants to take a close look at. And then there's you."

She allowed the final comment to fade away, as if she hoped he might not notice it at all. "Minerva. What does 'and then there's you,' mean?"

Raising her chin, she smiled at him, and her eyes glinted from her silver mask. "First of all, you are a mystery, a man who was presumed dead but who came back to life. Secondly, you are exceedingly eligible, and unmarried, and this is an area where there are very few eligible bachelors. And don't imagine your mask will save you from a great deal of attention. They will all know who you are."

Damn nuisance. He hadn't even thought of that. "Well, any candidate for my hand must be exceedingly intelligent, witty, good-looking, brown-haired, blue-eyed, inventive, an only child, her name must be Minerva, and she must be very, very fleet."

Minerva giggled. "Like Max's festerers?"

"Exactly." Gray smiled.

"Yes," she said, looking only at him, "this means, I think, that there is only one candidate for your hand, and I am she. We'd better show our costumes."

Gray took off his own cloak and reached for Minerva's. She pushed down her hood. A helmet fashioned of silver material cut into fish-scale-shaped pieces fitted her head closely. The effect was startling. Despite the mask, the fact that her eyes were exceedingly large was even more apparent, as were the pleasing curves of her face and the flat nature of her small ears.

"You look wonderful," Minerva told him. "But I shall have to insist that we get on with things at the first possible moment. The ladies will be all over you, and I shall be terribly jealous."

He looked down at tattered brown trousers cut off at the knee and long dark stockings. He'd procured an old pair of buckled shoes for the occasion.

Two women stopped to stare, one the ancient Mrs. Goddard, who took mincing little steps and chomped constantly on empty gums. Her costume consisted of what was probably her everyday black bombazine gown, but worn with a horned headdress of yellow velvet. She hadn't bothered to mask.

"Who is he?" Mrs. Goddard shouted.

Her companion, a spinster who had been the former village teacher, looked uncomfortable and said loudly in the old lady's ear, "I think this is Mr. Gray Falconer."

"No need to shout," Mrs. Goddard bellowed. "What's he doing wearing almost nothing in company, that's what I'd like to know? Couldn't you afford a whole shirt, young man? Disgraceful I call it. Never would have done when I was a girl."

"About the time your hat was new," Minerva muttered.

"What did you say?" Mrs. Goddard asked. "Speak up."

"I said your hat is wonderful. When was it new, do you think?"

"Fie. What do the young learn in the classroom these days. If she'd had you as a teacher she'd have known the period of my hat, Muriel. Early fourteen hundreds. See if you can't remember that. Henry the Fifth was on the throne."

"Knew him, did you?" Minerva said softly, and Gray saw her catch the teacher's eye, and saw the gleam of mirth there.

Mrs. Goddard sniffed and lost interest. Making her opinions of Gray loudly known, she allowed Muriel to guide her away. "Naked in public," she said. "You can see his chest. The idea. I may never recover from the shock. I was married for forty years and never saw my husband without a shirt."

Gray chuckled, and so did other guests close by. In fact he did wear a shirt, but it hung in shreds, revealing a good deal of his "nakedness."

He took Minerva's cloak and forgot to breathe. Then he

made to put the cloak back, but her glare warned him to do no such thing.

"Min," he said urgently. "You can't be here like that."

"I am here like this. I'll leave as quickly as possible, it can't be quick enough, but this has a purpose."

"Of course it has a purpose. To make every man stare at you and every woman hate you. They are *already* staring at you. Minerva, *who* are you supposed to be?"

"I'd have thought that was obvious to anyone who went to school. I'm Queen Boadicea. Get rid of the cloaks and let's circulate." She smiled around. "We have to be seen. And remembered."

"Oh, you'll be remembered," he told her, handing their cloaks off to a servant he didn't recognize. "For God's sake—can't you cover yourself more?"

"I can't help it if I'm somewhat—sturdy."

Sturdy. Her hair was loose and flowed from beneath the artfully stitched helmet. A red robe fashioned from a long length of silk was wound loosely about her body. Very loosely. "*Minerva.* You cannot show yourself like that."

"Oh, don't be silly. No one will look at me."

No one would look at the contraption—the very abbreviated contraption—that didn't at all cover her breasts and was made of the same silver stuff as her headpiece?

"Why is . . . that thing necessary? The thing under the robe?"

"Breastplates," she said calmly, marching forth with her head held high, smiling regally from side to side. "If I take it off, I should think I might really cause a stir.

"I suggest we use the diversion we've made to allow us to take good measure of where the enemy may be."

The robe parted about her limbs—all the way up to her thighs. On her feet she wore odd black boots that reached her calves. Silver thongs crisscrossed the boots.

Women's mouths fell open.

Men jostled to get a better view.

He would call them out. All of them. Kill all of them. How dare they look at her like that?

Max appeared and fell in on the other side of Minerva. "Perfect," he told her. "Exactly the right touch. No one will fail to see you—or to remember how you look."

"Have a care, Max," Gray said.

"You've done a good job, too," Max said, obviously unmoved by Gray's hostility. "A pirate to remember. The ladies are loving glimpses of the forbidden." He chuckled, and marched along with them, his black robe billowing.

"Who have you seen so far?" Gray asked.

"Reverend Pumfrey's dressed as some sort of Roman. Bedsheet. Simple. But I told him he made a fine Roman."

"You know who I'm looking for, and it isn't Pumfrey."

"Eldora's in the ballroom," Max said, going with them into that room. "Lolling by that statue of Ramses they borrowed from somewhere."

Minerva sighted Eldora and said, "She does look striking."

"Good spot for her," Gray said. "Just in case someone doesn't immediately guess she's supposed to be Cleopatra. Let's keep our distance from her. We don't have time."

"The McSporrans," Minerva said. She bit her bottom lip.

"What about them?" Gray asked, but the couple bore down upon them almost at once.

"Good evening," Minerva said.

Drucilla sniffed. "I take it your poor mother hasn't seen you."

"What exactly are you and Mr. McSporran supposed to be?" Gray interrupted. "If you don't mind my asking." The pair wore simple black garb, McSporran with a stiff wing collar and black tie, Drucilla's hair covered with a white lace cap. Keys swung from her waist.

"We came as a butler and housekeeper," McSporran said. "We thought we'd make a dashin' pair an' be sure no one else had the same idea."

Gray was too preoccupied to be much amused at the deception. A very tall man with a harshly angular face stepped before him and said, "Good evening. I don't believe we've met." His black hair was worn in a queue, but a considerably longer queue than Gray's. Behind his black mask, his eyes were so light as to be almost transparent. "Captain Smith. I knew your father, Mr. Falconer."

Gray inclined his head. "Pleased to meet you. This is my fiancée, Minerva Arbuckle."

Smith made a leg in an old-fashioned manner and swept off the plumed hat that matched a generic blue and gold uniform of some bygone era.

"How did you know my father, Captain Smith?" Gray asked.

"We had some business dealings years ago. Nothing significant, but I admired him greatly."

"Thank you."

"There you are. Here they are, Cadzy." Eldora rushed up, all aquiver in her gold satin, and with Cadzow looking pale and dressed in normal evening clothes. "Cadzy isn't up to too much, but he's made the effort to come and be with me. Isn't that sweet?" Eldora avoided looking at Max and gave Captain Smith only a cursory glance.

"I wouldn't have been here if I hadn't received some very disturbing news from Ratley," Cadzow said distinctly. "Evidently Ratley got it from Mrs. Hatch, who heard Minerva's parents talking about it. Honestly, Gray, one would think that after all I've been through, you'd have discussed such a matter with me first."

Gray looked at Eldora, who became interested in adjusting her sleeves. So Eldora had not gone to Cadzow with the news of Gray's plans. He couldn't imagine why.

Rather than draw discreetly away, as Max instantly did, Smith held his ground and turned the signet ring on his right small finger around and around. The man had neither charm nor grace, Gray decided, but had no idea how to ask him to move along without creating unpleasantness.

"Gray, why didn't you tell me?" Cadzow asked.

Gray felt guilty for putting his uncle through this sham, but there was no help but to do so if all were to be fair. "I had no intention of anyone finding out at all," he said. "The whole thing has been a disaster. But don't worry. You will approve heartily when I explain. But this isn't the place."

"Since this is where we are, this is the place," Cadzow said, his pallor becoming almost green. "I cannot consider being left here in England to deal with matters again."

Gray caught his uncle's arm. "Look, I'm not . . . Trust me. I shall need your support in the days and weeks to come. There are a great many matters in which I will turn to you for help and advice."

Porteous and Janet Arbuckle chose that moment to press into the group. Porteous pirouetted and said, "I decided to be really clever. I came as a famous painter. In other words—I came as myself."

The man, Smith, leaned his weight on one leg and regarded Porteous from head to foot, then repeated the process with Janet Arbuckle. And Janet Arbuckle was well worth the effort.

"Let me guess," Smith said, pointing a long forefinger at her. "Moll Flanders?"

Janet turned a shade of red that didn't complement her green mask. "I am Elizabeth the First," she said haughtily, her neck held stiff inside a wired, lace-edged white collar that stood up behind her neck, curved above her shoulders, and swept to outline either side of her bodice as far as her waist. Between that collar and the tight, flat bodice, lay only a rope of pearls and most of the flesh that should have been inside the bodice.

"Oh, my," Eldora said, striking a more provocative pose. "Almost the stuff of an Arbuckle painting."

"*Almost,*" Janet snorted. "I'll have you know—"

"You look marvelous," Porteous told his wife, whose pearl-encrusted gown complete with stiffened panniers was really quite a masterpiece. "Wouldn't you say your mother looks marvelous, Minerva?"

"Yes," Minerva said quietly, and Gray wondered if she was noticing that neither of her parents mentioned knowing that she and Gray supposedly intended to marry and go to America.

He felt eyes upon him and turned in time to catch Smith staring once more. The other nodded and averted his face. There was about his features an unmoving quality. When he spoke, his thin lips barely parted. He had no brows, and his forehead was smooth. The color of the man's skin surprised Gray, a yellowish cast that seemed out of place entirely.

The music swelled, and a number of the assembly broke into song. Gray cared only that it was time to finish setting the scene—as soon as he had all possible players within sight.

"Who's that?" Max asked, coming forward again. "That man."

Gray saw immediately whom he meant. "Don't know. Seems determined to make a cake of himself, though."

The man in question pulled forward one of the chairs that had been collected from houses around the area and leaped onto its seat. Dressed in a long white tunic, but wearing a medieval fool's hat, green and yellow, with gold bells jingling, and a matching bicolored mask, he threw wide an arm and shouted.

What he said was indecipherable until Reverend Pumfry, a large glass of champagne in one hand, came forward, set the glass at his feet, and beat on a copper warming pan with a fire poker.

Silence was instant.

"Thank you, sir, thank you," the speaker said to the clergyman.

Minerva elbowed Gray and indicated someone who hovered not far away. Despite an excellent beggar's costume, complete with streaked face and a tattered scarf over his head, Gray recognized Brumby McSporran but not his companion, who was a beautiful, serene-faced young woman wearing a nun's black habit complete with starched white wimple. Brumby held her hand and kept her close to his side.

"A welcome sight," Minerva remarked.

Gray agreed and said, "As you say."

"Mr. Clack has asked me to pass along his most sincere regrets," the part fool, part East Indian of some kind announced, his bells jingling. "Some of you know he was injured in India and suffers from his old wounds. Inconveniently, they are causing him great pain at the moment."

Murmurs of sympathy wafted about the big room.

"If we can believe that," Gray said, "then the entire cast is accounted for."

"Except for Micky Finish," Minerva said, looking around again. "Don't see him."

"Damn." Why hadn't he noticed the boy was missing? "Of course, maybe he's tucked up in bed like all good children should be."

"Perhaps," Max said from behind him. "Perhaps he is. But I'd rather be sure, wouldn't you?"

Before Gray could respond, the man on the chair said, "However, Mr. Clack will not be happy if you are not happy. And, of course, Mr. Gray Falconer, who is also host of this wonderful event, also insists that you enjoy yourself."

Many faces, some of them avid with curiosity, turned toward Gray, and there was applause. He bowed slightly and noted that Captain Smith looked not at the speaker but at Cadzow. Cadzow looked back—until he lowered his eyes and turned away.

"So," the man on the chair said, brushing at his black mustache and beard, "to that end we will proceed with some of the more exotic events we have devised for you this evening." He flipped his hand, and Gray saw black smudges on his skin. From his dyed facial hair, no doubt.

Meaner, Gray realized with surprise. Silas Meaner, no less. The man was transformed more by the change in coloring than by his unlikely costume. One might almost think he'd been intended to be dark-haired rather than blond.

"We are going to have a *treasure hunt!*"

Whoops of glee went up.

Meaner signaled for silence. "Mr. Gray Falconer has very kindly agreed to provide . . . the *treasure,* and I'm assured that it is treasure indeed."

More cheers.

"Did you?" Minerva asked without looking at Gray.

"Wait and see," Gray said, then, more loudly, he called, "There are clues, correct, Silas?"

Meaner stared, unsmiling, at him.

"Clues," Gray repeated, his heart beginning to beat faster. "At first they may take most of you beautiful people in similar directions. Later they will divide you because your interpretations will vary. Think long and hard. Follow your whims—or be logical, if you must."

A smattering of laughter went through the ballroom.

"Be careful of your neighbor. No one shall be without some treasure in the end. Take particular care on staircases and the like. Now, here is the first clue." He found Minerva's hand and squeezed it. "Look where water turned to stone."

There was a buzz of conversation.

Somewhere a voice called, "The River's away far for a cold night, sir."

Apparently that was also humorous, for more laughter followed.

"There's water closer at hand," Reverend Pumfry, now thoroughly in a party mood, shouted, and loped off toward the foyer with a snaking crowd winding behind him. "The fountains."

Gray drew a deep breath and said, "It's time."

Drawing Minerva with him, and checking around to make sure Max was close at hand—and that the most important members of the audience were, as well—he fell into the surging band heading for the front doors.

Once outside, they were swept into a throng that strained toward the fountains.

"Now," Gray whispered to Minerva, releasing her hand. "Go. But be careful, my dearest one."

She moved forward, away from him, as if anxious to get near to the fountain, and Gray turned to Max, laughing and gesturing—while he checked yet again for the faces he needed to see, and found them all present, and all diverted. True, Cadzow continued to look at him with deeply troubled eyes, but the rest jumped up and down to try to see what was happening closer to the front.

Max stood beside Gray now. "Perhaps we should begin too," he said, and when Gray nodded, stood on his toes and searched about in all directions. Then he turned away and walked, with every appearance of openness, to the right until he reached a group of holly bushes, stripped of most of their berries for the decorations, but still dense.

Gray stayed where he was and exchanged a few comments with Porteous Arbuckle, complimenting the man on his wife's spectacular costume and making a point of saying, in Janet's hearing, that their daughter must get her ingenuity in that area from her mother.

Both seemed pleased with his comments.

Who wanted him dead?

Was he misguided in his suspicions?

Could there be someone he'd missed entirely?

A cry went up from the crowd, and Gray knew someone had seen the "clue" of which he spoke. Instantly he shifted, nonchalantly, in the direction Max had taken, and when he was clear of the group he must watch, he stood still again and studied them—and found that they hadn't noticed his departure.

A few more steps and he was between the greedy thorned leaves of the holly bushes, taking the black robe from Max. Once the switch had been made, the two of them watched from their cover.

"Och, I see the clue," a voice shouted. In fact, Fergus Drummond's voice shouted.

"Let's have it, then," someone roared.

"Gi' a man a chance," Fergus demanded. "It's cut in the ice. Ah, now I see what it says."

"What?" the cry went up.

"The lady will tell it," Fergus announced. "That's it. The lady will tell it."

"Daft," a guest said loudly.

A grumble ensued, and another called, "What good is a clue if we've all got it?"

"Speak up then, *Lady,"* yet another voice demanded, and there was more laughter.

Then, flashing beneath the moon, a vehicle with the appearance of gold tore up the driveway toward the manor and the crowd scattered, ran back, squealing and screaming, and shouting to each other that it was "the lady."

"Look at her," Max said when Minerva became clear in her clever "chariot," which was a borrowed farm cart with cloth of gold draped about it, and huge wooden knives attached to the wheels. "Boadicea."

"She didn't tell me what she'd decided to be until we got here, probably because she wanted to shock me. My wild one will never bore me."

Urging on a single white horse, Minerva circled the fountain and called out, "You sat upon it!" before heading back down the driveway.

Making himself stay where he was became unbearable, but Gray knew he must be sure all had gone as planned. If he'd had any doubt, the presence of the Arbuckles and the

McSporrans on the front steps would have convinced him. They would be sure to see what they were intended to see.

A few minutes passed and the cart made a return up the driveway, at a more leisurely pace. In the back, flipping the reins, a girl in red and silver stood, quietly making her way now that the crowd had dispersed.

Gray watched as the McSporrans and the Arbuckles promptly retreated into the manor before Max, in a pirate costume that matched Gray's, went to the front door and pressed into the crowd.

The girl in the cart looked neither right nor left, but she raised a hand in a wave before heading for the side of the manor. Iona Drummond was, as Minerva asserted, a dear friend.

Gray ran then. From the holly bushes, into the pines that edged the woods, and deeper into the trees. Exactly where he knew it would be, a narrow path beaten down by poachers led to a wider trail in poor condition, but passable enough if a man knew his way.

Gray Falconer knew his way.

A whinny sounded, and the clink of tack. Hoofs pawed the frozen ground.

"Minerva?"

"Here," she called, and opened her arms when she saw him coming to her.

Gray went into those dear arms, lifted her, swung her around. "My darling girl. My all. We did it. They will not miss us until we are well away. Then the note will explain our elopement and our plan to return to Ballyfog in due course. Those who must be sure I never return will set out to find us. It will take time—perhaps a long time. And when they come, I shall be ready for them. Think of it, Minerva. The waiting will be hard, but we must hope to finally confront them, and then be free of the fear that has stalked us."

"Yes," she agreed, "but most of all I am thinking of being with you."

They wrapped themselves in the warm clothes they had provided for the journey, and mounted their horses.

With a final backward glance toward the manor, Gray waited for Minerva to ride ahead before wheeling about and following her. "Edinburgh," he said, rejoicing. "You're going to love the Rossmara house in Charlotte Square."

His heart soared, and he felt strong enough to combat any foe. The enemy lay behind, and ahead was a nest, a stronghold where he could protect his love and himself.

Chapter Twenty-four

Minerva had visited Edinburgh often enough, but had never arrived with the dawn, or on horseback and exhausted.

The snowfall here had been light, and it remained as grimy sludge beside the roads. A heavy frost iced every surface, and decorated windowpanes in patterns no mere painter could achieve.

"We'll be there very soon now," Gray said. Anxiety furrowed his brow and made his words of encouragement sound hollow. "The house belongs to the Marquis of Stonehaven. Max's uncle. I spent a half-term holiday there when I was at Eton."

"You don't have to cheer me, Gray," Minerva said, "I'm well enough. It's the horses I'm concerned for."

They'd changed mounts once, at a small inn where fresh horses had been ready for them. Minerva hadn't asked how Gray had made such arrangements. She began to believe he could do almost anything.

"The horses will get their rest soon enough, too," he said. "My challenge will be to make sure the house shows no sign of my presence. The ones I seek will come stealthily. I would not want curious neighbors to call, or friends of the

Rossmaras or Stonehavens who happened to think that they were in residence."

They rode along one of Edinburgh's elegantly curved crescents. Houses, three or four stories high, formed these pleasing terraces. Minerva spared distracted glances for front steps scrubbed and whited by industrious servants, for black railings rimed with ice, and for polished doors with bright brass knockers and letter boxes that glimmered in the misty light of early morning.

"You're certain the one you want will come?" Minerva asked. "What if he doesn't?"

"They will come," he said, and their eyes met.

He suspected, as she did, that one of them would suffer a grave disappointment before their drama ended. "I am troubled," she told him. "Deeply so. You understand me, don't you, Gray?"

His gentle smile warmed her, despite the accompanying tense flicker of muscles in his face. "I understand. It's that bond between us, the knowing of each other's heart, that will keep us strong together. But let's try to move as quickly as we can now. First I must be sure you are well rested. I have little fear that unwelcome company will arrive too soon."

Minerva slowed her horse until Gray had ridden ahead some distance. He stopped and looked back, then trotted to meet her. "Are you . . . Min, what's the matter?"

"I must be more tired than I thought. You must be sure I am well rested? *You* must make sure the house doesn't appear lived in? The ones *you* seek will come stealthily? No, no, Gray, we must both attend to these matters. What concerns you concerns me."

Gray wheeled about, and Minerva guessed he was deciding how to explain himself. "We should get on, Min," he said. "The fewer people about when we arrive, the better. It's already later than I'd hoped."

"Gray—"

"*Please,* Min. In this you must allow me to do what I know is best. I cannot expose you to the kind of danger I expect to encounter."

A few moments earlier, she'd decided she would like to lie down and sleep, on the horse if necessary! Now she couldn't imagine sleeping again, anywhere. "How dare you." No, no, she cautioned herself. No enraged outbursts here. If she hoped for success against the male obsession with its wretched, perceived need to protect the "weaker" sex, then she must give him no opportunity to suggest she was hysterical.

He watched her with his infuriating calm.

She would watch and wait also.

"Can we get on?" he asked at last.

"I don't think so," she told him evenly. "Not until I fully understand your intentions."

His long, long sigh tested her resolve to be reasonable. "I intend," he said, "to take you to Charlotte Square, feed you as best I can, and put you to bed."

This was, Minerva thought, the ultimate test of her will. "Do go on," she suggested.

"When you have slept I shall do what Max and I arranged, and send you to his sister, Ella, who should shortly be in residence at a small, discreet hotel. If there had been time, I should have sent you away before any of this occurred. There wasn't time, and I cannot simply take you to the hotel, not at this hour, and not until I'm certain Ella is there."

"You could not have sent me away before," she said, clinging to false calm. "You needed me to help you with your escape."

He reached for her reins, but Minerva spurred her horse on and passed him.

"All right," he said, catching up at once. "Yes, you are right. Right about everything. Will you forgive me for wishing that I could have saved you from this? Will you allow me to be a simple man in this way? I would protect the woman I love from any danger if I could."

If she gave in completely, he would try to send her away. "There is nothing to forgive. But I shall not leave you."

"Min . . ." He let out an exasperated breath, then closed his mouth and rode with purpose.

She smiled privately and followed his lead. They turned into a handsomely proportioned square arranged around a central garden where leafless beech trees stood, stiff and still, and clumps of stubby growth crouched spiderlike in their frigid coats.

Gray led the way to the mews behind the northerly side of the square and dealt efficiently with stabling the horses. With Minerva's help, he rubbed them down, blanketed and fed them.

Carrying their supplies from the mews to the gardens behind one of the imposing three-story houses, they moved swiftly to the back entrance into the kitchens.

After unlocking the door, Gray locked and bolted it from the inside and they walked past kitchen and scullery, butler's pantry and buttery, and took a flight of stairs to the ground floor.

"We can't risk lights," Gray said. "Soon enough we won't need them. It'll be gloomy, but we'll manage. I'm going to light a fire—after I make sure it won't alert anyone from the outside. We'll pray the smoke will not be noticed."

Minerva followed him through an entrance hall too dim for her to make out more than a longcase clock, and that only because it ticked loudly.

Very quickly Gray climbed the stairs and made his way to a suite of rooms at the back of the house. He went directly into the bedroom, to the window, where he made certain wooden shutters were tightly closed before drawing heavy drapes.

All light was closed out, and Minerva's eyes took seconds

to adjust before the gray pall seeping from the corridor allowed her to see shapes again.

"Sit," Gray said shortly. "I must light the fire. I cannot risk you becoming ill. If you are not already ill."

"Pah," she said, although not as sharply as she would have liked. "Have you forgotten that I am very—"

"Sturdy?" he said, shoveling coals into the grate. "No, sweet, I haven't forgotten that you are, as you say, sturdy. I haven't forgotten anything about you. I never could."

Minerva felt a wash of heat and closed her mouth. They had procured food from the inn where they'd changed horses. While they'd journeyed she'd been too anxious to arrive at their destination to consider hunger. Now she realized she was famished. "Shall I prepare us something to eat?"

He tossed off his cloak and laughed shortly. "Prepare? I fear we'll be eating bread and cheese. And drinking whatever that robber baron of a landlord provided for us to drink. Get into bed. You'll warm up faster there. I'll bring you something to eat."

"I'm dirty."

"Dirty?" Looking over his shoulder, shadows made by the young flames played over his face, and his eyes glinted. "Of course. I'll heat water over the fire to take the chill off for you."

"And for you," she said, feeling the rise of irritation again. "My needs are no different from yours."

"As you say." His tone didn't convince her that he agreed with a word he spoke. "Take off your shoes—boots. They must be soaked."

Minerva remembered her marvelous boots. "Not a bit of it. They are an experiment—to help me decide if I have found the perfect new medium for my Mud Thwarter Hems. Actually it will be an old medium that is becoming much improved."

"Yes," Gray said. "Take them off and sit here where you can warm those toes." He pulled a chair close to the fire.

"You aren't listening, but it doesn't matter. Some other time will do. Then I shall tell you all about rubber and the improvements made over the efforts of MacIntosh and Hancock by two unknown American gentlemen, Mr. Haywood and Mr. Goodyear. It seems that sulfur may prove the answer to all the problems in using rubber. You know how they find it cracks in winter and melts in summer, well . . . Anyway, my boots are rubber."

She stopped and looked into Gray's face.

"You are wonderful, Min. If I don't stop myself I'm going to say something really stupid, like 'you should have been born a man.' Which you certainly should not, because you are perfect as you are, and you are mine. But you have an enviable mind."

His admiration confused her somewhat. "Thank you," she said, but he left the room without another word.

Still wrapped in her cloak, she sat down and obediently pulled off her ugly boots in order to extend her feet to the fire's warmth.

He was right, of course. She could not expect him to be other than a man, a man with the instincts bred into such as he. A gentleman. A gentle man, but also a warrior who could not countenance taking a woman into battle. Gray was readying himself for battle.

Would she hamper him?

Could she leave him?

If the answers were no, then how could she help him, and how could she persuade him to allow her to stay?

Gray's footsteps sounded in the passage outside, and she couldn't help smiling. Just listening to the manner in which he scuffed one heel shot the vision of the slight but unconscious swagger with which he walked. The desert sheikh's robes discarded so that he might ride with more ease, he still wore his ragtag pirate costume and it suited him a deal too well.

He entered with a large kettle of water and placed it on the trivet over the fire. "It won't take long," he told her. "We'll eat. And then I'll leave you to wash."

Minerva made no comment. He brought one of the bags that had been slung across his horse, and produced exactly what he'd promised: bread and cheese. Further exploration revealed a jug of wine, of which Gray took a swallow and winced. "Awful. But it'll have to do."

It was, indeed, dreadful, but Minerva had lost her interest in either food or drink. She did eat some bread and cheese, and drink a little of the wine, but she thought only of what Gray must be planning to say, and what she would say in return.

He sat on a chair opposite hers and ate silently, his gaze on the fire.

Minerva broke off a crumb of bread and rolled it between finger and thumb.

"Wine?" Glancing toward her, he offered the jug.

She shook her head, no.

"More cheese?"

"No, thank you."

"Very well." He stood and went to the washstand. Returning with the bowl, he went down on one knee and poured out a little water to test. "Still chill," he said, preparing to replace the kettle.

"It will do," she told him. "Cool water invigorates me."

"You must sleep, not be invigorated."

"I disagree. With you, my dearest friend, I need all of the fine mind you say I have, and I need it very much awake."

He hesitated, then set down the bowl before her and filled it. "If you insist on cold water, then at least use it before the fire." He gathered the scarcely touched food back into its wrappings and replaced them in the bag.

Minerva continued to study every move he made, a pleasant task if each one did not take him closer to leaving her.

Standing over her again, he said, "I'll be in the sitting

room. You have nothing to fear. I am practiced in the art of little sleep when the need arises."

When she didn't answer, he left her, and she let him go without protest.

He closed the door that was to separate them.

And there was no sound, not the sound of his heels scuffing as he swaggered just a little. Unconsciously. On his way to . . .

Minerva pushed to her feet and turned toward the door that separated them.

And there was no sound.

She approached slowly until she must touch the door or walk away.

And she rested her flattened palms on cool wood, and her brow, and then her cheek, her ear.

And there was no sound.

Oh, yes, he was practiced in the art of little sleep, but so was she. Did he imagine for one moment that in the days, and the months, and the years as his absence had yawned, a void, that she had slept like a babe?

If she let him send her away and there was another void, this a void without end, then what?

Nothing.

Minerva closed her eyes and knew she would not go, not ever, no matter how hard he tried to send her, and no matter the cost. "I will not go," she said softly to the wood. "I will never be parted from him again. He is my life."

All was still, utterly still.

"You are my life," she cried. "Do you understand?"

She made fists against that wood.

"Yes!" Gray told her as if nothing stood between them. "And you are mine. I must send you where you will be safe." He tore open the door and stood, a dark silhouette against a dusky drop, but with his shirt a tattered white banner.

For the first time, Minerva knew fear, fear of this man. "I

will not leave you," she said, dropping her arms to her sides. "If you die here, I die with you."

He swore, and braced himself in the doorway, his head hanging forward. "I have but a few hours to get you to safety and make myself ready for whatever comes. If you are here, I cannot for one moment forget that you are."

"In other words, if I insist upon remaining, I am selfish?"

"You—"

"You have weapons, don't you? Pistols?"

"Of course."

"Then let me use one of them."

He laughed, a fatigued laugh. "So that it could be used against you? Weapons are not for the uninitiated, my dear, nor are they the simple playthings they appear—even if you could bear the weight and hold the pistol steady."

"How long do you think it will be before he comes?"

"Max and I devised a plan. He will watch and listen in Ballyfog. He is astute and knows what he must look for. Questions will be asked. The note I have left says that we have gone to a place of our choosing to be married before the two witnesses required by Scottish law. Then to a friend's Edinburgh house to begin our honeymoon. We will, as I've written, return to Ballyfog in our own good time. It would not have been found until some hours after we left. By then, since our marriage was considered inevitable by most, everyone should be expected to go about their business and be ready to submit us to some good-natured chastisement upon our return.

"Naturally I expect to be followed. And since my connection to Max and the Rossmaras is well known, I expect to be followed here. Probably by as early as this evening."

"What a clear head you have, Gray. I declare, I shall always be glad that the man who is my husband can be relied upon in any eventuality."

He looked at her. "Thank you. I am not yet your husband, but I intend to be."

"How are you to know that Max's cousin is at her hotel?"

"She is there." He produced a slip of paper from his pocket. "This was slipped beneath the front door. She will wait there until you come."

"Good." A gambler she had never been, but she would become an excellent one if need be. "Good, then Ella will be satisfied to have her quarters to herself until this evening, don't you think?"

"I would prefer—"

"Would you? Would you prefer to send me away as quickly as you can?"

"It would be best."

"For whom?" she asked, offering him her hand. "Not for me, certainly. Will you give me a few hours of your time? While we can have them?"

Gray whirled suddenly, violently, away from her. "You do not understand," he shouted. "Why must you torment me so? I am a man, Minerva, not a mewling thing who cannot control . . . No, no, a lie. I cannot control what I feel, what I need anymore. I cannot be with you like this and sit with you like a brother. I am dangerous to you. Do you hear me?"

She took a step backward and said, "I hear you," regretting that her voice shook.

"Then have pity on me, woman, for I am in *pain*. I cannot be sure what lies ahead, and I would as well rip out my eyes as think that you might suffer horror because of me."

Trembling overtook her, but she didn't retreat farther. Rather, she placed a hand on his back, expecting him to fling her away, but determined that she would pursue him until he stopped denying her.

He did not fling her away.

"What do you want from me?" he said, and his quietly spoken question was more ominous than his raging shouts. "Be very clear in your answer."

"I want you to let me lead you."

Beneath her hand the muscles in his back stiffened. "Lead me? Lead me where?"

"Wherever I choose to take you. And if you trust me, you will come. Do you trust me?"

The sitting-room floor was cold to her feet, the air musty and damp to her cheeks. "Do you trust me, Gray?"

"Yes," he whispered.

"Then let me hold your hand and take you with me."

When he remained where he was, she gripped his arms and turned him to face her, and took the hand he didn't offer, and led him back into the bedroom, where she closed the door.

Standing with him before the fire, the bowl of water between them, she took off her cloak and let it fall, and then she knelt and indicated for him to follow.

When they faced each other across the cool, clean water, Minerva said, "Give me your shirt," and he did so, with measured gestures, never taking his eyes from hers now. And when the ruined material rested in her hands he looked at her in the firelight, looked long into her eyes, and at her mouth. He looked only briefly at her body, where the outrageous scarlet and silver of her costume must make a garish picture.

She tore the remnants of his shirt into pieces and handed him one. "I've read of many wedding rituals," she told him. "Why should we not design our own? We are baptized in water because water symbolizes life. With water we can symbolize life again, our life together as man and wife."

His lips parted, but he seemed speechless.

"In this bowl, with this water," she bent to dip in her cloth, "we could join with our promises to each other."

"A promise of the marriage to come?" he said, his voice still soft.

"A marriage to be solemnized as the law of God and man requires, as soon as is expedient."

"It is for me to take care of you," he said.

"And for me to take care of you." She wrung out the cloth and reached to touch his face. Minerva washed his face and his neck. She cupped water in both hands, and he bent his head over the bowl to allow her to wet his hair, and slick it back. He was naked to the waist, and she stood and went to his side to cleanse him.

With each caress of her fingers, he shuddered.

Very firmly, he removed her to the other side of the bowl again and lowered her gently back to her knees. Using his fingertips, dipped into the water, he smoothed back tendrils of hair and traced her face.

"Use the cloth," she told him, and began removing the red robe. "I have ministered to you, and now you must minister to me."

Awkwardly, Gray wrung out a piece of his shirt and shook it.

Minerva loosed the silver garment she had fashioned and took it off.

Gray made a choked sound and averted his face.

The right words, Minerva begged of her memory, *please give me the right words.* "I give you my heart, Gray Falconer."

"Oh, Min." He looked to her again. "And I give you mine."

"I give you my soul, Gray Falconer."

"And I give you my soul, Minerva." His gaze remained on her face. "And my body, all that I am or can be, I give to you."

"My body, and all I can be, I give to you, Gray."

"Until we are parted by forces we cannot quell."

"Yes," she agreed.

He reached for his cloak and spread it before the fire, and spread hers on top, and held out his arms.

She went to him, knelt, knee to knee, thigh to thigh, bared breast to bared breast. And she rested her head on his shoulder.

Gray stretched her out on the cloaks and finished removing her scant clothing. And when she lay before him, naked, he ministered to her, washing her body slowly, slowly, with intense care. He turned her onto her face and smoothed the cooling water over her back, her bottom, the sensitive undersides of her thighs, her calves and ankles, the soles of her feet until she giggled. But when he took the water to the sides of her breasts she stopped giggling, and when he turned her again and rose to remove his breeches and stand with feet braced apart, watching for her reaction to the man she had claimed as her own . . . well, then, when he did that, she pressed a fist to her mouth and tears slipped silently from her wide-open eyes.

"Love," he said simply, lowering himself beside her. "Oh, my love, do I make you cry from anguish?"

"From wonder," she told him. "There is nothing about you that is not a wonder to me."

Stretched out on his side, he settled a hand on her stomach and touched the dips beside her hipbones. "I can see your veins here. You skin is so pale."

She tried to reach for him, but he pushed her gently back. "No, love, allow me to lead you where we must go now. Will you do that just this once—or at least this time?"

Minerva rested her arms at her sides and nodded.

"In here," he stroked her belly, "if God wills it, our children will grow."

Her heart must surely break from emotion. "Surely he wills it."

"And here," he kneaded one of her breasts and gently pinched the nipple, "here our children will suckle. Ah, I shall look forward to seeing that." And he bent to take that nipple into his own mouth and pull on it until her hips rose from the heavy wool beneath them, and a blaze swept from the tip of his tongue to the tip of her breast, into her belly, and into places she could not name.

Ignoring her own vow to let him lead her, Minerva began

her own soft, sensuous search of his powerful body. He tried only once to stop her, but she took his Part into her hands and, just as she had expected, he could not deny her the pleasure of enjoying him. He fell quite easily to his back and filled his own hands with cloak, while his head rolled from side to side and his teeth clenched.

"Enough," he said suddenly, and not at all softly. "We are husband and wife?"

She whispered, "Yes."

"We have given ourselves to each other and will do so again in front of God and man?"

"Yes."

"Then I hope God will forgive me for taking what is evidently mine."

So quickly did he tip her to her back that she forgot to breathe. He kissed her breasts with such urgency that she cried out at the force of his sucking and the answering squeezing deep within her, and the release of warm moisture.

His eyes blazed, and he was, for that time, a beautiful stranger. When he moved between her thighs and lifted her legs over his shoulders, her eyes flew wide open and she gasped. Gray smiled at her, a grimly determined smile filled with the same desire she felt.

"To make my way easier," he told her. "It will open you to me."

He was going to enter her. She tried to relax, to relax the muscles that tightened as if to exclude him.

Velvet and iron nudged against her private place. With his hand he took that slick hardness and played it back and forth, back and forth, and too quickly a glorious torment rippled into her loins.

Thrashing, reaching for him, she cried out Gray's name, over and over. Or thought she did. She cried out and urged him with her body to complete what she did not know but knew she must have.

He joined with her.

She could not countenance that she could hold so much of him. The first gliding entry pressed deep, and she felt the slightest resistance within herself before she accepted him completely.

Wind and fire.

She heard the wind, felt the fire, and gave herself up to the body that brought them. Sweat bathed her, and when she felt again the breaking free of the sweet little death of sensation that led to bucking demands for more and more, she pulled him down on top of her and rolled with him until his keening cries joined her own.

Panting, they lay tangled together, no end, no beginning—all one.

He said, "I love you, Minerva."

"I love you," she told him.

Gray held her so tightly she could scarce catch a breath.

"It feels as if I died a little to become one with you. And it was beautiful. And perhaps there will be new life from it?"

"You steal my breath," he told her. "And my mind. I thank God you waited for me."

Chapter Twenty-five

G ray's limbs were heavy, heavy from the punishment he'd heaped upon them during the ride from Ballyfog, and heavy in the best possible way from all that had transpired in the hours since he'd brought Minerva to Edinburgh.

The longcase clock in the hall had sounded the hours faithfully. Eleven in the morning had passed, and noon. Minerva slept beside him in the big four-poster, her hair tousled and all but covering her face, her arms thrown over her head. Grinning to himself, he pulled the bedcovers to her waist and indulged himself in a leisurely examination of her "sturdy" breasts.

Beautiful, beautiful, beautiful girl.

His girl. His lover. His friend. His all.

But someone would come. Tonight, or tomorrow, or tomorrow night, or whenever, someone would come, and he must be ready.

He fondled her breasts, and she arched her back up from the mattress and murmured in her sleep. She smiled and kicked away the covers until she was naked before him.

A sensualist, his lover and friend.

"Minerva," he said into her ear. "Minerva, it's time to wake up."

"Uh-uh."

"It is most definitely time to wake up, my love. We must find some clothing we can move around in without drawing attention."

Her eyes snapped open. She frowned at him, then at the canopy above the bed, then at him again. "Of course we don't have to wake up. We're tired."

Gray continued to stroke her until she became aroused. Then, knowing he was despicable, he stopped and leaped from the bed.

"Gray!" She rose to her elbows. "Come back here at once."

"No. Absolutely not. This has all been most irregular. Honeymoons before weddings are not at all the thing."

"We're married."

He regarded her solemnly then, and nodded. "Yes. Yes, Min. But I'll not pretend that I won't be most happy to stand before old Pumfrey and have him say the words. Now, my darling, please get up and put on what I give you. We'll find something, Max assured me we should."

And Max hadn't lied. A wardrobe offered a selection of gowns—all of them rather too elaborate for the probable events of the day. Gray selected the plainest of them all, a lavender silk, and spread it on the bed. Drawers contained the rest of what he sought, but Minerva stopped him as he tried to assemble small clothes for her.

"Attend to yourself," she told him, efficiently finding what she needed. "I suggest the mint green taffeta and matching slippers."

"Very funny, sweet. I'll return soon enough."

He went to Max's rooms and availed himself of service-able trousers, a dark coat, and clean linen, and dressed quickly.

Upon returning to Minerva, he was surprised to see that

she had accomplished all but the fastenings at the back of her bodice. This he did for her, straining somewhat since the gown obviously belonged to a slightly less "sturdy" female.

Breathless from his tugging, she giggled and said, "Perhaps we should give up and leave it unfastened. There must be a pelisse I can wear to disguise what a large person I am."

Gray moaned. "Large," he said, "very large. These dresses probably belong to the Marchioness, who is a tiny woman."

"Excuses," Minerva said, and grew still. She put a finger to her lips, but Gray had heard the same sound as she—a swift brush, perhaps of fabric, against the passage wall.

He should, Gray thought in that instant, have sent Min away. He should have been too strong to give in to what she wanted, what he'd allowed to become the excuse for what he'd wanted himself.

Too late for recriminations.

The fire had burned out while they slept and despite the hour, the bedroom remained washed in gray light. For that at least he was grateful.

Pointing, he directed Minerva to crawl beneath the bed and smiled when, rather than protest, she followed his instructions at once. She disappeared in a froth of lavender silk, white petticoats, and drawers.

He went to the slightly open door on tiptoe, stopped, and listened.

Not a sound.

Nothing.

Not a stealthy footstep, or the swish of clothing, or the hint of a drawn breath.

Nothing.

Flattening himself to the wall, he peered into the passage, where he could see portraits of Rossmaras, and of Rossmara horses and dogs.

No living soul gave away his—or her—presence.

Gray removed the pistol he'd replaced in the waist of his

trousers and used the tip of the barrel to fling the door open wide.

He was rewarded with a clear view of a larger portion of the passage. Just to the left of the door, silver jugs in descending sizes stood upon a heavily carved chest.

It could be that something, somewhere, had fallen. A piece of clothing in a closet, a curtain, any one of so many things, but he must find out for sure.

A room opposite, at the front of the house, stood open, and this, too, was gloomy. With a glance back at the bed, where Min remained obediently out of sight, Gray stepped into the passage and looked to his left. All was exactly as it should be.

More portraits lined the walls to the right, in the direction of the stairs. An Aubusson runner rested atop dark wood the entire length of the passage.

All still.

All as it should be.

Except for a knot of some blue stuff crumpled on the floor at the right, almost at the far end of the passage.

As he'd assumed, something had fallen.

He took several steps away from the bedroom door. Specks of gold glimmered amid the blue. Probably a hanging. Min would feel better if he brought her some evidence of what had caused the sound.

Gray sped to retrieve what was a blue military coat trimmed with gold. He frowned and turned it over. The wall showed no sign of where such an item would have hung, and, since the coat showed no signs of distinction, he could not imagine why it should hang anywhere other than in a wardrobe.

The coat had not been there when he'd last left the bedroom. That had been when he went in search of water for Minerva.

Holding the coat, he hurried forward to look into the inner hall. He went quietly down the stairs, searching from side to side, searching for any sign of an intruder. The hall was shrouded in the same heavy silence he'd left above.

The clock struck one in the afternoon, causing him a violent jolt.

Gray spun about and broke into a run. He dashed up the stairs. Premonition of danger made him desperate to get Minerva away from here quickly.

He skidded to a halt at the bedroom door. The closed bedroom door. He'd left it open.

Flaring his nostrils, he took a slow, shallow breath and stepped away—and caught sight of movement reflected in the row of silver jugs.

He spun around, and fell back.

"Afternoon, Mr. Falconer. Do join us."

In the room opposite stood a very tall man. Gray could not make him out clearly, except for his dark hair, his lack of a coat, and the horrifying fact that he held Minerva against him with one hand, and aimed a pistol at her head with the other.

"Come, come, now, Mr. Falconer. Don't keep me waiting. I've a great many things to do today, but I decided to spare a little time to get to know you and this . . . this creature, better."

Gray noted the distaste with which the fellow referred to Minerva, but he could not be concerned with such matters now. "Who are you, sir?" he said, aware that the pistol in his own hand was presently useless to him. "Kindly unhand my . . . my wife."

"Wife?" A guttural laugh sickened Gray. "I've been gone from these shores some considerable time. That must be a new term for 'doxy,' I suppose."

Minerva gave a small cry, and Gray took a step toward the room.

"Yes, yes," the man said. "Come along, do, Mr. Falconer. We shall have a jolly little interlude before I'm forced to wish you both goodbye."

"Don't," Minerva cried. "Go, Gray. Go quickly. He intends to kill us."

"Foolishness," the man said in happy tones. "Silly imaginings. We'll have to drink to our health. Of course, if you should decide to show any sign of leaving, Mr. Falconer, I shall simply shoot the little doxy, and still manage to dispose of you, too."

"Go, Gray!"

Gray walked steadily into the room until he was within a few feet of the newcomer. The palest of eyes regarded him steadily, this time without the partial barrier of a black mask. Long black hair was still tied back in a queue, and in the veiled light, the angular lines of Captain Smith's face were even less appealing than they'd been the previous evening at Maudlin Manor.

"I see you think you know me," the man said.

"At the masquerade," Minerva said breathlessly. "You remember him, Gray?"

"I remember him, my love."

"Touching," Smith said.

Gray looked at the coat and knew it had been used to lure him away from Minerva. He tossed it aside.

"You'd as well send the pistol the same way," Smith said, and Gray felt another turning in his belly at the way the man's thin-lipped mouth barely moved.

"Don't do it," Minerva said. "As long as you keep it, you have a chance. Why should we both die?"

"You, my dearest, are the most logical woman in the world," Gray said, while his mind chased after possible ways of escape for both of them.

"Pour drinks for all of us," Smith said. He pointed. "Over there. I brought a bottle of fine Madeira. Pour three glasses."

Gray saw the bottle and the glasses. They stood atop a cabinet. Keeping an eye on Smith, he did as the man suggested. The bottle was full and showed no sign of having been previously opened. Gray wondered what this part of the game was intended to achieve.

That was when he saw what he should have noted earlier. Two large trunks stood open and empty against the wall beneath the windows.

Gray averted his eyes and pretended to be engrossed in pouring Madeira. There was little doubt as to the proposed use of the trunks. They would make very adequate coffins.

Keeping the pistol at Minerva's temple, Smith reached back and loosened the queue. Shaking out his long, curly hair, he shifted the pistol to the hand that curved around his captive's body and pressed it into her left breast. She gritted her teeth, and Gray made to go to her.

"Stay," Smith said. "Unless you want your toy ruined."

To Gray's horrible fascination, the man bent forward, allowing the hair to fall like a cape and throwing his face into deep shadow. He moved sideways with Minerva until he could pick up a cane that rested against a chair, a cane with a handle in the shape of a boot. He laughed and banged the cane on the floor. "Eunuch, I am," he said, laughing as he did so, "and proud to disport meself."

"Olaf Clack," Gray murmured. "No wonder you made a point of hiding your face."

Clack straightened. "I didn't hide it because I think it's ugly," he snapped, raising his hooked beak of a nose. "I hid because I'd thought you might know me, you *fool*. Don't you know me?"

"Clack," Gray said, feeling stupid.

"We know you, sir," Minerva said. She wore no slippers, and her bare feet added to her vulnerable appearance. "You are Mr. Olaf Clack of Maudlin Manor, and you are so clever."

"*Don't* try to sweeten me, *doxy*. What do you think I am? A fool? I am a gentleman and a scholar, and I had a better woman than you for my own—until she chose to die giving birth to that wretched girl who is my daughter."

Minerva's eyes grew so large, they seemed to be all of her face. "I'm sure your dear wife didn't *choose* to die. She wouldn't have wanted to leave you and your daughter."

Who was this man? Gray searched his memory for some hint but found none, none but the vaguest sense that they had met somewhere, sometime, and other than in Scotland.

"She was a *lady*," Clack said. "Never spoke a word to me. Can you imagine that? Just because I took her against her will, she'd never speak to me."

Minerva's already pale face took on the quality of chalk.

"Left me with a brat, and a *girl* to boot." Clack shook back his hair, and the fury in his face ebbed, leaving it smooth. "Drinks! Let us drink a toast! To reconciliation. There's nothing to be gained by all this unpleasantness. Mistakes were made, but they won't be repeated. You and I are fair-minded men, Falconer. You understand, as I do, that civilized men accept the inevitable. It's inevitable that you two have to die. But that doesn't mean we can't drink to our health first, does it?" He cackled afresh, and put the head of his cane between his teeth.

"Where is your daughter?" Minerva asked.

Clack mumbled, and appeared to be struggling to unscrew the top of his cane.

"You'll break your teeth, Clack," Gray remarked.

"Never mind my teeth," Clack roared. "We'll have a toast anyway, and I'll get my strength up. This is going to be done my way. I've waited too long for the pleasure. Hush! Listen. What the blazes is that? Get over there, Falconer. Against the wall. One sound and she dies."

Thudding footsteps climbed the stairs and started along the passageway.

Gray knew an instant of hope before a voice called, "Olaf, old friend, are you here? Oh, Olaf! Olaf, Olaf, old friend! Help on the way. Didn't think I'd find out you'd sneaked away, did you? Thought you'd pull this off all on your own and collect the booty from—"

"Silence!" Clack roared. "Get in here, Meaner. And shut up!"

Silas Meaner appeared at the door. A floor-length cloak accentuated his narrow frame. Beneath the garment he still wore his long white tunic. The fool's cap was gone, but his brows, mustache, and beard remained blackened, and much of the dye was now smeared over his face.

"How did you know where to come?" Clack said.

Meaner winced, and clutched his silver cane close. "Please don't shout, Olaf. Hurts the brain. Bit in me cups last night."

"I asked you how you found me. And to you, I have never been Olaf, Number *Two*."

Gray put his hands behind him and leaned on the wall. *Number Two.*

"Is Lord Ice Eyes all tucked up safe, then, Number Two?"

"That he is indeed, Number Nine."

"The Cap'n will be pleased to hear that."

An island on a hot, hot night. A fire burning bright, illuminating capering shadows that darted closer to the compound each time they cried out something they wanted Gray, their helpless captive, to hear.

By heaven, here he was, face-to-face with some of the very pirates who had taken him from that damnable ship. He should have known. He should have guessed. That he'd never seen them closely wasn't an acceptable excuse today.

"All right, *Cap'n*," Meaner said. "I wasn't aware you wanted him to know who we are."

"Why not? When he leaves here he won't be talking."

Meaner looked at Gray and nodded. "Of course he won't. So silly of me. He never would play the games, would he? Too upright and honest. Wouldn't even ship a few harmless seeds among all that sugar when I asked him. Imagine that."

Gray longed to react, to shake his head, to demand that all the mysteries be revealed, but his hands were behind his back, and in one hand he held a pistol. He said, "You've confounded me until now. Damnably clever of you. You were the chap who came to me at the plantation—bumwallow seeds. Wasn't that the case? You wanted us to ship them out with our sugar."

"Correct," Meaner said, slapping his knees with glee, then wincing again. "Like a member of your family did before you. You know, I even put on one of my old robes for the salon last night. I enjoyed risking that you would recognize me, Falconer. But I didn't really expect you to make the connection. Different surroundings change a man, don't they? Different surroundings and different trappings. Shave the old pate and so on. Amazing what a difference being bald makes."

Gray wasn't pleased to be reminded of his failure to note things that could have spared him and Min this.

"Enough talk," Clack said. "Let's get on with it. I see you've got your trusty stick there, Number Two." He winked, keeping the eye closed so long that Gray couldn't look away from it.

"Trouble with your eye, Cap'n?" Meaner asked. "Got something in it? Let me take a look."

"Nothing in my eye, you *dolt*," Clack said. "I want to give these two a drink. Civilized stuff, Number Two. You *know*, civilized. Makes things quick—er, more pleasant, and *quicker*. I see you've got your *trusty stick*." He closed one eye again and jerked his head in the direction of the glasses of Madeira.

"Oh," Meaner said, and his mouth remained open. "My *stick*. Yes, yes, I've got it with me. Now, let me think. Where did I put it."

"In your hand, you fool. The hand you don't have."

Meaner bowed, presenting the top of his head, where Gray now saw black stubble. Too bad he hadn't caught sight of him without a shave before now.

Turning his back, Meaner grunted, obviously working with something. He stopped, flung around, and said, "Damn that Micky. She's done it again." In his hand he held the top of his cane. With the hand he didn't have, he clamped the stick to his chest, revealing a small hollow compartment where the top would screw in. "She's emptied them out again. Soft all the way through, she is."

"Don't speak of my daughter in that tone of voice," Clack said. "It's your job to look after her, not revile her, and don't you forget it."

"Oh, I wasn't reviling the dear girl. It was Micky who pointed out to me that you'd decided to follow these two lovelies all on your own to get the money from—"

"Enough!" Clack interrupted.

"Micky's a girl?" Minerva said. "Poor little thing."

"Bane of my life," Clack growled.

"The demure little nun at the salon," Gray said, smiling despite himself. "Very fitting. I hope I get the opportunity to thank her for her assistance."

"She didn't assist you," Clack said.

"She took my bumwallow," Meaner said sulkily. "Not the first time, either. Plague of my life since she was born."

"Don't talk about my daughter in that manner," Clack said. "I've warned you often enough."

"Let me marry her, then."

Clack went to slap a hand to his brow, but thumped it with the wooden boot on his cane instead. "Argh! My daughter will marry no one. Now. I've got to get this damn boot off this bloody cane."

"Shoot 'em instead," Meaner said, smiling brightly.

"Messy," Clack said. "Don't want to leave any mess. We'll make them stand in the trunks, give them a little drinkie with a . . . you-know-what in it. Shut the trunks and heave-ho them downstairs and into the carriage."

"Good thought," Meaner said. "Saw that carriage and wondered, I must say."

"Where's Micky?"

"Ballyfog. Likes that mooning fool, Brumby."

"Micky doesn't like anyone," Clack said. "Highfalutin like her mother. Good job I kept her in disguise, or men like young McSporran would be sniffing around."

"He *is* sniffing around," Meaner said, not hiding his pleasure at annoying Clack.

Gray assessed the room, the position of the glasses, the distance between Clack, with Minerva in his grasp, and Meaner. The pistol was in the back of his trousers, at his waist. Stuffed inside each boot was a knife. Opportunity was the only missing ingredient.

Clack backed away, dragging Minerva with him. When he drew level with the smaller of the two trunks, he lifted her and set her down inside.

Horror tightened the skin on her face, but she made no sound.

"Get down," Clack told her. "Go on!"

"I get ill in small spaces," she said.

Clack laughed, pulling his ugly mouth wide. "Hear that, Number Two, she gets ill in small spaces. Isn't that good, because we intend for her to get very ill in this small space, don't we?"

Gray thought he saw Meaner swallow before he said, "We certainly do."

More footsteps were heard from below, these slower but just as heavy as Meaner's.

"Did you bring someone with you?" Clack whispered, baring sharp little teeth at Meaner. "Can't I trust you to do anything right?"

"Not with me," Meaner said, turning toward the door in time for Cadzow to arrive, panting.

"Cadzow," Gray said, immeasurably relieved. "God bless you for coming, man. We're in a pretty pickle. Do you know who these men are? Of course you don't."

"Thanks to Eldora, I found out what you were up to, Clack," Cadzow said. "Not that I know how she discovered your game."

"Cadzow—"

"Hold your tongue," Cadzow told Gray. "I didn't have time to hang about questioning Eldora. That will come later. Damn you, Clack. I suppose you and Meaner planned to pull this off, then come to me to clean up the mess you'd made. *And* ask me to keep paying."

"There'll be no mess," Clack said defensively. "But you'll pay."

Minerva stood very straight and still in the steamer trunk. She stared at Cadzow and said, "Mr. Falconer, we are very pleased to see you. Have you brought some constables?"

"Shut up," Cadzow said succinctly. "You were always a stupid, headstrong girl. Not that you are of any interest to me. No more interest than Gray, except that he has come close to ruining my plans. You were supposed to die on that island," he said without looking at Gray. "I paid handsomely for you to die there. But these ruffians decided you were worth more if they kept you alive. They kept milking me for more blunt by threatening to expose that it was I who arranged for your abduction. Said they could produce you if they had to, and I couldn't afford to call their bluff."

Gray felt betrayed, but he also felt strong, the strength of intense anger running through his veins, hot and dangerous. The trick was to harness the anger and use it well.

"Meaner," Cadzow said sharply, producing a small pistol of his own. "Clack has messed everything up. He's going to die for it."

Gray all but panicked. If Cadzow shot Clack, he could kill Minerva in the process.

"Be my guest," Meaner said to Cadzow. "Fire away!"

"This pistol is for my protection should it become necessary," Cadzow said. "Take that very fine cane of yours and break the fool's skull. Do it *now*."

Gray saw Clack's eyes widen, and Meaner's cane rise— in his good right arm. And he saw the silver streak down.

But it was Cadzow who cried out, Cadzow who fell in an ungainly heap on the floor.

"Got him," Meaner shouted, capering about. "Look at that, Olaf. I got him."

Clack grunted.

Gray looked at Minerva, who lowered her eyes. "Cadzow," he said quietly. "Of course. You were right. He had the most to gain."

"And the most to lose," she said softly, "because he lost you."

"Ah, how sweet," Meaner said, sweeping up a glass of Madeira and draining it. "Better get on, then, Olaf. What about your stash of . . . you know."

"Yes, yes," Clack said. "Take this off, would you?"

Meaner availed himself of Clack's wooden cane and clamped it beneath the arm that had no hand while he attempted to unscrew the boot.

"I say," Meaner said, frowning up at Clack, "who's going to pay us all the money, then, with him gone?" He indicated Cadzow's still form.

Clack twitched his long nose. "Just do as I've told you. Getting rid of them has got to be worth a great deal to someone. Give me time to think."

Meaner managed to remove the boot and peer into the secret compartment at the top of the stick. "Damnable Micky. You never could control her, Olaf. She's been at your stash too. Not a seed in sight."

Clack jumped into the air and came down with a great crash. He yelled, "Ow," and gingerly lifted first one foot, and then the other. "She'll know the flat of my hand when she sees me. Your fault, Meaner, she's your responsibility."

"Minerva?" A very familiar, high male voice called from the lower regions of the house. "Are you here, daughter? Answer me at once."

"Papa," Min said quietly, looking at Gray with trepidation. "Oh, do tell him to get away before he is hurt."

Dutifully Gray called out, "Kindly wait outside the house, Mr. Arbuckle."

"Arbuckle?" Clack said. "Arbuckle?"

"Her father," Meaner remarked, drinking another glass of Madeira. "You know. Squat little chap in a silly hat. Thinks he's a painter."

"Papa is a painter," Minerva said. "He's famous."

Clack pointed at nothing in particular. "Yes, yes, the fool whose wife helped with the masquerade."

"My mama," Minerva said, very firmly for a woman being held at gunpoint.

"Money!" Clack bellowed. "Of course. You can always rely on me, Number Two. Mr. Arbuckle." His voice rose. "Come along up and join us, Mr. Arbuckle. Minerva's with us." In a whisper, he added, "Arbuckle will pay if he thinks it'll save his daughter's life."

Gray opened his mouth to shout again, but saw Meaner's silver stick flash. The next second he was struck on top of his left shoulder, a blow that sent him to his knees.

"Not another word from you unless you're spoken to," Meaner said pleasantly.

Rapid steps echoed in the passage, then stopped.

"In here, Mr. Arbuckle," Clack said. "Minerva's so glad you could come."

Porteous Arbuckle's head, complete with blue beret, appeared around the doorjamb. Wearing his dark-lensed spectacles, he took a very long time to register the consternation that eventually contorted his face. "I'll thank you to unhand my daughter, sir," he said. "Can't imagine what you're thinkin' of, Meaner. Standin' after all my wife and I have done to help you and your friend. Who is this villain, then?"

"You can't help here, Mr. Arbuckle," Gray said, very aware that he had misjudged the man. "It would be better if you left while you can."

"Left? Left, with my daughter held at gunpoint? I should think not."

Gray closed his eyes and prayed for patience. The entire situation was out of control and becoming more so. His only hope rested on some diversion that would make Clack take the pistol away from Minerva.

Arbuckle all but fell into the room, evidently propelled by Angus McSporran, who came in red-faced and sputtering.

"More of them," Clack muttered.

"Ye scum," McSporran said, pointing at Meaner. "She came t'Ballyfog wi' ye, damn ye. That Micky. An' she's made away wi' my boy, Brumby. His mother's beside hersel'. Eloped, they have."

"Brumby came to us, Minerva," Arbuckle said. "This, er, Micky was disturbed at Brumby's distress over you. Because you'd disappeared. She . . . we'd all thought she was a he, most strange, but she told Brumby you'd come here and that Clack was following you."

"See," Meaner said, shaking his stick, "wretched girl, I tell you. She's told all of Ballyfog."

"Don't speak of my daughter—"

"In that manner," Meaner finished for Clack. "You tell me how we're going to get out of this in one piece, Cap'n. Tell me that, then."

"That's Clack," Gray said for Arbuckle and McSporran's benefit. "He's been pretending to be crippled. As you see, he isn't doubled over at all."

"And he kidnapped Gray and took him to a horrible island," Minerva said, and gasped at a fresh poke from Clack's gun.

"Porteous," McSporran said, his voice hushed. "It's Cadzow Falconer. Look."

Arbuckle took a cautious step closer to Cadzow's crumpled form and said, "Egads. What's he doing here?"

"Eldora told him to come," Gray said. "He didn't seem sure about her part in things."

Arbuckle scratched his chin. "Is that so? Dead, is he?"

"Of course he's dead." Meaner brandished his stick. "And so will anyone else be dead if they get in my way."

Arbuckle grinned and rubbed his hands together. "Shouldn't dream of it. Too bad about Cadzow, what, Angus?"

McSporran smiled with equal enthusiasm, enough enthusiasm to make Gray frown.

"I say," Arbuckle said, "you don't have a thing to worry about with us, I can assure you. The Falconers mean nothing to us."

"Papa!" Minerva actually struggled against Clack. "Papa, how can you say such a thing about Gray?"

"Be still, my love," Gray said. "Please. I'm sure your father doesn't mean exactly that."

"I most certainly do," Arbuckle said, widening his stance. "We'll take Minerva and leave, Clack. What you do here is your affair. Never spoken of again, I assure you."

Minerva's face flamed. Tears stood in her eyes.

"You and I are our own family," Gray said, longing to go to her. "Please don't cry."

Heaving up from where he'd lain, Cadzow dealt the assembly another shock. "You'll all cry! I'll make sure of that." His pistol, aimed at Clack's stomach, sent the man scrambling, blessedly away from Minerva.

Gray said, "Come to me," and leveled his own pistol on Clack—until Minerva turned, hopped from the trunk, and flew at the villain.

"Min. For God's sake, *Min*." She beat him with her fists until he covered his head. After lashing out at Meaner and knocking him to the ground, Gray went for Clack's outstretched right arm and wrestled the pistol from his fingers.

"Kill him, Number Two," Clack howled, batting at Min. "Ouch! Kill them all. Ouch! Cut out their guts. String 'em from the yardarm. Ouch! Make 'em walk the plank, and feed the fish."

Minerva's nails found Clack's colorless eyes, and the man screamed and stumbled. He tripped backward over the edge of a trunk and fell inside.

"Come, love," Gray said, lifting Minerva away, despite her still-flailing fists. "Move a muscle and you're dead, Clack. Stay where you are, Meaner. You too, Cadzow."

Hauling Minerva with him, Gray backed up until he had a clear sight on the entire room and all its occupants. "Stand behind me," he told Minerva. As soon as she did as she was told, he confronted their enemies with a weapon in each hand.

"I say," Cadzow said querulously, "I just saved your hide."

"Not because you wanted to," Gray said. "Put the pistol on the floor. Stand still, you two." Arbuckle and McSporran had each taken a stealthy sidestep toward the door.

"Kill them," Cadzow said, setting down his firearm and scrambling to his feet. "All of them. Clack's a pirate, y'know. So's Meaner. They took you to that island and kept you there."

"And you paid us," Clack said.

Meaner nodded. "You did. And you took our money to make shipments for us when you were in the Indies."

"We're nothin' t'do wi' any of this," Angus McSporran said. "We'll wait for ye outside."

"Nothing to do with it," Cadzow blustered. "You came to me for a damnable marriage settlement you said I owed you, Arbuckle. Even though my nephew was thought dead."

Minerva popped forward to retrieve Cadzow's pistol and returned to clutch Gray's coat.

"And you extorted money from me for years," Cadzow continued.

"Couldn't have if you hadn't been guilty," Arbuckle said, sneering. "Trying it out was all I had in mind. You were enjoying what should have been his, and you didn't seem sorry about it. So I said you'd had him offed, as if I knew for sure you had. If you'd had your wits about you, you'd never have let me scare you into paying me to keep quiet."

"Stop it," Minerva cried. "Papa? What did you do? I don't understand."

"Of course you don't, my dear," Arbuckle said. "Don't worry your little head about these matters."

"Your father asked for a large settlement," Cadzow said. "When I refused, he accused me of arranging for your beloved Gray to disappear, and I believed he knew I had. So I paid for his silence. Paid well. And he went around telling everyone he was growing rich from selling his awful paintings."

Wedged, rear first, into the smaller of the two trunks, Clack tried to heave himself out, but caught Gray's eye and went limp again.

"Papa," Minerva said, moving beside Gray, "how could you?"

"Expenses," Arbuckle muttered, "miscellaneous."

"Oh, yes," she said, and Gray felt her mounting rage, "the famous miscellany. All that time I was keeping your books. You gave me receipts for supposedly sold paintings. And you made your own entries for expenses that were miscellany."

"Och, well," McSporran said, edging away from his friend, "seems as if we've all our wee troubles. I'll leave ye t'yours, Porteous. I'd better be gettin' back to Drucilla. She's beside hersel' over the boy."

"*You*," Arbuckle shouted, his jowls wobbling. "You'd just sidle out of here as if it's none of your business. Oh, no. Why don't you tell Minerva where the miscellaneous money went, McSporran?"

"Now, now," Mc Sporran said, waving his hands in a placating gesture. "No point in muddyin' the waters."

"No . . . That money went to you! You know very well it did."

McSporran whirled about, setting his kilt swinging. "You

had to do it, didn't you, Porteous? You had to open up something that could have been left as it was."

"So you could crawl away unscathed? I think not. You sold off priceless furnishings from Maudlin Manor. You sold them to me." Arbuckle's chin rose. "There. Now the truth's out."

"Except for the fact that ye bought them from me for next t'nothing and ye've been sellin' them here in Edinburgh—and in London—for a fortune, ye crook. And because I hadn't the contacts, I let ye. Ye took money from Falconer. Paid a pittance to me. And got a great deal more money from sellin' what ye weaseled out o' me."

"Look here, my friends," Cadzow said, a little color returning to his pudgy face, "we can all deal together and come to a most satisfactory arrangement. Of course, these . . . these ruffians must be disposed of." His gesture took in Clack, folded in his trunk, and Meaner, who cowered near the Madeira. "They'd be bound to cause problems."

"I'd never be a bother, I assure you," Silas Meaner said, mincing somewhat unsteadily forward. "But I do agree about Clack. He simply can't be trusted."

Gray felt as much as saw the tensing of Clack's body, and renewed his grip on the pistols. One great, ungainly shove and the pirate captain gained his feet, and his cane. "Away with you, Cadzow," he cried, raising the cane in both hands and lunging.

A single blow felled Cadzow.

Another single blow, from Meaner, sent Clack into a dazed stagger, and Meaner smiled in all directions. "You see, I'm on your side, gentlemen."

The last blow of the afternoon was Clack's. He found the strength to lift his booted cane once more, and he rendered Meaner senseless.

Minerva sat on a footstool enjoying fresh air through the windows Gray had opened. She kept Cadzow's pistol trained on the jumble of men sprawled upon the floor. Cadzow had stirred and pulled himself a distance from the other two. "How long shall we have to wait?" she asked Gray. She really was exhausted, and would very much like to curl up and sleep—with Gray.

"Not long, I think," Gray said, looking from the window to the street. "I hesitate to create a disturbance, since I expect reinforcements at any time."

On Gray's orders, Papa and Mr. McSporran had made a creditable job of tying up Mr. Clack and Mr. Meaner. Minerva looked at the two pirates and shuddered. "I never thought I should actually see a pirate, much less be taken captive by one, and keep company with *two*. Don't you think Cadzow should be tied?"

"No," Gray said shortly. "No more than these other two need to be tied. They'll all be dealt with appropriately. Ah, here he comes."

She heard another carriage draw up below, and very shortly another set of heavy boots climbed the stairs, these at a slower pace.

"Will you look at the mess here?" Max Rossmara said, holding Drucilla McSporran's arm when he entered. "I found Mrs. McSporran hovering below. Seems in quite a state, so I thought I'd bring her up."

"Glad to see you," Gray said, offering Max a pistol.

Max declined, producing his own.

"Pistols everywhere," Minerva said, propping her head and studying the one she held.

"A disgrace," Drucilla McSporran said. "And you're a disgrace, McSporran. The coachman wants to be paid at once, and says he'll not wait a moment longer than five minutes more unless he is paid. It's as well Janet insisted on staying at home. She'd have been hysterical by now. Have you got what you came for, husband?"

"Hush, my dear," McSporran said. "There'll be time enough for that."

"There will not," his wife informed him. "I've tried to spare you, but I can't anymore. Arbuckle, unless you want us to reveal all, you'll get the money we need from your future son-in-law, and get it at once."

Arbuckle moaned.

"Very well." Drucilla sniffed loudly. "You must give your future father-in-law money, Mr. Falconer, so that he can give it to us, so that we can go to Edinburgh and London to buy back all the furniture we allowed Mr. Arbuckle to talk us into selling him from the manor—for a pittance, I might add."

"You offered me the furniture," Arbuckle said. "My future son-in-law and I don't owe you a farthing."

"Have you told your future son-in-law that you agreed to help Eldora Makewell murder him so that her intended would be lord of the manor again?" Drucilla asked. "No, I don't suppose you have. Well, that dreadful woman has run off, they say, but the truth is the truth. The old lady who owned the manor has died, and we've got to get the furniture back before the new owner arrives with his inventory of all that's supposed to be there. He's bound to be unpleasant about everything. A nasty sort of person, we understand. We've been warned that he's a hard, silent, bitter man by the name of North, Devlin North."

"Then I suggest," Gray said, "that you and Mr. McSporran prepare to make some difficult explanations to Mr. North. Meanwhile, if I could trouble you to go for some constables, Max, we'll get these three into custody. As for the McSporrans and the Arbuckles? Well, we'll have to bring charges—once we've decided the best course to take."

Oddly silent, Max surveyed the chaos before sauntering from the room.

"Cadzy! Cadzy, where are you? Come to me."

Gray and Minerva looked at each other and said "Eldora" in unison.

"Dreadful woman," Drucilla remarked, sinking to sit on a small chaise. "Completely dreadful."

Cadzow's eyes opened wide. He got up and tottered to the window.

"Cadzy," Eldora called again. "Oh, Cadzy."

"Give it up, Cadzow," Gray said. "It's all over now."

"It is, isn't it?" Cadzow agreed. Before the amazed eyes of all, he hooked a leg over the sill and jumped.

Seconds of appalled hush followed before Drucilla McSporran said, "Good riddance. That man didn't have an honorable bone in his body."

Epilogue

L ove and loss. How sweet, yet sad, was this, the day
she had dreamed of.

In the silver-soft early morning of Christmas Eve,
Minerva slipped along the main street in Ballyfog, making
her way to St. Aldhelm's.

Again snow fell, flitting gently onto downy mounds
heaped almost to the ledges of the shop windows.

Today, in every kitchen, wives and mothers would scurry
about preparations for the Christmas feast. Children would
squeal, and chase, and be admonished, but good-naturedly
so. And the smells. Oh, the smells of pies, apple and cinna-
mon, and mince, of precious ginger and cloves hoarded for
this feast, and of warm brandy in the pudding, and pungent
lemons in the custards.

At Willieknock there were no Christmas smells. Hatch
was still there, but quiet in the aftermath of the shock they'd
all received only days earlier. Fergus and Iona hadn't arisen
yet for the day, but would be with Minerva when she needed them—Fergus to give her away and Iona to stand with
her.

Windows stood open at the Flying Drum and Pig Inn.
From inside came the raised voice of the innkeeper, who

cheerfully bellowed the garbled words of "The Holly and the Ivy."

Drawing her cloak firmly over her gown and pulling her hood forward, Minerva went as quickly as she could. She needed some time alone to think about all that had happened, and about what she intended to undertake this day.

"Of all the trees that are in the wood . . ." The innkeeper's voice followed her. "The holly bears the crown."

Under her cloak she carried slippers to replace the rubber boots she'd employed for the journey to the church.

In the yard, white drifts made the graves new, clean. A gray marble angel perched atop a plinth wore a pretty white cap on her head and a kindly coating on her little wings and folded hands.

Minerva had always found peace here, partly because Reverend Pumfrey and Mrs. P. had welcomed her, and walked with her, telling her stories, encouraging her to come whenever she pleased. Their unpretentious home gathered all who came to the door into its warmth, and not one was turned away.

With the Pumfreys there were no people who were more important than other people, not a soul to be more impressed than another.

The flicker of light inside the church disappointed her. She needed to be alone.

Her parents were lost to her, at least for the present while legal matters were dealt with. And Gray was alone at Drumblade. She hoped he slept soundly and without dreams.

Minerva smiled and hugged herself, and could not stem the rush of tears to her eyes. Perhaps there had been a love such as that which she felt for Gray, but she couldn't imagine how. If many people loved as she did, well, then the world would be a happy place, but a useless place where very little was accomplished.

Stamping her feet in the vestibule, she opened the door very carefully and peeked inside. The light she'd seen came from candles near the altar. Drawn forward by the wonder of what she saw, she tilted her head to study garlands of holly looped between the ends of pews. On the altar itself stood a single crystal ewer filled with creamy roses and more holly, its dark, shining leaves and scarlet berries turned to spots of brilliance against the velvet pallor of the roses.

In readiness for the service to welcome the Christ Child.

She turned about and left the church quickly, seeking her solitude on the far side of the building from the Pumfreys' house.

Beyond the wall here, a gentle slope rose to hills where sheep grazed for most of the year. Minerva climbed slowly, holding her skirts out of the damp as she went. She set her eyes on the place where a dry stone made a line against the heavy sky. Once over the stile she could be certain of seclusion.

Gray had guessed that her parents were involved in the plot against him. They had not been guilty of the first part of the crime, but they did not even deny their later involvement.

She clambered awkwardly over the stile and was grateful that earlier footsteps, no doubt a shepherd searching for lost sheep, had given her a place to walk.

Was it fair to Gray to marry him when she was the child of people who had wished him dead?

Finding a bouquet of wildflowers in the dead of winter proved a grueling task, but one worth accomplishing. Gray had not seen Minerva for three days, since the final preparations for their marriage ceremony had been made, and she had asked for time alone to get ready.

He believed she wanted time alone.

He did not believe she intended to use it to get ready.

Gray knew fear again, the fear that somehow, after going through so much, he would lose the woman he longed to claim for all time.

When they'd been very young—she much younger than he—they had wandered the hills outside Ballyfog. In the first years of their confessed love for one another, those wanderings had consumed him. He thought only of being with her, and being removed from the constraints of home and family.

He still thought only of being with her.

Her withdrawal drove a cold spike into his heart. There had been something he felt in her, something distant as if, after Edinburgh, she blamed him for the revelations that had changed her life forever.

But what of *his* life? What of the changes he must bear? True, he had begun to think of himself as alone some years earlier. But he hadn't expected to learn that his only relative had betrayed him, utterly betrayed him.

Cadzow had died in his leap from the house in Charlotte Square. Clack and Meaner were in custody and would probably be transported afterward—unless there was proof that they had committed even more serious crimes of which he was not aware.

He would start back to the village.

Max had promised to stand up for him—had insisted, in fact. Nevertheless, their—Minerva's and his—wedding would be a quiet affair and the following celebration must, necessarily, be subdued.

"Damn." He looked to a sky that drooped to meet the land. Perhaps he was wrong to push Minerva to marry at once, but he could not risk her sinking into some deeper self-disgust that he'd already sensed in her. If that happened, she might try to refuse him forever. Then he would lose all that mattered to him, and her parents would have won anyway.

He climbed a hill to the top and started down the other side, and drew to a halt. In the distance, trudging upward, came a figure he'd know in the dark.

Minerva, swathed in heavy clothing and with her head

down, made her way toward him without knowing he was there.

With slow but deliberate steps, he went to meet her. The next hour would be nine, two hours before their wedding. She should be at home doing whatever brides did to prepare for such occasions.

A wind arose, whipping up snow from the ground to meet the falling snow. Flakes took on an icy quality that stung the eyes and the face, and bit into the lips.

A surge of anger shocked him, but he tamped it down and held it close. He had been cruelly used, and so had this girl of his, and those who had sought to injure them should not be allowed to take away their happiness.

When they drew within yards of each other, Minerva looked up. Her footsteps slowed, and she swayed a little against the wind-driven snow. Then she turned in each direction, and for an instant he thought she might run from him.

"Minerva," he called out. "Stay where you are. I'll come to you."

Gray.

He was a tall, dark figure against the winter's landscape. She heard him call, but couldn't make out the words. A large man. Forceful even at a distance. He insisted he wanted her, took it for granted that nothing had changed between them, despite the horror that their time in Edinburgh had become.

She wasn't ready to see him.

Minerva ran. She whirled about and ran downhill, her rubber boots slipping and sliding. In the dash, she lost her slippers, but didn't care. The faster she ran, the harder her heart beat and the louder became the humming sound in her ears.

She began to draw breaths that hurt as they entered her throat, and exhaled in sobs. Her cloak billowed and her hood fell back. Soon her hair slipped from the clusters of curls each side of her head, and she felt it whip behind her like a banner.

"Minerva!" That word was very clear now. "Stop. You will fall. You will hurt yourself."

She didn't care, didn't care, didn't care.

Gray's hand closed on her arm. Hard, strong fingers enclosed her flesh and bone and he swung her toward him, and crushed her to his chest, and wrapped her beneath his own cloak—and held her. "Hush, love, hush," he said against her temple while he pulled her hood over her hair once more. "Quiet—be quiet in your heart. I feel it thumping. Minerva, you're afraid."

Yes, she was afraid. "I have every right to be afraid," she told him, keeping her face buried in his coat. "I am the child of monsters, and I cannot bear it. You will always know what my parents tried to do, and that they are shallow, deeply dishonest people."

"You are mine and I am yours. Nothing will ever change that. Those people went astray. My uncle went astray and paid dearly for his sins. We must put them all behind us and live for each other."

She trembled in his arms. And she mumbled something.

"Min, I can't hear you. Look at me."

She shook her head.

Gray eased up her head, but she kept her eyes lowered.

"What did you say?"

"That I am ashamed," she murmured. "Deeply, deeply ashamed. And if we marry, I bring that shame on you. There is no one who doesn't know what Papa and Mama did."

"Or what Cadzow did," he pointed out. "And if there is one among the people here who condemns us for the acts of our relatives, then we do not care to count him as a friend or acquaintance."

"And what of our children?" she asked, her eyes awash in

tears. "How will they feel when they're told the story by others?"

"They will be told the story by us," Gray told her gently. "As soon as they are old enough to understand. We are not such empty, proud people that we cannot deal with this, are we?"

She pulled away from him, and he let her go.

Standing before him, she sniffed, and wiped the backs of her hands over her eyes. "I am not proud, simply practical."

He smiled at her. "I have pride of a sort. Pride in what my family accomplished before me. And pride in having you. Say what you will, I will never let you go."

She turned from him again, without haste this time, and continued downhill. Once more her hood deserted her head and her hair streamed behind her. Gray grinned. At this rate, his bride would make a most unusual sight—an appropriate sight, given that she was not at all a conventional woman.

Abruptly she halted, and looked at him over her shoulder. "I cannot marry you," she said. "Or I cannot allow you to marry me. It would not be fair."

He breathed deeply to calm the thunder of his heart. "You have already promised."

"You may say that because of recent developments, it is only appropriate to call off the event."

"You aren't listening. I said *you* have promised to marry me. And I do not release you."

"You are willful, Gray Falconer. And a foolish romantic. You will not find success with me at your side. My family is a laughingstock."

"As is mine. Let people laugh. Laughter is good for them."

"I will not do this to you."

He caught her when she would have run from him again, and swept her up into his arms. Silently cursing the slippery ground underfoot, he carried her to the stile and climbed over with her, and marched downhill, ignoring her pleas to be released and her occasional cross pokes—painful pokes—at his chest when she especially wished to make a point.

The answer here was to contain her, and marry her before she could get away. That would be best accomplished by gathering the little wedding party and proceeding at once.

"Now," he said, setting her down in the shelter of the stone vestibule. "I think that will be quite enough of that, wife. You do remember our first wedding ceremony."

She turned pink, but eventually nodded.

"Good, because I shall never forget it." He held out what he'd spent a good deal of time finding for her. "There are roses and holly on the altar."

"I know. I saw them, and they are beautiful."

"From Drumblade. But you are a woman who complements natural things, so I gathered these."

She stared at his higgle-piggle bouquet and cried again.

"What?" he asked. "What is it now?"

"I cannot do it, I tell you."

His composure broke and he thrust the flowers upon her. "I will never let you go."

"I am difficult. Ask anyone. The difficult child of difficult parents, and best forgotten, especially by you." She allowed the wildflowers to fall to the flagstones. "I intend to sell Willieknock, and good riddance. And I must take care of Fergus and Iona, and poor old Hatch. There won't be much left, but I shall manage."

"You're right," he said quietly. "You will manage, miss, because you will live up to your contractual obligations. Do I make myself clear?"

She took a single step backward and would have dodged around him, but she made the error of looking into the eyes that would have earned him his name. A storm gathered there, and determination—and love.

She looked into his eyes and grew still. She could not turn from him again, never again.

Gray went to his knees and picked up what must have been so difficult to find, the flowers of winter, the flowers of Christmas, and he held them up to her.

This time she took the bundle to her breast and held it, and looked down into their fragile faces.

"A poor bouquet, really," he said.

"No," Minerva told him. "The most beautiful of bouquets. Yellow groundsel and ragwort. Purple speedwell. The witch hazel blossoms are early."

"They knew I needed them."

"And mistletoe. I love them all. You must have taken a long time to find them."

"It helped pass the time this morning."

She looked questioningly at him.

"Until our wedding." He offered her a hand and said, "Come with me?"

The time for trust had come. With not a word, she threaded her fingers in his and they entered the church side by side, but stopped on the very threshold.

Gathered before them was a small knot of dear faces: Iona and Fergus, Max, Mrs. Hatch hovering sheepishly with Ratley at her side, Reverend and Mrs. Pumfrey, and, to Gray's amazement, Brumby McSporran and the small woman, Micky, whose appearance was entirely changed by smoothly combed black hair that revealed an elegant face and intelligent brown eyes.

Minerva found her voice first and asked, "What are you all doing here?"

"Come to celebrate a wedding," Brumby said. "I've become an expert. This is my wife, Micky."

Congratulations were said, and hugs exchanged, and Gray saw in Minerva's face that she was thinking how Brumby had also suffered the shock of seeing his parents arrested, but that he'd managed to find joy.

Scuffling and muttering drew the group's attention to the front rows of pews where, to Gray's amazement, several dozen familiar Ballyfog faces were assembled—and smiling, and murmuring, "Ah."

"We're not supposed to do this until eleven," Minerva said, and Gray heard her panic.

"Best to do what needs to be done as soon as it needs to be done," Reverend Pumfrey said. "Why don't we take our places. Iona, if you would remove Minerva's cloak. And Max—"

"Of course," Max said, winking a deal too broadly as he took both Gray's and Minerva's cloaks and put them on a back pew.

"Right," the reverend said. "Let's get to it. Got the ring, have you, Gray?"

For an instant his mind became blank.

"Got it," Max said, patting a pocket.

"And you know to take the bride's bouquet at the appropriate moment, Iona?"

"Oh, yes, I do know."

Iona, Minerva couldn't fail to note, looked a deal too long at Max Rossmara.

Reverend Pumfrey walked majestically up the aisle and faced the congregation. "Very will, then," he said. "It's about time we got Gray Falconer and Minerva Arbuckle wed."

A titter passed through the congregation.

"Here, if you please, Gray. And Max beside you." To his happy audience he remarked, "They tend to forget everything if you don't tell them what to do. That's why I have to have them repeat everything after me."

More laughter followed.

Gray, with Max at his side, stood to the reverend's left and looked down the aisle at Minerva. Even at a distance he could tell she'd blanched again.

"You can play now, Mrs. Pumfrey," Reverend Pumfrey

said. "We thought since it's almost Christmas, we'd practice for that, too. Minerva will enter to 'Hark! The Herald Angels Sing.' Unsung."

Mrs. Pumfrey played the organ with more gusto than skill, her small form rising from the seat with almost every enthusiastic chord.

Pumfrey beckoned, and Minerva walked forward as if in a trance, until she stood before him with Fergus at her side and Iona just behind her.

She touched her wet hair, trying to restore order, but gave up and let it trail about the shoulders of her damp, pale yellow dress. That was when Iona darted forward and pulled a single rose from the ewer on the altar. This she broke off and placed in the wild disarray of her cousin's hair.

And Minerva was beautiful. Unspoiled because her heart was unspoiled.

"Well," Pumfrey said. "Very nice, too. Natural, you both look."

Gray chose to ignore the next round of giggles and stand beside the woman who would be his bride.

Pumfrey rushed through the preliminary formalities of the occasion and held out his Bible for Max to place a simple gold band upon it. The ring had been Gray's mother's and it pleased him to think of Minerva wearing it.

"Repeat after me," Pumfrey began. "I, Gray Falconer—"

"I, Gray Falconer, love you, Minerva. I want you to be my wife. You are my first love, and my last. I shall always put you first, knowing that our love is my most precious possession."

He heard a sigh, felt stillness settle.

"I, Minerva Arbuckle, love you, Gray," Minerva said, her voice shaky. "You are everything I ever hoped for in a husband. You are my first love, and my last. I shall always put you first, knowing that our love is my most precious possession."

"Today," Gray said, "I marry you, my best friend."

Minerva smiled gently and repeated, "And today, I marry my best friend."

Pumfrey's voice continued. Gray answered, and listened to Minerva answer. He placed the ring upon her finger, and, when the time came, kissed his bride.

Clinging together, they retraced their steps down the aisle to a rousing rendition of "While Shepherds Watched Their Flocks by Night."

Just inside the church they waited to receive congratulations from the congregation, and invited everyone back to Drumblade for the wedding breakfast Ratley and Hatch had announced was prepared.

That was when Minerva stared at Gray with amused horror and said, "We waited all this time to do this, and I'm wearing *rubber boots*."

AUTHOR'S NOTE

Every story has a story, a starting place. So it was with *Wait for Me*.

My father was a wanderer, and I am my father's daughter. He wandered the world in ships. I have wandered in planes, and trains, and automobiles, and the occasional ship—but even more so, especially to places I don't think I'll go—I have traveled there, and lingered there, in my mind.

And so, in a way, the seed of this story began to sprout when a young man looked over the side of a ship at anchor off Pitcairn Island. This beautiful, lush, and forbidden island lies close to the Tropic of Capricorn, close to French Polynesia, to the Marquesas Islands, and the Tuamotu Arch.

A mysterious place, a pirate kind of place.

No, I definitely don't think I'll go there, but my father did—or he went as close as the descendants of Fletcher Christian of the ill-fated ship *Bounty* would allow. No stranger could go ashore. Some of those people, many by the name of Christian, rowed out to the big ship at anchor to trade. They offered handcrafts, mostly fashioned of wood. And like my father, and my father's daughter, they were curious about the rest of the world, and they coveted any new proof that there was, indeed, a great deal more beneath the skies than Pitcairn Island where no stranger might come, and no native might leave.

That was why, for a bar of soap and three pencils, my father became the owner of a wondrous piece of wood, a piece of wood I stroked, and craved to own from childhood.

Two years ago I finally told my father that I'd always

admired his prize from Pitcairn—where giant ferns and palms nodded at a turquoise ocean, and shy people lined the beach to stare at outsiders they would never meet.

"Why didn't you say so?" Dad asked.

I didn't tell him, "Because you taught me that one shouldn't ask for gifts," but said, "You mean I can have it?"

Well, he gave me his cane from Pitcairn, the one he paid for with a bar of soap and three pencils. That cane is right here beside me. The handle is carved in the shape of a boot.

Stella Cameron
Frog Crossing
Nether Piddle

Look for **Stella Cameron**'s
upcoming releases:

The Best Revenge, Zebra Books, in
February 1998

The Wish Club, Warner Books, in
May 1998
****
Enjoy the following previews from
both books.

Please read on for
a preview of
Stella Cameron's

The Best Revenge

Coming from
ZEBRA BOOKS
in
February 1998

PROLOGUE

Glad Times, Georgia

"You just keep your filthy, lyin' mouth shut, Rae Faith. Hear?"

Rae sat on the floor in the hot windowless room she shared with the baby. With her back against the thin door, she felt vibrations from every stumbling move Willie Skeggs made in the single room that was cooking, eating, and living space on the other side of the door.

Baby Ginny whimpered. Rae cradled her high on her shoulder and made little love noises. Willie got real mad if Ginny cried, and that made Rae scared, especially when Willie was drunk. Willie was drunk tonight. Again.

"Hear?" Willie shouted. "I asked if you heard me, girl. No more lyin' to your momma. No more tellin' her I done things when I didn't." He pounded on the door.

Rae wedged her feet against the bottom of the old trundle bed where she and Ginny slept. The bed, with its threadbare patchwork quilt, and two wooden crates where she kept clothes, her own and the baby's, were the only furniture.

The baby let out a gurgling cry that screwed up her pretty pink face. Rae loved Ginny so much it hurt her heart to think about it. A good kind of hurt.

"Rae! You leave that snivelin' brat in there and get out here. You're a big girl now. Seventeen years old, for cryin' out loud. You gotta take care of your daddy now."

Rae breathed harder, yet felt more breathless.

"You aren't my daddy," she said very softly to herself. "I don't know my daddy, but you aren't him."

1

"Rae Faith. Your momma told you to take care of me, didn't she? Answer me." More thumping on the door. "Get out here before I come in and get you. Your momma's gone and left me again. I'm lonely, Rae Faith."

He was starting to whine. A bad sign. Once the whining started, the rage was only minutes away.

Ginny nuzzled her soft face against Rae's neck. Hungry again. Rae needed to go get a bottle, but that would mean getting within grabbing range of Willie Skeggs.

She felt so sick she could vomit. Momma had left hours ago to go dancing in Atlanta. Rae had been hiding out ever since. She hadn't eaten since breakfast when she'd scrambled an egg in bacon grease and stacked it between two slices of Wonderbread. Wearing only his shorts, Willie had then been stretched out on the bed he shared with Momma, asleep, several empty beer bottles scattered around the second bedroom in the cabin. His straight blond hair needed a wash and hung over his face. Beard stubble darkened his slack jaw. Rae had watched him while she gulped down the congealed egg and damp bread, and while she warmed a bottle for Ginny. Momma'd been out all night, and Rae had known there'd be another fight when Betty Skeggs came home and Willie woke up.

Tangled in a grimy sheet, one of Willie's long legs had trailed off the bed. Momma never stayed home long enough to make that bed, and Willie sure wouldn't do women's work. Willie was tall and muscular but going to fat because he didn't do anything but lie around the cabin all the time. When he splayed his legs like that, Rae couldn't help seeing up inside his loose shorts, seeing things she didn't want to see, but couldn't help staring at.

Then she'd looked at Ginny and thought how that

2

sweet baby had come from there. From there and from her gentle sister, Cassie. Willie had always called Cassie "droolin' idiot," but he'd done things to her whenever Momma was out and made Cassie pregnant. And now Cassie was dead five months from the seizure she'd had when Ginny was born. Cassie had been eighteen.

"I'm countin' to ten, Rae Faith." Willie's words ran together. "You get out here. Now. *One.*"

Five months Cassie had been dead. She wasn't an idiot, Rae thought defensively. Cassie had got brain trouble from hitting her head when she was real little. That made her kind of slow, but gentle-slow, not stupid-slow. And Willie Skeggs had watched Cassie grow up and get breasts. He'd started going after her then. Cassie got big breasts, not like Rae's small ones. The two sisters were different like that. Cassie had grown into a beautiful, curvy, blond young woman while Rae just got a bit taller, and what Momma called "dark and secretive." Willie Skeggs hadn't looked at Rae while Cassie was alive—or not until she got too big with Ginny anyway.

Then he'd begun trying to get Rae alone. He'd made it a few times, but he'd always been too drunk, and she'd always been too quick.

"Rae Faith," Willie wheedled, and Rae could tell he'd put his mouth to the crack between the door and the jamb. "Come on out and let me be nice to you, Rae Faith. I got somethin' for you. Time you had a little fun. You spend too much time holed up in that cupboard of a room like that."

Experience had taught her that argument only inflamed him. Her best hope was that he'd get tired and go fall on the bed.

"Your momma's treatin' me mean," Willie said, his breathing heavy. "She don't give me what I need no more."

3

Rae opened her mouth to say her momma paid for the beer Willie was drinking, but clamped her teeth together just in time.

"She doesn't let me feel like a man. You know what I mean, Rae Faith. A man's gotta be allowed to be a man, or he ain't nothin'. Come on out, little honey, and let Willie be a man with you. You know you're ready. More'n ready."

He wanted to do that to her. Like he used to do to Cassie every day after their Momma left for work at the broiler plant. Willie never even bothered to close the door when he used to take Cassie in there. He'd said he wanted Rae to see how much Cassie enjoyed it so she'd know he wasn't hurting her sister.

At first Cassie cried. Willie'd hit her then, but he still did it to her.

Later Cassie went without being told and sat on the bed all quiet—waiting.

Rae's eyes stung and she blinked. She ought to have been able to stop Willie from doing that to her sweet sister.

"Speak to me, Rae Faith!" He had to shout to make himself heard above music coming from a car parked outside the cabin next door.

Her skin prickled. Willie was mad now.

"Answer me. Tell me you're comin' to keep me company."

Ginny started to sob. She swallowed air and hiccuped, and her face turned bright red. Beneath Rae's hand she could feel that the baby's diaper needed changing. The smell of ammonia hung in the close air. Ginny should have been changed some time ago.

"Betty said she's not coming back this time." Willie was crying. Sometimes he cried, but only until he drank some more and got angry some more. "She's left me, Rae Faith, and she knows I can't do for myself with this bad back of mine."

Ginny reared backward and screamed.

"Shut her up," Willie said. "Shut her *up*." He threw a shoulder against the door and it rattled.

Rae's heart beat harder and harder. "Go away," she said. "Ginny's got a fever. She needs to be quiet."

"She shoulda died with her idiot momma."

"Cassie wasn't an idiot," Rae cried. "And Ginny's your—" She mustn't say it.

The screaming grew louder. The baby's body was hot, and she writhed.

"Willie," Rae said in a deliberately calm voice. "I need to get Ginny some water. And I want to give her a cool bath. She's real hot, Willie. Why don't you go to bed?"

"I'm gonna do that." He laughed, then burped. "I'm gonna do that, and you're gonna come with me, sweet thing. Time I gave you something real nice to think about."

He wanted to do that to her, that thing he used to do with Cassie. The thing he and Momma did after the fighting, and before Willie fell drunk asleep and Momma went into the cramped bathroom to soak in the tub.

Rae had listened to girls at school laughing together about it, and she'd watched boys talking about the same thing while they eyed the girls. The boys she could understand. They'd be like Willie who couldn't get enough, but Rae tended to think none of the girls would do it willingly, not if they knew how ugly it was. Some girls did get pregnant and have babies. Rae couldn't believe they did it again after that.

Sammy Joe Phipps had tried to put a hand up Rae's shirt once. Rae slapped him so hard he looked like he was going to cry. He never tried it again. Nope—she wasn't having anything to do with any of it if she had her way.

Thunderous banging on the door set Ginny to screaming.

5

"Get your skinny ass out here," Willie yelled. "I'm gonna show you who's boss and it ain't you, little girl. Little girls was put here to drive men crazy. It's up to men to show 'em how they've only got one thing that's any good and it's between their legs."

"Hush," Rae said, hating how her voice shook. "You're upsetting the baby and she's sick, Willie." The door hammered against her back. Rae's knees started to buckle. She opened her mouth, and the air hurt her throat.

Willie gave the door another shove and bent Rae's knees some more. Her bottom inched along the linoleum.

Willie's fingers forced a way around the edge of the door.

Rae shifted Ginny to her other shoulder and cast about, silently begging for the Lord to show her a way out to safety. She'd have left for good before, only there'd been Cassie who needed her, then Ginny. She didn't know how she'd take care of Ginny if she went now, but she'd just have to find a way.

Willie grunted and put his weight on the door. His dirty fingernails dug into the wood on Rae's side. "You're trying my patience, Rae Faith. All I want is to show you a good time, but I'm losin' my temper, I tell you."

"Momma is coming home soon," Rae said, breathless. "You were asleep when she left. She said she'd be back by two. It's almost two now."

"Lyin' *bitch*," Willie said, and in a lull in the music from outside, Rae heard him pour more beer down his throat. "Both of you. Both lyin' bitches. Mother and daughter. I oughta walk out and see how you get on without me. Lyin' no-good bitches. Like mother, like daughter. My daddy always warned me about that. S'true. She's out there now. Puttin' out for some no

6

good who's tellin' her lies. She was always a sucker for them pretty lies."

Rae tried to cover her ears.

"Tell her she's sexy and she can't open her legs fast enough. Never mind if she's got a husband at home who needs her."

Ginny's screams ripped through Rae's head. She jiggled the baby faster and faster, but the screams only got louder.

Sweat ran down Rae's neck and between her breasts and shoulder blades. Her thin cotton tank top and shorts were soaked.

A crashing blow hit the cheap wood above Rae's head. With a splintering sound, Willie's right hand smashed through.

Rae's scream joined Ginny's. She stared upward and saw bloody gashes well on the protruding fist.

"Christ," Willie shouted. He tried to yank his wrist back, but shrieked when frayed slivers embedded in his flesh.

Rae felt the moment when he turned crazed.

The door pummeled her back, scooting her forward until her knees folded, and Ginny was crushed between Rae's thighs and her chest.

Rae searched frantically for something that might help. The only solid implement within reach was a big old flashlight that had once been painted orange, but was now mostly coated with rust.

To reach the flashlight, she had to give up her spot on the floor.

Holding Ginny tight, Rae shifted to grab the flashlight.

The instant her resistance left the door it flew open with such force it ripped from its hinges and crashed over the trundle bed. Naked to the waist of his jeans, Willie lay spread-eagle on top.

"Help me," he yelled. "Help me, bitch. Get this door off of me."

"You're on the door," Rae said. She felt tears on her face. They must have been Ginny's. "I've got to see to Ginny."

When she made to climb past Willie, he kicked at her with a silver-toed boot and she shot backward.

"Help me." He gasped aloud and panted. "I'm bleedin' to death."

She had to think, to do things really carefully. "It's okay, Willie. You stay real still. If you don't, you're going to bleed worse."

"Make the goddamn hole bigger. Put the brat down and help me, will ya?"

"Sure I will," Rae said soothingly. Her teeth chattered. Ginny stopped crying and shuddered, banging her face against Rae's sharp collarbone. "I'm going to go into the kitchen and find something to help you with."

"Like hell." Willie spat out his words. He turned his head to see her, and she saw tears running from his reddened eyes. "You think I'm as stupid as that drooling idiot sister of yours was? You'd leave me here. Put down the brat and hold this door still. "

She'd got through high school, Rae thought, her head beating inside. Done it early. Even with Momma wanting her at home, and Willie demanding she look after him, and Cassie when she was alive, Rae had graduated. Not with the gown and stuff. There hadn't been money for that. But she had the certificate hidden under the mattress on the trundle part of the bed. Right under Willie Skeggs' no-good body and the door.

"You listenin' to me?" He cried openly now, and sobs tore sounds from his throat. "I'm bleedin' to death here."

The diploma was her treasure. And the transcript that showed she'd had a 3.6 grade point average. The principal had asked if she was going to college. He'd been kind, and smiled at her. She never told anyone how hard it was to do her homework. Rae swallowed hard. She wanted to go to college. Maybe she would one day.

"Rae Faith!"

Why was she thinking about all that stuff now?

Because it was time to do something about it, that's why. For Ginny and herself. And in memory of sweet Cassie who never had any chance at all.

"I'm going into the kitchen," Rae told Willie firmly. Once more she started to climb over him.

Once more he kicked at her, and this time he connected. Rae crumpled to the brown linoleum, barely managing to keep her grip on Ginny.

"Hold the goddamn door steady," Willie said.

The slam of the outside screen door silenced him. Ginny sniffled.

"Now you're in for it," Willie said, drawing his lips back in a grimacing smile. "Your momma's home. In here, Betty, baby. Come and see what your pet did to her daddy."

An unshaded overhead light in the main room of the cabin showed piles of newspapers on the couch where stuffing bubbled free from rings worn open over springs. Unwashed dishes littered a table wedged between the couch and the end of the counter by the sink.

"Betty," Willie called. "Come here, sweetcakes."

After a few moments' hesitation, Betty Skeggs' high heels tapped a fast track to the destroyed doorjamb. She took in the scene, looking from Willie lying on top of the door, to Rae cowering against the wall with Ginny clutched in her arms, and blood from Willie's kick seeping down her shin.

"What's happenin' here?" Like Willie's, Betty's

9

accent was pure Tennessee, which was where they'd lived before leaving in the middle of the night for some reason Rae had never been told—or dared to ask about. "What's wrong with your leg, Rae Faith?"

"She went for me," Willie said, starting to pull his arm back, then howling and slumping down again with his face hidden. "Wouldn't do what I told her. Ran in here and slammed the door when I came after her. I tried to stop the door from hitting me, and my hand went right through."

"Liar!" Rae couldn't close her mouth. She stared at him. "He was breaking the door down, Momma. He wanted to do it to me like he did to Cassie."

Betty Skeggs wasn't a small woman, but she was strong. Working over dead chickens all day kept her agile. She leaped across her husband's legs in a single stride, and her closed fist connected with Rae's jaw so hard Rae's head snapped up and she heard something crack.

"You teach her, Betty. You show her, honeycakes." Willie slid sideways to kneel on the floor. "She's a devil. Needs teachin'. Get me free of this, and I'll make sure she never opens her mouth like that again."

With pain exploding in her brain, Rae concentrated on holding Ginny. The baby had shrieked, a shocked shriek that rose into fresh, hysterical cries.

"What d'you think you're doing with that flashlight?" Betty said. She took a handful of Rae's long dark hair and pulled her head sideways. "You're no good. Your father was no good. I thank God you're no child of mine. Don't know why I ever dragged you along with me."

Rae held the hair closest to her scalp and tried to free it from Momma's fingers. "I'm yours, Momma." She never wanted to hurt her mother, her flamboyant, sometimes mean, sometimes affectionate mother.

"Don't say I'm not yours. We're all we've got. Remember how you used to say that before him?" She looked at Willie.

"Smack her mouth, Betty," Willie said, gingerly working his wrist out, inch by inch.

Betty brought her face close to Rae's. The baby squirmed between them. "You aren't mine, I tell you." Stale liquor loaded her breath. Green shadow clung in the laugh lines around her blue eyes. Navy blue mascara clumped her lashes together and smeared her cheeks. "Your daddy—Windy, we called him. He blew in. He blew out. Never stayed long, and one day he blew out and never came back. Only he left you with me. And I was dumb enough to be sorry for you, scraggly little thing that you were."

"Betty," Willie moaned.

"But Cassie was my sister," Rae said, her thoughts running together. The cabin was so hot her clothes could have been wet tissue plastered on her skin. "You always said sisters had to stick together."

"You had the same mother. So Windy said. Cassie wasn't his kid, but you were. Left the pair of you."

"But I thought—"

"Don't matter what you thought," Willie moaned, dragging the door with him as he managed to sit on the edge of the bed. "Betty's got a soft heart. Sure wasn't for the puny relief money they give for a couple of brats. Right, doll? But I wouldn't have let you be taken advantage of if you'd told me the way of it."

"Not even to get your hands on Cassie's big boobs?" Momma said.

Rae closed her eyes and whispered, "Don't."

"Grow up." Momma's lipstick was gone, and she turned the corners of her full mouth down. Everything about Momma was full, including her thighs beneath the short skirt of her fringed denim outfit. That's why

11

men lined up for a little of her time, so she said. Her body and her brain—that's what they wanted, Momma said

"Goddamn you, Betty," Willie said suddenly, explosively. "Shut your fuckin' mouth and help me, will ya?"

Betty stared at him for a long time. Very slowly, she took off a red shoe with a four-inch heel that made her well over six feet tall. "Sure I'll help you, Willie," she said, and brought the heel down on the door, breaking away some of the wood—and gouging Willie's arm at the same time.

He opened his mouth, but no sound came out. His sallow cheeks turned gray and his eyelids lowered.

Blood gushed.

Betty raised the shoe and struck again.

More blood pumped, but she'd freed Willie. She pulled out his hand and picked up the door as if it weighed nothing. Rae watched, mute, as Momma carried the door through the cabin and hurled it outside.

When she returned, Willie was clasping the wounds in his arm and blubbering. He glared at Momma, then at Rae. His eyes narrowed on Rae and he said, "It's her fault. She came from trash and she acts like trash. Violent trash. She's got to be taught a lesson, I tell you. Then she's gotta be made to do what we need here."

Momma stood with her hands on her hips. "Get out," she told Rae. "Go. Now. While Willie's not up to doing nothin' about it."

Confused, Rae stared at the woman she'd known as her mother for all her remembered life. "Go where?" she asked in a small voice.

"Anywhere," Betty Skeggs said. "I gotta take a pee. Go before I get back. And take the brat with you."

Rae watched her go and heard the bathroom door close.

"Not so fast," Willie said with a sneer. "I got a little something I promised you first. "

Rae rushed for the door, but despite his wounds, Willie was faster. He tore Ginny from her arms, and threw the baby onto the mattress. "Take off your shorts," he said, advancing, wiping blood off on his flabby gut.

"Momma," Rae shouted, but the sound was silly, small. "Let me go, Willie. Momma'll be mad if you touch me."

"You heard her, girl. She ain't your momma. Take 'em off." While he approached, he unsnapped the waist of his jeans and unzipped them. Then he reached for the elastic waistband of Rae's homemade shorts.

Ginny began to slip from the bed.

"Help!" Rae called. "Please help us!"

Willie laughed and gathered her tank top in his fist. The fabric started to give at the side seams. Willie twisted, managing to push his knuckles into her nipples as he did so.

"Momma," Rae shouted brokenly. "Ginny's falling off the bed. She'll hurt her head like Cassie did."

"Too bad you ain't got what Cassie had," Willie said, using both hands to squeeze her breasts. "They'll do. And what else you got'll do just fine. All the same to me."

Rae heard Betty's voice before she saw her. "Sonuvabitch," Betty Skeggs said in a hissing tone. "I told you what I'd do to you if you tried it again."

"Ah, give it up, Betty," Willie said, pushing a hand inside Rae's shorts. "She ain't nothin' to us except what she's good for. Go get some beauty sleep for that lovely face of yours. I'll be there soon enough."

Then Rae saw Betty. The woman jumped on Willie's back like a big kid going for a piggyback ride. And with short nails broken from long hours working

13

over the carcasses of chickens, she clawed at Willie's eyes. He released Rae and bucked, and grappled with Betty's fingers. His blood smeared her hands and his own face.

With a huge heave, he swung her around his body and threw her to the floor. Then he was upon her, beating her with his fists, not caring where his blows landed.

Betty tried to fend him off, but she was no match for Willie Skeggs when he didn't have a door on his arm.

Rae retrieved terrified Ginny and set her in one of the crates filled with clothes.

"Stop it, Willie," Rae said, plucking at the waistband of his jeans. "Stop. You're hurting her."

"I'm fuckin' killin' the bitch," he said and punched Betty again, this time in the stomach. He landed another blow to her belly, and another.

Betty retched, and blood ran from the corner of her mouth.

"No, Willie," Rae said.

He wasn't listening. Betty still fought, but weakly now. She tried to find some place to hold Willie's bare chest, his pumping arms.

When she fell back, Willie wrenched her skirt up, revealing that Momma wasn't wearing panties. He slapped her face, and finished opening his jeans. While Momma made awful noises and choked up more blood, Willie concentrated on getting his thing inside her.

Rae knew she was going to throw up.

She retrieved the flashlight she'd dropped.

Willie began to move over Momma, whose chin sagged toward her shoulder. Her eyes were closed.

"You've killed her," Rae whispered.

Soon he'd kill her, too, Rae thought, and then Ginny, sweet Ginny.

Rae gathered up the baby and reached into the trundle beneath the mattress until she felt the envelope. She pulled it out and stuck it inside her tank top with Ginny pressed against it.

She could do it. She had her diploma. The principal said as long as you graduated and kept your nose clean, you could be what you wanted to be. One day Rae would go to college, but first she'd make money and look after Ginny for Cassie.

Creeping, she made her way around Willie, who sweated and grunted over Momma's limp body.

Once outside she could vomit, but not here, not while she needed to get away.

Carefully, Rae stepped into the other room and rose to tiptoe.

And yelling, howling like an animal, Willie Skeggs came after her along the floor. He grabbed her ankle and brought her down. Somehow she kept hold of Ginny, held her close and safe.

"Now you, bitch. That one's no good. Won't be no good till she sobers up. Then she's gonna learn who's boss. First I'm teachin' you, though."

Ignoring the baby, he found the waist of Rae's shorts once more and pulled.

Rae lifted her right arm and brought it down.

The heavy, rusty old flashlight hit the base of Willie's skull with a sound like breaking open a coconut with a hammer.

Rae threw the flashlight away.

Willie fell face down on the linoleum.

He didn't move again.

"Momma," Rae whispered, crawling to the woman. "Momma, help." Momma didn't answer. Her eyelids fluttered, but that's all.

With Ginny held in one arm, Rae shuffled to Willie and felt his neck the way she'd seen them do on TV. She couldn't feel anything.

She'd killed him.

So shaky she thought she'd fall over, Rae got to her feet. They didn't have a phone so she couldn't call for help. Not that anyone would come out here. Even the police were afraid of the gangs in Glad Times.

She knew what she had to do.

In a corner of the kitchen, Momma kept plastic bags from grocery shopping. Rae gathered some and filled them with clothes for her and Ginny. She took a couple of baby bottles, a carton of milk, some cookies, and a box of disposable diapers. What was left of the loaf of Wonderbread joined the rest of the supplies, and a shriveled apple and a bunch of spoiled bananas. Several crumpled bills and some change lay on the kitchen counter. Rae scooped the money into the pocket of her shorts.

She checked Momma and Willie one more time. They were the same, except Momma moaned and muttered.

Fingerprints.

Locating the flashlight, Rae pushed it in with the clothes. If the police questioned her she'd say she was scared and ran away with the baby. Before then, she'd lose the light. Everyone knew Betty and Willie Skeggs fought a lot—they'd think this had been one more of their fights. Except Momma—who wasn't Momma— would probably send them after the child she'd never wanted.

Rae made it through the heated darkness, through the straggle of mean cabins where music blared and people shouted, to the road.

West went toward Atlanta. Rae had been there a couple of times. She didn't like it. Momma always got drunk there, and met men.

South must go toward Savannah. She'd read about it, and it sounded nice. She'd go that way, and maybe

16

find some place where she could get a job with her diploma.

Rae started walking. The handles of the plastic bags cut into her elbows, but she didn't care. It was hot, but there was a little breeze, and Ginny wasn't crying anymore.

Sooner or later she'd get a ride with some trucker, and she'd pray he was a good man. Couldn't be so much worse than the man she'd left behind.

Rae lengthened her stride and bounced Ginny the way she liked to be bounced.

She'd be okay. Ginny would be okay.

Rae Faith was a good girl who'd kept her nose clean.

She would forget the man on his face on the dirty floor, and the woman who said she'd never wanted her anyway.

Rae Faith was a good girl who'd kept her nose clean.

She kissed Ginny's cheek and checked to make sure the diploma was safe in its envelope beneath her own tank top.

Please read on for
a preview of
Stella Cameron's

The Wish Club

Coming from
WARNER BOOKS
in
May 1998

Chapter One

Scotland, spring 1834. On Kirkcaldy land.

Max was the only name he knew was truly his. Just Max. Nothing more. He'd become Max Rossmara because a good man had rescued a desperate boy destined for a London workhouse, or worse, and given him a family name to call his own. He was nobody, not really, yet he'd been made part of a great family tradition and he was expected to bear its standard high.

Did he really want to call that standard his own?

If he took it up with his entire heart and bore it with the weight of all it meant, might he pay for the shelter of its privilege wth his soul?

Yes.

Would he do so anyway?

Answering yes again would likely cost him what he loved most.

He scanned the wild countryside he'd come to love so well. Overshadowing the sur-

1

rounding landscape, Castle Kirkcaldy rose atop its mount, a massive many-towered and castellated bastion, harsh against a crystal-blue spring sky.

Presently the home of his father's older brother, Arran, Marquess of Stonehaven, Kirkcaldy had been held by the noble family of Rossmara for generations.

And Max, the boy who had once picked pockets in London's Covent Garden, had been given the right to move about that castle with as much freedom as had he been born there.

In its sharp, gorse-scented snap, the air bore the memory of winter. The breeze tossed his hair and stung his eyes. He turned his back on Kirkcaldy's hill to regard instead the simple croft where Robert and Gael Mercer lived with their children, Kirsty and Niall. She was inside— Kirsty was inside. He knew because he always knew when she was near. And she would feel his presence soon enough, if she hadn't already.

Robert Mercer was also near, watching from the chicken coop, while pretending not to watch, and worrying about his beloved daughter, and what he perceived as the danger of her being hurt by a man above her station.

Max could never hurt his sweet Kirsty, not if there was a choice. And the choice was his unless he allowed that choice to be taken from him.

His boots making no sound, he entered the croft.

The flood of feeling in every part of him grew stronger each time he saw her, and he was not fool enough to pretend that those feelings were entirely of the higher nature he'd have sworn to as a boy.

The boy had become a man.

With her back to him, Kirsty bent over the table in what served as the Mercers' rude kitchen. She hummed and plunged her hands into a bowl of water.

Max walked softly across the earthen floor of the croft until he stood behind her.

Sunlight through the open door made a halo of the fair hair she wore in long braids pinned on top of her head. Curls sprang at the nape of her thin neck. The soft, vulnerable skin there brought Max another rush of emotion and need.

The stuff of her blue-and-white-checked dress was cheap, but on Kirsty it looked fresh and pretty. Slightly made, she was neither tall nor short, and although she didn't have her mother's red-gold hair there was much about Kirsty that reflected her pretty, fragile mother's aura of sensitive inner strength.

He could not give her up.

Max stopped. He couldn't loosen the fists

3

he'd made or fight down the swell of tenderness that mixed with anger in his breast.

"Master Max," Robert Mercer had said not ten minutes earlier, doffing his battered woolen bonnet and winding it in work-scarred hands. *"It's no my place t'say as much, but ye'd be doin' me a favor if ye left my lassie alone the now. Ye're no a laddie anymore, a laddie who wants t'play bairns' games. Ye're a gentleman. A gentleman, and kin t'the lairds o' this great estate. My lassie's—my lassie's no for the likes o' ye."*

What Robert Mercer had meant was that he feared Max would use his daughter as other men of means sometimes used humble young females. He also meant he'd guessed that a childhood friendship had grown into something more, something so much more, and that he didn't approve any more than Max's own father would approve. Well, what he and Kirsty shared was more than a childhood friendship, but less than Max longed for it to be.

A gentleman? He was a bastard. He was Struan Rossmara, Viscount Hunsgore's adopted son.

"I feel ye sneakin', Max Rossmara," Kirsty said without looking at him. "And I feel ye standin' there, starin' at me."

Of course she did. They'd often confided how they felt close even when they were actual-

4

ly far apart. He hadn't told Kirsty how he sometimes reached for her in the night and awoke
expecting to find her in his arms.

"Ye're troubled." She held her soapy
hands out of the water and twisted to see him.

He smiled, easy enough to do when he
looked into her startlingly blue eyes. "Not a bit
of it, Miss Mercer. Not troubled at all. Only puzzled. Why would a sensible girl of sixteen be
playing with a bowl of water for no reason at
all?"

She grew a little pink and used a forearm
to push strands of hair away from her face.
"There's a reason for everythin', Mr. Rossmara.
Why, if ye'd eyes t'see, ye'd know I was about an
important creation."

Her voice, a trifle husky, sounded as if
laughter couldn't be far away. "I would, would I?"
he said, going to her side and bending low over
the water. "Are there kelpies in there? Are you
bathing kelpies?"

"No," she told him, giggling. "I'm makin'
bubbles. An' dinna laugh, or ye'll have me
cryin'."

Max straightened slowly and studied her
face. Intelligence shone there and how well he
knew it. He was the older by years, yet she'd
badgered him to teach her to read, to learn her
numbers, to study whatever he studied—and

between the two of them she'd often been the quicker to comprehend.

He'd never kissed her. He'd wanted to often enough, but her innocence and her trust in him gave him the strength to resist—so far. Would they never kiss? Never know even that small, exquisite pleasure?

"Whist?" she said, frowning a little. "Ye're thinkin' if ye'll laugh at me?"

He inclined his head and allowed himself the pleasure of staring at each of her features. "I'll never laugh at you," he said. He looked at her mouth and knew he must not kiss her, for if he did he'd surely lose all power to make the decisions, take the actions he must pursue for both of them.

Her gaze didn't waver from his, but she lifted her right hand, the tips of her thumb and first finger touching, and blew softly until a bubble trembled between them. Sunlight stroked its rainbow colors.

Her generous mouth remained pushed out in a soft "ooh."

He felt his own lips part.

"Make a wish," she whispered. "Go on, Max, make a wish and blow t'bubble away."

"A wish?"

"Aye. We should always have somethin' t'wish for. Haste ye, before it pops."

He closed his eyes and blew, and felt minute droplets scatter his face.

"What did ye wish for?"

"I thought you weren't supposed to tell."

Her smile wobbled a little. "Maybe it'd be all right for the two o' us t'know? If we kept t'secret between us, d'ye think?"

He thought being twenty-two and in love with sixteen-year-old Kirsty was the sweetest, yet the most painful thing in the world. "I think it would be all right."

"Tell me then." The top of her head reached his chin. She'd inherited her mother's light skin and freckles. The end of her nose tipped up just a little. "*Tell* me," she begged.

"I wished for time to stand still. Right now. I wished to be standing here with you— looking at you—forever."

Her smile fled and her throat jerked as she swallowed. "I see."

She knew.

"Ye've come t'say ye're leavin' again."

"For a few months. My father and Uncle Arran want me to study estate management on the Yorkshire properties."

"Yes." Nodding, she bowed until he couldn't see her face anymore.

He ought to say something about it being time for them to see less of each other, about

7

how she should think about looking for a husband, but he said, "You'll read those books I brought for you? So that we can talk about them when I get back?" And he thought he would die if he ever had to see her with another man and know that man was her husband.

"I'll read them," she said.

He heard tears in her voice now and said, "Will you make a wish before I go?"

Silently she dipped her hand into the water again, swished it around, and raised her joined finger and thumb to blow. Then she closed her eyes tightly and he saw her lips move.

The bubble separated from her fingers and floated toward the roof.

"And what did you wish for, Kirsty?"

Her arms fell to her sides. She pressed her lips tightly together and stood quite still. Her eyes glittered.

"Oh, Kirsty." Not caring who might come, who might see, or that he must find a way to let her go, Max enfolded her in his arms and held her close. "My Kirsty. Please don't cry."

She shuddered, but slowly returned his hug. "I wished for t'same as ye. I want t'stay here like this. I never want it t'end."

"Sounds as if we've one mind, then," he told her. "We ought to form a club for people who think alike."

"Aye, a club o' two." She nudged her sharp chin into his chest. "A club for wishin'."

His smile, the smile she couldn't see, was bitter. A man and a girl could have their wishes, couldn't they? At least they could keep those.

Max said, "A wish club."

*   *   *